D0775773

Great Short Stories

BY

English and Irish Women

Edited by
Candace Ward

DOVER PUBLICATIONS, INC.
Mineola, New York

Bibliographical Note

Great Short Stories by English and Irish Women is a new work, first published by Dover Publications, Inc., in 2007.

"The Demon Lover" by Elizabeth Bowen is reproduced with the permission of Curtis Brown Group Ltd., London, on behalf of the estate of Elizabeth Bowen.
Copyright © 1945 by Elizabeth Bowen.

Library of Congress Cataloging-in-Publication Data

Great short stories by English and Irish women / edited by Candace Ward.
    p. cm.
   ISBN 0-486-45232-8 (pbk.)
    1. Short stories, English. 2. English fiction—Women authors. I. Ward, Candace.

PR1286.W6G74 2006
823'0108—dc22

2006050286

Manufactured in the United States of America
Dover Publications, Inc., 31 East 2nd Street, Mineola, N.Y. 11501

Contents

Introduction

The question that immediately arises when considering the contents of an anthology of writings by English and Irish women is, whose writings should be included? Although all compilers of anthologies ask a similar question, in this case conceptions of national identity complicate matters. How, that is, does one define "English" and "Irish"? Now as in the nineteenth and twentieth centuries—a period that saw the short story rise in significance as a literary form and during which the stories here were first published—the question is hotly debated, particularly given the vexed history of England's attempts to rule Ireland, dating as far back as 1172 when Henry II of England became feudal lord of Ireland by papal decree. Colonization of Ireland became more formalized under Henry VIII, who declared himself King of Ireland in 1541, and Elizabeth I, who adopted a plantation policy. Under this system the Crown "planted" colonists, transferring Irish (particularly Catholic) ownership of land to the English settlers, a policy vigorously pursued by Oliver Cromwell later in the seventeenth century. By 1780, ninety-five percent of the land in Ireland was owned by English (Protestant) landlords. The Irish did not passively accept English rule, however, as demonstrated by numerous revolts and rebellions, from the rebellion of Hugh O'Neill, Earl of Tyrone, in 1595 to the bloody Rebellion of 1798, waged against the British by the Society of United Irishmen, a group founded in 1791. The society consisted of Irish Protestants and Catholics of all classes, who came together in an attempt to establish self-rule; the revolt ultimately failed, and in 1800 the

British Parliament passed the Act of Union, which brought Ireland under even tighter control. The political and religious divisions that fuelled such rebellions persisted well into the twentieth century, from the Civil War (1922–23) to the "Troubles," that violent period of conflict between Union loyalists and the Irish Revolutionary Army (1956–1998).

All of the writers included here, particularly those whose work is set in Ireland or features Irish characters, were aware of this fraught history and understood how contentious questions of national and colonial identity could be, as did editors of their work. Often these questions have been subsumed (rightly or wrongly) by using "British" as an encompassing adjective, a problematic rhetorical move that can be read as a kind of cultural imperialism. The 1985 *Signet Classic Book of British Short Stories*, for example, contains many works by Irish writers, from James Joyce and Frank O'Connor to Elizabeth Bowen and Edna O'Brien, and by others not necessarily associated with England, like the Caribbean-born Jean Rhys and the South African Nadine Gordimer.

Classifying the writers in this anthology has presented a similar challenge. Should Maria Edgeworth be considered an Irish writer? Her work is included in several collections of Irish women's writings, for even though she was born in Oxfordshire, England, she lived in Ireland from the age of fourteen or fifteen until her death in 1849. But she was also a member of the Protestant landed gentry, some of whom could trace their ancestry, as did Edgeworth, back to those English who had held Irish lands and lived in Ireland since Elizabeth's time. As Edgeworth biographer James Newcomer puts it, she "had not one drop of native Irish blood," yet Edgeworth and other Anglo-Irish writers like her considered themselves Irish. Anna Maria Fielding Hall was born in Dublin in 1800, but left at fifteen. Her writing, however, focuses almost exclusively on Ireland and the Irish, and even though her books "were never popular in Ireland," they display (according to her husband and collaborator) a deeply felt sympathy for "her country and its people." Writing under the pen-names E. Œ. Somerville and Martin Ross, Edith Somerville and her cousin Violet Martin displayed their intimate knowledge of Irish customs and manners in novels like *An Irish Cousin* (1889) and *The Real Charlotte* (1894) and in the enormously popular collections of stories revolving around the Irish Resident Magistrate, Major Sinclair Yeates. The writings of Elizabeth Bowen, whose Anglo-Irish ancestry can be traced to an officer in Cromwell's occupying army, are remarkable for what critic Neil Corcoran calls her "ceaseless return to Ireland," evident even in stories set elsewhere.

Literary crosscurrents between England and Ireland did not flow strictly east-to-west, of course, but from west to east as well. Critics and biographers of Mary Shelley and Charlotte Brontë, for example, have identified the imaginative powers of these two iconic Englishwomen as part of their Celtic legacy: Shelley's mother, Mary Wollstonecraft, is described as an Anglo-Irish feminist and philosopher by virtue of her Irish mother, Elizabeth Dixon of the Ballyshannon Dixons; Brontë's father Patrick immigrated to England from County Down, Ireland, around the turn of the nineteenth century. Then, of course, there are the women whose backgrounds bespeak a continental cosmopolitanism, like Ella D'Arcy, who was born to Irish parents in London circa 1856, was educated in Germany and France, and who lived in the Channel Islands and in Paris before returning to London, where she died in 1937. Her cross-cultural experiences were critical to her development as a writer, one who, according to literary scholar James Fleming, was a leading figure in the development of late nineteenth-century experimental fiction and, more broadly, in the transition from Victorianism to Modernism.

Clearly, questions of national and cultural identity must be acknowledged and recognized as central to an appreciation of the English and Irish women writers in this collection. They are particularly evident in Edgeworth's "The Limerick Gloves," which ridicules English prejudice against the Irish by exposing a suspected plot to blow up a Protestant church as nothing more than a child's game. Anna Hall's "The Last of the Line" deals explicitly with political and religious divisions in Ireland in the early nineteenth century but without assigning blame—illustrating that author's desire to "blend the orange and the green." But if questions of nationalism need to be acknowledged, they also are too complex to settle in this brief introduction—if they can be settled at all. Another approach, then, is to consider the writings themselves. A wide range of settings, styles, and themes are exhibited in the fifteen stories here, from Edgeworth's "The Limerick Gloves," with its overt didacticism ("an Irishman born may be as good, almost, as an Englishman born") couched in the witty and often biting language of early nineteenth-century comedies of manners, to Mary Anne Hoare's sentimental treatment of one of the most tragic events in Irish history, the great famine of 1845–49, to Jane Barlow's local-color depiction of Irish rural life, to Charlotte Riddell's semi-autobiographical account of a gentlewoman's struggle to support herself by writing.

Despite the breadth of technique and subject matter, from Shelley's Romanticism to D'Arcy's and Sinclair's Modernism, there are also similarities between the works, most notably the gothic strain evident in the stories by Shelley, Brontë, Elizabeth Gaskell, Mary Braddon, Rosa Mulholland, and Bowen. As literary historians have noted, the rise of gothic fiction during the last decades of the eighteenth century roughly coincided with and was central to the development of the English novel; but as is evident from the gothic tales here, it also contributed to the development of the short story as a genre, and women's short fiction in particular. Part of the gothic's appeal is the protagonists' emotional vulnerability, a modern sensibility that renders them susceptible not only to supernatural dangers but to the psychological terrors associated with alienation. This is most apparent when the gothic tale is communicated by narrators like Shelley's "mortal immortal" and Eliot's poetic Latimer, individuals who are excluded from sympathetic communion with others because of their special "gifts." Shelley's protagonist has lived for centuries and, though he longs to die, fears the ultimate loneliness death brings; Latimer also desires and fears death. Possessed of the ability to read other people's thoughts, he is at once isolated from and intimately connected to those around him. This paradoxical condition does not allow for the typical give and take associated with sympathetic connections, but serves instead to alienate him further. The sense of alienation explored by Shelley and Eliot is also related to humankind's problematic relationship with science, as illustrated by the mortal immortal's participation in the experiments of Cornelius Agrippa and Latimer's role in a blood transfusion experiment performed at the end of "The Lifted Veil." In both cases, scientific miracles carry surprising and disastrous consequences.

Whereas Shelley and Eliot evoke terror through their exploration of psychological distress heightened by scientific advancement, Brontë, Gaskell, Braddon, and Bowen rely on more traditional gothic conventions to achieve that end. Of their four tales, Gaskell's is perhaps the most conventional, involving as it does an old family curse, a gloomy and isolated country manor house, and not one but three ghosts—one of whom plays eerie music on an organ that in the daylight proves to be "all broken and destroyed inside." Although Gaskell's basic plot is somewhat formulaic, it also includes some interesting (proto), feminist twists. The female characters, including the mother and child ghost who haunt the manor's inhabitants, suffer under the oppressive control of a tyrannical father, whose reach extends beyond the grave. Until, that is, the "old nurse" breaks the curse by braving the ghosts and saving the young girl in her care. This character, who narrates events that took place when she was a young woman, represents a different kind of servant than those typically found in gothic novels. Rather than functioning as a simple-minded loyal retainer, she embodies a courage and resourcefulness that anticipates the mother-savior who rescues her daughter from Bluebeard in the title story of Angela Carter's *The Bloody Chamber and Other Stories* (1992).

Bowen reworks the gothic more explicitly in "The Demon Lover," a story loosely based on Celtic legends of a demon lover who returns after a long absence to claim the promises of a young woman, as happens in Sir Walter Scott's retelling of the ballad in *Minstrelsy of the Scottish Border.* Initially unwilling to run away with her old lover because of her "husband dear" and "her two little babes," she is soon persuaded to leave them to travel the world with the rich mariner:

> She set her foot upon the ship,
> No [other] mariners could she behold;
> But the sails were o' the taffetie,
> And the masts o' the beaten gold. . . .
>
> They had not saild a league, a league,
> A league but barely three,
> Until she espied his cloven foot,
> And she wept right bitterlie. . . .

Rather than depicting a fickle, thoughtless young woman enticed by the promise of riches and adventures, Bowen's chilling story features a middle-aged, middle-class London housewife caught, as it were, between the two world wars of the twentieth century. She has no desire to reunite with the lover reportedly killed in 1916, and when he reappears twenty-five years later, it is to drive her away screaming "into the hinterland" of bombed out, deserted London streets.

Madness is another staple of gothic fiction, one used to great effect in Rosa Mulholland's "Not To Be Taken at Bedtime." But whereas madness in traditional gothic fiction is often the punishment inflicted on wayward women—for example, the raving Signora Laurentini in Ann Radcliffe's classic *Mysteries of Udolpho* (1794) confesses that the indulgence of her "evil passions" have driven her mad—in Mulholland's tale Evleen Blake has done nothing to "deserve" her fate. Indeed, her would-be lover, unable to restrain *his* passions, employs the services of a local witch to cast a spell on Evleen, a love potion that, as happens so often, backfires and results in tragedy for her and Coll Dhu ("Black-Coll").

Ill-fated lovers are found not only in the gothic stories here but also in Hall's sentimental "The Last of the Line" and the modernist writings of Ella D'Arcy and May Sinclair. Both Sinclair, whose aging protagonist Lena Wrace struggles to keep her dilettante husband from straying, and D'Arcy examine the modern marriage. But whereas Sinclair focuses on Lena's ability to delude herself from feeling the despair of betrayal, D'Arcy's "Irremediable" is remarkable for its intense depiction of marital frustration. As it traces the courtship and marriage of Willoughby and Esther, who marry despite wide differences in their social backgrounds, the story appears to privilege Willoughby's suffering, both because we are privy to his thoughts and because the text appears unsympathetic to the working-class Esther, who drops her h's and hates books. But D'Arcy doesn't spare Willoughby: if Esther is slatternly and manipulative, Willoughby is condescending, trapped as much by his vanity as her wiles. D'Arcy's concern, however, is less with assigning blame than with portraying the barrenness of a completely unsympathetic relationship. The reader feels, along with Willoughby, "the terror of his Hatred" and so clearly does D'Arcy communicate his "agonizing, unavailing regret" that despite William Blackwood's admiration of her talents, he rejected "Irremediable" for *Blackwood's Magazine* on the grounds that it was too bleak for its readers.

✿ ✿ ✿

Short Stories by English and Irish Women represents a very small sampling of women's short fiction of the last two hundred years. But from this sampling we can draw some conclusions, primarily that women's writings were absolutely critical to the literary arts, both in terms of popular appeal and the development of the writer's craft. Fortunately for us, despite various obstacles—of being dismissed as *women* writers, of writing under a patriarchal eye, like Maria Edgeworth, whose father closely monitored her literary career, and Mary Shelley, whose father William Godwin was often distant and unsympathetic; of the anonymity of writing under pseudonyms like "Currer Bell" (Charlotte Brontë) and "George Eliot" (Mary Ann Evans); of suffering critical neglect in life (as in Charlotte Riddell's case, described in "Out in the Cold") and in death (as happened to Mary Anne Hoare, whose short story collection *Shamrock Leaves* was erroneously attributed to another writer in the National Union Catalogue) these women persisted.

THE LIMERICK GLOVES°

Maria Edgeworth
(c. 1767–1849)

Chapter I

It was Sunday morning, and a fine day in autumn; the bells of
Hereford Cathedral rang, and all the world, smartly dressed,
were flocking to church.

"Mrs. Hill! Mrs. Hill!—Phoebe! Phoebe! There's the cathedral bell, I say, and neither of you ready for church, and I a
verger," cried Mr. Hill, the tanner, as he stood at the bottom of
his own staircase. "I'm ready, papa," replied Phoebe; and down
she came, looking so clean, so fresh, and so gay, that her stern
father's brows unbent, and he could only say to her, as she was
drawing on a new pair of gloves, "Child, you ought to have had
those gloves on before this time of day."

"Before this time of day!" cried Mrs. Hill, who was now coming downstairs completely equipped—"before this time of day!
She should know better, I say, than to put on those gloves at all:
more especially when going to the cathedral."

"The gloves are very good gloves, as far as I see," replied Mr.
Hill. "But no matter now. It is more fitting that we should be in
proper time in our pew, to set an example, as becomes us, than
to stand here talking of gloves and nonsense."

He offered his wife and daughter each an arm, and set out for

°From *Popular Tales*, 1804.

1

the cathedral; but Phoebe was too busy in drawing on her new gloves, and her mother was too angry at the sight of them, to accept of Mr. Hill's courtesy. "What I say is always nonsense, I know, Mr. Hill," resumed the matron: "but I can see as far into a millstone as other folks. Was it not I that first gave you a hint of what became of the great dog that we lost out of our tan-yard last winter? And was it not I who first took notice to you, Mr. Hill, verger as you are, of the hole under the foundation of the cathedral? Was it not, I ask you, Mr. Hill?"

"But, my dear Mrs. Hill, what has all this to do with Phoebe's gloves?"

"Are you blind, Mr. Hill? Don't you see that they are Limerick gloves?"

"What of that?" said Mr. Hill, still preserving his composure, as it was his custom to do as long as he could, when he saw his wife was ruffled.

"What of that, Mr. Hill! why don't you know that Limerick is in Ireland, Mr. Hill?"

"With all my heart, my dear."

"Yes, and with all your heart, I suppose, Mr. Hill, you would see our cathedral blown up, some fair day or other, and your own daughter married to the person that did it; and you a verger, Mr. Hill."

"God forbid!" cried Mr. Hill; and he stopped short and settled his wig. Presently recovering himself, he added, "But, Mrs. Hill, the cathedral is not yet blown up; and our Phoebe is not yet married."

"No; but what of that, Mr. Hill? Forewarned is forearmed, as I told you before your dog was gone; but you would not believe me, and you see how it turned out in that case; and so it will in this case, you'll see, Mr. Hill."

"But you puzzle and frighten me out of my wits, Mrs. Hill," said the verger, again settling his wig. "*In that case and in this case!* I can't understand a syllable of what you've been saying to me this half-hour. In plain English, what is there the matter about Phoebe's gloves?"

"In plain English, then, Mr. Hill, since you can understand

nothing else, please to ask your daughter Phoebe who gave her those gloves. Phoebe, who gave you those gloves?"

"I wish they were burnt," said the husband, whose patience could endure no longer. "Who gave you those cursed gloves, Phoebe?"

"Papa," answered Phoebe, in a low voice, "they were a present from Mr. Brian O'Neill."

"The Irish glover!" cried Mr. Hill, with a look of terror.

"Yes," resumed the mother; "very true, Mr. Hill, I assure you. Now, you see, I had my reasons."

"Take off the gloves directly: I order you, Phoebe," said her father, in his most peremptory tone. "I took a mortal dislike to that Mr. Brian O'Neill the first time I ever saw him. He's an Irishman, and that's enough, and too much for me. Off with the gloves, Phoebe! When I order a thing, it must be done."

Phoebe seemed to find some difficulty in getting off the gloves, and gently urged that she could not well go into the cathedral without them. This objection was immediately removed by her mother's pulling from her pocket a pair of mittens, which had once been brown, and once been whole, but which were now rent in sundry places; and which, having been long stretched by one who was twice the size of Phoebe, now hung in huge wrinkles upon her well-turned arms.

"But, papa," said Phoebe, "why should we take a dislike to him because he is an Irishman? Cannot an Irishman be a good man?"

The verger made no answer to this question, but a few seconds after it was put to him observed that the cathedral bell had just done ringing; and, as they were now got to the church door, Mrs. Hill, with a significant look at Phoebe, remarked that it was no proper time to talk or think of good men, or bad men, or Irishmen, or any men, especially for a verger's daughter.

We pass over in silence the many conjectures that were made by several of the congregation, concerning the reason why Miss Phoebe Hill should appear in such a shameful shabby pair of gloves on a Sunday. After service was ended, the verger went, with great mystery, to examine the hole under the foundation of the cathedral; and Mrs. Hill repaired, with the grocer's and the stationer's ladies, to take a walk in the Close, where she boasted to all her female acquaintance, whom she called her friends, of her maternal discretion in prevailing upon Mr. Hill to forbid her daughter Phoebe to wear the Limerick gloves.

In the meantime, Phoebe walked pensively homewards; endeavouring to discover why her father should take a mortal dislike to a man at first sight, merely because he was an Irishman; and why her mother had talked so much of the great dog which had been lost last year out of the tan-yard; and of the hole under the foundation of the cathedral! "What has all this to do with my Limerick gloves?" thought she. The more she thought, the less connection she could perceive between these things: for as she had not taken a dislike to Mr. Brian O'Neill at first sight, because he was an Irishman, she could not think it quite reasonable to suspect him of making away with her father's dog, nor yet of a design to blow up Hereford Cathedral. As she was pondering upon these matters, she came within sight of the ruins of a poor woman's house, which a few months before this time had been burnt down. She recollected that her first acquaintance with her lover began at the time of this fire; and she thought that the courage and humanity he showed, in exerting himself to save this unfortunate woman and her children, justified her notion of the possibility that an Irishman might be a good man.

The name of the poor woman whose house had been burnt down was Smith: she was a widow, and she now lived at the extremity of a narrow lane in a wretched habitation. Why Phoebe thought of her with more concern than usual at this instant we need not examine, but she did; and, reproaching herself for having neglected it for some weeks past, she resolved to go directly to see the widow Smith, and to give her a crown which she had long had in her pocket, with which she had intended to have bought play tickets.

It happened that the first person she saw in the poor widow's kitchen was the identical Mr. O'Neill. "I did not expect to see anybody here but you, Mrs. Smith," said Phoebe, blushing.

"So much the greater the pleasure of the meeting; to me, I mean, Miss Hill," said O'Neill, rising, and putting down a little boy, with whom he had been playing. Phoebe went on talking to the poor woman; and, after slipping the crown into her hand, said she would call again. O'Neill, surprised at the change in her manner, followed her when she left the house, and said, "It would be a great misfortune to me to have done anything to offend Miss Hill, especially if I could not conceive how or what it was, which is my case at this present speaking." And as the spruce glover spoke, he fixed his eyes upon Phoebe's ragged gloves. She drew them up in vain; and then said, with her natural simplicity and gentleness, "You have not done any thing to offend me, Mr. O'Neill; but you are some way or other displeasing to my father and mother, and they have forbid me to wear the Limerick gloves."

"And sure Miss Hill would not be after changing her opinion of her humble servant for no reason in life but because her father and mother, who have taken a prejudice against him, are a little contrary."

"No," replied Phoebe; "I should not change my opinion without any reason; but I have not yet had time to fix my opinion of you, Mr. O'Neill."

"To let you know a piece of my mind, then, my dear Miss Hill," resumed he, "the more contrary they are, the more pride and joy it would give me to win and wear you, in spite of 'em all; and if without a farthing in your pocket, so much the more I should rejoice in the opportunity of proving to your dear self, and all else whom it may consarn, that Brian O'Neill is no fortune-hunter, and scorns them that are so narrow-minded as to think that no other kind of cattle but them there fortune-hunters can come out of all Ireland. So, my dear Phoebe, now we understand one another, I hope you will not be paining my eyes any longer with the sight of these odious brown bags, which are not fit to be worn by any Christian arms, to say nothing of Miss Hill's, which are the handsomest, without any compliment, that ever I saw, and, to my mind, would become a pair of Limerick gloves beyond anything: and I expect she'll show her generosity and proper spirit by putting them on immediately."

"You expect, sir!" repeated Miss Hill, with a look of more indignation than her gentle countenance had ever before been seen to assume. "Expect!" "If he had said hope," thought she, "it would have been another thing: but expect! what right has he to expect?"

Now Miss Hill, unfortunately, was not sufficiently acquainted with the Irish idiom to know that to expect, in Ireland, is the same thing as to hope in England; and, when her Irish admirer said I" expect," he meant only in plain English, "I hope." But thus it is that a poor Irishman, often, for want of understanding the niceties of the English language, says the rudest when he means to say the civillest things imaginable.

Miss Hill's feelings were so much hurt by this unlucky "I expect" that the whole of his speech, which had before made some favourable impression upon her, now lost its effect: and she replied with proper spirit, as she thought, "You expect a great deal too much, Mr. O'Neill; and more than ever I gave you reason to do. It would be neither pleasure nor pride to me to be won and worn, as you were pleased to say, in spite of them all; and to be thrown, without a farthing in my pocket, upon the protection of one who expects so much at first setting out.—So I assure you, sir, whatever you may expect, I shall not put on the Limerick gloves."

Mr. O'Neill was not without his share of pride and proper spirit; nay, he had, it must be confessed, in common with some others of his countrymen, an improper share of pride and spirit. Fired by the lady's coldness, he poured forth a volley of reproaches; and ended by wishing, as he said, a good morning, for ever and ever, to one who could change her opinion, point blank, like the weathercock. "I am, miss, your most obedient; and I expect you'll never think no more of poor Brian O'Neill and the Limerick gloves."

If he had not been in too great a passion to observe anything, poor Brian O'Neill would have found out that Phoebe was not a weathercock: but he left her abruptly, and hurried away, imagining all the while that it was Phoebe, and not himself, who was in a rage. Thus, to the horseman who is galloping at full speed, the hedges, trees, and houses, seem rapidly to recede, whilst, in reality, they never move from their places. It is he that flies from them, and not they from him.

On Monday morning Miss Jenny Brown, the perfumer's daughter, came to pay Phoebe a morning visit, with face of busy joy.

"So, my dear!" said she: "fine doings in Hereford! But what makes you look so downcast? To be sure you are invited, as well as the rest of us."

"Invited where?" cried Mrs. Hill, who was present, and who could never endure to hear of an invitation in which she was not included. "Invited where, pray, Miss Jenny?"

"La! have not you heard? Why, we all took it for granted that you and Miss Phoebe would have been the first and foremost to have been asked to Mr. O'Neill's ball."

"Ball!" cried Mrs. Hill; and luckily saved Phoebe, who was in some agitation, the trouble of speaking. "Why, this is a mighty sudden thing: I never heard a tittle of it before."

"Well, this is really extraordinary! And, Phoebe, have you not received a pair of Limerick gloves?"

"Yes, I have," said Phoebe, "but what then? What have my Limerick gloves to do with the ball?"

"A great deal," replied Jenny. "Don't you know that a pair of Limerick gloves is, as one may say, a ticket to this ball? for every lady that has been asked has had a pair sent to her along with the card; and I believe as many as twenty, besides myself, have been asked this morning."

Jenny then produced her new pair of Limerick gloves, and as she tried them on, and showed how well they fitted, she counted up the names of the ladies who, to her knowledge, were to be at this ball. When she had finished the catalogue, she expatiated upon the grand preparations which it was said the widow O'Neill, Mr. O'Neill's mother, was making for the supper, and concluded by condoling with Mrs. Hill for her misfortune in not having been invited. Jenny took her leave to get her dress in readiness: "for," added she, "Mr. O'Neill has engaged me to open the ball in case Phoebe does not go; but I suppose she will cheer up and go, as she has a pair of Limerick gloves as well as the rest of us."

There was a silence for some minutes after Jenny's departure, which was broken by Phoebe, who told her mother that, early in the morning, a note had been brought to her, which she had returned unopened, because she knew, from the handwriting of the direction, that it came from Mr. O'Neill.

We must observe that Phoebe had already told her mother of her meeting with this gentleman at the poor widow's, and of all that had passed between them afterwards. This openness on her part had softened the heart of Mrs. Hill; who was really inclined to be good-natured, provided people would allow that she had more penetration than anyone else in Hereford. She was, moreover, a good deal piqued and alarmed by the idea that the perfumer's daughter might rival and outshine her own. Whilst she had thought herself sure of Mr. O'Neill's attachment to Phoebe, she had looked higher, especially as she was persuaded by the perfumer's lady to think that an Irishman could not be a bad match; but now she began to suspect that the perfumer's lady had changed her opinion of Irishmen, since she did not object to her own Jenny's leading up the ball at Mr. O'Neill's.

All these thoughts passed rapidly in the mother's mind, and, with her fear of losing an admirer for her Phoebe, the value of that admirer suddenly rose in her estimation. Thus, at an auction, if a lot is going to be knocked down to a lady who is the only person that has bid for it, even she feels discontented, and despises that which nobody covets; but if, as the hammer is falling, many voices answer to the question, "Who bids more?" then her anxiety to secure the prize suddenly rises, and, rather than be outbid, she will give far beyond its value.

"Why, child," said Mrs. Hill, "since you have a pair of Limerick gloves; and since certainly that note was an invitation to us to this ball; and since it is much more fitting that you should open the ball than Jenny Brown; and since, after all, it was very handsome and genteel of the young man to say he would take you without a farthing in your pocket, which shows that those were misinformed who talked of him as an Irish adventurer; and since we are not certain 'twas he made away with the dog, although he said its barking was a great nuisance; there is no great reason to suppose he was the person who made the hole under the foundation of the cathedral, or that he could have such a wicked thought as to blow it up; and since he must be in a very good way

of business to be able to afford giving away four or five guineas'
worth of Limerick gloves, and balls and suppers; and since, after
all, it is no fault of his to be an Irishman, I give it as my vote and
opinion, my dear, that you put on your Limerick gloves and go
to this ball; and I'll go and speak to your father, and bring him
round to our opinion, and then I'll pay the morning visit I owe
to the widow O'Neill and make up your quarrel with Brian.
Love quarrels are easy to make up, you know, and then we shall
have things all upon velvet again, and Jenny Brown need not
come with her hypocritical condoling face to us anymore."

After running this speech glibly off, Mrs. Hill, without waiting to hear a syllable from poor Phoebe, trotted off in search
of her consort. It was not, however, quite so easy a task as his
wife expected to bring Mr. Hill round to her opinion. He was
slow in declaring himself of any opinion; but when once he had
said a thing, there was but little chance of altering his notions.
On this occasion Mr. Hill was doubly bound to his prejudice
against our unlucky Irishman; for he had mentioned with great
solemnity at the club which he frequented the grand affair of
the hole under the foundation of the cathedral, and his suspicions that there was a design to blow it up. Several of the club
had laughed at this idea; others, who supposed that Mr.
O'Neill was a Roman Catholic, and who had a confused notion
that a Roman Catholic must be a very wicked, dangerous
being, thought that there might be a great deal in the verger's
suggestions, and observed that a very watchful eye ought to be
kept upon this Irish glover, who had come to settle at Hereford
nobody knew why, and who seemed to have money at command nobody knew how.

The news of this ball sounded to Mr. Hill's prejudiced imagination like the news of a conspiracy. Ay! ay! thought he; the
Irishman is cunning enough! But we shall be too many for him:
he wants to throw all the good sober folks of Hereford off their
guard, by feasting, and dancing, and carousing, I take it, and so
to perpetrate his evil design when it is least suspected; but we
shall be prepared for him, fools as he takes us plain Englishmen
to be, I warrant.

In consequence of these most shrewd cogitations, our verger

silenced his wife with a peremptory nod, when she came to persuade him to let Phoebe put on the Limerick gloves and go to the ball. "To this ball she shall not go, and I charge her not to put on those Limerick gloves, as she values my blessing," said Mr. Hill. "Please to tell her so, Mrs. Hill, and trust to my judgment and discretion in all things, Mrs. Hill. Strange work may be in Hereford yet: but I'll say no more; I must go and consult with knowing men who are of my opinion."

He sallied forth, and Mrs. Hill was left in a state which only those who are troubled with the disease of excessive curiosity can rightly comprehend or compassionate. She hied her back to Phoebe, to whom she announced her father's answer and then went gossiping to all her female acquaintance in Hereford, to tell them all that she knew, and all that she did not know, and to endeavour to find out a secret where there was none to be found.

There are trials of temper in all conditions, and no lady, in high or low life, could endure them with a better grace than Phoebe. Whilst Mr. and Mrs. Hill were busied abroad, there came to see Phoebe one of the widow Smith's children. With artless expressions of gratitude to Phoebe, this little girl mixed the praises of O'Neill, who, she said, had been the constant friend of her mother, and had given her money every week since the fire happened. "Mammy loves him dearly for being so good-natured," continued the child; "and he has been good to other people as well as to us."

"To whom?" said Phoebe.

"To a poor man who has lodged for these few days past next door to us," replied the child; "I don't know his name rightly, but he is an Irishman, and he goes out a-haymaking in the daytime, along with a number of others. He knew Mr. O'Neill in his own country, and he told mammy a great deal about his goodness."

As the child finished these words, Phoebe took out of a drawer some clothes, which she had made for the poor woman's children, and gave them to the little girl. It happened that the Limerick gloves had been thrown into this drawer; and Phoebe's favourable sentiments of the giver of those gloves were revived by what she had just heard, and by the confession Mrs. Hill had made, that she had no reasons, and but vague suspicions, for thinking ill of him. She laid the gloves perfectly smooth, and strewed over them, whilst the little girl went on talking of Mr. O'Neill, the leaves of a rose which she had worn on Sunday.

Mr. Hill was all this time in deep conference with those prudent men of Hereford who were of his own opinion, about the perilous hole under the cathedral. The ominous circumstance of this ball was also considered, the great expense at which the Irish glover lived, and his giving away gloves, which was a sure sign he was not under any necessity to sell them, and consequently a proof that, though he pretended to be a glover, he was something wrong in disguise. Upon putting all these things together, it was resolved by these over-wise politicians that the best thing that could be done for Hereford, and the only possible means of preventing the immediate destruction of its cathedral, would be to take Mr. O'Neill into custody. Upon recollection, however, it was perceived that there was no legal ground on which he could be attacked. At length, after consulting an attorney, they devised what they thought an admirable mode of proceeding.

Our Irish hero had not that punctuality which English tradesmen usually observe in the payment of bills; he had, the preceding year, run up a long bill with a grocer in Hereford, and, as he had not at Christmas cash in hand to pay it, he had given a note, payable six months after date. The grocer, at Mr. Hill's request, made over the note to him, and it was determined that the money should be demanded, as it was now due, and that, if it was not paid directly, O'Neill should be that night arrested. How Mr. Hill made the discovery of this debt to the grocer agree with his former notion that the Irish glover had always money at command we cannot well conceive, but anger and prejudice will swallow down the grossest contradictions without difficulty.

When Mr. Hill's clerk went to demand payment of the note, O'Neill's head was full of the ball which he was to give that evening. He was much surprised at the unexpected appearance of the note: he had not ready money by him to pay it; and, after swearing a good deal at the clerk, and complaining of this ungenerous and ungentleman-like behaviour in the grocer and the tanner, he told the clerk to be gone, and not to be bothering him at such an unseasonable time: that he could not have the money then, and did not deserve to have it at all.

This language and conduct were rather new to the English clerk's mercantile ears: we cannot wonder that it should seem to him, as he said to his master, more the language of a madman than a man of business. This want of punctuality in money transactions, and this mode of treating contracts as matters of favour and affection, might not have damned the fame of our hero in his own country, where such conduct is, alas! too common; but he was now in a kingdom where the manners and customs are so directly opposite, that he could meet with no allowance for his national faults. It would be well for his countrymen if they were made, even by a few mortifications, somewhat sensible of this important difference in the habits of Irish and English traders before they come to settle in England.

But to proceed with our story. On the night of Mr. O'Neill's grand ball, as he was seeing his fair partner, the perfumer's daughter, safe home, he felt himself tapped on the shoulder by no friendly hand. When he was told that he was the king's prisoner, he vociferated with sundry strange oaths, which we forbear to repeat. "No, I am not the king's prisoner! I am the prisoner of that shabby rascally tanner, Jonathan Hill. None but he would arrest a gentleman in this way, for a trifle not worth mentioning."

Miss Jenny Brown screamed when she found herself under the protection of a man who was arrested; and, what between her screams and his oaths, there was such a disturbance that a mob gathered.

Among this mob there was a party of Irish haymakers, who, after returning late from a hard day's work, had been drinking in a neighbouring ale-house. With one accord they took part with their countryman, and would have rescued him from the civil officers with all the pleasure in life if he had not fortunately possessed just sufficient sense and command of himself to restrain their party spirit, and to forbid them, as they valued his life and reputation, to interfere, by word or deed, in his defence.

He then despatched one of the haymakers home to his

mother, to inform her of what had happened, and to request that she would get somebody to be bail for him as soon as possible, as the officers said they could not let him out of their sight till he was bailed by substantial people, or till the debt was discharged.

The widow O'Neill was just putting out the candles in the ball-room when this news of her son's arrest was brought to her. We pass over Hibernian exclamations: she consoled her pride by reflecting that it would certainly be the most easy thing imaginable to procure bail for Mr. O'Neill in Hereford, where he had so many friends who had just been dancing at his house; but to dance at his house she found was one thing, and to be bail for him quite another. Each guest sent excuses, and the widow O'Neill was astonished at what never fails to astonish everybody when it happens to themselves. "Rather than let my son be detained in this manner for a paltry debt," cried she, "I'd sell all I have within half an hour to a pawnbroker." It was well no pawnbroker heard this declaration: she was too warm to consider economy. She sent for a pawnbroker, who lived in the same street, and, after pledging goods to treble the amount of the debt, she obtained ready money for her son's release.

O'Neill, after being in custody for about an hour and a half, was set at liberty upon the payment of his debt. As he passed by the cathedral in his way home, he heard the clock strike; and he called to a man, who was walking backwards and forwards in the churchyard, to ask whether it was two or three that the clock struck. "Three," answered the man; "and, as yet, all is safe."

O'Neill, whose head was full of other things, did not stop to inquire the meaning of these last words. He little suspected that this man was a watchman whom the over-vigilant verger had stationed there to guard the Hereford Cathedral from his attacks. O'Neill little guessed that he had been arrested merely to keep him from blowing up the cathedral this night. The arrest had an excellent effect upon his mind, for he was a young man of good sense: it made him resolve to retrench his expenses in time, to live more like a glover and less like a gentleman; and to aim more at establishing credit, and less at gaining popularity. He found, from experience, that good friends will not pay bad debts.

Chapter II

On Thursday morning our verger rose in unusually good spirits, congratulating himself upon the eminent service he had done to the city of Hereford by his sagacity in discovering the foreign plot to blow up the cathedral, and by his dexterity in having the enemy held in custody, at the very hour when the dreadful deed was to have been perpetrated. Mr. Hill's knowing friends farther agreed it would be necessary to have a guard that should sit up every night in the churchyard; and that as soon as they could, by constantly watching the enemy's motions, procure any information which the attorney should deem sufficient grounds for a legal proceeding, they should lay the whole business before the mayor.

After arranging all this most judiciously and mysteriously with friends who were exactly of his own opinion, Mr. Hill laid aside his dignity of verger, and assuming his other character of a tanner, proceeded to his tan-yard. What was his surprise and consternation, when he beheld his great rick of oak bark levelled to the ground; the pieces of bark were scattered far and wide, some over the close, some over the fields, and some were seen swimming upon the water! No tongue, no pen, no muse can describe the feelings of our tanner at this spectacle—feelings which became the more violent from the absolute silence which he imposed on himself upon this occasion. He instantly decided in his own mind that this injury was perpetrated by O'Neill, in revenge for his arrest; and went privately to the attorney to inquire what was to be done, on his part, to secure legal vengeance.

The attorney unluckily—or at least as Mr. Hill thought, unluckily—had been sent for, half an hour before, by a gentleman at some distance from Hereford, to draw up a will: so that our tanner was obliged to postpone his legal operations.

We forbear to recount his return, and how many times he walked up and down the Close to view his scattered bark, and to estimate the damage that had been done to him. At length that hour came which usually suspends all passions by the more imperious power of appetite—the hour of dinner: an hour of which it was never needful to remind Mr. Hill by watch, clock, or dial; for he was blessed with a punctual appetite, and powerful as punctual: so powerful, indeed, that it often excited the spleen of his more genteel, or less hungry wife. "Bless my stars! Mr. Hill," she would oftentimes say, "I am really downright ashamed to see you eat so much; and when company is to dine with us, I do wish you would take a snack by way of a damper before dinner, that you may not look so prodigious famishing and ungenteel."

Upon this hint, Mr. Hill commenced a practice, to which he ever afterwards religiously adhered, of going, whether there was to be company or no company, into the kitchen regularly every day, half an hour before dinner, to take a slice from the roast or the boiled before it went up to table. As he was this day, according to his custom, in the kitchen, taking his snack by way of a damper, he heard the housemaid and the cook talking about some wonderful fortune-teller, whom the housemaid had been consulting. This fortune-teller was no less a personage than the successor to Bampfylde Moore Carew, king of the gipsies, whose life and adventures are probably in many, too many, of our readers' hands. Bampfylde, the second king of the gipsies, assumed this title, in hopes of becoming as famous, or as infamous, as his predecessor: he was now holding his court in a wood near the town of Hereford, and numbers of servant-maids and 'prentices went to consult him—nay, it was whispered that he was resorted to, secretly, by some whose education might have taught them better sense.

Numberless were the instances which our verger heard in his kitchen of the supernatural skill of this cunning man; and whilst Mr. Hill ate his snack with his wonted gravity, he revolved great designs in his secret soul. Mrs. Hill was surprised, several times during dinner, to see her consort put down his knife and fork, and meditate. "Gracious me, Mr. Hill! what can have happened to you this day? What can you be thinking of, Mr. Hill, that can make you forget what you have upon your plate?"

"Mrs. Hill," replied the thoughtful verger, "our grandmother Eve had too much curiosity; and we all know it did not lead to good. What I am thinking of will be known to you in due time, but not now, Mrs. Hill; therefore, pray, no questions, or teasing, or pumping. What I think, I think; what I say, I say; what I know,

I know; and that is enough for you to know at present: only this, Phoebe, you did very well not to put on the Limerick gloves, child. What I know, I know. Things will turn out just as I said from the first. What I say, I say; and what I think, I think; and this is enough for you to know at present."

Having finished dinner with this solemn speech, Mr. Hill settled himself in his arm-chair, to take his after-dinner's nap: and he dreamed of blowing up cathedrals, and of oak bark floating upon the waters; and the cathedral was, he thought, blown up by a man dressed in a pair of woman's Limerick gloves, and the oak bark turned into mutton steaks, after which his great dog Jowler was swimming; when, all on a sudden, as he was going to beat Jowler for eating the bark transformed into mutton steaks, Jowler became Bampfylde the Second, king of the gipsies; and putting a horsewhip with a silver handle into Hill's hand, commanded him three times, in a voice as loud as the town-crier's, to have O'Neill whipped through the market-place of Hereford: but, just as he was going to the window to see this whipping, his wig fell off, and he awoke.

It was difficult, even for Mr. Hill's sagacity, to make sense of this dream: but he had the wise art of always finding in his dreams something that confirmed his waking determinations. Before he went to sleep, he had half resolved to consult the king of the gipsies, in the absence of the attorney; and his dream made him now wholly determined upon this prudent step. From Bampfylde the Second, thought he, I shall learn for certain who made the hole under the cathedral, who pulled down my rick of bark, and who made away with my dog Jowler; and then I shall swear examinations against O'Neill, without waiting for attorneys. I will follow my own way in this business: I have always found my own way best.

So, when the dusk of the evening increased, our wise man set out towards the wood to consult the cunning man. Bampfylde the Second, king of the gipsies, resided in a sort of hut made of the branches of trees; the verger stooped, but did not stoop low enough, as he entered this temporary palace, and, whilst his body was almost bent double, his peruke was caught upon a twig. From this awkward situation he was relieved by the consort of the king; and he now beheld, by the light of some embers, the person of his gipsy majesty, to whose sublime appearance this dim light was so favourable that it struck a secret awe into our wise man's soul; and, forgetting Hereford Cathedral, and oak bark, and Limerick gloves, he stood for some seconds speechless. During this time, the queen very dexterously disencumbered his pocket of all superfluous articles. When he recovered his recollection, he put with great solemnity the following queries to the king of the gipsies, and received the following answers:—

"Do you know a dangerous Irishman of the name of O'Neill, who has come, for purposes best known to himself, to settle at Hereford?"

"Yes, we know him well."

"Indeed! And what do you know of him?"

"That he is a dangerous Irishman."

"Right! And it was he, was it not, that pulled down, or caused to be pulled down, my rick of oak bark?"

"It was."

"And who was it that made away with my dog Jowler, that used to guard the tan-yard?"

"It was the person that you suspect."

"And was it the person whom I suspect that made the hole under the foundation of our cathedral?"

"The same, and no other."

"And for what purpose did he make that hole?"

"For a purpose that must not be named," replied the king of the gipsies, nodding his head in a mysterious manner.

"But it may be named to me," cried the verger, "for I have found it out, and I am one of the vergers; and is it not fit that a plot to blow up the Hereford cathedral should be known *to* me, and *through* me?"

> "Now, take my word,
> Wise men of Hereford,
> None in safety may be,
> Till the bad man doth flee."

These oracular verses, pronounced by Bampfylde with all the enthusiasm of one who was inspired, had the desired effect upon our wise man; and he left the presence of the king of the gipsies with a prodigiously high opinion of his majesty's judgment and of his own, fully resolved to impart, the next morning, to the mayor of Hereford his important discoveries.

Now it happened that, during the time Mr. Hill was putting the foregoing queries to Bampfylde the second, there came to the door or entrance of the audience chamber an Irish haymaker, who wanted to consult the cunning man about a little leathern purse which he had lost whilst he was making hay in a field near Hereford. This haymaker was the same person who, as we have related, spoke so advantageously of our hero O'Neill to the widow Smith. As this man, whose name was Paddy M'Cormack, stood at the entrance of the gipsies' hut, his attention was caught by the name of O'Neill; and he lost not a word of all that passed. He had reason to be somewhat surprised at hearing Bampfylde assert it was O'Neill who had pulled down the rick of bark. "By the holy poker!" said he to himself, "the old fellow now is out there. I know more o' that matter than he does—no offence to his majesty; he knows no more of my purse, I'll engage now, than he does of this man's rick of bark and his dog: so I'll keep my tester in my pocket, and not be giving it to this king o' the gipsies, as they call him: who, as near as I can guess, is no better than a cheat. But there is one secret which I can be telling this conjuror himself; he shall not find it such an easy matter to do all what he thinks; he shall not be after ruining an innocent countryman of my own whilst Paddy M'Cormack has a tongue and brains."

Now, Paddy M'Cormack had the best reason possible for knowing that Mr. O'Neill did not pull down Mr. Hill's rick of bark; it was M'Cormack himself who, in the heat of his resentment for the insulting arrest of his countryman in the streets of Hereford, had instigated his fellow haymakers to this mischief; he headed them, and thought he was doing a clever, spirited action.

There is a strange mixture of virtue and vice in the minds of the lower class of Irish; or rather, a strange confusion in their ideas of right and wrong, from want of proper education. As soon as poor Paddy found out that his spirited action of pulling down the rick of bark was likely to be the ruin of his countryman, he resolved to make all the amends in his power for his folly—he went to collect his fellow haymakers and persuaded them to assist him this night in rebuilding what they had pulled down.

They went to this work when everybody except themselves, as they thought, was asleep in Hereford. They had just completed the stack, and were all going away except Paddy, who was seated at the very top, finishing the pile, when they heard a loud voice cry out, "Here they are! Watch! Watch!"

Immediately, all the haymakers who could, ran off as fast as possible. It was the watch who had been sitting up at the cathedral who gave the alarm. Paddy was taken from the top of the rick and lodged in the watchhouse till morning. "Since I'm to be rewarded this way for doing a good action, sorrow take me," said he, "if they catch me doing another the longest day ever I live."

Happy they who have in their neighbourhood such a magistrate as Mr. Marshal! He was a man who, to an exact knowledge of the duties of his office, joined the power of discovering truth from the midst of contradictory evidence, and the happy art of soothing or laughing the angry passions into good-humour. It was a common saying in Hereford that no one ever came out of Justice Marshal's house as angry as he went into it.

Mr. Marshal had scarcely breakfasted when he was informed that Mr. Hill, the verger, wanted to speak to him on business of the utmost importance. Mr. Hill, the verger, was ushered in; and, with gloomy solemnity, took a seat opposite to Mr. Marshal.

"Sad doings in Hereford, Mr. Marshal! Sad doings, sir."

"Sad doings? Why, I was told we had merry doings in Hereford. A ball the night before last, as I heard."

"So much the worse, Mr. Marshal—so much the worse: as those think with reason that see as far into things as I do."

"So much the better, Mr. Hill," said Mr. Marshal, laughing, "so much the better: as those think with reason that see no farther into things than I do."

"But, sir," said the verger, still more solemnly, "this is no laughing matter, nor time for laughing, begging your pardon. Why, sir, the night of that there diabolical ball our Hereford Cathedral, sir, would have been blown up—blown up from the foundation, if it had not been for me, sir!"

"Indeed, Mr. Verger! And pray how, and by whom, was the cathedral to be blown up? and what was there diabolical in this ball?"

Here Mr. Hill let Mr. Marshal into the whole history of his early dislike to O'Neill, and his shrewd suspicions of him the first moment he saw him in Hereford: related in the most prolix manner all that the reader knows already, and concluded by saying that, as he was now certain of his facts, he was come to swear examinations against this villanous Irishman, who, he hoped, would be speedily brought to justice, as he deserved.

"To justice he shall be brought, as he deserves," said Mr. Marshal; "but, before I write, and before you swear, will you have the goodness to inform me how you have made yourself as certain, as you evidently are, of what you call your facts?"

"Sir, that is a secret," replied our wise man, "which I shall trust to you alone;" and he whispered into Mr. Marshal's ear that his information came from Bampfylde the Second, king of the gipsies.

Mr. Marshal instantly burst into laughter; then composing himself, said, "My good sir, I am really glad that you have proceeded no farther in this business; and that no one in Hereford, beside myself, knows that you were on the point of swearing examinations against a man on the evidence of Bampfylde the Second, king of the gipsies. My dear sir, it would be a standing joke against you to the end of your days. A grave man like Mr. Hill! and a verger too! Why, you would be the laughing-stock of Hereford!"

Now Mr. Marshal well knew the character of the man to whom he was talking, who, above all things on earth, dreaded to be laughed at. Mr. Hill coloured all over his face, and, pushing back his wig by way of settling it, showed that he blushed not only all over his face, but all over his head.

"Why, Mr. Marshal, sir," said he, "as to my being laughed at, it is what I did not look for, being, as there are, some men in Hereford to whom I have mentioned that hole in the cathedral, who have thought it no laughing matter, and who have been precisely of my own opinion thereupon."

"But did you tell these gentlemen that you had been consulting the king of the gipsies?"

"No, sir, no: I can't say that I did."

"Then I advise you, keep your own counsel, as I will."

Mr. Hill, whose imagination wavered between the hole in the cathedral and his rick of bark on one side, and between his rick of bark and his dog Jowler on the other, now began to talk of the dog, and now of the rick of bark; and when he had exhausted all he had to say upon these subjects, Mr. Marshal gently pulled him towards the window, and putting a spy-glass into his hand, bade him look towards his own tan-yard, and tell him what he saw. To his great surprise, Mr. Hill saw his rick of bark rebuilt. "Why, it was not there last night," exclaimed he, rubbing his eyes. "Why, some conjuror must have done this."

"No," replied Mr. Marshal, "no conjuror did it: but your friend Bampfylde the Second, king of the gipsies, was the cause of its being rebuilt; and here is the man who actually pulled it down, and who actually rebuilt it."

As he said these words, Mr. Marshal opened the door of an adjoining room and beckoned to the Irish haymaker, who had been taken into custody about an hour before this time. The watch who took Paddy had called at Mr. Hill's house to tell him what had happened, but Mr. Hill was not then at home.

It was with much surprise that the verger heard the simple truth from this poor fellow; but no sooner was he convinced that O'Neill was innocent as to this affair, than he recurred to his other ground of suspicion, the loss of his dog.

The Irish haymaker now stepped forward, and, with a peculiar twist of the hips and shoulders, which those only who have seen it can picture to themselves, said, "Plase your honour's honour, I have a little word to say too about the dog."

"Say it, then," said Mr. Marshal.

"Plase your honour, if I might expect to be forgiven, and let off for pulling down the jontleman's stack, I might be able to tell him what I know about the dog."

"If you can tell me anything about my dog," said the tanner, "I will freely forgive you for pulling down the rick: especially as you have built it up again. Speak the truth, now: did not O'Neill make away with the dog?"

"Not at all, at all, plase your honour," replied the haymaker:

"and the truth of the matter is, I know nothing of the dog, good or bad; but I know something of his collar, if your name, plase your honour, is Hill, as I take it to be."

"My name is Hill: proceed," said the tanner, with great eagerness. "You know something about the collar of my dog Jowler?"

"Plase your honour, this much I know, anyway, that it is now, or was the night before last, at the pawnbroker's there, below in town; for, plase your honour, I was sent late at night (that night that Mr. O'Neill, long life to him! was arrested) to the pawnbroker's for a Jew by Mrs. O'Neill, poor creature! She was in great trouble that same time."

"Very likely," interrupted Mr. Hill: "but go on to the collar; what of the collar?"

"She sent me—I'll tell you the story, plase your honour, *out of the face*—she sent me to the pawnbroker's for the Jew; and, it being so late at night, the shop was shut, and it was with all the trouble in life that I got into the house anyway: and, when I got in, there was none but a slip of a boy up; and he set down the light that he had in his hand, and ran up the stairs to waken his master: and, whilst he was gone, I just made bold to look round at what sort of a place I was in, and at the old clothes and rags and scraps; there was a sort of a frieze trusty."

"A trusty!" said Mr. Hill; "what is that, pray?"

"A big coat, sure, plase your honour: there was a frieze big coat lying in a corner, which I had my eye upon, to trate myself to: I having, as I then thought, money in my little purse enough for it. Well, I won't trouble your honour's honour with telling of you now how I lost my purse in the field, as I found after; but about the big coat—as I was saying, I just lifted it off the ground to see would it fit me; and, as I swung it round, something, plase your honour, hit me a great knock on the shins: it was in the pocket of the coat, whatever it was, I knew; so I looks into the pocket, to see what was it, plase your honour, and out I pulls a hammer and a dog-collar: it was a wonder, both together, they did not break my shins entirely: but it's no matter for my shins now; so, before the boy came down, I just out of idleness spelt out to myself the name that was upon the collar: there were two names, plase your honour, and out of the first there were so many letters hammered out I could make nothing of it at all, at all; but the other name was plain enough to read anyway, and it was Hill, plase your honour's honour, as sure as life: Hill, now."

This story was related in tones and gestures which were so new and strange to English ears and eyes, that even the solemnity of our verger gave way to laughter.

Mr. Marshal sent a summons for the pawnbroker, that he might learn from him how he came by the dog-collar. The pawnbroker, when he found from Mr. Marshal that he could by no other means save himself from being committed to prison, confessed that the collar had been sold to him by Bampfylde the second, king of the gipsies.

A warrant was immediately despatched for his majesty; and Mr. Hill was a good deal alarmed by the fear of its being known in Hereford that he was on the point of swearing examinations against an innocent man upon the evidence of a dog-stealer and a gipsy.

Bampfylde the second made no sublime appearance when he was brought before Mr. Marshal nor could all his astrology avail upon this occasion. The evidence of the pawnbroker was so positive as to the fact of his having sold to him the dog-collar, that there was no resource left for Bampfylde but an appeal to Mr. Hill's mercy. He fell on his knees, and confessed that it was he who stole the dog, which used to bark at him at night so furiously, that he could not commit certain petty depredations by which, as much as by telling fortunes, he made his livelihood.

"And so," said Mr. Marshal, with a sternness of manner which till now he had never shown, "to screen yourself, you accused an innocent man; and by your vile arts would have driven him from Hereford, and have set two families for ever at variance, to conceal that you had stolen a dog."

The king of the gipsies was, without further ceremony, committed to the house of correction. We should not omit to mention that, on searching his hut, the Irish haymaker's purse was found, which some of his majesty's train had emptied. The whole set of gipsies decamped upon the news of the apprehension of their monarch.

Mr. Hill stood in profound silence, leaning upon his walking-stick, whilst the committal was making out for Bampfylde the second. The fear of ridicule was struggling with the natural positiveness of his temper. He was dreadfully afraid that the story of his being taken in by the king of the gipsies would get abroad; and, at the same time, he was unwilling to give up his prejudice against the Irish glover.

"But, Mr. Marshal," cried he, after a long silence, "the hole under the foundation of the cathedral has never been accounted for—that is, was, and ever will be, an ugly mystery to me; and I never can have a good opinion of this Irishman till it is cleared up, nor can I think the cathedral in safety."

"What!" said Mr. Marshal, with an arch smile, "I suppose the verses of the oracle still work upon your imagination, Mr. Hill. They are excellent in their kind. I must have them by heart, that when I am asked the reason why Mr. Hill has taken an aversion to an Irish glover, I may be able to repeat them:

> "Now, take my word,
> Wise men of Hereford,
> None in safety may be,
> Till the bad man doth flee."

"You'll oblige me, sir," said the verger, "if you would never repeat those verses, sir, nor mention, in any company, the affair of the king of the gipsies."

"I will oblige you," replied Mr. Marshal, "if you will oblige me. Will you tell me honestly whether, now that you find this Mr. O'Neill is neither a dog-killer nor a puller-down of bark-ricks, you feel that you could forgive him for being an Irishman, if the mystery, as you call it, of the hole under the cathedral was cleared up?"

"But that is not cleared up, I say, sir," cried Mr. Hill, striking his walking-stick forcibly upon the ground with both his hands. "As to the matter of his being an Irishman, I have nothing to say to it; I am not saying anything about that, for I know we all are born where it pleases God, and an Irishman may be as good as another. I know that much, Mr. Marshal, and I am not one of those illiberal-minded, ignorant people that cannot abide a man that was not born in England. Ireland is now in his majesty's dominions. I know very well, Mr. Marshal; and I have no manner of doubt, as I said before, that an Irishman born may be as good, almost, as an Englishman born."

"I am glad," said Mr. Marshal, "to hear you speak—almost as reasonably as an Englishman born and every man ought to speak; and I am convinced that you have too much English hospitality to persecute an inoffensive stranger, who comes amongst us trusting to our justice and good nature."

"I would not persecute a stranger, God forbid!" replied the verger, "if he was, as you say, inoffensive."

"And if he was not only inoffensive, but ready to do every service in his power to those who are in want of his assistance, we should not return evil for good, should we?"

"That would be uncharitable, to be sure; and, moreover, a scandal," said the verger.

"Then," said Mr. Marshal, "will you walk with me as far as the widow Smith's, the poor woman whose house was burnt last winter? This haymaker, who lodged near her, can show us the way to her present abode."

During his examination of Paddy M'Cormack, who would tell his whole history, as he called it, *out of the face,* Mr. Marshal heard several instances of the humanity and goodness of O'Neill, which Paddy related to excuse himself for that warmth of attachment to his cause that had been manifested so injudiciously by pulling down the rick of bark in revenge for the rest. Amongst other things, Paddy mentioned his countryman's goodness to the widow Smith. Mr. Marshal was determined, therefore, to see whether he had, in this instance, spoken the truth; and he took Mr. Hill with him, in hopes of being able to show him the favourable side of O'Neill's character.

Things turned out just as Mr. Marshal expected. The poor widow and her family, in the most simple and affecting manner, described the distress from which they had been relieved by the good gentleman and lady—the lady was Phoebe Hill; and the praises that were bestowed upon Phoebe were delightful to her father's ear, whose angry passions had now all subsided.

The benevolent Mr. Marshal seized the moment when he saw Mr. Hill's heart was touched, and exclaimed, "I must be

acquainted with this Mr. O'Neill. I am sure we people of
Hereford ought to show some hospitality to a stranger who has
so much humanity. Mr. Hill, will you dine with him tomorrow at
my house?"

Mr. Hill was just going to accept of this invitation, when the
recollection of all he had said to his club about the hole under
the cathedral came across him, and, drawing Mr. Marshal aside,
he whispered, "But, sir, sir, that affair of the hole under the
cathedral has not been cleared up yet."

At this instant the widow Smith exclaimed, "Oh! here comes
my little Mary," (one of her children, who came running in);
"this is the little girl, sir, to whom the lady has been so good.
Make your curtsey, child. Where have you been all this while?"

"Mammy," said the child, "I've been showing the lady my rat."

"Lord bless her! Gentlemen, the child has been wanting me
this many a day to go to see this tame rat of hers; but I could
never get time, never—and I wondered, too, at the child's liking
such a creature. Tell the gentlemen, dear, about your rat. All I
know is that, let her have but never such a tiny bit of bread for
breakfast or supper, she saves a little of that little for this rat of
hers; she and her brothers have found it out somewhere by the
cathedral."

"It comes out of a hole under the wall of the cathedral," said
one of the older boys; "and we have diverted ourselves watching
it, and sometimes we have put victuals for it—so it has grown,
in a manner, tame-like."

Mr. Hill and Mr. Marshal looked at one another during this
speech; and the dread of ridicule again seized on Mr. Hill, when
he apprehended that, after all he had said, the mountain might
at last bring forth—a rat. Mr. Marshal, who instantly saw what
passed in the verger's mind, relieved him from this fear by
refraining even from a smile on this occasion. He only said to
the child, in a grave manner, "I am afraid, my dear, we shall be
obliged to spoil your diversion. Mr. Verger, here, cannot suffer
rat-holes in the cathedral; but, to make you amends for the loss
of your favourite, I will give you a very pretty little dog, if you
have a mind."

The child was well pleased with this promise; and, at Mr.

Marshal's desire, she then went along with him and Mr. Hill to the cathedral, and they placed themselves at a little distance from that hole which had created so much disturbance. The child soon brought the dreadful enemy to light; and Mr. Hill, with a faint laugh, said, "I'm glad it's no worse, but there were many in our club who were of my opinion; and, if they had not suspected O'Neill too, I am sure I should never have given you so much trouble, sir, as I have done this morning. But, I hope, as the club know nothing about that vagabond, that king of the gipsies, you will not let anyone know anything about the prophecy, and all that? I am sure I am very sorry to have given you so much trouble, Mr. Marshal."

Mr. Marshal assured him that he did not regret the time which he had spent in endeavouring to clear up all those mysteries and suspicions; and Mr. Hill gladly accepted his invitation to meet O'Neill at his house the next day. No sooner had Mr. Marshal brought one of the parties to reason and good humour, than he went to prepare the other for a reconciliation. O'Neill and his mother were both people of warm but forgiving tempers—the arrest was fresh in their minds; but when Mr. Marshal represented to them the whole affair, and the verger's prejudices, in a humorous light, they joined in the good-natured laugh; and O'Neill declared that, for his part, he was ready to forgive and to forget everything, if he could but see Miss Phoebe in the Limerick gloves.

Phoebe appeared the next day, at Mr. Marshal's, in the Limerick gloves; and no perfume ever was so delightful to her lover as the smell of the rose-leaves in which they had been kept.

Mr. Marshal had the benevolent pleasure of reconciling the two families. The tanner and the glover of Hereford became, from bitter enemies, useful friends to each other; and they were convinced by experience that nothing could be more for their mutual advantage than to live in union.

THE LAST OF THE LINE[*]
Anna Maria Fielding Hall
(1800–1881)

It was on a tranquil evening, in the sweet summer-month of
June, that a lady of no ordinary appearance sat at an open
casement of many-coloured glass, and overlooked a wild, but singularly beautiful, country. From the window, a flight of steep stone
steps led to a narrow terrace, that, in former times, had been carefully guarded by high parapets of rudely-carved granite; but they
had fallen to decay, and lay in mouldering heaps on the shrubby
bank, which ran almost perpendicularly to a rapid stream that
danced like a sunny spirit through the green meadows, dotted and
animated with sheep and their sportive lambs. In the distance,
rude and rugged mountains towered in native dignity, "high in air,"
their grim and sterile appearance forming an extraordinary, but
not unpleasing, contrast to the pure and happy-looking valley at
their base, where, however, a few dingy peasant-cottages lay thinly
scattered, injuring, rather than enlivening, a scene that nature had
done much to adorn, and man nothing to preserve. Half way up
the nearest mountain, a little chapel, dedicated to "our Lady of
Grace," hung, like a wren's nest, on what seemed a point of rock;
but even its rustic cross was invisible from the antique casement.
Often and anxiously did the lady watch the distant figures who
trod the hill-side towards the holy place, to perform some act of
penance or devotion.

---

[*]From *Sketches of Irish Character*, 1829.

It was impossible to look on that interesting woman without affection; one might have almost thought her destined—

"To come like truth, and disappear like dreams."

Though she was young, there was much of the dignity of silent sorrow in her aspect; and it was difficult to converse with her, without feeling her influence—not to overpower, but to soften. Her form was slight, but rounded to the most perfect symmetry, and an extraordinary quantity of hair, black as the raven's wing, was braided, somewhat after the fashion of other lands, over a high and well-formed brow; although, such was the style of the time; she wore no head-dress, except what nature had bestowed; a golden rosary, and cross of the same metal, gemmed with many precious jewels, hung over a harp-stand of antique workmanship; a few of the strings of the harp were broken, and a pile of richly-bound music gave no token of being often disturbed. Silken ottomans, gilded vases, fresh-gathered flowers, and a long embroidered sofa, filled up, almost to crowding, the small apartment. In a little recess, opposite the window, a child's couch was fitted with much taste and care; the hangings were of blue damask, curiously inwrought with silver, such as the nuns in France and Flanders delight to emboss; there was also a loose coverlet of the same material, and a tasseled oblong cushion at either end. I have said that the lady was seated at the casement; sometimes she pressed her small white fingers to her brow, and then passed them, over its rounded surface, as if to dispel, by that simple movement, thoughts, the unbidden guests of anxious hours—but still it was only for a moment her gaze was turned from her best treasure, her only child; her eye followed it as, in its nurse's arms, it enjoyed the evening breeze that played amid its light and clustering hair; the baby had blue eyes and a fair skin; and if it sometimes, in the infantine seriousness that passed as airy shadows over a smiling landscape, resembled its mother, now, as it laughed and shouted, in broken accents, "Mamma! mamma!" she thought how like its father it spoke and looked. Clavis Abbey—as the strange mixture of ancient and modern building, inhabited by the household of Sir John Clavis, was called—was wisely situated. The monks of old always chose

happily for their monasteries; the sites of their ruined aisles tell
of the good taste, as well as good sense, of their projectors. Hill,
wood, and water, were ever in their neighbourhood, and the reel
deer and salmon were always near, to contribute to their repast.

But the fair possessions had, nearly two centuries before our
tale commences, passed from the hands of holy Mother Church.
The marvellous tale of its exchange of masters is still often
repeated, and always credited; it is said and believed that the
stream, which runs through the valley I have described, is, every
midsummer-night, of a deep-red hue, in mysterious commelio-
ration of the massacre of the priests of that abbey, which took
place as late as the Elizabethan reign. Certain it is that the pro-
jector of such indiscriminate slaughter never reaped the rich
harvest he anticipated; for, unable from severe illness to visit the
court of the maiden queen, he despatched his son's tutor on the
mission, with communications of the services he had rendered
to the state, and a petition for a grant of the lands he had rescued from "popery." The tutor, however, made himself so agreeable to the royal lady, that she either was, or affected to be,
severely angered by the unnecessary effusion of blood; and, so
far from approving, testified her displeasure, and bestowed the
fair lands of the murdered monks upon Oliver Clavis, the false,
but handsome, accessary of the priest-slayer. But no family
could take possession of consecrated ground in Ireland, without
falling under the ban of both church and people; and, notwithstanding the bland and liberal conduct of the new owner of the
estate, then called Clavis Abbey, Oliver lived and died unpopu-
lar. Tradition says that none of the heirs male of the family ever
departed peaceably in their beds, and much learned and
unlearned lore is still extant upon the subject.

Somewhat about the year 1783, Sir John Clavis entered upon
his title and property, in consequence of the sudden demise of
his father, Sir Henry, who was drowned on a moonshiny night,
when the air and the sea were calm, and he was returning from
an excursion to one of those fairy islands that at once beautify
and render dangerous the Irish coast. The people who accompanied him, on that last day of his existence, say that he had
been in unusual health and spirits during the morning, and

had fished, and sung, and drank as usual—that as the night advanced he became reserved and gloomy, and, as they neared the coast, insisted on taking the helm—that, suddenly yielding the guidance of his little vessel, he sprang overboard—that immediately the crew crowded to save him, but a black cloud descended on the waters, and hid his form from their eyes, and it was not until the boat had driven an entire mile (as well as they could calculate) from the spot, they were enabled to behold the sea and the sky. Some laughed, some surmised, but many credited the tale; for superstition had hardly, at that period, resigned any of her strongholds; and the peasantry, to this day, believe that Sir Henry Clavis acted under the influence of a spirit-guide, that had lured him to sudden death, conformably with the old prophecy—

> "The party shall fail by Clavis led,
> And none of the name shall die in their bed."

Sir John had just completed his college course when he was called upon to support the honours of his house and name. At Trinity he was considered more as an amiable, gentlemanly young man, than an esprit fort, or one likely to lead in public life. At that period the college lads were a very different set of youths from what they are at present. The rude but generous hospitality, the thoughtless daring, the angry politics, the feudal feeling that characterized the gentry of the time, were not likely to send forth subjects submissive to college rule; and the citizens of Dublin were too often insulted and aggrieved by the insolent aristocratic airs of unfledged boys, ripe for mischief, who, half in earnest, half in jest, sported with their comforts, and often with their lives. Party feeling, also, ran (as unhappily there it always does) to a dreadful height; and the young baronet, whose father had invariably drank "The Glorious Memory," and "Protestant Ascendancy," every day after dinner, was frequently called upon to defend or support his party, although he invariably declared that as yet he was of none—that he must wait to make up his mind, &c. &c. It must be confessed that this extraordinary irresolution, at such a period, was more the effect of constitutional apathy than of reflection; he had a good deal of the consciousness of birth and wealth about him, but he disliked either mental or bodily exertion. As an only child, he had suffered nothing like contradiction; and had he horsewhipped and abused his servants (when, at the age of twelve, he sported two of his own racers at the Curragh of Kildare), instead of speaking to them as fellow-creatures in a mild and kindly voice, it would have elicited no rebuke from his father, who secretly regretted that the youth was neither likely to become a five-bottle man, a staunch Orangeman, nor a Member of Parliament—the only three things he considered worth living for.

The young baronet never could have resolved upon visiting the Continent—an exploit he had long talked of—but that an anticipated general election frightened him away, as he would certainly, if at home, have been expected to offer himself as a candidate, and make speeches. He hated trouble, and of the two exertions chose the least—committed his affairs, for twelve calendar months, to the management of Denny Dacey, his nurse's son, who had acted satisfactorily, as steward, since the second childhood of the old and respected man who had for sixty years filled the situation; and left the Abbey, attended by only two servants and one travelling-carriage. This was a matter of surprise and conversation to many, more particularly as Sir Henry and his neighbour, Mr. Dorncliff, a Cromwellian settler, had arranged that their children should be united, when of sufficient age. Miss Dorncliff was handsome, and an heiress, and, it was said, in no degree averse to the union; they had been companions in childhood, but the lady, it would appear, was of too unromantic a disposition to remove the young baronet's indifference. As his carriage rolled past the avenue that led to her dwelling, he merely leaned forward, and cast a fleeting glance towards the house. Where he met, and to what precise circumstance he owed the possession of so lovely a wife as the lady I have endeavoured to describe, is still a mystery; his business-letters conveyed no intelligence of his marriage; nor was it until the arrival of gay furniture, from a fashionable Dublin upholsterer, that the idea of such an event occurred to the inhabitants of Clavis. When the baronet returned, and announced, as his lady, her who leaned upon his arm; when the domestics received her with that warm-hearted and affectionate respect for which Irish servants are so justly celebrated; and when the rumour went abroad that Sir John Clavis had married a Spanish lady, a Catholic, and "one who had little more English than a Kerry-man," great was the consternation, and many and various the conjectures. "What will become of the 'Protestant Ascendancy,' and the 'Glorious and Immortal Memory,' now that a popish mistress is come to Clavis?" said one party. "Some chance of luck and grace turning to the ould Abbey, now that the right sort's in it," observed the other. Not a few affirmed that the lady had absconded from a convent; others asserted that she was picked off, with a few other survivors, from a wrecked vessel in the Mediterranean; those who had not seen her whispered that she was no better than she should be; but Miss Dorncliff—who, at first, perhaps, to show she was heart-whole, and afterwards from real regard, was often Lady Clavis's guest—generously declared that she was the most charming woman she had ever met, that she was highly accomplished, and, although a Catholic and a Spaniard, anything but a bigot.

Her want of knowledge of the language, when she arrived, prevented her joining in conversation either with those who visited her, or those at whose houses she was received. Perfectly unconscious of the rules and etiquette of society in our colder regions, she was sure to commit some grievous fault in the arrangement of her guests, which invariably threw her husband into an ill temper, that, after the honey-moon was over, he seldom thought it necessary to conceal. Sir John had shaken off a good deal of his ennui by journeying; and when he came home he no longer stood on neutral ground, but suffered the excitement of politics to take the place of that which is the accompaniment of travelling. He had now discovered that, for the honour of the house, it was necessary he should adopt his father's side of the question; and accordingly the gardener was ordered to fill the flower-beds with orange lilies, and the hangings of the spare rooms were garnished with orange bindings. Unfortunately, the members of an Orange Lodge were invited to dine at the Abbey, and Lady Clavis positively refused to wear their colour, in any way, because she considered it as the symbol of persecution to the Catholic religion, of which she was a devout and faithful member. When her husband, after much contention, gave up the point, she ordered a green velvet dress for the occasion, embroidered with golden shamrocks; she did this with a view to gratify him, never imagining that the colour which emblems the beauty and fertility of Ireland, could be obnoxious to any body of Irishmen. What, then, was her astonishment, when he, whom she had been so anxious to please, expressed a most angry opinion of her costume—which occasioned a flood of tears from one party, and from the other, an over hastily expressed desire that, as she could never understand the customs of the country, she would give up trying to do so. Matrimonial disputes are dreadfully uninteresting in the recital—not entertaining as are lovers' quarrels, simply because there is no danger of a heart-breaking separation arising from them; it is only the two engaged in those unhappy differences that can understand their bitterness; the world has, for them, but little sympathy. Enough, then be it, that the innocent green velvet was the commencement of much real disagreement: the lady insisting that she had the dress made as a compliment to his party; the gentleman protesting that it could not be so, as green was always opposed to orange. This he repeated over and over again, without troubling himself to inquire whether his wife understood him or not. Many an unpleasantness grew out of this trifle, that continued silently, like the single drop of rain, to wear the rock of domestic happiness. Sir John persevered in drinking deeply of the bitter cup of politics, that universal destroyer of society and kindly feeling. He soon discovered, or imagined he had discovered, how perfectly a continental education unfits the most amiable woman in the world for the society and habits of our islands; and the very efforts Lady Clavis made to appear cheerful, were silent reproaches to him for not endeavouring to make her so; they had, however, still one feeling in common—affection for their child.

While the mistress of Clavis Abbey was engaged in watching every movement of her beloved daughter, as the nurse paced slowly beneath her turret-window, the baronet was sitting *tête-à-tête* with no other than Deimy Dacey, who, from being what in England is termed bailiff to the estate, had risen to the rank of agent, under the title, as his correspondents set forth, of "Dionysius Dacey, Esq.," &c. &c. How this person ever acquired the influence he possessed over his patron, must now remain a mystery: it is to be supposed that he insinuated himself into his good graces, as a weasel does into a rabbit-burrow, by various twists and windings, of which nobler animals are incapable. It was no secret in the county that, although Sir John's political apathy no longer existed, he had not acquired the active habits that are so especially necessary where a gentleman's affairs are embarrassed, and where nothing but good sense, and steady economy, can retrieve them. During the young baronet's residence abroad, Dacey had exceedingly prospered; and though one or two shrewd landholders suspected he used means, not consistent with his employer's interests, to obtain both, influence and wealth, there was so much plausibility about the man, that the most watchful could bring nothing home to him; his bearing was blunt and open; he affected honesty, but his look belied the utterance of his tongue, for his eye lacked the expression of truth, and instead of looking forth straightly from beneath its pent-house lid, was everlastingly twisting into corners—with cat-like quickness, watching a fitting opportunity, when those with whom he conversed were busied about other matters, to scan and observe their countenances. It has been to me an entertaining, though often an unpleasing, study, to attend to the varied expressions conveyed by the mere action of the eye, almost without reference to the other features; and I would avoid, as I would a poisoned adder, the person whose eye quivers or looks down.

The two friends (such is the usual term given to those who eat meat at the same board) were seated at either end of a somewhat long table, on which were piled papers of various dates and dimensions; a huge bowl of punch had been nearly emptied of its contents, and the baronet did not appear particularly fit for business. He leaned listlessly on the table, as if in reverie, and it was only Dacey's voice that roused him from his reflections.

"But, my dear Sir John," he commenced, with his peculiar drawl, while his eye was fixed on the punch-ladle; "My dear Sir John, 'pon my sowl it weighs upon my conscience, so it does, to be managing here, and you to the fore, with such a fine head and so much cleverness (a sly glance to see how the flattery took); 'tis a shame you don't turn to it yourself, for by-'n-by you'll, may-be, find things worse nor you think 'em, as I have told you before, God knows—"

"And will my looking over these cursed papers make things better? It is positively enough to set me mad—just at a time, too, when our grand county meeting is coming on, and the general election, and so much exertion expected from me; and the house will be full of English company from the castle, and Lady C. has not an idea how English people should be entertained."

"But sure Miss Dorncliff is coming to stop with my lady while they stay."

"Very true; she is a capital, good-natured girl, 'faith, and much better looking than she was eight years ago, when I left Ireland. Oh, dear! I wonder young men of fortune marry, Dacey!"

"Sir John, it is very necessary."

"Well, well, I suppose it is, but say no more about it; there are enough of disagreeable subjects on the table already." The baronet looked upon the pile of papers, and the agent glanced keenly up, but his eye was quickly withdrawn. "My lady was in a convent, I believe, Sir John?"

"Ay; it was a fine exploit to get her out of it. Well, poor thing, she trusted to my honour, and was not deceived."

"Of course you were married by a priest?" (This was said cautiously.)

"To be sure we were, and by a jovial fellow too; he went with me to the convent-wall, and performed the ceremony at the foot of a beautiful old cross, by the way-side, as the moon was sailing over our heads, and the orange-trees were showering perfume around us. Poor Madelina!" he continued, almost involuntarily, "I found the withered orange-blossoms, which that night I bound upon her maiden brow, encased in a casket, with the hair of our child, only this morning."

"You had the ceremony repeated on your arrival in England?" inquired Dacey.

Sir John Clavis fixed his eyes upon the reptile, and, in a sterner tone of voice than was his wont, in his turn became the querist.

"Why do you ask?"

"For no reason, only that if you had a son it would be well to see that the marriage was firm and legal."

"Thank you," replied the baronet, drily, "there is not much chance of that being the case; and if there was—"

A long pause followed the last sentence, which neither seemed inclined to disturb. Dacey gathered the papers towards him, and, pulling his spectacles from his forehead to his nose, occupied himself in sorting and placing them in separate piles; every five or ten minutes a heavy sigh escaped from his lips, the last of which was so audible, that Sir John exclaimed, "What the devil, man alive, do you growl for in that manner?—one would think that you expected the ghost of your uncle, the priest, to start forth from the papers, and upbraid you with your apostacy!"

"Sorra a ghost at all, then, Sir John, among the papers; only the reality of botherin' debts, custodiums, thrown-up leases on account of the rackrent, and the Lord knows what!"

"And whose fault is it?" replied the gentleman, angrily; "did I not leave it all to your management? The property was a good property, and why should it not continue so? I'm sure I can't think how the money goes; to do Lady C. justice, she spends nothing."

"There's the hounds, the hunters, and five grooms, of one sort or other, Sir John; to say nothing of town-houses, and carriages, and—"

"My father always had the same establishment," interrupted Sir John, "and never kept an agent to overlook matters either."

"More's the pity!" ejaculated the manager (the exclamation might have been taken in two ways).

"There's no manner of use in my keeping you, if I am to be pestered with these eternal accounts—accounts—accounts—morning, noon, and night. The simple fact is," continued Sir John, rising from his seat, "the simple fact is, money I want, and money I must have. After flying to the Continent to avoid an election, I find that now, at this particular crisis, I cannot help running into the very strait I endeavoured to steer clear of. My friends say it is necessary, and would even subscribe (if I permitted) to return me free of expense; that I will never do—so money, Dacey, money *I* must have, that's certain."

"It's easy say money," retorted the agent; "will you sell, Sir John?"

"What?" interrogated the baronet.

"There's the Corner estate, that long strip, close by Ballyraggan; your cousin Corney of the hill has long had an eye to it, and would lav down something handsome."

"You poor, pitiful scoundrel!" exclaimed Sir John, "do you think it's come to that, for me to sell land, like a huckster?—and to Corney too, a fellow that gathers inches off every estate, as a magpie picks rl'pennies!—a fellow so basely born, and basely bred, has, nevertheless, managed to accumulate wealth like a pawnbroker, on the miseries of others! I know he has had an eye on that property these eight years, but look-sooner than he should have it, I'll beg my bread—I'll sell the estate to a stranger to prevent the possibility of his ever possessing an acre of the land."

"Please yerself, sir," replied the manager, sweeping some of the papers into a wide-mouthed canvass sack which he drew from under his chair. "Here's Mr. Damask's, the upholsterer's, letter—swears, if he's not paid, he'll clap on an execution like lightning; it's as good as £2,500 now, with costs."

"Fire and fury!" exclaimed the baronet, who, his apathy once shaken off, became terrible in his violence; "do you want to drive me mad?"

"Then I'll say nothing of Mr. Barry Mahon's little letter," continued the man of business, quietly, "who writes, that as you've decided on standing, in opposition to him, he'll trouble you for the money he lent you as good as four years ago, to complete some purchase or another; it ends very civilly though, by saying that it's only the knowledge that a gentleman like you will be a formidable adversary, which obliges him to strain every nerve to make his own step firm."

"A blight upon him and his civility!"

"Then here is—." Mr. Dacey was prevented from finishing his sentence, by Sir John's striking the table so violently with his clenched hand, that the very punch-bowl trembled, and the agent ejaculated, "Lord, save us!"

"Look here!" said the baronet, "you have, I know—means, somehow or other, of raising money when you like; find me the sum of ten thousand pounds by this day week, and that very estate, so coveted by my cousin Corney, shall be yours for ever, at a peppercorn rent, provided the matter be kept secret; mind, provided it be kept secret, and you bind yourself never to let a twig of it into Corney's possession."

"It's easy to keep secret a thing that never happens," observed Dacey, rolling the cord of the bag between his finger and thumb; "is it me get money when I like?—and I obliged to go at credit even for these brogues on my feet!"—and he put forth a topped boot, well-polished and shining, as he spoke.

"The Corner estate, as it is called," repeated Sir John.

"At a peppercorn rent," pondered Dacey; "if a body could any way make up the money, I'd do a dale to oblige you, sir; and, though I've neither cross nor coin to bless myself with, to be sure I know them that has, who, may-be, for a valuable consideration, might—though I don't know—the little estate—eh!—ten thousand—it's badly worth that, Sir John, unless, indeed, you'd throw the fourteen acres of pasture by the loch into it."

"Well!" exclaimed the indolent baronet, though perfectly conscious that the land was worth double the sum; "we'll talk about that, provided you insure me the money; and now gather your parchments, and vanish; I've had enough of arithmetic to last me for some months—and, Dacey S."

"Yes, sir."

"After the election, I will really look into matters myself; but, at present, when the good of my country is at stake—when we are threatened from without, and with rebellion from within—the man must be basely selfish who thinks of self.—Oh, Dacey—did you see the Madeira safely into the cellar?"

"Yes, Sir John."

"Good night, Dacey!—there—good night—you won't forget—ten thousand—hard gold—none of your flimsy paper—the Corner estate."

"And the pasture."

"There, good night," repeated the baronet, as the wily agent bowed himself out of the apartment. Sir John Clavis rose from his seat, and threw open the window which was directly under the turret that formed the boudoir of his Spanish wife; indeed, it was the sound of her guitar that had drawn him to it; and he recognised a favourite *seguidilla*, to which he had written words; he remembered having taught her to repeat them; and the full rich voice that had given them so much beauty—if in that twilight hour it sounded less melodious—had never fallen upon his ear so full of tenderness; its simple burthen—

"Sweet olive-groves of Spain,"

brought the remembrance of what Madelina was to him, in the days when he playfully chid the mispronunciation of his poetry; and as the prospect of receiving the ten thousand, and not being plagued about money matters, had somewhat softened his temper (the idea that he was diminishing his property had no share whatever in his thoughts—possessing, as he did, the dangerous—nay, fatal, faculty of looking only on to-day), he thought, I say, of his wife, with more complacency than he had done since the affair of the green velvet. He was pleased when he heard Miss Dorncliif (of whose arrival he was unconscious) urge her to repeat the strain. She commenced, but at a line which he well remembered—

"I know no blessing but thy smile."

Her voice faltered, and the next moment he heard her friend chiding away her tear; his first impulse was to proceed to her apartment, and inquire their cause; but then he hated scenes; and vanity or curiosity, or both, prompted him to remain; and the broken dialogue which followed, happily for the repose of his soul, roused, in his wife's cause, the best feelings of his heart. Many were the affectionate expressions lavished by Miss Dorncliff on her friend, and many the entreaties that she would cease to agitate herself upon what, she insisted, was a surmise without foundation.

"You would not say so," replied Madelina, "if you had seen his attentions, his tenderness, on the Continent—or heard his

repeated promises that my religion should be held sacred; the little silver shrine, that my sainted so often knelt to, I have been
obliged to remove, even from this which it is mockery to all my
own; and though I cannot understand all he says—and though
his eye is bright, and his lip smiles, sometimes, yet he never looks
upon me as he used; to me his countenance is sadly changed."

"I'll tell you what, my dear," replied her friend, taking advantage of a pause in her complaint, "adopt the course I should
have taken, if my good father's scheme had, unfortunately for
me, been carried into effect. Assert your own dignity; if he looks
as cold as snow, do you look as cold as ice—if he stamps, do you
storm—if he orders, do you counter-order—if he says, 'I will,'
do you say 'you shan't.' My life on it!—such conduct for one
week would bring him sighing to your feet. Here you sit, with
your baby, which, if he had the common feelings of a man, he
would worship you for presenting to him—"

"Stop, my dear Margaret," said Lady Clavis; "do him not
injustice; he loves his child as fondly as father ever loved a child;
he has not changed to it—"

"Yet," interrupted, in her turn, the indignant Margaret, "he
has not changed yet, but who can tell how soon he may? The
man who would change to you must be base indeed."

"He is not base," replied the wife, in a sweet, low tone, which
penetrated into the inmost recesses of Sir John's heart, "not
base, only weak; he is surrounded by a parcel of flatterers, many
of whom hate me because of my religion, and others for reasons
which I cannot define; but look, Margaret, were he to treat me
as a dog, were he to spurn me from him, and trample me to
dust, even that dust would rise to heaven's own gate to ask for
blessings on his head."

"She is an angel after all!" thought Sir John.

"You are a fool, my dear!" both thought and exclaimed Miss
Dorncliff; "and I only wish I were big enough to throw him over
the terrace of this old musty place, and I would soon choose you
a husband worthy of your love."

"Upon my word, I am much obliged to you, Miss Minx!"
murmured the baronet, as he cautiously closed the window,
resolving to turn over a new leaf, and station himself, for the

remainder of the evening, in his wife's dressing-room. He could not avoid thinking, as he passed through the winding corridors and up the staircases, "a very pretty wife I should have had, if it had been as my worthy agent seems to think it might be even now. The fellow means well, but he is mistaken; I should not have been able to call my life my own—the termagant! Thank goodness, I escaped her! I never valued my blessing before!"

He met his child in the lobby, and took the laughing cherub from the nurse's to his own arms. As he prepared to enter, "You may go down, Mary," he said, seeing the maid waiting to receive the child. "I will take Miss Madeline in myself."

How easily can a man make the woman who truly loves him happy! It was enough for Lady Clavis that her husband was at her side—enough that he smiled upon her—enough that he called her "darling:" although it would have been better for them both, had she possessed the strength of mind to entitle her to the name of "friend," the most sacred, yet the most abused of all endearing terms. Miss Dorncliff exulted in her happiness, though her more cool and deliberate temperament led her to believe that Sir John's "love-fit," as she termed it in her own mind, would not be of long duration. She little knew the service she had rendered Lady Clavis by her somewhat intemperate advice; nor the dread of the baronet lest any portion of that advice should be followed by his gentle wife.

As Mary Conway, Madelina's nurse, descended to the vestibule, she heard a voice, whose sound was familiar to her ear, repeat her name two or three times, and in various tones; she lingered for a moment, and then, as if gladly remembering that her infant charge was committed to its parent's care, turned into an abrupt passage, leading from the great hall to one of the archways, where dews and damps mouldered from day to day upon the massive walls.

"What are ye after wantin' now, Mister Benjy?" she inquired, as the outline of her lover's (for there is no use in concealing the fact) figure became visible to her laughing eyes.

"Nothing particular, that is to say very particular," replied the youth, who was no other than Dacey's nephew; "only I'm going a journey to-night, and I thought I'd be all the better for your

God speed, or, may-be, a bit of prayer to the saints you think so much of."

"A journey—where to?" inquired Mary, with a palpitating heart.

"Why, thin, just to Dublin, Mary, honey. And it's glad enough I'd be to get out of this murderin' grand ould place, only just for one single thing."

"And might a body know what that is?" again inquired the maiden.

"Honour bright, Mary, because I shan't see yer sweet smilin' face for many a long day, may-be; for uncle says he has a dale o' business to transact in Dublin, and that he'll be wanting me to look afther it; indeed, I'm thinkin' that hie has a notion we're keeping company, and don't over like it; though, Mary, darlin', it's more nor he can do to put between us."

Mary covered her face with her hand, and, though no sigh or sound escaped her lips, tears bedewed her cheeks. She was nothing more nor less than a frank-hearted, good-natured girl, with only three or, perhaps, four definite ideas in her pretty round head—the first of which was decided love for her mistress, and her mistress's child—a great portion of affection for Benjamin Dacey—and no small regard for finery, in all its branches and bearings; she consequently had not a multiplicity of objects to divide her attention, which was therefore steadily devoted to the service of her three or four several propensities. The idea of her lover's being sent away, and to Dublin too, overwhelmed her with grief, to which she would have given more audible vent, but that Benjamin had unwittingly observed, his "uncle didn't over like his keeping company with her," which aroused the maiden's pride; she therefore said, "that, indeed, Mr. Dacey ought to remimber when he once held two or three acres of land under her father," and that, "though she was at the Abbey, she was far from being a rale sarvant; she took care of Miss Maddy more from pure love nor anything else. May-be, it was Mister Benjy himself that wanted to be off the promise—if so, she was willing and ready," &c. &c. But, in fact, these lovers' quarrels are the same in all cases; I could give a recipe by which people might quarrel, agreeably, ten times a week on an average—only, as love would be the principal ingredient in my prescription, I fear the misunderstandings would be too soon understood for your genuine downright-in-earnest quarrellers. I must not tarry with those young people, during their parting scene, but only recount that "Mary," as she afterwards expressed it, "got a dale out of Benjy, which no one should be the wiser for; only her heart was fairly crushed—thinkin' what a misfortune it was to a boy like him to have such an uncle;" even this she only communicated to her particular friend and companion, Patty Grace.

When the expected company arrived from Dublin—from "the Castle," as it has been familiarly termed for ages—it was evident that Sir John had nerved his mind to some great undertaking to which he was secretly urged by Dennis Dacey. Indeed, the particular party which had once been led by his father, were anxious he should tread in the same steps, and they again regretted that his union with a Catholic was likely to cool his ardour in "the good cause;" they, however, did their best to urge him forward—and "the glorious and immortal memory" was drank so often after dinner, that those who sacrificed to the sentiment had neither glorious nor inglorious memory left. The humble parish priest never joined in these revels; and when Dacey, in Lady Clavis's presence, hinted at this circumstance, and had, moreover, the audacity to assert that his absence was a tacit acknowledgment of disloyalty, the lady roused herself in defence of her ancient friend, and told the agent that, if religion was a proof of loyalty, he must be the worst of traitors, for he was a renegade from the faith of his father's, and had changed for the love of filthy lucre. Dacey trembled and turned pale; but as he quitted the apartment he muttered a deep and bitter curse against the lady of Clavis Abbey. Not only had "the little estate" been secretly transferred to Dacey, along with the fourteen acres of pasture, and the ten thousand pounds paid for present relief, but other sums must, at this crisis, be advanced to relieve the necessities of the proprietor, and other lands sacrificed to feed the rapacity of the agent. Mr. Barry Mahon resolved to stand as the people's champion, and already were the addresses of the several candidates duly printed in the county papers. The

Abbey became such a scene of interminable bustle and confusion, as the day for the commencement of the election approached, that it would be difficult to convey an idea of the strange persons and objects which crowded on each other. To Mary Conway's great delight, Benjamin unexpectedly returned; and, from the manner in which his uncle received him, it might be supposed that he was not particularly pleased at the circumstance; he, however, carved out for him the task of managing (dare I say bribing?) a few refractory freeholders at some distance; but the young man did not depart until he had whispered some words of moment into his true love's ear. The same evening, when Mary was undressing the little Madeline, Lady Clavis entered the room, happy to escape from a tumult she could hardly understand.

"I'm so glad yer honourable ladyship's come in," said the girl; "I wanted so much to know what you'd have packed up to take into town to-morrow, my lady—as, in course, you mean to go with his honour to see the election and all that?"

"Indeed, Mary," replied Lady Clavis, "I have no such intention; I shall be but too glad to escape the bustle of it here—and I should be only in the way, Sir John says."

"Och, my grief! does his honour, the masther, say that? But, no matter, Madam, dear; for the love o' God, as ye value yer own honour, and the honour of this sweet baby, go!—go, for God's sake!—or you'll be sorry for it—mark my words!"

Lady Clavis was astonished at the girl's vehement manner and gestures, but still she remained firm to her purpose. She was suffering acutely from mental anxiety and bodily exertion; and as Sir John had continued to treat her with great kindness, she was anxious to show how willingly she would yield to his wishes— even where they were opposed to her own. But Mary was not to be thus satisfied. She "hushowed" her little charge to sleep, and descended to the lobby that led to her master's study. She paused for a few moments at the entrance, and inclined her head so as to catch any sound that might pass along, having ascertained that persons were speaking within. I cannot avoid lamenting that she was led away, by what might be called "natural curiosity," to draw near—very near; so near that her ear covered the key-hole—and listen—systematically listen—to whatever conversation was going on. She might have remained some fifteen minutes, in no very comfortable attitude, when she suddenly started up; but had hardly receded three steps from the door, when it was opened, and the round vulgar face of Dacey appeared, carefully prying into the darkness. Mary saw she could not escape unnoticed, so, with ready wit, she inquired, "Oh, Misther Dacey, have you seen my lady's Finny? I've been huntin' all the evenin' after the ugly baste, and can get neither tale nor tidings of it?—Finny!—Finny!—Finny!"

"Can ye see in the dark, like the cats, Miss Mary, with yer fine red topknot?" said Dacey, earnestly.

"Troth, ye may ask that," she replied, "for my candle went out."

"And where's the candlestick, Miss Mary?" persisted the keen querist.

"No wonder ye'd inquire, but sorra one have we been able to lay hands on these three weeks, for the shoals o' company, so I just used the same candlestick my father and your father, Misther Dacey, war best acquainted with—my fingers, why!——Finny!—Finny!—Finny!"

She was receding, calling the dog at the same time; when Dacey, whose ire was roused, followed her nearly to the end, and said, "You'd better not turn yer tongue against my family, Miss Impudence, for ye're mighty anxious to get into it, I'm thinkin'."

"Not into your family, Misther Dacey," retorted Mary, proudly. "Anxious, indeed! I don't deny that Benjy and I have been keepin' company, though my true belief is, he's no nevvy of yours. Ye'd think little of adoptin' any man's child or property either."

"Hah!" he exclaimed, seizing her arm, and pressing it firmly, "is that the news ye're afther?—ye'd better———" but the girl prevented his finishing his threat by screaming "Murder!" so loudly, that Sir John Clavis rushed out, with a candle in his hand, to inquire into the nature of the disturbance.

Dacey looked extremely foolish, while Mary lifted her apron to her eyes, and, with well-feigned tears, declared, "It's a shame—and I'll tell my lady, so I will, that when I was looking for little Finny, he came out of your honour's study to kiss me, yer honour—a dacent girl like me—I'll tell my lady, so I will. Finny!—Finny!—Finny!" And off she marched triumphantly, leaving Dacey to explain his equivocal situation as he best could.

The night had become dark and stormy, and when Mary put her head from under the archway, before-mentioned, large drops of rain were drifted on her face. She hastily folded her grey mantle round her, and stepping from parapet to parapet of the ancient enclosure, gained a particular elevation that overlooked the entire country. Here she paused for a moment, and then pushed into the brushwood that covered the slope leading to the meadows. Having reached the stream, that partook of the agitation of the evening gale, she seemed puzzled how to make her passage good; but her perplexity was not of long duration, although the stepping-stones were perfectly covered by the swollen waters. She seated herself on the wet grass, took off her shoes and stockings, and, folding her clothes round her, prepared to cross the river—. Having achieved her purpose, after much buffeting with both wind and water, she re-adjusted her dress, and proceeded on her way so intently, and with so much resolution, that I doubt if she would have stayed her course had she even met the bogle that frightened the good Shepherd of Ettrick—

> "Its face was black as Briant coal,
> Its nose was o' the whunstane;
> Its mou' was like a borel-hole—
> That puffed out fire and brimstane."

Regardless of banshees, cluricauns, or any of the fairy tribe, Mary pressed earnestly forward till she arrived opposite a small gate that opened into an extensive park; the lock was out of repair, so that she had but to apply her finger underneath, and push the bolt back. She only paused to inhale a long breath, and flew onward across the yielding grass, startling birds and herded deer from their early slumbers: this continued fleetness soon brought her opposite the gate of a noble modern mansion, but she preferred entering through a little postern-door, to ascending the stone steps.

"Where's her honour?" she inquired of an old serving-man, astonished at her untimely visit.

"Lord, Mary! you've frightened the senses out o' me."

"Why, then it's myself is glad to hear it."

"Why so, Mary?"

"Because it's the first time I've heard of yer havin' any in—but where's the lady?"

"Umph," replied the old servant, evidently annoyed, "find out!" and, turning on his heel, he was leaving the offended damsel alone, when she snatched the candle that maintained a very equivocal equilibrium in his hand, and ran up the back staircase.

"That one has the impudence of the ould boy in her, and makes as free in this house as if it was her own," he observed.

She tapped gently at the door of a small apartment, and a clear-toned voice responded, "Come in." In another moment Mary was in Miss Dorncliff's presence. She advanced, making a courtesy at every second step, until she stood opposite the young lady, who regarded her with much surprise.

"Why, Mary, is your mistress ill—or has anything happened to little Madeline?"

"No, God be thanked!—no thin'—to say nothin'—yet," replied the girl, laying her hand on the back of a chair for support, for she had traversed nearly five Irish miles in less than an hour.

"Sit down, sit down, my good girl," said the lady, kindly; "and, as soon as you can, tell me what has agitated you thus."

"Thank you, my lady—sure ye said that just like herself that's the angel intirely, if ever there was one, God knows!—and God counsel her, and you, my lady; for she won't be said or led by me, and more's the pity!"

"You speak of your mistress, Mary, I suppose," interrupted Miss Dorncliff, "but do come to the point at once, for I am all anxiety."

"I can't make a long story short, Madam, particular when my heart's all in it—but as fast as I can, I'll riddle it all out, for sure my heart's burstin' to tell it." The lady assumed the attitude of a patient listener, and Mary, again drawing a long breath, and pulling first one and then another of her red but taper fingers, commenced the disclosure of her mystery.

"Ye remember, when her ladyship first came over, the bobbery and the work there was about her; and the people—the protestant people (savin' yer favour—all but yerself) saying this, that, and t'other about her, as if she wasn't what she ought to be. Well, to my knowledge and belief, the one who kept this stirrin' was no other than that ould vagabond—that the beams of God's own sun and moon 'ud scorn to rest upon (savin' yer presence, for mentionin' him before ye)—ould Dacey; because ye're sensible he's a turn-coat in the first place—and my lady is so steady to her duty, that it was ever and always puttin' him to shame; and then to be sure my lady, seem', I suppose, that in foreign parts the poor are all negres, God save us! (may-be black bodies too) my lady was high to him—she has a high way with her, I grant, and sure so has the lilies, though they're so sweet and gentle when you come to know them—well, for that he hated her; and I'm sure it's more to get at the way of punishing her, than even securin' the property, that he's been goin' on as he has lately————"

"Securing what property?—going on how?" eagerly demanded Miss Dorncliff. "Let me tell ye my own way, Miss, agra! or I can't go on; besides, how would ye get at the rights of it, if ye didn't hear it from the beghinin'?"

Miss Dorncliff resumed her patient attitude.

"Ye see ould Dacey knows what he's afther, and Sir John has a way of his own of never seein' to anything—gentleman-like—though I can't but think it a bad fashion; arid while he was away, there was a dale of plunderin' roguery goin' on; and when he came home, sure the agent managed to keep him employed gettin' presentments, and eiitertaimn', an' making speeches about patriotism, and all that (I've been tould he's a powerful fine speaker, though I can't say I ever heard him)—and ever divartin' him with sich things, till the right time, when he turned, my dear! as quick as a merryman, and bothered him with debts and accounts. Now the masther, beiri' a classical scholard (as I've heard tell), didn't by coorse like the figures, which are only common larnin'; and the ould one played his cards so well, that he made him hate the sight of a bill, or a figure; till at last Sir John said, 'Manage it all yerself,' which he was glad to get the wind of the word to do, though all the time he was purtendin' he wanted the masther to look to it himself—the thief o' the world! As well as I can come at it, Madam (Miss, I ax yer pardon), Sir John agreed to let Dacey have pieces of estates, on the sly, for ready money, at half their valee—agreein' that Dacey should keep it to himself; for the pride, ye see, wouldn't let him own it; and the ould one, 'cute like, got sich another rogue as himself, in Dublin, to go somethin' in it. You're sinsible, Miss, my lady? Bein' not a well larned girl, never havin' got beyarit my read-a-me-daisy, I can't understand the rights of it, only that these two was cochering together, and procurin' money—for what I know, unlawful money—from foreign parts, and gettin' bit by bit of the poor masther's property from him, and tyin' him down, as Benjy said."

"As who said?" interrupted Miss Dorncliff.

"Why Benjy said so," stammered forth the girl, confused at committing her lover's name.

"Then Benjy, as you call him, was your informant as to these pretty villanous plots, I suppose?" interrogated the lady.

"I didn't say that, Miss Dorncliff: sure a body may make a remark, as the poor boy did, when they hear a thing, without being the one to tell it?" retorted the girl, keenly looking into her face; and the lady, wisely, seeing that Mary was now put on the *qui vive* to prevent her lover being suspected as the informer, merely replied, "Go on."

"Ye've put me out ever so many times! but all I've got to say's asy said now; it isn't enough for that ould devil's pippin that he has custolied, or some sich thing, the whole land, so as to make the noble gentleman all as one as a genteel beggar, but now that the election is come on, and Sir John goin' to stand for the county and all—what d'ye think, but he's laid a plan to get the poor gentleman into W————, to give the word to some thraythors of vagabonds, and get him arrested and shamed fore'nent the whole county, unless—(oh, the black villain!)—unless—(the sneakin' ditch-hopper!)—unless—(oh, indeed I can't say it, for the chokin' of my throat!)—unless he puts away his dar-lin' wife— who can be made ont not his wife, on account of the religion, as I'm creditably informed; and that, if he doesn't give in to this,

he'll expose him in the face of the people, which I know the masther 'ud rather die than stand. Well, Miss, ye see, he's got Sir John
to promise intirely that he'll not take my lady with him, because
she's delicate like; and he's persuaded masther she'd be in the
way. And I want her to go—for look," continued Mary, giving full
scope to the action and energy of her country, "if she was with
him, he couldn't desart her, and look in her sweet patient face,
and her two darlint eyes, that send the bames of true and pure
love right to his soul; he couldn't look at that, ma'am dear, and
consent to stick a knife in her heart, and send the blessin' of the
poor, the light of one's eyes—the fond craythur that trusted him,
as if she was a thing of shame, abroad into the could, could,
world!—but—" and here the poor girl's voice sank from the highest tones of hope, to the low and feeble ones of uncertainty—"
if she's not with him, and that villain at his shoulder—and the
disgrace—and lose the election—and all that; and if he agrees—
plinty o' money—and the seat—and ivery thing smooth, and
keep him more than half or whole mad, betwixt the fame and the
whisky!—it 'ill be all over with my poor lady!—Oh, she little
thinks!—this blessed night—she'll lay down her head and die!"
Mary hid her face in her hands, and sobbed bitterly.

"My poor friend!—my dear Madelina!" exclaimed Miss
Dorncliff; as she hastily passed up and down the apartment;
"how worthy of a better fate!—Mary, there is no use in your
denying it; Benjy has given you this information, and he must
give it publicly."

"D'ye want ruin on him too?" returned the subdued girl;
"sure he's above a trade, and has been brought up like a born
gentleman to do nothin'—and, even if he had a mind, how can
he turn agin the ould villain, his uncle, when sorra a penny he'd
have in the world, and doesn't know how to make one?"

"Look," said the lady; "if Benjamin will bring forward such
proof of trickery as can force conviction on Sir John's mind, I
will settle upon him a sufficiency for life; and there," she continued, throwing her purse into Mary's lap, "is the earnest of my
promise." For a moment, the girl forgot her mistress's interest in
her own, as she eyed the glittering treasure; but soon she
reverted to what, with true Irish fidelity, was nearest her heart.

"My lady, you'll come to her now, and persuade the masther to take her, and make out something to oblige him to take her. Och! my heart never warmed to ye as much as it does at this minute!—for they said——." She stopped before the conclusion of the sentence.

"What did they say, Mary?" inquired Miss Dorncliff.

"That you, my lady—only I'm loath to repeat a lie—that, may-be, you'd marry the masther, if he'd put away his wife."

Miss Dorncliff's face and forehead crimsoned to the deepest dye at this villanous insinuation. "Me!" she ejaculated, as if to herself, "Me!—the base-born churls! But I will save her, come what may. Mary," she continued, after a pause, "Mary, do not say a word of your having been here—mind, not a syllable. You will see me in the morning."

"Before masther goes?" inquired Mary.

"No, but soon—immediately after. Fear not, my good girl, your mistress shall be safely cared for."

When Miss Dorncliff was again alone, she resolved her plans as she paced along her chamber. For the last three years she had had the sole management and control of her father's affairs, whose age had, in a great degree, swallowed up his mind; and a large property was also at her sole command, which she had already inherited from her uncle. That night she neither slumbered nor slept; repose came not to her body or her spirit; and, from the highest window of the dwelling, she watched until she saw Sir John's equipage, with his troop of noisy retainers, pass the great gate on its way to W———. She then ordered her own carriage, and in a little time was at Clavis Abbey. The first person she inquired for was Mary, and doubtless she derived some information from her, for they were long together. She then proceeded to Lady Clavis's dressing-room, and found her in tears.

"I cannot tell why," she said, "but I feel a sad anticipation of evil hanging over me. It was so strange, John kissed me this morning when he thought I was asleep; and, do you know, he attempted to kneel at Madelina's cradle, but he rushed, like a madman, from the room, despite my efforts to recall him."

"We must follow him, then," observed Miss Dorncliff, assuming an air of gaiety—"we must follow him; I want most sadly to go to the election—my presence will cheer on my own tenants to his service; and there is no saying but that some of them, were I not on the spot, might dare to think for themselves. Besides, I can only go under the protection of a matron, you know. No interruption—I must be obeyed; we will set off this afternoon, so as to hear his maiden speech from the hustings."

Lady Clavis offered a very weak opposition to what her heart longed to engage in, and they arrived in W——at about half-past ten at night. The little Madelina was left in Mary's care at the Abbey.

There was no difficulty in finding the inn, or, as it was called, hotel, where the Orange member put up; for he had steadily refused going to the house of either of his constituents.

The waiters immediately recognised Lady Clavis, and, with many bows, conducted her into the passage, which was empty at the time, though the sounds of music, singing, and loud debate, were clearly distinguished by the ladies, even before they alighted from their carriage.

"You can show us to a sitting-room, where we can wait till Sir John is disengaged. We wish to surprise him," said Miss Dorncliff.

"I can't tell him ye're here just now, my lady," replied the man, "for Mr. Dacey said they war not to be disturbed; and there's two gentlemen, I'm thinkin' from Dublin, besides two or three others, waitin' to get speakin' with him. And it's myself don't know where to put yer ladyships, barrin' ye'll go into a purty tidy room jist off where his honour's settlin' a little affair of business with Mr. Dacey. Sure, if I'd known you war comin', it's the great grand committee-place I'd have had redied out for ye."

"Be firm and cautious now, my dear friend, for the hour of trial is come," observed Miss Dorncliff, in French, as she pressed her friend's arm closely to her heart;—"the men from Dublin, and all: we have just arrived in the right time—depend upon it, all will be well."

The waiter stared with stupid astonishment, and said, "May-be ye'd have the goodness, my lady, not to speak out much, as Sir John's at business in the next room, and he mightn't like to be disturbed; it 'ill do to tell him by-'n-by, won't it, my lady? But what'll you please to take?"

"Nothing—nothing, now," replied Miss Dorncliff; for Lady Clavis appeared incapable of either mental or bodily exertion. Her friend had revealed to her a considerable portion of her plans and anxieties during their brief journey, and her elegant but weak mind, unable to arrive at any conclusion, remained in a state of passive obedience.

Communicating with the next apartment was a small door, which hung very loosely on its hinges; the cracks and chinks were many; and through the principal one Miss Dorncliff saw Sir John sitting at a table, his face buried in his hands; while Dacey, whose head was approached close to his, was talking in a low, eager tone—so low that only broken syllables reached her ear.

At last Sir John removed his hands, and, lifting his eyes slowly, while his pale and sunken features expressed the painful struggles he endured, said, "It must not be, Dacey; do you think I want to insure damnation to my soul? What possible difference can it make to you, that you thus stipulate for her destruction? Men are seldom so desperately wicked without a motive."

"Hasn't she scorned me, and ordered me out of the room as if I was a neagre?—hasn't she treated me with the contempt which a man never forgives?—hasn't she————but the short and the long of it is, Sir John, that you know my determination: disgrace her, or disgrace yourself!—disclaim your marriage, or go to jail!—to jail, instead of to parliament!—to the jail, where Mr. Mahon can point, as he passes it, at the last of the house of Clavis! There's the pen, and the ink; I don't force ye—do as ye please—it's no business of mine." The fellow pushed some parchments and papers towards the unfortunate baronet, and gathered unto himself a pile of rouleaus that were filled with gold, while his eyes gloated and glared on the agonized face of his patron! "Sure, there's no harm in life in keeping a foreigner like her," continued the brute; "many has done the same, and will again. Send her back to the 'olive-groves of Spain,' she's so fond of singing about, and————"

"Peace, miscreant!" roared Sir John, in a voice of thunder, quite forgetting the time and place.

"Whisht!" exclaimed the coward, "never call names so loud—you know I'm yer best friend. If these sheriff's officers hear ye, it will be high mass with us all!" The baronet sank back in a state of stupefaction, and the agent advanced towards him, pen in hand. Almost mechanically Sir John took the little instrument in his fingers—its point touched the paper—even the letter J was traced, when Miss Dorncliff pushed strongly against the door; and, in the same instant, both Sir John and Dacey were trembling in her presence. For some moments, all parties remained silent—gazing at each other with such varied expression as would be difficult to describe. With the politeness with which Nature has endowed every Irishman, from the prince to the peasant, both pushed seats towards the young heiress, which she declined; at last Sir John inquired, as the pen dropped from his fingers, "to what circumstance they were indebted for the honour of her visit?"

"I came, Sir John," she replied—and the first sentence was uttered in a trembling voice, which gained strength as she proceeded, "I came to save the husband of my friend, Lady Clavis, from destruction!"

Sir John's pride mounted, as he replied, stiffly and formally, "that he was not aware to what Miss Dorncliff could allude."

"This, Sir John," she continued, heedless of his interruption, "is a bad time for compliments; you were about to sign a paper repudiating your wife, in order that that bad man might relieve your present necessities, and save you from arrest. I cannot now bring forward the proofs that I possess, of his villanies, and the various arts he has used to dupe your understanding, while he ruined your property. I pledge my word to do so; and to redeem all, even the little Corner estate from his clutches, if, instead of signing his paper, you will sign mine—and, to relieve your present embarrassment, I will tell down guinea for guinea of the money you are to receive from that person! Need I say more?—Need I urge the love you have tried?—Need I ask if you will consign your child to shame?—Need I———"

She was interrupted by a loud and piercing shriek from Lady Clavis, as with one strong effort she rushed from the outer room, and threw herself into her husband's arms. He was so unprepared, so astonished, that he did not appear able to support her, and she sank gradually on her knees—her hands clasped—her hair falling in heavy masses over her neck and shoulders—and her eyes shining with unnatural brightness, from amid the bursting tears that flowed incessantly down her cheeks. It is impossible to describe the mingled look of hope and anxiety with which she regarded Sir John; Miss Dorncliff advanced to her side; and, as her tall, commanding figure towered over the bending form of her friend, she laid her hand on the baronet's arm, and, in a low, impressive tone, said, "Can you look upon and crush her?" The appeal was decisive. He pressed his wife convulsively to his bosom, and it is no disgrace to his manhood to confess that his tears mingled with hers.

"This is all mighty fine," at length exclaimed Dacey, whose vulgar perplexity was beginning to subside into assurance, "but I don't understand it."

"And who supposed that the wallowing swine comprehended the sweetness of the ringdove's note?" replied Miss Dorncliff, casting upon him a withering look of contempt and scorn.

"I don't deserve that from you, Miss," said the savage, interpreting the expression of her countenance, "for I meant to help you to a husband."

"Sir John Clavis—I call upon you to turn that man out of the room!" replied the lady; "let him and his gold vanish—and trust for this night to the agency of your wife's friend!"

Bitter and deep were the curses he muttered, while depositing the coin in his leathern wallet; he would have formed no unapt representation of Satan preparing baits for sin—but foiled even in this effort.

"I recommend you, Dacey, to be silent," said the baronet.

"But others won't be so," growled forth the menial, as he retired. He had hardly closed the door, when he remembered the papers and parchments he had left on the table, and returned with a view of securing them. Miss Dorncliff had anticipated the movement, and, placing her hand firmly on the documents, signified so decidedly her intention of not suffering their removal, that, baffled at all points, he finally withdrew. He could hardly have reached the hall, when the officers, who had been waiting outside, made their appearance, in no very gentle manner, to make good their seizure. This, however, Miss Dorncliff prevented, by paying the amount demanded, and the room was soon cleared of such graceless company.

"Now, then," said the generous girl, looking round her with a happy and cheerful countenance, "now, Sir John, my document must be signed. I claim that as my reward. My own lawyer will settle other matters at some future date, but that must be done before I either slumber or sleep—the physician demands her fee."

The baronet seized the pen, which, a short time before, he had taken to perform a very different office, and affixed his name to the paper she presented. After placing it within her bosom, she remained sometime silent, while the vacillating man was endeavouring to explain his conduct to his wife, who, loving much, forgave all.

"It is well," thought Miss Dorncliff, "that such men should be wedded to such gentle women. My affection would always expire with my esteem; but now, she loves and believes, as if he had never been about to ruin her reputation, and to stigmatize for ever their innocent child! There must be something mysterious in this love, which I cannot comprehend." She could, however, comprehend the heights and depths of the noblest friendship. Her sleep that night was light and refreshing; and it was not till the morning was far advanced, that the shouts and bustle of an Irish election woke her to consciousness and activity.

It is not to be supposed that Dacey's bad but enterprising spirit would rest composedly, under detection and consequent exposure. He conjectured, truly, that Miss Dorncliff, through some means, which at present he could only suspect, had obtained information of his intentions, and was prepared to render null and void his basely-earned bargains and nefarious schemes. He was aware that, until the election was over, no investigation could be systematically gone into; and he hit upon a cold and villanous design to prevent the inquiry he had so much reason to dread. He knew well the character of the opposing candidate—a fearless, careless, man—vigorous and imprudent—

> "Jealous of honour,
>   Sudden and quick in quarrel;"

who had fought more duels than any man in the county; and was as often called "Bullet Mahon," as "Barry Mahon." He existed only in an atmosphere of democracy; and his hot, impatient aspect, firm tread, blustering voice, and arrogant familiarity, formed a very striking contrast to the polished, weak, but gentlemanly, bearing of Sir John Clavis. It was not at all unlikely that a quarrel would ensue, before the termination of the election, and many had even betted upon it. With the generality of Irishmen, it would have been unavoidable. But, though Sir John had never shown the white feather, he was a decidedly peaceable man—and was known to be so. Dacey, however, resolved not to trust to chance in the matter, and, on the morning of the second day, he was closeted with Mahon for nearly an hour. When the candidates appeared on the ill-constructed hustings, to greet their respective constituents, it appeared evident that Mahon was overboiling with rage at some known or supposed injury. Sir John's address was mild, and more than usually facetious—a style better understood and appreciated in England than in the sister island; he alluded to, without exulting at, the favourable state of the poll; and, after a short and cheering exhortation to his friends, resumed his seat.

When Mahon prepared to address the crowd, he swung his body uneasily from side to side, looking, when wrapt up in his huge white coat, as the personification of those unhappy polar bears who suffer confinement in our menageries. At last, elevating his right arm, as if threatening total annihilation to all who even differed from him in opinion, he began one of those inflammatory addresses that have been followed up by so many second-rate agitators in modern times; he talked of the distresses of the people, until those who had just eaten a hearty dinner imagined they were literally starving—and assured them so often that they were in a debased state of bondage, that at last they fancied they were sinking under their fetters' weight. "I would have you beware," he said, exerting to their utmost power his stentorian lungs, "I would have you all, green as well as orange, beware of those who would purchase your votes by bribery! If a man gives a bribe, he will take one!—and I wonder my opponent is not ashamed—I say, ashamed—to show his face here, after the conduct he has practised in private!" Sir John Clavis called upon Mr. Mahon to explain.

Mr. Barry Mahon said he did not come there to explain—he came to speak—and speak he would—no descendant of an impostor should put him down—if Sir John Clavis wished for explanation, he could seek it elsewhere—if he did not do so, he was a coward!

The language had grown too violent, or, as the interfering parties called it, "too warm," even for an Irish election; and the friends of both candidates endeavoured to put an end to it, or, at all events, to conclude it in another place. As Mr. Mahon refused to make any apology, or even give any explanation, it became necessary, according to the received and approved code of honour, for Sir John Clavis to send a message to the gentleman who had so grossly insulted him.

It was sent, but Clavis so worded it as to leave the matter open to apology. This, however, was not taken advantage of, and a "meeting" for the next morning was, of course, agreed upon.

Since their reconciliation, poor Lady Clavis had been suffering severely from agitation; her mind and body had received a severe shock; and though the happy termination, through her friend's kind sacrifice, had set her trembling heart at ease, her health had not yet mastered the struggle; she had been confined to her chamber, unceasingly attended by Miss Dorncliff.

About seven o'clock on the evening of the distressing quarrel between the candidates, Lady Clavis had just requested her friend to open the window, that she might feel the breath of heaven on her fevered cheek, even for a few moments; her fine dark eyes were fixed on the setting of a rich autumnal sun, which shed its glories over the scattered houses, and converted them into dwellings of molten gold. She was reclining on a couch formed of the high-backed chairs of the rude apartment, and, as her husband entered, she greeted him with inquiries as to the state of the poll. Miss Dorncliff thought within herself, that he looked pale and agitated, but did not allude to the circumstance. He was hardly seated, when a servant placed a note in Lady Clavis's hand; she just broke the wafer, and, glancing at the contents, burst into tears; Sir John perused it with almost the same agitation; and the intelligence it conveyed was well calculated to excite sorrow, for it said that the little Madelina had been taken dangerously ill, and Mary Conway, the writer, entreated Lady Clavis, "for God's sake, to come home, if she wished to see the child alive." The mother lost no time in her preparations; she thought not of herself; and to Sir John, under existing circumstances, her departure was a relief: he kissed and handed her into the carriage; the door was shut, and the coachman preparing to drive off, when Sir John called to him to stop. The evening sun had set, and the night wind was blowing sharply in the faces of the horses; the baronet pushed the footman away, and, unfastening the door, let the steps down, so that he could kneel upon them.

"Madelina," he said, in a low, agitated tone, and in her own dear native tongue—"Madelina, do join from your heart forgive me, for the unkindness I have shown—for the injury which, under the influence of a villain, I would have done you, and our innocent child?"

"My soul's life," she replied, "why do you ask? I cannot think of you and injury at the same time; from my heart, I have forgiven you." She bent her head forward to kiss her husband, and the wind blew one of the long locks of her raven hair across his face—he seized upon it, as on a treasure.

"How kind and affectionate he has grown!" observed Lady Clavis, as the carriage drove on; "when this dreadful election is over, and our darling recovered, we shall be so happy!—and to you, my dear, dear friend—my more than sister—I owe all this; his first love was not so sweet to me as his returning affection;" and, overcome with many contending feelings, the gentle creature sank into a troubled sleep.

The calm was but the prelude to a storm. How often, when our hopes are highest, and our certainties of happiness seem firmest, is the thunder-cloud gathering over us that will soon ruin both! Even at the very moment when the wife had the surest confidence in days of enjoyment and repose to come, and the friend was luxuriating over the consciousness of a good deed done, they were on the very brink of a precipice, from which there was, alas! no retreat. Alas! still more, that a vile hand should have had the power to force them over it. But thus it is—

> "————Sorrow and guilt,
> Like two old pilgrims guised, but quick and keen
>
> Of vision, evermore plod round the world,
> To spy out pleasant spots, and loving hearts;
> And never lack a villain's ready hand
> To work their purpose on them."

The roads were heavy, and the lumbering carriage and fatted horses little accustomed to hasty journeyings; they had proceeded at the rate of three miles, or three miles and a half, the hour, and were within five miles of the Abbey, when their progress was arrested by a figure on horseback seizing the reins, and commanding them to stop.

"God be thanked for his mercy!" ejaculated a well-known voice; "by his blessin 'it 'ill not be too late, and he may be saved yet."

"Who saved?—what do you mean, Mary?" eagerly demanded Miss Dorncliff, for Lady Clavis was not sufficiently collected to make any inquiry, and only looked wildly from the carriage-window.

"The masther! the masther!—turn the horses' heads, Leary, as ye value salvation, or the priest's blessin'!"

"Explain first, Mary, for this is madness," replied Miss Dorncliff; "where—how is the child?"

"Here," she replied, unfolding her cloak, and placing the smiling cherub on its mother's lap. "I knew misthress 'ud never believe it was alive and well, when I hard o' the trick just to get ye all out o' the way, my lady—and you too, Miss, who unriddled so much before, that he thought you'd be at it again—the villain! The short an' the long of it is, that ould rascal tould some lies to the other mimber that wants to be, and, on the strength of them lies, him, the other man, insulted master forenent the people; and they'd a row; and the upshot of it is that they're to fight a divil to-morrow morning—Lord save us!—like Turks or Frenchmen; and 'twas he wrote the note—as one let on to me, who rode a good horse to tell it—and, troth, grass didn't grow under my feet either. But turn, turn!—we'll may-be get a help of horses on the road; I'll gallop on and have 'em ready, though it's as much as we can to reach town by daylight."

The servants urged the jaded animals to their utmost speed; and prayers mingled, with the tears Lady Clavis shed, as she pressed her child to her bosom. Miss Dorncliff endeavoured to give what she did not possess—hope. She knew that Barry Mahon's bullet was unerring; and, from time to time, she let down the front glass to cheer forward the anxious coachman. The horses Mary procured on the road were more a hinderance than a help, so restive and ignorant were they as to carriage-harness. Never did culprits, who watch for, yet dread, the coming day, feel more bitterly than they did when the first thin stream of light appeared on the horizon; the stars, one by one, faded from their gaze; and at last the spire of the church of W———appeared like a dark speck on the clearing sky.

"Forward, forward, my good Leary!" said Miss Dorncliff; "there's the church-steeple—hasten now, and reward shall not be wanting."

"It isn't the reward—it's the masther I'm thinking of," replied the faithful fellow. "If we had the luck to be on the Dublin road itself, there'd be some chance of help; but here———" He groaned audibly, and by words of encouragement, and a more liberal application of the whip, forced the horses into something like a trot.

"I can see the masts of the vessels that are lying in the harbour," exclaimed Mary; "for God's sake, hasten, Leary!"

"I may as well throw down the reins," replied Leary; "they can only crawl; this one's sides are cut with the whip, and that one's fallen lame, too!" "I could walk faster than the horses can go now," said Miss Dorncliff. "And so could I, and we will walk," replied Lady Clavis, rousing all her energies.

"Do, do, my dearest friend," retorted Miss Dorncliff, "for I see figures on the bridge that cannot be mistaken; and if we could only get there in time, all could be explained."

Lady Clavis sprung from the carriage with a promptness that astonished her friend. She folded her child closely to her bosom, and took the path, across some meadows, which led, by a nearer way than the carriage-road, to the field that, for centuries, had been the duellist's meeting-place. The agony of her mind may be imagined, but cannot be described. There was her husband—every step rendered him more visible—she pressed onward—and her child was rocked by the panting of her bosom. The ground is measured—she flew without disturbing the dew that trembled on the grass—repeatedly she raised and waved her arm, eager to arrest attention—in vain!

Man to man stood opposed—not in spirited combat, but with cold murdering designs on each other. She screamed loud and fearfully, and her scream was answered by a fiendish laugh, which seemed to proceed from the hollow of a blighted tree that stood in her pathway; as she passed it, the bad face of Dacey glared upon her with bitter exultation. She shrank involuntarily from his ken, and the report of a pistol struck upon her ear with appalling distinctness; it was followed by another, and the next minute saw her kneeling by the side of him whom she had loved with all the fervour of the glowing south, and all the fidelity of our colder climes; the innocent child crept from her arms over his bosom, and pressed her little lips to those of her dead father. Lady Clavis motioned off the people, who wished to remove the body, and, with fearful calmness, unbuttoned the bosom of his shirt, and looked intently on the wound and the oozing blood. She attempted to unfasten it still more, but started back as if some new horror had been displayed, when the tress of hair he had severed from her head the night before, appeared literally resting on his heart. Tears did not dim her eyes, which became fixed and motionless; and her whole figure assumed a frightful rigidity. The scene was even too much for Ellen Dorncliffs firmness; she fainted while endeavouring to take the child from the remains of its ill-starred parent.

"It's the last o' the LINE, sure enough!" exclaimed an old keener, who had watched the melancholy proceeding; "for a girl, and such a girl, if report says true, has no hoult on the land; ill got—ill gone!"

My tale is told, and many will recognise it as over true. Lady Clavis's intellect never recovered the shock it received, and some years afterwards she died in a convent in Catalonia. The property of Clavis passed into other hands; and those who obtained it were generous and honourable enough to settle upon Lady Clavis and her child a larger income than they would have been entitled to, had there even been legal proof of the marriage, which, it was generally supposed, could not be obtained, or Miss Dorncliff would have procured it. So perfect, however, was the evidence she had collected of Dacey's villany, that he was never suffered to enjoy his ill-gotten wealth. I remember him in extreme old age—a hated, mischievous, drivelling idiot. Mary and Benjy were "as happy," to use the tale-telling phrase, "as the days were long;" and Miss Dorncliff—who was a living refutation of all the scandal ever heaped upon that most maligned class of persons called old maids—received, in her declining age, more than even a child's attention from Madelina Clavis.

THE MORTAL IMMORTAL:
A TALE°
Mary Shelley
(1797–1851)

JULY 16, 1833.—This is a memorable anniversary for me; on it I complete my three hundred and twenty-third year!

The Wandering Jew?—certainly not. More than eighteen centuries have passed over his head. In comparison with him, I am a very young Immortal.

Am I, then, immortal? This is a question which I have asked myself, by day and night, for now three hundred and three years, and yet cannot answer it. I detected a gray hair amidst my brown locks this very day—that surely signifies decay. Yet it may have remained concealed there for three hundred years—for some persons have become entirely white-headed before twenty years of age.

I will tell my story, and my reader shall judge for me. I will tell my story, and so contrive to pass some few hours of a long eternity, become so wearisome to me. For ever! Can it be? to live for ever! I have heard of enchantments, in which the victims were plunged into a deep sleep, to wake, after a hundred years, as fresh as ever: I have heard of the Seven Sleepers—thus to be immortal would not be so burthensome: but, oh! the weight of never-ending time—the tedious passage of the still-succeeding hours! How happy was the fabled Nourjahad!——But to my task.

°From *The Keepsake* for 1834, 1833.

All the world has heard of Cornelius Agrippa. His memory is as immortal as his arts have made me. All the world has also heard of his scholar, who, unawares, raised the foul fiend during his master's absence, and was destroyed by him. The report, true or false, of this accident, was attended with many inconveniences to the renowned philosopher. All his scholars at once deserted him—his servants disappeared. He had no one near him to put coals on his ever-burning fires while he slept, or to attend to the changeful colours of his medicines while he studied. Experiment after experiment failed, because one pair of hands was insufficient to complete them: the dark spirits laughed at him for not being able to retain a single mortal in his service.

I was then very young—very poor—and very much in love. I had been for about a year the pupil of Cornelius, though I was absent when this accident took place. On my return, my friends implored me not to return to the alchymist's abode. I trembled as I listened to the dire tale they told; I required no second warning; and when Cornelius came and offered me a purse of gold if I would remain under his roof, I felt as if Satan himself tempted me. My teeth chattered—my hair stood on end—I ran off as fast as my trembling knees would permit.

My failing steps were directed whither for two years they had every evening been attracted—a gently bubbling spring of pure living waters, beside which lingered a dark-haired girl, whose beaming eyes were fixed on the path I was accustomed each night to tread. I cannot remember the hour when I did not love Bertha; we had been neighbours and playmates from infancy—her parents, like mine, were of humble life, yet respectable—our attachment had been a source of pleasure to them. In an evil hour, a malignant fever carried off both her father and mother, and Bertha became an orphan. She would have found a home beneath my paternal roof, but, unfortunately, the old lady of the near castle, rich, childless, and solitary, declared her intention to adopt her. Henceforth Bertha was clad in silk—inhabited a marble palace—and was looked on as being highly favoured by fortune. But in her new situation among her new associates, Bertha remained true to the friend of her humbler days; she often visited the cottage of my father, and when forbidden to go thither, she would stray towards the neighbouring wood, and meet me beside its shady fountain.

She often declared that she owed no duty to her new protectress equal in sanctity to that which bound us. Yet still I was too poor to marry, and she grew weary of being tormented on my account. She had a haughty but an impatient spirit, and grew angry at the obstacles that prevented our union. We met now after an absence, and she had been sorely beset while I was away; she complained bitterly, and almost reproached me for being poor. I replied hastily—

"I am honest, if I am poor!—were I not, I might soon become rich!"

This exclamation produced a thousand questions. I feared to shock her by owning the truth, but she drew it from me; and then, casting a look of disdain on me, she said—

"You pretend to love, and you fear to face the Devil for my sake!"

I protested that I had only dreaded to offend her—while she dwelt on the magnitude of the reward that I should receive. Thus encouraged—shamed by her—led on by love and hope, laughing at my late fears, with quick steps and a light heart, I returned to accept the offers of the alchymist, and was instantly installed in my office.

A year passed away. I became possessed of no insignificant sum of money. Custom had banished my fears. In spite of the most painful vigilance, I had never detected the trace of a cloven foot; nor was the studious silence of our abode ever disturbed by demoniac howls. I still continued my stolen interviews with Bertha, and Hope dawned on me—Hope—but not perfect joy; for Bertha fancied that love and security were enemies, and her pleasure was to divide them in my bosom. Though true of heart, she was somewhat of a coquette in manner; and I was jealous as a Turk. She slighted me in a thousand ways, yet would never acknowledge herself to be in the wrong. She would drive me mad with anger, and then force me to beg her pardon. Sometimes she fancied that I was not sufficiently submissive, and then she had some story of a rival, favoured by her protectress. She was surrounded by silk-clad youths—the rich and gay——What chance had the sad-robed scholar of Cornelius compared with these?

On one occasion, the philosopher made such large demands upon my time, that I was unable to meet her as I was wont. He was engaged in some mighty work, and I was forced to remain, day and night, feeding his furnaces and watching his chemical preparations. Bertha waited for me in vain at the fountain. Her haughty spirit fired at this neglect; and when at last I stole out during the few short minutes allotted to me for slumber, and hoped to be consoled by her, she received me with disdain, dismissed me in scorn, and vowed that any man should possess her hand rather than he who could not be in two places at once for her sake. She would be revenged!—And truly she was. In my dingy retreat I heard that she had been hunting, attended by Albert Hoffer. Albert Hoffer was favoured by her protectress, and the three passed in cavalcade before my smoky window. Methought that they mentioned my name—it was followed by a laugh of derision, as her dark eyes glanced contemptuously towards my abode.

Jealousy, with all its venom, and all its misery, entered my breast. Now I shed a torrent of tears, to think that I should never call her mine; and, anon, I imprecated a thousand curses on her inconstancy. Yet, still I must stir the fires of the alchymist, still attend on the changes of his unintelligible medicines.

Cornelius had watched for three days and nights, nor closed his eyes. The progress of his alembics was slower than he expected: in spite of his anxiety, sleep weighed upon his eyelids. Again and again he threw off drowsiness with more than human energy; again and again it stole away his senses. He eyed his crucibles wistfully. "Not ready yet," he murmured; "will another night pass before the work is accomplished? Winzy, you are vigilant—you are faithful—you have slept, my boy—you slept last night. Look at that glass vessel. The liquid it contains is of a soft rose-colour: the moment it begins to change its hue, awaken me—till then I may close my eyes. First, it will turn white, and then emit golden flashes; but wait not till then; when the rose-colour fades, rouse me." I scarcely heard the last words, muttered, as they were, in sleep. Even then he did not quite yield to nature. "Winzy, my boy," he again said, "do not touch the vessel—do not put it to your lips; it is a philter—a philter to cure love; you would not cease to love your Bertha—beware to drink!"

And he slept. His venerable head sunk on his breast, and I scarce heard his regular breathing. For a few minutes I watched the vessel—the rosy hue of the liquid remained unchanged. Then my thoughts wandered—they visited the fountain, and dwelt on a thousand charming scenes never to be renewed—never! Serpents and adders were in my heart as the word "Never!" half formed itself on my lips. False girl!—false and cruel! Never more would she smile on me as that evening she smiled on Albert. Worthless, detested woman! I would not remain unrevenged—she should see Albert expire at her feet—she should die beneath my vengeance. She had smiled in disdain and triumph—she knew my wretchedness and her power. Yet what power had she?—the power of exciting my hate—my utter scorn—my—oh, all but indifference! Could I attain that—could I regard her with careless eyes, transferring my rejected love to one fairer and more true, that were indeed a victory!

A bright flash darted before my eyes. I had forgotten the medicine of the adept; I gazed on it with wonder: flashes of admirable beauty, more bright than those which the diamond emits when the sun's rays are on it, glanced from the surface of the liquid; an odour the most fragrant and grateful stole over my sense; the vessel seemed one globe of living radiance, lovely to the eye, and most inviting to the taste. The first thought, instinctively inspired by the grosser sense, was, I will—I must drink. I raised the vessel to my lips. "It will cure me of love—of torture!" Already I had quaffed half of the most delicious liquor ever tasted by the palate of man, when the philosopher stirred. I started—I dropped the glass—the fluid flamed and glanced along the floor, while I felt Cornelius's gripe at my throat, as he shrieked aloud, "Wretch! you have destroyed the labour of my life!"

The philosopher was totally unaware that I had drunk any portion of his drug. His idea was, and I gave a tacit assent to it, that I had raised the vessel from curiosity, and that, frighted at its brightness, and the flashes of intense light it gave forth, I had let it fall. I never undeceived him. The fire of the medicine was quenched—the fragrance died away—he grew calm, as a philosopher should under the heaviest trials, and dismissed me to rest.

I will not attempt to describe the sleep of glory and bliss which bathed my soul in paradise during the remaining hours of that memorable night. Words would be faint and shallow types of my enjoyment, or of the gladness that possessed my bosom when I woke. I trod air—my thoughts were in heaven. Earth appeared heaven, and my inheritance upon it was to be one trance of delight. "This it is to be cured of love," I thought; "I will see Bertha this day, and she will find her lover cold and regardless: too happy to be disdainful, yet how utterly indifferent to her!"

The hours danced away. The philosopher, secure that he had once succeeded, and believing that he might again, began to concoct the same medicine once more. He was shut up with his books and drugs, and I had a holiday. I dressed myself with care; I looked in an old but polished shield, which served me for a mirror; methought my good looks had wonderfully improved. I hurried beyond the precincts of the town, joy in my soul, the beauty of heaven and earth around me. I turned my steps towards the castle—I could look on its lofty turrets with lightness of heart, for I was cured of love. My Bertha saw me afar off, as I came up the avenue. I know not what sudden impulse animated her bosom, but at the sight, she sprung with a light fawn-like bound down the marble steps, and was hastening towards me. But I had been perceived by another person. The old high-born hag, who called herself her protectress, and was her tyrant, had seen me, also; she hobbled, panting, up the terrace; a page, as ugly as herself, held up her train, and fanned her as she hurried along, and stopped my fair girl with a "How, now, my bold mistress? whither so fast? Back to your cage—hawks are abroad!"

Bertha clasped her hands—her eyes were still bent on my approaching figure. I saw the contest. How I abhorred the old crone who checked the kind impulses of my Bertha's softening heart. Hitherto, respect for her rank had caused me to avoid the lady of the castle; now I disdained such trivial considerations. I was cured of love, and lifted above all human fears; I hastened forwards, and soon reached the terrace. How lovely Bertha

looked! her eyes flashing fire, her cheeks glowing with impatience and anger, she was a thousand times more graceful and
charming than ever—I no longer loved—Oh! no, I adored—
worshipped—idolized her!

She had that morning been persecuted, with more than usual
vehemence, to consent to an immediate marriage with my rival.
She was reproached with the encouragement that she had
shown him—she was threatened with being turned out of doors
with disgrace and shame. Her proud spirit rose in arms at the
threat; but when she remembered the scorn that she had
heaped upon me, and how, perhaps, she had thus lost one whom
she now regarded as her only friend, she wept with remorse and
rage. At that moment I appeared. "O, Winzy!" she exclaimed,
"take me to your mother's cot; swiftly let me leave the detested
luxuries and wretchedness of this noble dwelling—take me to
poverty and happiness."

I clasped her in my arms with transport. The old lady was
speechless with fury, and broke forth into invective only when
we were far on our road to my natal cottage. My mother
received the fair fugitive, escaped from a gilt cage to nature and
liberty, with tenderness and joy; my father, who loved her, wel-
comed her heartily; it was a day of rejoicing, which did not need
the addition of the celestial potion of the alchymist to steep me
in delight.

Soon after this eventful day, I became the husband of Bertha.
I ceased to be the scholar of Cornelius, but I continued his
friend. I always felt grateful to him for having, unawares, procured me that delicious draught of a divine elixir, which, instead
of curing me of love (sad cure! solitary and joyless remedy for
evils which seem blessings to the memory), had inspired me
with courage and resolution, thus winning for me an inestimable
treasure in my Bertha.

I often called to mind that period of trance-like inebriation
with wonder. The drink of Cornelius had not fulfilled the task
for which he affirmed that it had been prepared, but its effects
were more potent and blissful than words can express. They had
faded by degrees, yet they lingered long—and painted life in
hues of splendour. Bertha often wondered at my lightness of

heart and unaccustomed gaiety; for, before, I had been rather serious, or even sad, in my disposition. She loved me the better for my cheerful temper, and our days were winged by joy.

Five years afterwards I was suddenly summoned to the bedside of the dying Cornelius. He had sent for me in haste, conjuring my instant presence. I found him stretched on his pallet, enfeebled even to death; all of life that yet remained animated his piercing eyes, and they were fixed on a glass vessel, full of a roseate liquid.

"Behold," he said, in a broken and inward voice, "the vanity of human wishes! a second time my hopes are about to be crowned, a second time they are destroyed. Look at that liquor—you remember five years ago I had prepared the same, with the same success—then, as now, my thirsting lips expected to taste the immortal elixir—you dashed it from me! and at present it is too late."

He spoke with difficulty, and fell back on his pillow. I could not help saying—

"How, revered master, can a cure for love restore you to life?"

A faint smile gleamed across his face as I listened earnestly to his scarcely intelligible answer.

"A cure for love and for all things—the Elixir of Immortality. Ah! if now I might drink, I should live for ever!"

As he spoke, a golden flash gleamed from the fluid; a well-remembered fragrance stole over the air; he raised himself, all weak as he was—strength seemed miraculously to re-enter his frame—he stretched forth his hand—a loud explosion startled me—a ray of fire shot up from the elixir, and the glass vessel which contained it was shivered to atoms! I turned my eyes towards the philosopher; he had fallen back—his eyes were glassy—his features rigid—he was dead!

But I lived, and was to live for ever! So said the unfortunate alchymist, and for a few days I believed his words. I remembered the glorious drunkenness that had followed my stolen draught. I reflected on the change I had felt in my frame—in my soul. The bounding elasticity of the one—the buoyant lightness of the other. I surveyed myself in a mirror, and could perceive no change in my features during the space of the five years which had elapsed. I remembered the radiant hues and grateful scent of that delicious beverage—worthy the gift it was capable of bestowing——I was, then, IMMORTAL!

A few days after I laughed at my credulity. The old proverb, that "a prophet is least regarded in his own country," was true with respect to me and my defunct master. I loved him as a man—I respected him as a sage—but I derided the notion that he could command the powers of darkness, and laughed at the superstitious fears with which he was regarded by the vulgar. He was a wise philosopher, but had no acquaintance with any spirits but those clad in flesh and blood. His science was simply human; and human science, I soon persuaded myself, could never conquer nature's laws so far as to imprison the soul for ever within its carnal habitation. Cornelius had brewed a soul-refreshing drink—more inebriating than wine—sweeter and more fragrant than any fruit: it possessed probably strong medicinal powers, imparting gladness to the heart and vigor to the limbs; but its effects would wear out; already were they diminished in my frame. I was a lucky fellow to have quaffed health and joyous spirits, and perhaps long life, at my master's hands; but my good fortune ended there: longevity was far different from immortality.

I continued to entertain this belief for many years. Sometimes a thought stole across me—Was the alchymist indeed deceived? But my habitual credence was, that I should meet the fate of all the children of Adam at my appointed time—a little late, but still at a natural age. Yet it was certain that I retained a wonderfully youthful look. I was laughed at for my vanity in consulting the mirror so often, but I consulted it in vain—my brow was untrenched—my cheeks—my eyes—my whole person continued as untarnished as in my twentieth year.

I was troubled. I looked at the faded beauty of Bertha—I seemed more like her son. By degrees our neighbours began to make similar observations, and I found at last that I went by the name of the Scholar bewitched. Bertha herself grew uneasy. She became jealous and peevish, and at length she began to question me. We had no children; we were all in all to each other; and though, as she grew older, her vivacious spirit became a little allied to ill-temper, and her beauty sadly diminished, I cherished her in my heart as the mistress I had idolized, the wife I had sought and won with such perfect love.

At last our situation became intolerable: Bertha was fifty—I twenty years of age. I had, in very shame, in some measure adopted the habits of a more advanced age; I no longer mingled in the dance among the young and gay, but my heart bounded along with them while I restrained my feet; and a sorry figure I cut among the Nestors of our village. But before the time I mention, things were altered—we were universally shunned; we were—at least, I was—reported to have kept up an iniquitous acquaintance with some of my former master's supposed friends. Poor Bertha was pitied, but deserted. I was regarded with horror and detestation.

What was to be done? we sat by our winter fire—poverty had made itself felt, for none would buy the produce of my farm; and often I had been forced to journey twenty miles, to some place where I was not known, to dispose of our property. It is true we had saved something for an evil day—that day was come.

We sat by our lone fireside—the old-hearted youth and his antiquated wife. Again Bertha insisted on knowing the truth; she recapitulated all she had ever heard said about me, and added her own observations. She conjured me to cast off the spell; she described how much more comely grey hairs were than my chestnut locks; she descanted on the reverence and respect due to age—how preferable to the slight regard paid to mere children: could I imagine that the despicable gifts of youth and good looks outweighed disgrace, hatred, and scorn? Nay, in the end I should be burnt as a dealer in the black art, while she, to whom I had not deigned to communicate any portion of my good fortune, might be stoned as my accomplice. At length she insinuated that I must share my secret with her, and bestow on her like benefits to those I myself enjoyed, or she would denounce me—and then she burst into tears.

Thus beset, methought it was the best way to tell the truth. I revealed it as tenderly as I could, and spoke only of a *very long life,* not of immortality—which representation, indeed, coincided best with my own ideas. When I ended, I rose and said,

"And now, my Bertha, will you denounce the lover of your youth?—You will not, I know. But it is too hard, my poor wife, that you should suffer from my ill-luck and the accursed arts of Cornelius. I will leave you—you have wealth enough, and friends will return in my absence. I will go; young as I seem, and strong as I am, I can work and gain my bread among strangers, unsuspected and unknown. I loved you in youth; God is my witness that I would not desert you in age, but that your safety and happiness require it."

I took my cap and moved towards the door; in a moment Bertha's arms were round my neck, and her lips were pressed to mine. "No, my husband, my Winzy," she said, "you shall not go alone—take me with you; we will remove from this place, and, as you say, among strangers we shall be unsuspected and safe. I am not so very old as quite to shame you, my Winzy; and I dare say the charm will soon wear off, and, with the blessing of God, you will become more elderly-looking, as is fitting; you shall not leave me."

I returned the good soul's embrace heartily. "I will not, my Bertha; but for your sake I had not thought of such a thing. I will be your true, faithful husband while you are spared to me, and do my duty by you to the last."

The next day we prepared secretly for our emigration. We were obliged to make great pecuniary sacrifices—it could not be helped. We realised a sum sufficient, at least, to maintain us while Bertha lived; and, without saying adieu to anyone, quitted our native country to take refuge in a remote part of western France.

It was a cruel thing to transport poor Bertha from her native village, and the friends of her youth, to a new country, new language, new customs. The strange secret of my destiny rendered this removal immaterial to me; but I compassionated her deeply, and was glad to perceive that she found compensation for her misfortunes in a variety of little ridiculous circumstances. Away from all tell-tale chroniclers, she sought to decrease the apparent disparity of our ages by a thousand feminine arts—rouge, youthful dress, and assumed juvenility of manner. I could not be angry—Did not I myself wear a mask? Why quarrel with hers, because it was less successful? I grieved deeply when I remembered that this was my Bertha, whom I had loved so fondly, and won with such transport—the dark-eyed, dark-haired girl, with smiles of enchanting archness and a step like a fawn—this mincing, simpering, jealous old woman. I should have revered her gray locks and withered cheeks; but thus!——It was my work, I knew; but I did not the less deplore this type of human weakness.

Her jealousy never slept. Her chief occupation was to discover that, in spite of outward appearances, I was myself growing old. I verily believe that the poor soul loved me truly in her heart, but never had woman so tormenting a mode of displaying fondness. She would discern wrinkles in my face and decrepitude in my walk, while I bounded along in youthful vigour, the youngest looking of twenty youths. I never dared address another woman: on one occasion, fancying that the belle of the village regarded me with favouring eyes, she bought me a gray wig. Her constant discourse among her acquaintances was, that though I looked so young, there was ruin at work within my frame; and she affirmed that the worst symptom about me was my apparent health. My youth was a disease, she said, and I ought at all times to prepare, if not for a sudden and awful death, at least to awake some morning white-headed, and bowed down with all the marks of advanced years. I let her talk—I often joined in her conjectures. Her warnings chimed in with my never-ceasing speculations concerning my state, and I took an earnest, though painful, interest in listening to all that her quick wit and excited imagination could say on the subject.

Why dwell on these minute circumstances? We lived on for many long years. Bertha became bed-rid and paralytic: I nursed her as a mother might a child. She grew peevish, and still harped upon one string—of how long I should survive her. It has ever been a source of consolation to me, that I performed my duty scrupulously towards her. She had been mine in youth, she was mine in age, and at last, when I heaped the sod over her corpse, I wept to feel that I had lost all that really bound me to humanity.

Since then how many have been my cares and woes, how few and empty my enjoyments! I pause here in my history—I will pursue it no further. A sailor without rudder or compass, tossed on a stormy sea—a traveller lost on a wide-spread heath, without landmark or star to guide him—such have I been: more lost, more hopeless than either. A nearing ship, a gleam from some far cot, may save them; but I have no beacon except the hope of death.

Death! mysterious, ill-visaged friend of weak humanity! Why alone of all mortals have you cast me from your sheltering fold? O, for the peace of the grave! the deep silence of the iron-bound tomb! that thought would cease to work in my brain, and my heart beat no more with emotions varied only by new forms of sadness!

Am I immortal? I return to my first question. In the first place, is it not more probable that the beverage of the alchymist was fraught rather with longevity than eternal life? Such is my hope. And then be it remembered that I only drank *half* of the potion prepared by him. Was not the whole necessary to complete the charm? To have drained half the Elixir of Immortality is but to be half immortal—my For-ever is thus truncated and null.

But again, who shall number the years of the half of eternity? I often try to imagine by what rule the infinite may be divided. Sometimes I fancy age advancing upon me. One gray hair I have found. Fool! do I lament? Yes, the fear of age and death often creeps coldly into my heart; and the more I live, the more I dread death, even while I abhor life. Such an enigma is man— born to perish—when he wars, as I do, against the established laws of his nature.

But for this anomaly of feeling surely I might die: the medicine of the alchymist would not be proof against fire—sword— and the strangling waters. I have gazed upon the blue depths of many a placid lake, and the tumultuous rushing of many a mighty river, and have said, peace inhabits those waters; yet I have turned my steps away, to live yet another day. I have asked myself, whether suicide would be a crime in one to whom thus only the portals of the other world could be opened. I have done all, except presenting myself as a soldier or duellist, an object of destruction to my—no, *not* my fellow-mortals, and therefore I have shrunk away. They are not my fellows. The inextinguishable power of life in my frame, and their ephemeral existence, place us wide as the poles asunder. I could not raise a hand against the meanest or the most powerful among them.

Thus I have lived on for many a year—alone, and weary of myself—desirous of death, yet never dying—a mortal immortal. Neither ambition nor avarice can enter my mind, and the ardent love that gnaws at my heart, never to be returned—never to find an equal on which to expend itself—lives there only to torment me.

This very day I conceived a design by which I may end all—without self-slaughter, without making another man a Cain—an expedition, which mortal frame can never survive, even endued with the youth and strength that inhabits mine. Thus I shall put my immortality to the test, and rest for ever—or return, the wonder and benefactor of the human species.

Before I go, a miserable vanity has caused me to pen these pages. I would not die, and leave no name behind. Three centuries have passed since I quaffed the fatal beverage: another year shall not elapse before, encountering gigantic dangers—warring with the powers of frost in their home—beset by famine, toil, and tempest—I yield this body, too tenacious a cage for a soul which thirsts for freedom, to the destructive elements of air and water—or, if I survive, my name shall be recorded as one of the most famous among the sons of men; and, my task achieved, I shall adopt more resolute means, and, by scattering and annihilating the atoms that compose my frame, set at liberty the life imprisoned within, and so cruelly prevented from soaring from this dim earth to a sphere more congenial to its immortal essence.

NAPOLEON AND THE SPECTRE*
Charlotte Brontë
(1816–1855)

Well, as I was saying, the Emperor got into bed.
"Chevalier," says he to his valet, "let down those window-curtains, and shut the casement before you leave the room."

Chevalier did as he was told, and then, taking up his candle-stick, departed.

In a few minutes the Emperor felt his pillow becoming rather hard, and he got up to shake it. As he did so a slight rustling noise was heard near the bed-head. His Majesty listened, but all was silent as he lay down again.

Scarcely had he settled into a peaceful attitude of repose, when he was disturbed by a sensation of thirst. Lifting himself on his elbow, he took a glass of lemonade from the small stand which was placed beside him. He refreshed himself by a deep draught. As he returned the goblet to its station a deep groan burst from a kind of closet in one corner of the apartment.

"Who's there?" cried the Emperor, seizing his pistols. "Speak, or I'll blow your brains out."

This threat produced no other effect than a short, sharp laugh, and a dead silence followed.

The Emperor started from his couch, and, hastily throwing on a *robe-de-chambre* which hung over the back of a chair, stepped courageously to the haunted closet. As he opened the door

---

*From the manuscript for *The Green Dwarf*, dated 1833.

something rustled. He sprang forward sword in hand. No soul or even substance appeared, and the rustling, it was evident, proceeded from the falling of a cloak, which had been suspended by a peg from the door.

Half ashamed of himself he returned to bed.

Just as he was about once more to close his eyes, the light of the three wax tapers, which burned in a silver branch over the mantlepiece, was suddenly darkened. He looked up. A black, opaque shadow obscured it. Sweating with terror, the Emperor put out his hand to seize the bell-rope, but some invisible being snatched it rudely from his grasp, and at the same instant the ominous shade vanished.

"Pooh!" exclaimed Napoleon, "it was but an ocular delusion."

"Was it?" whispered a hollow voice, in deep mysterious tones, close to his ear. "Was it a delusion, Emperor of France? No! all thou hast heard and seen is sad forewarning reality. Rise, lifter of the Eagle Standard! Awake, swayer of the Lily Sceptre! Follow me, Napoleon, and thou shalt see more."

As the voice ceased, a form dawned on his astonished sight. It was that of a tall, thin man, dressed in a blue surtout edged with gold lace. It wore a black cravat very tightly round its neck, and confined by two little sticks placed behind each ear. The countenance was livid; the tongue protruded from between the teeth, and the eyes all glazed and bloodshot started with frightful prominence from their sockets.

"*Mon Dieu!*" exclaimed the Emperor, "what do I see? Spectre, whence cometh thou?"

The apparition spoke not, but gliding forward beckoned Napoleon with uplifted finger to follow.

Controlled by a mysterious influence, which deprived him of the capability of either thinking or acting for himself, he obeyed in silence.

The solid wall of the apartment fell open as they approached, and, when both had passed through, it closed behind them with a noise like thunder.

They would now have been in total darkness had it not been for a dim light which shone round the ghost and revealed the damp walls of a long, vaulted passage. Down this they proceeded with mute rapidity. Ere long a cool, refreshing breeze, which rushed wailing up the vault and caused the Emperor to wrap his loose nightdress closer round, announced their approach to the open air.

This they soon reached, and Nap found himself in one of the principal streets of Paris.

"Worthy Spirit," said he, shivering in the chill night air, "permit me to return and put on some additional clothing. I will be with you again presently."

"Forward," replied his companion sternly.

He felt compelled, in spite of the rising indignation which almost choked him, to obey.

On they went through the deserted streets till they arrived at a lofty house built on the banks of the Seine. Here the Spectre stopped, the gates rolled back to receive them, and they entered a large marble hall which was partly concealed by a curtain drawn across, through the half transparent folds of which a bright light might be seen burning with dazzling lustre. A row of fine female figures, richly attired, stood before this screen. They wore on their heads garlands of the most beautiful flowers, but their faces were concealed by ghastly masks representing death's-heads.

"What is all this mummery?" cried the Emperor, making an effort to shake off the mental shackles by which he was so unwillingly restrained, "Where am I, and why have I been brought here?"

"Silence," said the guide, lolling out still further his black and bloody tongue. "Silence, if thou wouldst escape instant death."

The Emperor would have replied, his natural courage overcoming the temporary awe to which he had at first been subjected, but just then a strain of wild, supernatural music swelled behind the huge curtain, which waved to and fro, and bellied slowly out as if agitated by some internal commotion or battle of waving winds. At the same moment an overpowering mixture of the scents of mortal corruption, blent with the richest Eastern odours, stole through the haunted hall.

A murmur of many voices was now heard at a distance, and something grasped his arm eagerly from behind.

He turned hastily round. His eyes met the well-known countenance of Marie Louise.

"What! are you in this infernal place, too?" said he."What has brought you here?"

"Will your Majesty permit me to ask the same question of yourself?" said the Empress, smiling.

He made no reply; astonishment prevented him.

No curtain now intervened between him and the light. It had been removed as if by magic, and a splendid chandelier appeared suspended over his head. Throngs of ladies, richly dressed, but without death's-head masks, stood round, and a due proportion of gay cavaliers was mingled with them. Music was still sounding, but it was seen to proceed from a band of mortal musicians stationed in an orchestra near at hand. The air was yet redolent of incense, but it was incense unblended with stench.

"*Mon dieu!*" cried the Emperor, "how is all this come about? Where in the world is Piche?"

"Piche?" replied the Empress. "What does your Majesty mean? Had you not better leave the apartment and retire to rest?"

"Leave the apartment? Why, where am I?"

"In my private drawing-room, surrounded by a few particular persons of the Court whom I had invited this evening to a ball. You entered a few minutes since in your nightdress with your eyes fixed and wide open. I suppose from the astonishment you now testify that you were walking in your sleep."

The Emperor immediately fell into a fit of catalepsy, in which he continued during the whole of that night and the greater part of the next day.

THE KNITTED COLLAR*
Mary Anne Hoare
(1818–1872)

One dark dismal morning in the month of November, 1846, a miserable group of human beings were assembled in the attic of an old crumbling house, situated in a filthy obscure lane in a large Irish city. The room contained no furniture save an old empty box, a broken pitcher, and a bundle of damp straw, on which lay a man pale and ghastly. His wife and four children were crouching on the ground, near a fireless grate; their tatted rags and famine-stricken faces testifying too surely the dreadful extremity to which they were reduced.

"Nelly," said the man, "give me a drink of water. Oh, then, if 'twas *that* I always drank, 't isn't this way we'd be now?"

"Denis, agra, don't fret yourself," replied the poor woman, rising feebly, and holding the jug to his parched lips. "If I had anything at all to give you, darling, you'd do well yet; but where to get even one halfpenny to buy a grain of meal, I don't know."

The eldest daughter, a girl of fourteen, who had been holding one of her little brothers in her wasted arms, and trying gently to hush the plaintive cries of the starving child, looked up, and said eagerly, "Oh! mother, I had the collar that Jane Brown gave me thread to knit, nearly finished, when little Denny began to cry; maybe I could put the last stitch to it now, if you'd take him in your arms, and then I might be able to sell it in the streets."

---

*From *Shamrock Leaves; or, Tales and Sketches of Ireland*, 1851.

"Do, darling," said her mother, "in the name of God, though He knows this blessed minute that 'tis badly able you are either to work or to walk."

Mary Sullivan, like many Irish girls, had much taste and facility in executing fine knitting; she had learned the art in happier days, while attending an excellent charity-school, and now she tried to make her talent available for the support of her family. They had once been well off. Denis Sullivan was a journeyman shoemaker, and earned a sufficiency for their wants. In an evil hour he was persuaded by a fellow workman to enter a public-house and take a glass of whiskey; then the common oft-repeated fate was his— his earnings squandered, his family reduced to want, and finally his own health totally destroyed. Things were in this state, when bitter famine visited the land in 1846. Then the Sullivans were literally left to perish, for those who had charity to dispense could scarcely reach one half the cases of heartrending misery which they witnessed; and therefore justly selected as objects of relief those who were brought to destitution by the pressure of the times, and not by any fault of their own. A drunken journeyman shoemaker could not hope for assistance while so many sober industrious men were perishing; and Sullivan's unfortunate family of course suffered with him. His wife, a poor weakly woman, in a spirit of almost Turkish apathy, was content to lie down and die; and when all their little articles of clothing and furniture had been pawned, the three young children pined away from hunger in slow but sure decay.

Mary alone of all the family tried *to do something*. She was a gentle, dark-eyed girl, with a look of patient suffering in her thin pale face, and a soft low voice which few, one would think, could listen to unmoved. The sale of work, however, had become almost hopeless; so many were trying to live by it, and so few had money to buy. The delicate fabrics, both in knitting and embroidery, which many a bony finger worked at till the hollow eye grew dim, were often disposed of for two or three pence beyond the price of the materials. The collar which poor Mary had now finished was beautifully fine, and had cost her many hours of toil; yet she almost despaired of selling it, as she sallied forth at eleven o'clock, shivering with cold and hunger.

About four o'clock the same day, as a fashionably dressed lady was walking along a road at the western end of the city, she heard a plaintive voice behind her saying, "Will you please, ma'am, to buy a knitted collar?"

She turned, and poor Mary, now almost fainting from exhaustion, offered the lace-like piece of work for her inspection.

"What do you ask for it, child?"

"Two shillings, ma'am."

"Oh, that's much too dear! I'll give you one for it."

"It took me several days to knit, and my parents and brothers are starving," said poor Mary, bursting into tears.

"Oh, yes; I suppose the old story. Well, child, if you don't like to give it for a shilling, you can sell it elsewhere."

"Take it, ma'am," said Mary, giving it to the lady, and eagerly seizing the offered shilling. There was life to her and those she loved in that bit of silver, that paltry coin which its former possessors would have squandered without a thought for any unneeded trifle, yet now considered well-spent in securing a *bargain*.

Let us change the scene to a baker's shop, in——street. It was a large establishment, and the deep shelves were piled with the crisp, fresh loaves of every shape, size, and quality, from the fine light French roll, to the dark, compact "household brick;" and the wide window displayed biscuits, cakes, and confectionery, in various tempting forms. It was half-past four o'clock, and the space outside the counter was filled with purchasers, very different in their rank and appearance. Two richly dressed ladies, whose carriage was in waiting, were selecting, with jewelled fingers, some of the prettiest *bon-bons* which the attentive master of the shop produced, and mirthfully discussing which kind "baby" was likely to prefer: near them stood a stout, fresh-coloured country-woman, wrapped in a blue cloak, and holding up her checked apron, while she impatiently called out—"Ah, then, good luck to you, honest man, and don't be keeping me this way, but just give me them two lumps, and three bricks I axed you for: here's the money ready, and 'tis three miles of the road home I ought to have over me by this."

The master of the shop had but two boys to assist him behind

Mary Anne Hoare

the counter, and though they hurried and toiled and "did the impossible" to content their clamorous customers, the latter were by no means satisfied to wait for their turn to be served. There were but two individuals in the shop who appeared to possess the very un-Irish quality of patience. One of them seemed to have learned it in a hard school; she was a thin, pale girl, barefooted, and clothed in miserable, scanty rags, which, however, were clean, and as tidily put on as they would admit of. She held a shilling tightly grasped in her slender fingers, and advancing through an opening in the crowd, asked the youngest shop-boy for a stale loaf of "thirds"—(the coarsest kind of bread manufactured). He had just finished serving a farmer, and hastily giving her what she wanted, took the shilling, and returned her the change. There had been standing next the girl, a pleasing-looking, neatly-dressed lady, who now advanced, and asked for some Naples biscuits.—The boy was busy weighing them, when the girl came back, and said to him, "If you please, what did you charge for the loaf?"

"Threepence, and I gave you the change."

"But you gave me sixpence and a fourpence, so you kept a penny too little."

The boy looked vexed at his blunder, which he probably feared his master might observe; so hastily taking the silver fourpence, and giving the girl threepence, he said, "'Tis all right now, you may go."

She was hastening away, when the gentle-looking lady next her said, "Stay, you have been very honest; good principle may be shown as well about a penny as a pound—here is a shilling for you."

The girl involuntarily raised her clasped hands.

"Oh, thank you, thank you, ma'am," she said, "God for ever bless you!" and then hastened out of the shop, before the lady could again address her.

Miss Saville had only moderate means, but possessed a truly benevolent heart. She usually resided in a remote part of the country, with her brother, who was a clergyman, and who was wont to assert, that in attention to the schools, and visiting the sick in his parish, his sister Sarah was worth two curates, "aye, and hard-working ones, too."

She was now staying on a visit with a married sister, who resided near——; and who, although blessed with an excellent husband, and several fine children, could not be called as truly happy as her maiden sister; for though, in the main, a good-natured woman, she lacked that generous, thoughtful benevolence of spirit which distinguished Miss Saville. On this day, however, the latter walked home to dinner in a self-reproaching frame of mind.

"How very thoughtless I was," she said to herself, "not to ask that poor child where she lives, and something of her history. I'm sure she's in great distress, and she seemed so honest and so grateful. I wish very much I could find her out."

A few hours afterwards, a happy family party were assembled in Mr. Elliott's drawing-room.—His sister-in-law, Miss Saville, held her youngest nephew on her knee, and was surrounded by four other bright-eyed little ones, among whom she had just distributed her purchase of Naples biscuits; and as they ate, they listened with much interest to Aunt Sarah's account of the honest girl, who, "though she looked so very poor, would not keep a penny which did not belong to her."

Mrs. Elliott, who was seated at her work-table, arranging some lace trimming on a cap, now got up, and handing a small collar to her sister, said—

"Look, Sarah, did you ever see any knitting so fine as that?"

"It is, indeed, beautiful—quite like lace; where did you get it, Eliza?"

"I bought it to-day in the street—such a bargain! Just fancy—the girl who had it asked two shillings; and when I offered her one, seemed quite glad to take it. Really, there's no knowing what to offer; for now money is so scarce, people who live by knitting and needlework, are willing to take almost anything. I dare say Miss Wilson, the milliner, would charge me five shillings for that collar."

Miss Saville looked very grave, and was silent, but Mr. Elliott, who had been reading the newspaper, now laid it down, and said—

"Do you think it honest, Eliza, to take the fruit of a poor girl's industry for one-fifth of its value?"

"Really, James, you men have the strangest notions!—why

should it not be honest to purchase an article for the price at which its owner is willing to sell it?"

"Not *willing*, Eliza. By your own account it is wrung from them by the direst want; and perhaps the other shilling which you withheld from the poor maker of that little article, and which to you is nothing, might have given food and comfort to a starving family."

Mrs. Elliott blushed, but did not speak. Her conscience told her her husband was right, yet she did not like—what woman does?—to own herself in the wrong.

Mr. Elliott did not wish to give his wife pain; and her sister felt glad to see that an impression, which she hoped might prove lasting, had been made on her mind; so, after a momentary pause, the conversation turned on other subjects, and the evening concluded happily. In the silence of night, however, ere they fell asleep, perhaps the last reflection of each was something of this kind:

"How I wish," thought Miss Saville, "I knew where that poor girl lives. I shall not forget her pale face and gentle voice for some time."

"Well," thought her brother, "I blamed Eliza for not being charitable, and I fear I'm not half enough so myself. When I'm paying my subscriptions next week, I think I'll double them."

"I wish I had given the shilling to that poor girl," was Mrs. Elliott's reflection. "James is right. I'll never again bargain with a poor work-woman."

Let us now return to the wretched attic inhabited by the Sullivans.

A month had elapsed since the day when our story commenced, and their miserable resources were utterly exhausted. Denis and his youngest child lay dead; they had both expired of hunger the preceding day, and as yet no one came to bury them. The wife lay gasping at the corpses' feet, and a low, dull moaning proceeded from the white, drawn lips of the two little skeletons lying on the floor, who, but for that sign of life, could scarcely be distinguished from their dead brother.

Where was Mary? Day after day, when the last halfpenny was expended, had she crawled forth to beg alms for her perishing family: often she returned to them empty. Her failing strength and eyesight, together with the long December nights, unlighted by fire or candle, forbade her resuming her ill-rewarded knitting. This day she went out, almost frantically, to beseech a morsel of bread; for she felt that ere another sun went down, they must all perish. We will leave her tottering towards a crowded thoroughfare, where she thought, perchance, even one halfpenny might be obtained.

About two o'clock, that day, Mr. and Mrs. Elliott, and their sister, emerged from a haberdasher's shop, in a street where the ladies had been making various purchases, and the gentleman—as gentlemen always have done and always will do—amused himself by commenting on their proceedings, and thanking his stars that masculine costume is so much more easily arranged than that pertaining to the softer portion of the creation. They were about to cross the street, when Mr. Elliott said—

"There's a crowd on the opposite footpath; we had better wait till it disperses."

"'Tis only a poor hungry crathur that fainted," said a man who was passing, "and she's lying now like dead."

"Let us go," said Miss Saville, "and see what can be done." And on she went, followed by her brother and sister.

There lay poor Mary, apparently lifeless, her head resting against a lamp post. Miserably death-like as she looked, Miss Saville immediately recognised the girl she had met at the baker's; and her sister the same moment knew the poor seller of the knitted collar.

No time was lost by Mr. Elliott in getting her conveyed to the nearest apothecary's shop; where, after some time, she was restored to consciousness. A few words sufficed to make known her story, and to direct her benefactor to the miserable dwelling where her parents lay. Thither Mr. Elliott went, and found that Nelly Sullivan had breathed her last since morning. The little boys were still alive, and able to swallow the cordial he offered them. He summoned some of the neighbours to his assistance, and provided for the decent burial of the dead. He then had the poor children wrapped up, and conveyed to a house inhabited by an old woman who had nursed his family, and who readily undertook the charge of them and of Mary. After some time, they all recovered their bodily health, but it was long before Mary could be roused from a state of deep dejection. At length Miss Saville took her to the country, and there the grateful girl lives with her as a servant, each day become more useful. The boys, through Mr. Elliott's interest, have been placed at school, where they promise to do well. Their benefactors found that such giving was indeed "twice blessed," for they experienced an abundant enlargement of their own hearts, while doing good to others. Mrs. Elliott especially, though thrifty, as a housewife should be, in buying from rich tradespeople, has never been known to cheapen the work of the poor, since the day on which she purchased the *knitted collar.*

THE OLD NURSE'S STORY°
Elizabeth Gaskell
(1810–1865)

You know, my dears, that your mother was an orphan, and an only child; and I dare say you have heard that your grandfather was a clergyman up in Westmoreland, where I come from. I was just a girl in the village school, when, one day, your grandmother came in to ask the mistress if there was any scholar there who would do for a nurse-maid; and mighty proud I was, I can tell ye, when the mistress called me up, and spoke to my being a good girl at my needle, and a steady, honest girl, and one whose parents were very respectable, though they might be poor. I thought I should like nothing better than to serve the pretty young lady, who was blushing as deep as I was, as she spoke of the coming baby, and what I should have to do with it. However, I see you don't care so much for this part of my story, as for what you think is to come, so I'll tell you at once. I was engaged and settled at the parsonage before Miss Rosamond (that was the baby, who is now your mother) was born. To be sure, I had little enough to do with her when she came, for she was never out of her mother's arms, and slept by her all night long; and proud enough was I sometimes when missis trusted her to me. There never was such a baby before or since, though you've all of you been fine enough in your turns; but for sweet, winning ways, you've none of you come up to your mother. She

°From *Household Words*, 1852.

took after her mother, who was a real lady born; a Miss Furnivall, a granddaughter of Lord Furnivall's, in Northumberland. I believe she had neither brother nor sister, and had been brought up in my lord's family till she had married your grandfather, who was just a curate, son to a shopkeeper in Carlisle—but a clever, fine gentleman as ever was—and one who was a right-down hard worker in his parish, which was very wide, and scattered all abroad over the Westmoreland Fells. When your mother, little Miss Rosamond, was about four or five years old, both her parents died in a fortnight—one after the other. Ah! that was a sad time. My pretty young mistress and me was looking for another baby, when my master came home from one of his long rides, wet and tired, and took the fever he died of; and then she never held up her head again, but just lived to see her dead baby, and have it laid on her breast, before she sighed away her life. My mistress had asked me, on her death-bed, never to leave Miss Rosamond; but if she had never spoken a word, I would have gone with the little child to the end of the world.

The next thing, and before we had well stilled our sobs, the executors and guardians came to settle the affairs. They were my poor young mistress's own cousin, Lord Furnivall, and Mr. Esthwaite, my master's brother, a shopkeeper in Manchester; not so well-to-do then as he was afterwards, and with a large family rising about him. Well! I don't know if it were their settling, or because of a letter my mistress wrote on her death-bed to her cousin, my lord; but somehow it was settled that Miss Rosamond and me were to go to Furnivall Manor House, in Northumberland; and my lord spoke as if it had been her mother's wish that she should live with his family, and as if he had no objections, for that one or two more or less could make no difference in so grand a household. So though that was not the way in which I should have wished the coming of my bright and pretty pet to have been looked at—who was like a sunbeam in any family, be it never so grand—I was well pleased that all the folks in the Dale should stare and admire, when they heard I was going to be young lady's maid at my Lord Furnivall's at Furnivall Manor.

But I made a mistake in thinking we were to go and live

where my lord did. It turned out that the family had left
Furnivall Manor House fifty years or more. I could not hear that
my poor young mistress had ever been there, though she had
been brought up in the family; and I was sorry for that, for I
should have liked Miss Rosamond's youth to have passed where
her mother's had been.

My lord's gentleman, from whom I asked as many questions
as I durst, said that the Manor House was at the foot of the
Cumberland Fells, and a very grand place; that an old Miss
Furnivall, a great-aunt of my lord's, lived there, with only a few
servants; but that it was a very healthy place, and my lord had
thought that it would suit Miss Rosamond very well for a few
years, and that her being there might perhaps amuse his old
aunt.

I was bidden by my lord to have Miss Rosamond's things
ready by a certain day. He was a stern, proud man, as they say
all the Lords Furnivall were; and he never spoke a word more
than was necessary. Folk did say he had loved my young mistress; but that, because she knew that his father would object,
she would never listen to him, and married Mr. Esthwaite; but
I don't know. He never married, at any rate. But he never took
much notice of Miss Rosamond; which I thought he might have
done if he had cared for her dead mother. He sent his gentleman with us to the Manor House, telling him to join him at
Newcastle that same evening; so there was no great length of
time for him to make us known to all the strangers before he,
too, shook us off; and we were left, two lonely young things (I
was not eighteen), in the great old Manor House. It seems like
yesterday that we drove there. We had left our own dear parsonage very early, and we had both cried as if our hearts would
break, though we were travelling in my lord's carriage, which I
thought so much of once. And now it was long past noon on a
September day, and we stopped to change horses for the last
time at a little smoky town, all full of colliers and miners. Miss
Rosamond had fallen asleep, but Mr. Henry told me to waken
her, that she might see the park and the Manor House as we
drove up. I thought it rather a pity; but I did what he bade me,
for fear he should complain of me to my lord. We had left all

signs of a town, or even a village, and were then inside the gates of a large wild park—not like the parks here in the north, but with rocks, and the noise of running water, and gnarled thorn-trees, and old oaks, all white and peeled with age.

The road went up about two miles, and then we saw a great and stately house, with many trees close around it, so close that in some places their branches dragged against the walls when the wind blew, and some hung broken down; for no one seemed to take much charge of the place—to lop the wood, or to keep the moss-covered carriageway in order. Only in front of the house all was clear. The great oval drive was without a weed; and neither tree nor creeper was allowed to grow over the long, many-windowed front; at both sides of which a wing projected, which were each the ends of other side fronts; for the house, although it was so desolate, was even grander than I expected. Behind it rose the Fells, which seemed unenclosed and bare enough; and on the left hand of the house, as you stood facing it, was a little, old-fashioned flower-garden, as I found out after-wards. A door opened out upon it from the west front; it had been scooped out of the thick, dark wood for some old Lady Furnivall; but the branches of the great forest trees had grown and overshadowed it again, and there were very few flowers that would live there at that time.

When we drove up to the great front entrance, and went into the hall, I thought we should be lost—it was so large, and vast, and grand. There was a chandelier all of bronze, hung down from the middle of the ceiling; and I had never seen one before, and looked at it all in amaze. Then, at one end of the hall, was a great fireplace, as large as the sides of the houses in my country, with massy andirons and dogs to hold the wood; and by it were heavy, old-fashioned sofas. At the opposite end of the hall, to the left as you went in—on the western side—was an organ built into the wall, and so large that it filled up the best part of that end. Beyond it, on the same side, was a door; and opposite, on each side of the fireplace, were also doors leading to the east front; but those I never went through as long as I stayed in the house, so I can't tell you what lay beyond.

The afternoon was closing in, and the hall, which had no fire

lighted in it, looked dark and gloomy, but we did not stay there
a moment. The old servant, who had opened the door for us,
bowed to Mr. Henry, and took us in through the door at the further side of the great organ, and led us through several smaller
halls and passages into the west drawing-room, where he said
that Miss Furnivall was sitting. Poor little Miss Rosamond held
very tight to me, as if she were scared and lost in that great
place, and as for myself, I was not much better. The west drawing-
room was very cheerful-looking, with a warm fire in it, and
plenty of good, comfortable furniture about. Miss Furnivall was
an old lady not far from eighty, I should think, but I do not know.
She was thin and tall, and had a face as full of fine wrinkles as if
they had been drawn all over it with a needle's point. Her eyes
were very watchful, to make up, I suppose, for her being so deaf
as to be obliged to use a trumpet. Sitting with her, working at
the same great piece of tapestry, was Mrs. Stark, her maid and
companion, and almost as old as she was. She had lived with
Miss Furnivall ever since they both were young, and now she
seemed more like a friend than a servant; she looked so cold,
and grey, and stony as if she had never loved or cared for anyone; and I don't suppose she did care for anyone, except her
mistress; and, owing to the great deafness of the latter, Mrs.
Stark treated her very much as if she were a child. Mr. Henry
gave some message from my lord, and then he bowed good-bye
to us all—taking no notice of my sweet little Miss Rosamond's
outstretched hand—and left us standing there, being looked at
by the two old ladies through their spectacles.

I was right glad when they rung for the old footman who had
shown us in at first, and told him to take us to our rooms. So we
went out of that great drawing-room, and into another sitting-
room, and out of that, and then up a great flight of stairs, and
along a broad gallery—which was something like a library, having books all down one side, and windows and writing-tables all
down the other—till we came to our rooms, which I was not
sorry to hear were just over the kitchens; for I began to think I
should be lost in that wilderness of a house. There was an old
nursery that had been used for all the little lords and ladies long
ago, with a pleasant fire burning in the grate, and the kettle boil-

ing on the hob, and tea-things spread out on the table; and out
of that room was the night-nursery, with a little crib for Miss
Rosamond close to my bed. And old James called up Dorothy,
his wife, to bid us welcome; and both he and she were so hos-
pitable and kind, that by and by Miss Rosamond and me felt
quite at home; and by the time tea was over, she was sitting
on Dorothy's knee, and chattering away as fast as her little
tongue could go. I soon found out that Dorothy was from
Westmoreland, and that bound her and me together, as it were;
and I would never wish to meet with kinder people than were
old James and his wife. James had lived pretty nearly all his life
in my lord's family, and thought there was no one so grand as
they. He even looked down a little on his wife; because, till he
had married her, she had never lived in any but a farmer's
household. But he was very fond of her, as well he might be.
They had one servant under them, to do all the rough work.
Agnes they called her; and she and me, and James and Dorothy,
with Miss Furnivall and Mrs. Stark, made up the family; always
remembering my sweet little Miss Rosamond! I used to wonder
what they had done before she came, they thought so much of
her now. Kitchen and drawing-room, it was all the same. The
hard, sad Miss Furnivall, and the cold Mrs. Stark, looked
pleased when she came fluttering in like a bird, playing and
pranking hither and thither, with a continual murmur, and
pretty prattle of gladness. I am sure, they were sorry many a
time when she flitted away into the kitchen, though they were
too proud to ask her to stay with them, and were a little surprised at her taste; though to be sure, as Mrs. Stark said, it was
not to be wondered at, remembering what stock her father had
come of. The great, old rambling house was a famous place for
little Miss Rosamond. She made expeditions all over it, with me
at her heels; all, except the east wing, which was never opened,
and whither we never thought of going. But in the western and
northern part was many a pleasant room; full of things that were
curiosities to us, though they might not have been to people
who had seen more. The windows were darkened by the sweeping boughs of the trees, and the ivy which had overgrown them;
but, in the green gloom, we could manage to see old China jars

and carved ivory boxes, and great heavy books, and, above all, the old pictures!

Once, I remember, my darling would have Dorothy go with us to tell us who they all were; for they were all portraits of some of my lord's family, though Dorothy could not tell us the names of every one. We had gone through most of the rooms, when we came to the old state drawing-room over the hall, and there was a picture of Miss Furnivall; or, as she was called in those days, Miss Grace, for she was the younger sister. Such a beauty she must have been! but with such a set, proud look, and such scorn looking out of her handsome eyes, with her eyebrows just a little raised, as if she wondered how anyone could have the impertinence to look at her, and her lip curled at us, as we stood there gazing. She had a dress on, the like of which I had never seen before, but it was all the fashion when she was young: a hat of some soft white stuff like beaver, pulled a little over her brows, and a beautiful plume of feathers sweeping round it on one side; and her gown of blue satin was open in front to a quilted white stomacher.

"Well, to be sure!" said I, when I had gazed my fill. "Flesh is grass, they do say; but who would have thought that Miss Furnivall had been such an out-and-out beauty, to see her now?"

"Yes," said Dorothy. "Folks change sadly. But if what my master's father used to say was true, Miss Furnivall, the elder sister, was handsomer than Miss Grace. Her picture is here somewhere; but, if I show it you, you must never let on, even to James, that you have seen it. Can the little lady hold her tongue, think you?" asked she.

I was not so sure, for she was such a little sweet, bold, open-spoken child, so I set her to hide herself; and then I helped Dorothy to turn a great picture, that leaned with its face towards the wall, and was not hung up as the others were. To be sure, it beat Miss Grace for beauty; and, I think, for scornful pride, too, though in that matter it might be hard to choose. I could have looked at it an hour, but Dorothy seemed half frightened at having shown it to me, and hurried it back again, and bade me run and find Miss Rosamond, for that there were some ugly places

about the house, where she should like ill for the child to go. I
was a brave, high-spirited girl, and thought little of what the old
woman said, for I liked hide-and-seek as well as any child in the
parish; so off I ran to find my little one.

As winter drew on, and the days grew shorter, I was sometimes almost certain that I heard a noise as if someone was playing on the great organ in the hall. I did not hear it every evening;
but, certainly, I did very often; usually when I was sitting with
Miss Rosamond, after I had put her to bed, and keeping quite
still and silent in the bedroom. Then I used to hear it booming
and swelling away in the distance. The first night, when I went
down to my supper, I asked Dorothy who had been playing
music, and James said very shortly that I was a gowk to take the
wind soughing among the trees for music; but I saw Dorothy
look at him very fearfully, and Bessy, the kitchen-maid, said
something beneath her breath, and went quite white. I saw they
did not like my question, so I held my peace till I was with
Dorothy alone, when I knew I could get a good deal out of her.
So, the next day, I watched my time, and I coaxed and asked her
who it was that played the organ; for I knew that it was the organ
and not the wind well enough, for all I had kept silence before
James. But Dorothy had had her lesson, I'll warrant, and never
a word could I get from her. So then I tried Bessy, though I had
always held my head rather above her, as I was evened to James
and Dorothy, and she was little better than their servant. So she
said I must never, never tell; and if ever told, I was never to say
she had told me; but it was a very strange noise, and she had
heard it many a time, but most of all on winter nights, and
before storms; and folks did say it was the old lord playing on the
great organ in the hall, just as he used to do when he was alive;
but who the old lord was, or why he played, and why he played
on stormy winter evenings in particular, she either could not or
would not tell me. Well! I told you I had a brave heart; and I
thought it was rather pleasant to have that grand music rolling
about the house, let who would be the player; for now it rose
above the great gusts of wind, and wailed and triumphed just
like a living creature, and then it fell to a softness most complete, only it was always music, and tunes, so it was nonsense to

call it the wind. I thought at first that it might be Miss Furnivall who played, unknown to Bessy; but one day, when I was in the hall by myself, I opened the organ and peeped all about it and around it, as I had done to the organ in Crosthwaite Church once before, and I saw it was all broken and destroyed inside, though it looked so brave and fine; and then, though it was noonday, my flesh began to creep a little, and I shut it up, and run away pretty quickly to my own bright nursery; and I did not like hearing the music for some time after that, any more than James and Dorothy did. All this time Miss Rosamond was making herself more and more beloved. The old ladies liked her to dine with them at their early dinner; James stood behind Miss Furnivall's chair, and I behind Miss Rosamond's all in state; and, after dinner, she would play about in a corner of the great drawing-room, as still as any mouse, while Miss Furnivall slept, and I had my dinner in the kitchen. But she was glad enough to come to me in the nursery afterwards; for, as she said, Miss Furnivall was so sad, and Mrs. Stark so dull; but she and I were merry enough; and, by-and-by, I got not to care for that weird rolling music, which did one no harm, if we did not know where it came from.

That winter was very cold. In the middle of October the frosts began, and lasted many, many weeks. I remember, one day at dinner, Miss Furnivall lifted up her sad, heavy eyes, and said to Mrs. Stark, "I am afraid we shall have a terrible winter," in a strange kind of meaning way. But Mrs. Stark pretended not to hear, and talked very loud of something else. My little lady and I did not care for the frost; not we! As long as it was dry, we climbed up the steep brows, behind the house, and went up on the Fells, which were bleak, and bare enough, and there we ran races in the fresh, sharp air; and once we came down by a new path that took us past the two old gnarled holly-trees, which grew about half-way down by the east side of the house. But the days grew shorter and shorter and the old lord, if it was he, played more and more stormily and sadly on the great organ. One Sunday afternoon—it must have been towards the end of November—I asked Dorothy to take charge of little Missey when she came out of the drawing-room, after Miss Furnivall had had her nap; for it was too cold to take her with me to

church, and yet I wanted to go, And Dorothy was glad enough
to promise, and was so fond of the child, that all seemed well;
Bessy and I set off very briskly, though the sky hung heavy and
black over the white earth, as if the night had never fully gone
away; and the air, though still, was very biting and keen.

"We shall have a fall of snow," said Bessy to me. And sure
enough, even while we were in church, it came down thick, in
great large flakes so thick it almost darkened the windows. It
had stopped snowing before we came out, but it lay soft, thick
and deep beneath our feet, as we tramped home. Before we got
to the hall, the moon rose, and I think it was lighter then—what
with the moon, and what with the white dazzling snow—than it
had been when we went to church, between two and three
o'clock. I have not told you that Miss Furnivall and Mrs. Stark
never went to church: they used to read the prayers together, in
their quiet, gloomy way; they seemed to feel the Sunday very
long without their tapestry-work to be busy at. So when I went
to Dorothy in the kitchen, to fetch Miss Rosamond and take her
upstairs with me, I did not much wonder when the old woman
told me that the ladies had kept the child with them, and that
she had never come to the kitchen, as I had bidden her, when
she was tired of behaving pretty in the drawing-room. So I took
off my things and went to find her, and bring her to her supper
in the nursery. But when I went into the best drawing-room,
there sat the two old ladies, very still and quiet, dropping out a
word now and then, but looking as if nothing so bright and
merry as Miss Rosamond had ever been near them. Still I
thought she might be hiding from me; it was one of her pretty
ways—and that she had persuaded them to look as if they knew
nothing about her; so I went softly peeping under this sofa, and
behind that chair, making believe I was sadly frightened at not
finding her.

"What's the matter, Hester?" said Mrs. Stark, sharply. I don't
know if Miss Furnivall had seen me for, as I told you, she was
very deaf, and she sat quite still, idly staring into the fire, with
her hopeless face. "I'm only looking for my little Rosy-Posy,"
replied I, still thinking that the child was there, and near me,
though I could not see her.

"Miss Rosamond is not here," said Mrs. Stark. "She went away more than an hour ago, to find Dorothy." And she, too, turned and went on looking into the fire.

My heart sank at this, and I began to wish I had never left my darling. I went back to Dorothy and told her. James was gone out for the day, but she, and me, and Bessy took lights and went up into the nursery first, and then we roamed over the great, large house, calling and entreating Miss Rosamond to come out of her hiding-place, and not frighten us to death in that way. But there was no answer; no sound.

"Oh!" said I, at last. "Can she have got into the east wing and hidden there?"

But Dorothy said it was not possible, for that she herself had never been in there; that the doors were always locked, and my lord's steward had the keys, she believed; at any rate, neither she nor James had ever seen them: so I said I would go back, and see if, after all, she was not hidden in the drawing-room, unknown to the old ladies; and if I found her there, I said, I would whip her well for the fright she had given me; but I never meant to do it. Well, I went back to the west drawing-room, and I told Mrs. Stark we could not find her anywhere, and asked for leave to look all about the furniture there, for I thought now, that she might have fallen asleep in some warm, hidden corner; but no! we looked, Miss Furnivall got up and looked, trembling all over, and she was nowhere there; then we set off again, everyone in the house, and looked in all the places we had searched before, but we could not find her. Miss Furnivall shivered and shook so much that Mrs. Stark took her back into the warm drawing-room; but not before they had made me promise to bring her to them when she was found. Well-a-day! I began to think she never would be found, when I bethought me to look into the great front court, all covered with snow. I was upstairs when I looked out; but it was such clear moonlight, I could see, quite plain, two little footprints, which might be traced from the hall door, and round the corner of the east wing. I don't know how I got down, but I tugged open the great, stiff hall door, and, throwing the skirt of my gown over my head for a cloak, I ran out. I turned the east corner, and there a black shadow fell on the snow; but when I came again into the moonlight, there were the little footmarks going up—up to the Fells. It was bitter cold; so cold that the air almost took the skin off my face as I ran, but I ran on, crying to think how my poor little darling must be perished, and frightened. I was within sight of the holly-trees, when I saw a shepherd coming down the hill, bearing something in his arms wrapped in his maud. He shouted to me, and asked me if I had lost a bairn; and, when I could not speak for crying, he bore towards me, and I saw my wee bairnie lying still, and white, and stiff, in his arms, as if she had been dead. He told me he had been up the Fells to gather in his sheep, before the deep cold of night came on, and that under the holly-trees (black marks on the hill-side, where no other bush was for miles around) he had found my little lady—my lamb—my queen—my darling—stiff and cold, in the terrible sleep which is frost-begotten. Oh! the joy and the tears of having her in my arms once again! for I would not let him carry her; but took her, maud and all, into my own arms, and held her near my own warm neck and heart, and felt the life stealing slowly back again into her little gentle limbs. But she was still insensible when we reached the hall, and I had no breath for speech. We went in by the kitchen-door.

"Bring the warming-pan," said I; and I carried her upstairs, and began undressing her by the nursery fire, which Bessy had kept up. I called my little lammie all the sweet and playful names I could think of—even while my eyes were blinded by my tears; and at last, oh! at length she opened her large blue eyes. Then I put her into her warm bed, and sent Dorothy down to tell Miss Furnivall that all was well; and I made up my mind to sit by my darling's bedside the live-long night. She fell away into a soft sleep as soon as her pretty head had touched the pillow, and I watched her till morning light; when she wakened up bright and clear—or so I thought at first—and, my dears, so I think now.

She said that she had fancied that she should like to go to Dorothy, for that both the old ladies were asleep, and it was very dull in the drawing-room; and that, as she was going through the west lobby, she saw the snow through the high window falling—falling—soft and steady; but she wanted to see it lying pretty and white on the ground; so she made her way into the great hall; and then, going to the window, she saw it bright and soft upon the drive; but while she stood there, she saw a little girl, not so old as she was, "but so pretty," said my darling, "and this little girl beckoned to me to come out; and oh, she was so pretty and so sweet, I could not choose but to go." And then this other little girl had taken her by the hand, and side by side the two had gone round the east corner.

"Now you are a naughty little girl, and telling stories," said I. "What would your good mamma, that is in heaven, and never told a story in her life, say to her little Rosamond, if she heard her—and I dare say she does—telling stories!"

"Indeed, Hester," sobbed out my child, "I'm telling you true. Indeed I am."

"Don't tell me!" said I, very stern. "I tracked you by your foot-marks through the snow; there were only yours to be seen: and if you had had a little girl to go hand-in-hand with you up the hill, don't you think the footprints would have gone along with yours?"

"I can't help it, dear, dear Hester," said she, crying, "if they did not; I never looked at her feet, but she held my hand fast and tight in her little one, and it was very, very cold. She took me up the Fell-path, up to the holly-trees; and there I saw a lady weeping and crying; but when she saw me, she hushed her weeping, and smiled very proud and grand, and took me on her knee, and began to lull me to sleep; and that's all, Hester—but that is true; and my dear mamma knows it is," said she, crying. So I thought the child was in a fever, and pretended to believe her, as she went over her story—over and over again, and always the same. At last Dorothy knocked at the door with Miss Rosamond's breakfast; and she told me the old ladies were down in the eating parlour, and that they wanted to speak to me. They had both been into the night-nursery the evening before, but it was after Miss Rosamond was asleep; so they had only looked at her—not asked me any questions.

"I shall catch it," thought I to myself, as I went along the north gallery. "And yet," I thought, taking courage, "it was in their charge I left her; and it's they that's to blame for letting her steal away unknown and unwatched." So I went in boldly, and told my story. I told it all to Miss Furnivall, shouting close to her ear; but when I came to the mention of the other little girl out in the snow, coaxing and tempting her out, and wiling her up to the grand and beautiful lady by the holly-tree, she threw her arms up—her old and withered arms—and cried aloud, "Oh! Heaven forgive! Have mercy!"

Mrs. Stark took hold of her; roughly enough, I thought; but she was past Mrs. Stark's management, and spoke to me, in a kind of wild warning and authority.

"Hester! keep her from that child! It will lure her to her death! That evil child! Tell her it is a wicked, naughty child." Then Mrs. Stark hurried me out of the room; where, indeed, I was glad enough to go; but Miss Furnivall kept shrieking out, "Oh, have mercy! Wilt Thou never forgive! It is many a long year ago—"

I was very uneasy in my mind after that. I durst never leave Miss Rosamond, night or day, for fear lest she might slip off again, after some fancy or other; and all the more, because I thought I could make out that Miss Furnivall was crazy, from their odd ways about her; and I was afraid lest something of the same kind (which might be in the family, you know) hung over my darling. And the great frost never ceased all this time; and whenever it was a more stormy night than usual, between the gusts, and through the wind, we heard the old lord playing on the great organ. But, old lord, or not, wherever Miss Rosamond went, there I followed; for my love for her, pretty, helpless orphan, was stronger than my fear for the grand and terrible sound. Besides, it rested with me to keep her cheerful and merry, as beseemed her age. So we played together, and wandered together, here and there, and everywhere; for I never dared to lose sight of her again in that large and rambling house. And so it happened, that one afternoon, not long before Christmas Day, we were playing together on the billiard-table in the great hall (not that we knew the right way of playing, but she liked to roll the smooth ivory balls with her pretty hands, and I liked to do whatever she did); and, by-and-by, without our notic- ing it, it grew dusk indoors, though it was still light in the open air, and I was thinking of taking her back into the nursery, when, all of a sudden, she cried out:

"Look, Hester! look! there is my poor little girl out in the snow!"

I turned towards the long narrow windows, and there, sure enough, I saw a little girl, less than my Miss Rosamond—dressed all unfit to be out-of-doors such a bitter night—crying, and beating against the window-panes, as if she wanted to be let in. She seemed to sob and wail, till Miss Rosamond could bear it no longer, and was flying to the door to open it, when, all of a sudden, and close upon us, the great organ pealed out so loud and thundering, it fairly made me tremble; and all the more when I remembered me that, even in the stillness of that dead-cold weather, I had heard no sound of little battering hands upon the window-glass, although the Phantom Child had seemed to put forth all its force; and, although I had seen it wail and cry, no faintest touch of sound had fallen upon my ears. Whether I remembered all this at the very moment, I do not know; the great organ sound had so stunned me into terror; but this I know, I caught up Miss Rosamond before she got the hall door opened, and clutched her, and carried her away, kicking and screaming, into the large, bright kitchen, where Dorothy and Agnes were busy with their mince-pies.

"What is the matter with my sweet one?" cried Dorothy, as I bore in Miss Rosamond, who was sobbing as if her heart would break.

"She won't let me open the door for my little girl to come in; and she'll die if she is out on the Fells all night. Cruel, naughty Hester," she said, slapping me; but she might have struck harder, for I had seen a look of ghastly terror on Dorothy's face, which made my very blood run cold.

"Shut the back-kitchen door fast, and bolt it well," said she to Agnes. She said no more; she gave me raisins and almonds to quiet Miss Rosamond: but she sobbed about the little girl in the snow, and would not touch any of the good things. I was thankful when she cried herself to sleep in bed. Then I stole down to the kitchen, and told Dorothy I had made up my mind. I would carry my darling back to my father's house in Applethwaite;

where, if we lived humbly, we lived at peace. I said I had been frightened enough with the old lord's organ-playing; but now that I had seen for myself this little moaning child, all decked out as no child in the neighbourhood could be, beating and battering to get in, yet always without any sound or noise—with the dark wound on its right shoulder; and that Miss Rosamond had known it again for the phantom that had nearly lured her to her death (which Dorothy knew was true); I would stand it no longer.

I saw Dorothy change colour once or twice. When I had done, she told me she did not think I could take Miss Rosamond with me, for that she was my lord's ward, and I had no right over her; and she asked me would I leave the child that I was so fond of just for sounds and sights that could do me no harm; and that they had all had to get used to in their turns? I was all in a hot, trembling passion; and I said it was very well for her to talk, that knew what these sights and noises betokened, and that had, perhaps, had something to do with the Spectre Child while it was alive. And I taunted her so, that she told me all she knew, at last; and then I wished I had never been told, for it only made me more afraid than ever.

She said she had heard the tale from old neighbours that were alive when she was first married; when folks used to come to the hall sometimes, before it had got such a bad name on the country side: it might not be true, or it might, what she had been told.

The old lord was Miss Furnivall's father—Miss Grace, as Dorothy called her, for Miss Maude was the elder, and Miss Furnivall by rights. The old lord was eaten up with pride. Such a proud man was never seen or heard of; and his daughters were like him. No one was good enough to wed them, although they had choice enough; for they were the great beauties of their day, as I had seen by their portraits, where they hung in the state drawing-room. But, as the old saying is, "Pride will have a fall;" and these two haughty beauties fell in love with the same man, and he no better than a foreign musician, whom their father had down from London to play music with him at the Manor House. For, above all things, next to his pride, the old lord loved music.

He could play on nearly every instrument that ever was heard of; and it was a strange thing it did not soften him; but he was a fierce, dour old man, and had broken his poor wife's heart with his cruelty, they said. He was mad after music, and would pay any money for it. So he got this foreigner to come; who made such beautiful music, that they said the very birds on the trees stopped their singing to listen. And, by degrees, this foreign gentleman got such a hold over the old lord, that nothing would serve him but that he must come every year; and it was he that had the great organ brought from Holland, and built up in the hall, where it stood now. He taught the old lord to play on it; but many and many a time, when Lord Furnivall was thinking of nothing but his fine organ, and his finer music, the dark foreigner was walking abroad in the woods, with one of the young ladies: now Miss Maude, and then Miss Grace.

Miss Maude won the day and carried off the prize, such as it was; and he and she were married, all unknown to anyone; and before he made his next yearly visit, she had been confined of a little girl at a farm-house on the Moors, while her father and Miss Grace thought she was away at Doncaster Races. But though she was a wife and a mother, she was not a bit softened, but as haughty and as passionate as ever; and perhaps more so, for she was jealous of Miss Grace, to whom her foreign husband paid a deal of court—by way of blinding her—as he told his wife. But Miss Grace triumphed over Miss Maude, and Miss Maude grew fiercer and fiercer, both with her husband and with her sister; and the former—who could easily shake off what was disagreeable, and hide himself in foreign countries—went away a month before his usual time that summer, and half-threatened that he would never come back again. Meanwhile, the little girl was left at the farm-house, and her mother used to have her horse saddled and gallop wildly over the hills to see her once every week, at the very least—for where she loved, she loved; and where she hated, she hated. And the old lord went on playing—playing on his organ; and the servants thought the sweet music he made had soothed down his awful temper, of which (Dorothy said) some terrible tales could be told. He grew infirm too, and had to walk with a crutch; and his son—that was the present Lord Furnivall's father—was with the army in America, and the other son at sea; so Miss Maude had it pretty much her own way, and she and Miss Grace grew colder and bitterer to each other every day; till at last they hardly ever spoke, except when the old lord was by. The foreign musician came again the next summer, but it was for the last time; for they led him such a life with their jealousy and their passions, that he grew weary, and went away, and never was heard of again. And Miss Maude, who had always meant to have her marriage acknowledged when her father should be dead, was left now a deserted wife— whom nobody knew to have been married—with a child that she dared not own, although she loved it to distraction; living with a father whom she feared, and a sister whom she hated. When the next summer passed over and the dark foreigner never came, both Miss Maude and Miss Grace grew gloomy and sad; they had a haggard look about them, though they looked handsome as ever. But by-and-by Miss Maude brightened; for her father grew more and more infirm, and more than ever carried away by his music; and she and Miss Grace lived almost entirely apart, having separate rooms, the one on the west side, Miss Maude on the east—those very rooms which were now shut up. So she thought she might have her little girl with her, and no one need ever know except those who dared not speak about it, and were bound to believe that it was, as she said, a cottager's child she had taken a fancy to. All this, Dorothy said, was pretty well known; but what came afterwards no one knew, except Miss Grace and Mrs. Stark, who was even then her maid, and much more of a friend to her than ever her sister had been. But the servants supposed, from words that were dropped, that Miss Maude had triumphed over Miss Grace, and told her that all the time the dark foreigner had been mocking her with pretended love—he was her own husband; the colour left Miss Grace's cheek and lips that very day for ever, and she was heard to say many a time that sooner or later she would have her revenge; and Mrs. Stark was for ever spying about the east rooms.

One fearful night, just after the New Year had come in, when the snow was lying thick and deep, and the flakes were still falling—fast enough to blind anyone who might be out and abroad—there was a great and violent noise heard, and the old lord's voice above all, cursing and swearing awfully, and the cries of a little child—and the proud defiance of a fierce woman—and the sound of a blow—and a dead stillness,—nd moans and wailings dying away on the hill-side! Then the old lord summoned all his servants, and told them, with terrible oaths, and words more terrible, that his daughter had disgraced herself, and that he had turned her out of doors—her, and her child—and that if ever they gave her help—or food—or shelter—he prayed that they might never enter Heaven. And, all the while, Miss Grace stood by him, white and still as any stone; and when he had ended, she heaved a great sigh, as much as to say her work was done, and her end was accomplished. But the old lord never touched his organ again, and died within the year; and no wonder! for, on the morrow of that wild and fearful night, the shepherds, coming down the Fell side, found Miss Maude sitting, all crazy and smiling, under the holly-trees, nursing a dead child, with a terrible mark on its right shoulder. "But that was not what killed it," said Dorothy; "it was the frost and the cold—every wild creature was in its hole, and every beast in its fold—while the child and its mother were turned out to wander on the Fells! And now you know all! and I wonder if you are less frightened now?"

I was more frightened than ever; but I said I was not. I wished Miss Rosamond and myself well out of that dreadful house for ever; but I would not leave her, and I dared not take her away. But oh! how I watched her, and guarded her! We bolted the doors, and shut the window-shutters fast, an hour or more before dark, rather than leave them open five minutes too late. But my little lady still heard the weird child crying and mourning; and not all we could do or say could keep her from wanting to go to her, and let her in from the cruel wind and snow. All this time, I kept away from Miss Furnivall and Mrs. Stark, as much as ever I could; for I feared them—I knew no good could be about them, with their grey, hard faces, and their dreamy eyes, looking back into the ghastly years that were gone. But, even in my fear, I had a kind of pity—for Miss Furnivall, at least. Those gone down to the pit can hardly have a more hopeless look than that which was ever on her face. At last I even got so sorry for her—who never said a word but what was quite forced from her—that I prayed for her; and I taught Miss Rosamond to pray for one who had done a deadly sin; but often, when she came to those words, she would listen, and start up from her knees, and say, "I hear my little girl plaining and crying very sad—Oh! let her in, or she will die!"

One night—just after New Year's Day had come at last, and the long winter had taken a turn, as I hoped—I heard the west drawing-room bell ring three times, which was the signal for me. I would not leave Miss Rosamond alone, for all she was asleep—for the old lord had been playing wilder than ever—and I feared lest my darling should waken to hear the spectre child; see her I knew she could not. I had fastened the windows too well for that. So I took her out of her bed, and wrapped her up in such outer clothes as were most handy, and carried her down to the drawing-room, where the old ladies sat at their tapestry-work as usual. They looked up when I came in, and Mrs. Stark asked, quite astounded, "Why did I bring Miss Rosamond there, out of her warm bed?" I had begun to whisper, "Because I was afraid of her being tempted out while I was away, by the wild child in the snow," when she stopped me short (with a glance at Miss Furnivall), and said Miss Furnivall wanted me to undo some work she had done wrong, and which neither of them could see to unpick. So I laid my pretty dear on the sofa, and sat down on a stool by them, and hardened my heart against them, as I heard the wind rising and howling.

Miss Rosamond slept on sound, for all the wind blew so; and Miss Furnivall said never a word, nor looked round when the gusts shook the windows. All at once she started up to her full height, and put up one hand, as if to bid us listen.

"I hear voices!" said she. "I hear terrible screams—I hear my father's voice!"

Just at that moment my darling wakened with a sudden start: "My little girl is crying, oh, how she is crying!" and she tried to get up and go to her, but she got her feet entangled in the blanket, and I caught her up; for my flesh had begun to creep at these noises, which they heard while we could catch no sound. In a minute or two the noises came, and gathered fast, and filled our ears; we, too, heard voices and screams, and no longer heard the winter's wind that raged abroad. Mrs. Stark looked at me, and I at her, but we dared not speak. Suddenly Miss Furnivall went towards the door, out into the ante-room, through the west lobby, and opened the door into the great hall. Mrs. Stark followed, and I durst not be left, though my heart almost stopped beating for fear. I wrapped my darling tight in my arms, and went out with them. In the hall the screams were louder than ever; they seemed to come from the east wing—nearer and nearer—close on the other side of the locked-up doors—close behind them. Then I noticed that the great bronze chandelier seemed all alight, though the hall was dim, and that a fire was blazing in the vast hearth-place, though it gave no heat; and I shuddered up with terror, and folded my darling closer to me. But as I did so, the east door shook, and she, suddenly struggling to get free from me, cried, "Hester, I must go! My little girl is there, I hear her; she is coming! Hester, I must go!"

I held her tight with all my strength; with a set will, I held her. If I had died, my hands would have grasped her still, I was so resolved in my mind. Miss Furnivall stood listening, and paid no regard to my darling, who had got down to the ground, and whom I, upon my knees now, was holding with both my arms clasped round her neck; she still striving and crying to get free.

All at once, the east door gave way with a thundering crash, as if torn open in a violent passion, and there came into that broad and mysterious light, the figure of a tall old man, with grey hair and gleaming eyes. He drove before him, with many a relentless gesture of abhorrence, a stern and beautiful woman, with a little child clinging to her dress.

"O Hester! Hester!" cried Miss Rosamond; "It's the lady! the lady below the holly-trees; and my little girl is with her. Hester! Hester! let me go to her; they are drawing me to them. I feel them—I feel them. I must go!"

Again she was almost convulsed by her efforts to get away; but I held her tighter and tighter, till I feared I should do her a hurt; but rather that than let her go towards those terrible phantoms. They passed along towards the great hall door, where the winds howled and ravened for their prey; but before they reached that, the lady turned; and I could see that she defied the old man with a fierce and proud defiance; but then she quailed—and then she threw up her arms wildly and piteously to save her child—her little child—from a blow from his uplifted crutch.

And Miss Rosamond was torn as by a power stronger than mine, and writhed in my arms, and sobbed (for by this time the poor darling was growing faint).

"They want me to go with them on to the Fells—they are drawing me to them. Oh, my little girl! I would come, but cruel, wicked Hester holds me very tight." But when she saw the uplifted crutch, she swooned away, and I thanked God for it. Just at this moment—when the tall old man, his hair streaming as in the blast of a furnace, was going to strike the little shrinking child—Miss Furnivall, the old woman by my side, cried out, "Oh father! father! spare the little innocent child!" But just then I saw—we all saw—another phantom shape itself, and grow clear out of the blue and misty light that filled the hall; we had not seen her till now, for it was another lady who stood by the old man, with a look of relentless hate and triumphant scorn. That figure was very beautiful to look upon, with a soft, white hat drawn down over the proud brows, and a red and curling lip. It was dressed in an open robe of blue satin. I had seen that figure before. It was the likeness of Miss Furnivall in her youth; and the terrible phantoms moved on, regardless of old Miss Furnivall's wild entreaty—and the uplifted crutch fell on the right shoulder of the little child, and the younger sister looked on, stony and deadly serene. But at that moment, the dim lights, and the fire that gave no heat, went out of themselves, and Miss Furnivall lay at our feet stricken down by the palsy—death-stricken.

Yes! she was carried to her bed that night never to rise again. She lay with her face to the wall, muttering low, but muttering always: "Alas! alas! what is done in youth can never be undone in age! What is done in youth can never be undone in age!"

THE LIFTED VEIL*
George Eliot
(1819–1880)

Give me no light, great Heaven, but such as turns
To energy of human fellowship;
No powers beyond the growing heritage
That makes completer manhood.

Chapter I

The time of my end approaches. I have lately been subject to attacks of *angina pectoris*; and in the ordinary course of things, my physician tells me, I may fairly hope that my life will not be protracted many months. Unless, then, I am cursed with an exceptional physical constitution, as I am cursed with an exceptional mental character, I shall not much longer groan under the wearisome burthen of this earthly existence. If it were to be otherwise—if I were to live on to the age most men desire and provide for—I should for once have known whether the miseries of delusive expectation can outweigh the miseries of true prevision. For I foresee when I shall die, and everything that will happen in my last moments.

Just a month from this day, on September 20, 1850, I shall be sitting in this chair, in this study, at ten o'clock at night, longing to die, weary of incessant insight and foresight, without delusions and without hope. Just as I am watching a tongue of blue

*Published in *Blackwood's,* July, 1859.

flame rising in the fire, and my lamp is burning low, the horrible contraction will begin at my chest. I shall only have time to reach the bell, and pull it violently, before the sense of suffocation will come. No one will answer my bell. I know why. My two servants are lovers, and will have quarrelled. My housekeeper will have rushed out of the house in a fury, two hours before, hoping that Perry will believe she has gone to drown herself. Perry is alarmed at last, and is gone out after her. The little scullery-maid is asleep on a bench: she never answers the bell; it does not wake her. The sense of suffocation increases: my lamp goes out with a horrible stench: I make a great effort, and snatch at the bell again. I long for life, and there is no help. I thirsted for the unknown: the thirst is gone. O God, let me stay with the known, and be weary of it: I am content. Agony of pain and suffocation—and all the while the earth, the fields, the pebbly brook at the bottom of the rookery, the fresh scent after the rain, the light of the morning through my chamber-window, the warmth of the hearth after the frosty air—will darkness close over them for ever?

Darkness—darkness—no pain—nothing but darkness: but I am passing on and on through the darkness: my thought stays in the darkness, but always with a sense of moving onward. . . .

Before that time comes, I wish to use my last hours of ease and strength in telling the strange story of my experience. I have never fully unbosomed myself to any human being; I have never been encouraged to trust much in the sympathy of my fellow-men. But we have all a chance of meeting with some pity, some tenderness, some charity, when we are dead: it is the living only who cannot be forgiven—the living only from whom men's indulgence and reverence are held off, like the rain by the hard east wind. While the heart beats, bruise it—it is your only opportunity; while the eye can still turn towards you with moist, timid entreaty, freeze it with an icy unanswering gaze; while the ear, that delicate messenger to the inmost sanctuary of the soul, can still take in the tones of kindness, put it off with hard civility, or sneering compliment, or envious affectation of indifference; while the creative brain can still throb with the sense of injustice, with the yearning for brotherly recognition—make haste—oppress it with your ill-considered judgements, your trivial comparisons, your careless misrepresentations. The heart will by and by be still—"ubi saeva indignatio ulterius cor lacerare nequit;" the eye will cease to entreat; the ear will be deaf; the brain will have ceased from all wants as well as from all work.* Then your charitable speeches may find vent; then you may remember and pity the toil and the struggle and the failure; then you may give due honour to the work achieved; then you may find extenuation for errors, and may consent to bury them.

That is a trivial schoolboy text; why do I dwell on it? It has little reference to me, for I shall leave no works behind me for men to honour. I have no near relatives who will make up, by weeping over my grave, for the wounds they inflicted on me when I was among them. It is only the story of my life that will perhaps win a little more sympathy from strangers when I am dead, than I ever believed it would obtain from my friends while I was living.

My childhood perhaps seems happier to me than it really was, by contrast with all the after-years. For then the curtain of the future was as impenetrable to me as to other children: I had all their delight in the present hour, their sweet indefinite hopes for the morrow; and I had a tender mother: even now, after the dreary lapse of long years, a slight trace of sensation accompanies the remembrance of her caress as she held me on her knee—her arms round my little body, her cheek pressed on mine. I had a complaint of the eyes that made me blind for a little while, and she kept me on her knee from morning till night. That unequalled love soon vanished out of my life, and even to my childish consciousness it was as if that life had become more chill. I rode my little white pony with the groom by my side as before, but there were no loving eyes looking at me as I mounted, no glad arms opened to me when I came back. Perhaps I missed my mother's love more than most children of seven or eight would have done, to whom the other pleasures of life remained as before; for I was certainly a very sensitive child. I remember

---

* "Where savage indignation can lacerate his heart no more." Epitaph appearing on the tombstone of Jonathan Swift (1667–1745), composed by Swift.

still the mingled trepidation and delicious excitement with which I was affected by the tramping of the horses on the pavement in the echoing stables, by the loud resonance of the groom's voices, by the booming bark of the dogs as my father's carriage thundered under the archway of the courtyard, by the din of the gong as it gave notice of luncheon and dinner. The measured tramp of soldiery which I sometimes heard—for my father's house lay near a county town where there were large barracks—made me sob and tremble; and yet when they were gone past, I longed for them to come back again.

I fancy my father thought me an odd child, and had little fondness for me; though he was very careful in fulfilling what he regarded as a parent's duties. But he was already past the middle of life, and I was not his only son. My mother had been his second wife, and he was five-and-forty when he married her. He was a firm, unbending, intensely orderly man, in root and stem a banker, but with a flourishing graft of the active landholder, aspiring to county influence: one of those people who are always like themselves from day to day, who are uninfluenced by the weather, and neither know melancholy nor high spirits. I held him in great awe, and appeared more timid and sensitive in his presence than at other times; a circumstance which, perhaps, helped to confirm him in the intention to educate me on a different plan from the prescriptive one with which he had complied in the case of my elder brother, already a tall youth at Eton. My brother was to be his representative and successor; he must go to Eton and Oxford, for the sake of making connexions, of course: my father was not a man to underrate the bearing of Latin satirists or Greek dramatists on the attainment of an aristocratic position. But, intrinsically, he had slight esteem for "those dead but sceptred spirits;" having qualified himself for forming an independent opinion by reading Potter's *Æschylus*, and dipping into Francis's *Horace*. To this negative view he added a positive one, derived from a recent connexion with mining speculations; namely, that a scientific education was the really useful training for a younger son. Moreover, it was clear that a shy, sensitive boy like me was not fit to encounter the rough experience of a public school. Mr. Letherall had said so very decidedly. Mr. Letherall was a large man in spectacles, who one day took my small head between his large hands, and pressed it here and there in an exploratory, suspicious manner— then placed each of his great thumbs on my temples, and pushed me a little way from him, and stared at me with glittering spectacles. The contemplation appeared to displease him, for he frowned sternly, and said to my father, drawing his thumbs across my eyebrows—

"The deficiency is there, sir—there; and here," he added, touching the upper sides of my head, "here is the excess. That must be brought out, sir, and this must be laid to sleep."

I was in a state of tremor, partly at the vague idea that I was the object of reprobation, partly in the agitation of my first hatred—hatred of this big, spectacled man, who pulled my head about as if he wanted to buy and cheapen it.

I am not aware how much Mr. Letherall had to do with the system afterwards adopted towards me, but it was presently clear that private tutors, natural history, science, and the modern languages, were the appliances by which the defects of my organization were to be remedied. I was very stupid about machines, so I was to be greatly occupied with them; I had no memory for classification, so it was particularly necessary that I should study systematic zoology and botany; I was hungry for human deeds and humane motions, so I was to be plentifully crammed with the mechanical powers, the elementary bodies, and the phenomena of electricity and magnetism. A better-constituted boy would certainly have profited under my intelligent tutors, with their scientific apparatus; and would, doubtless, have found the phenomena of electricity and magnetism as fascinating as I was, every Thursday, assured they were. As it was, I could have paired off, for ignorance of whatever was taught me, with the worst Latin scholar that was ever turned out of a classical academy. I read Plutarch, and Shakespeare, and *Don Quixote* by the sly, and supplied myself in that way with wandering thoughts, while my tutor was assuring me that "an improved man, as distinguished from an ignorant one, was a man who knew the reason why water ran downhill." I had no desire to be this improved man; I was glad of the running water; I could watch it and listen to it gurgling among the pebbles, and bathing the bright green water-plants, by the hour together. I did not want to know *why* it ran; I had perfect confidence that there were good reasons for what was so very beautiful.

There is no need to dwell on this part of my life. I have said enough to indicate that my nature was of the sensitive, unpractical order, and that it grew up in an uncongenial medium, which could never foster it into happy, healthy development. When I was sixteen I was sent to Geneva to complete my course of education; and the change was a very happy one to me, for the first sight of the Alps, with the setting sun on them, as we descended the Jura, seemed to me like an entrance into heaven; and the three years of my life there were spent in a perpetual sense of exaltation, as if from a draught of delicious wine, at the presence of Nature in all her awful loveliness. You will think, perhaps, that I must have been a poet, from this early sensibility to Nature. But my lot was not so happy as that. A poet pours forth his song and *believes* in the listening ear and answering soul, to which his song will be floated sooner or later. But the poet's sensibility without his voice—the poet's sensibility that finds no vent but in silent tears on the sunny bank, when the noonday light sparkles on the water, or in an inward shudder at the sound of harsh human tones, the sight of a cold human eye—this dumb passion brings with it a fatal solitude of soul in the society of one's fellow-men. My least solitary moments were those in which I pushed off in my boat, at evening, towards the centre of the lake; it seemed to me that the sky, and the glowing mountain-tops, and the wide blue water, surrounded me with a cherishing love such as no human face had shed on me since my mother's love had vanished out of my life. I used to do as Jean Jacques° did—lie down in my boat and let it glide where it would, while I looked up at the departing glow leaving one mountain-top after the other, as if the prophet's chariot of fire were passing over them on its way to the home of light. Then, when the white summits were all sad and corpse-like, I had to

---

°Jean-Jacques Rousseau (1712–1778), Geneva-born philosopher and novelist.

push homeward, for I was under careful surveillance, and was allowed no late wanderings. This disposition of mine was not favourable to the formation of intimate friendships among the numerous youths of my own age who are always to be found studying at Geneva. Yet I made *one* such friendship; and, singularly enough, it was with a youth whose intellectual tendencies were the very reverse of my own. I shall call him Charles Meunier; his real surname—an English one, for he was of English extraction—having since become celebrated. He was an orphan, who lived on a miserable pittance while he pursued the medical studies for which he had a special genius. Strange! that with my vague mind, susceptible and unobservant, hating inquiry and given up to contemplation, I should have been drawn towards a youth whose strongest passion was science. But the bond was not an intellectual one; it came from a source that can happily blend the stupid with the brilliant, the dreamy with the practical: it came from community of feeling. Charles was poor and ugly, derided by Genevese *gamins,* and not acceptable in drawing-rooms. I saw that he was isolated, as I was, though from a different cause, and, stimulated by a sympathetic resentment, I made timid advances towards him. It is enough to say that there sprang up as much comradeship between us as our different habits would allow; and in Charles's rare holidays we went up the Salève together, or took the boat to Vevay, while I listened dreamily to the monologues in which he unfolded his bold conceptions of future experiment and discovery. I mingled them confusedly in my thought with glimpses of blue water and delicate floating cloud, with the notes of birds and the distant glitter of the glacier. He knew quite well that my mind was half absent, yet he liked to talk to me in this way; for don't we talk of our hopes and our projects even to dogs and birds, when they love us? I have mentioned this one friendship because of its connexion with a strange and terrible scene which I shall have to narrate in my subsequent life.

This happier life at Geneva was put an end to by a severe illness, which is partly a blank to me, partly a time of dimly-remembered suffering, with the presence of my father by my bed from time to time. Then came the languid monotony of

convalescence, the days gradually breaking into variety and distinctness as my strength enabled me to take longer and longer
drives. On one of these more vividly remembered days, my
father said to me, as he sat beside my sofa—

"When you are quite well enough to travel, Latimer, I shall
take you home with me. The journey will amuse you and do you
good, for I shall go through the Tyrol and Austria, and you will
see many new places. Our neighbours, the Filmores, are come;
Alfred will join us at Basle, and we shall all go together to
Vienna, and back by Prague. . . ."

My father was called away before he had finished his sentence, and he left my mind resting on the word *Prague,* with a
strange sense that a new and wondrous scene was breaking upon
me: a city under the broad sunshine, that seemed to me as if it
were the summer sunshine of a long-past century arrested in its
course—unrefreshed for ages by dews of night, or the rushing
rain-cloud; scorching the dusty, weary, time-eaten grandeur of a
people doomed to live on in the stale repetition of memories,
like deposed and superannuated kings in their regal gold-
inwoven tatters. The city looked so thirsty that the broad river
seemed to me a sheet of metal; and the blackened statues, as I
passed under their blank gaze, along the unending bridge, with
their ancient garments and their saintly crowns, seemed to me
the real inhabitants and owners of this place, while the busy,
trivial men and women, hurrying to and fro, were a swarm of
ephemeral visitants infesting it for a day. It is such grim, stony
beings as these, I thought, who are the fathers of ancient faded
children, in those tanned time-fretted dwellings that crowd the
steep before me; who pay their court in the worn and crumbling
pomp of the palace which stretches its monotonous length on
the height; who worship wearily in the stifling air of the
churches, urged by no fear or hope, but compelled by their
doom to be ever old and undying, to live on in the rigidity of
habit, as they live on in perpetual midday, without the repose of
night or the new birth of morning.

A stunning clang of metal suddenly thrilled through me, and
I became conscious of the objects in my room again: one of the
fire-irons had fallen as Pierre opened the door to bring me my

draught. My heart was palpitating violently, and I begged Pierre to leave my draught beside me; I would take it presently.

As soon as I was alone again, I began to ask myself whether I had been sleeping. Was this a dream—this wonderfully distinct vision—minute in its distinctness down to a patch of rainbow light on the pavement, transmitted through a coloured lamp in the shape of a star—of a strange city, quite unfamiliar to my imagination? I had seen no picture of Prague: it lay in my mind as a mere name, with vaguely-remembered historical associations—ill-defined memories of imperial grandeur and religious wars.

Nothing of this sort had ever occurred in my dreaming experience before, for I had often been humiliated because my dreams were only saved from being utterly disjointed and commonplace by the frequent terrors of nightmare. But I could not believe that I had been asleep, for I remembered distinctly the gradual breaking-in of the vision upon me, like the new images in a dissolving view, or the growing distinctness of the landscape as the sun lifts up the veil of the morning mist. And while I was conscious of this incipient vision, I was also conscious that Pierre came to tell my father Mr. Filmore was waiting for him, and that my father hurried out of the room. No, it was not a dream; was it—the thought was full of tremulous exultation—was it the poet's nature in me, hitherto only a troubled yearning sensibility, now manifesting itself suddenly as spontaneous creation? Surely it was in this way that Homer saw the plain of Troy, that Dante saw the abodes of the departed, that Milton saw the earthward flight of the Tempter. Was it that my illness had wrought some happy change in my organization—given a firmer tension to my nerves—carried off some dull obstruction? I had often read of such effects—in works of fiction at least. Nay; in genuine biographies I had read of the subtilizing or exalting influence of some diseases on the mental powers. Did not Novalis feel his inspiration intensified under the progress of consumption?

When my mind had dwelt for some time on this blissful idea, it seemed to me that I might perhaps test it by an exertion of my will. The vision had begun when my father was speaking of our going to Prague. I did not for a moment believe it was really a representation of that city; I believed—I hoped it was a picture that my newly liberated genius had painted in fiery haste, with the colours snatched from lazy memory. Suppose I were to fix my mind on some other place—Venice, for example, which was far more familiar to my imagination than Prague: perhaps the same sort of result would follow. I concentrated my thoughts on Venice; I stimulated my imagination with poetic memories, and strove to feel myself present in Venice, as I had felt myself present in Prague. But in vain. I was only colouring the Canaletto engravings that hung in my old bedroom at home; the picture was a shifting one, my mind wandering uncertainly in search of more vivid images; I could see no accident of form or shadow without conscious labour after the necessary conditions. It was all prosaic effort, not rapt passivity, such as I had experienced half an hour before. I was discouraged; but I remembered that inspiration was fitful.

For several days I was in a state of excited expectation, watching for a recurrence of my new gift. I sent my thoughts ranging over my world of knowledge, in the hope that they would find some object which would send a reawakening vibration through my slumbering genius. But no; my world remained as dim as ever, and that flash of strange light refused to come again, though I watched for it with palpitating eagerness.

My father accompanied me every day in a drive, and a gradually lengthening walk as my powers of walking increased; and one evening he had agreed to come and fetch me at twelve the next day, that we might go together to select a musical box, and other purchases rigorously demanded of a rich Englishman visiting Geneva. He was one of the most punctual of men and bankers, and I was always nervously anxious to be quite ready for him at the appointed time. But, to my surprise, at a quarter past twelve he had not appeared. I felt all the impatience of a convalescent who has nothing particular to do, and who has just taken a tonic in the prospect of immediate exercise that would carry off the stimulus.

Unable to sit still and reserve my strength, I walked up and down the room, looking out on the current of the Rhone, just where it leaves the dark-blue lake; but thinking all the while of the possible causes that could detain my father.

Suddenly I was conscious that my father was in the room, but not alone: there were two persons with him. Strange! I had heard no footstep, I had not seen the door open; but I saw my father, and at his right hand our neighbour Mrs. Filmore, whom I remembered very well, though I had not seen her for five years. She was a commonplace middle-aged woman, in silk and cashmere; but the lady on the left of my father was not more than twenty, a tall, slim, willowy figure, with luxuriant blond hair, arranged in cunning braids and folds that looked almost too massive for the slight figure and the small-featured, thin-lipped face they crowned. But the face had not a girlish expression: the features were sharp, the pale grey eyes at once acute, restless, and sarcastic. They were fixed on me in half-smiling curiosity, and I felt a painful sensation as if a sharp wind were cutting me. The pale-green dress, and the green leaves that seemed to form a border about her pale blond hair, made me think of a Water-Nixie—for my mind was full of German lyrics, and this pale, fatal-eyed woman, with the green weeds, looked like a birth from some cold sedgy stream, the daughter of an aged river.

"Well, Latimer, you thought me long," my father said. . . .

But while the last word was in my ears, the whole group vanished, and there was nothing between me and the Chinese painted folding-screen that stood before the door. I was cold and trembling; I could only totter forward and throw myself on the sofa. This strange new power had manifested itself again. . . . But *was* it a power? Might it not rather be a disease—a sort of intermittent delirium, concentrating my energy of brain into moments of unhealthy activity, and leaving my saner hours all the more barren? I felt a dizzy sense of unreality in what my eye rested on; I grasped the bell convulsively, like one trying to free himself from nightmare, and rang it twice. Pierre came with a look of alarm in his face.

"Monsieur ne se trouve pas bien?" he said anxiously.

"I'm tired of waiting, Pierre," I said, as distinctly and emphatically as I could, like a man determined to be sober in spite of wine; "I'm afraid something has happened to my father—he's usually so punctual. Run to the Hôtel des Bergues and see if he is there."

Pierre left the room at once, with a soothing "Bien, Monsieur;" and I felt the better for this scene of simple, waking prose. Seeking to calm myself still further, I went into my bedroom, adjoining the *salon,* and opened a case of eau-de-Cologne; took out a bottle; went through the process of taking out the cork very neatly, and then rubbed the reviving spirit over my hands and forehead, and under my nostrils, drawing a new delight from the scent because I had procured it by slow details of labour, and by no strange sudden madness. Already I had begun to taste something of the horror that belongs to the lot of a human being whose nature is not adjusted to simple human conditions.

Still enjoying the scent, I returned to the *salon,* but it was not unoccupied, as it had been before I left it. In front of the Chinese folding-screen there was my father, with Mrs. Filmore on his right hand, and on his left—the slim, blond-haired girl, with the keen face and the keen eyes fixed on me in half-smiling curiosity.

"Well, Latimer, you thought me long," my father said. . . .

I heard no more, felt no more, till I became conscious that I was lying with my head low on the sofa, Pierre, and my father by my side. As soon as I was thoroughly revived, my father left the room, and presently returned, saying—

"I've been to tell the ladies how you are, Latimer. They were waiting in the next room. We shall put off our shopping expedition to-day."

Presently he said, "That young lady is Bertha Grant, Mrs. Filmore's orphan niece. Filmore has adopted her, and she lives with them, so you will have her for a neighbour when we go home—perhaps for a near relation; for there is a tenderness between her and Alfred, I suspect, and I should be gratified by the match, since Filmore means to provide for her in every way as if she were his daughter. It had not occurred to me that you knew nothing about her living with the Filmores."

He made no further allusion to the fact of my having fainted at the moment of seeing her, and I would not for the world have told him the reason: I shrank from the idea of disclosing to anyone what might be regarded as a pitiable peculiarity, most of all from betraying it to my father, who would have suspected my sanity ever after.

I do not mean to dwell with particularity on the details of my experience. I have described these two cases at length, because they had definite, clearly traceable results in my afterlot.

Shortly after this last occurrence—I think the very next day—I began to be aware of a phase in my abnormal sensibility, to which, from the languid and slight nature of my intercourse with others since my illness, I had not been alive before. This was the obtrusion on my mind of the mental process going forward in first one person, and then another, with whom I happened to be in contact: the vagrant, frivolous ideas and emotions of some uninteresting acquaintance—Mrs. Filmore, for example—would force themselves on my consciousness like an importunate, ill-played musical instrument, or the loud activity of an imprisoned insect. But this unpleasant sensibility was fitful, and left me moments of rest, when the souls of my companions were once more shut out from me, and I felt a relief such as silence brings to wearied nerves. I might have believed this importunate insight to be merely a diseased activity of the imagination, but that my prevision of incalculable words and actions proved it to have a fixed relation to the mental process in other minds. But this superadded consciousness, wearying and annoying enough when it urged on me the trivial experience of indifferent people, became an intense pain and grief when it seemed to be opening to me the souls of those who were in a close relation to me—when the rational talk, the graceful attentions, the wittily-turned phrases, and the kindly deeds, which used to make the web of their characters, were seen as if thrust asunder by a microscopic vision, that showed all the intermediate frivolities, all the suppressed egoism, all the struggling chaos of puerilities, meanness, vague capricious memories, and indolent make-shift thoughts, from which human words and deeds emerge like leaflets covering a fermenting heap.

At Basle we were joined by my brother Alfred, now a handsome, self-confident man of six-and-twenty—a thorough contrast to my fragile, nervous, ineffectual self. I believe I was held to have a sort of half-womanish, half-ghostly beauty; for the portrait-painters, who are thick as weeds at Geneva, had often asked me to sit to them, and I had been the model of a dying minstrel in a fancy picture. But I thoroughly disliked my own physique and nothing but the belief that it was a condition of poetic genius would have reconciled me to it. That brief hope was quite fled, and I saw in my face now nothing but the stamp of a morbid organization, framed for passive suffering—too feeble for the sublime resistance of poetic production. Alfred, from whom I had been almost constantly separated, and who, in his present stage of character and appearance, came before me as a perfect stranger, was bent on being extremely friendly and brother-like to me. He had the superficial kindness of a good-humoured, self-satisfied nature, that fears no rivalry, and has encountered no contrarieties. I am not sure that my disposition was good enough for me to have been quite free from envy towards him, even if our desires had not clashed, and if I had been in the healthy human condition which admits of generous confidence and charitable construction. There must always have been an antipathy between our natures. As it was, he became in a few weeks an object of intense hatred to me; and when he entered the room, still more when he spoke, it was as if a sensation of grating metal had set my teeth on edge. My diseased consciousness was more intensely and continually occupied with his thoughts and emotions, than with those of any other person who came in my way. I was perpetually exasperated with the petty promptings of his conceit and his love of patronage, with his self-complacent belief in Bertha Grant's passion for him, with his half-pitying contempt for me—seen not in the ordinary indications of intonation and phrase and slight action, which an acute and suspicious mind is on the watch for, but in all their naked skinless complication.

For we were rivals, and our desires clashed, though he was not aware of it. I have said nothing yet of the effect Bertha Grant produced in me on a nearer acquaintance. That effect was chiefly determined by the fact that she made the only exception, among all the human beings about me, to my unhappy gift of insight. About Bertha I was always in a state of uncertainty: I could watch the expression of her face, and speculate on its meaning; I could ask for her opinion with the real interest of ignorance; I could listen for her words and watch for her smile with hope and fear: she had for me the fascination of an unravelled destiny. I say it was this fact that chiefly determined the strong effect she produced on me: for, in the abstract, no womanly character could seem to have less affinity for that of a shrinking, romantic, passionate youth than Bertha's. She was keen, sarcastic, unimaginative, prematurely cynical, remaining critical and unmoved in the most impressive scenes, inclined to dissect all my favourite poems, and especially contemptous towards the German lyrics which were my pet literature at that time. To this moment I am unable to define my feeling towards her: it was not ordinary boyish admiration, for she was the very opposite, even to the colour of her hair, of the ideal woman who still remained to me the type of loveliness; and she was without that enthusiasm for the great and good, which, even at the moment of her strongest dominion over me, I should have declared to be the highest element of character. But there is no tyranny more complete than that which a self-centred negative nature exercises over a morbidly sensitive nature perpetually craving sympathy and support. The most independent people feel the effect of a man's silence in heightening their value for his opinion—feel an additional triumph in conquering the reverence of a critic habitually captious and satirical: no wonder, then, that an enthusiastic self-distrusting youth should watch and wait before the closed secret of a sarcastic woman's face, as if it were the shrine of the doubtfully benignant deity who ruled his destiny. For a young enthusiast is unable to imagine the total negation in another mind of the emotions which are stirring his own: they may be feeble, latent, inactive, he thinks, but they are there—they may be called forth; sometimes, in moments of happy hallucination, he believes they may be there in all the greater strength because he sees no outward sign of them. And this effect, as I have intimated, was heightened to its utmost intensity in me, because Bertha was the only being who remained for me in the mysterious seclusion of soul that renders such youthful delusion possible. Doubtless there was another sort of fascination at work—that subtle physical attraction which delights in cheating our psychological predictions, and in compelling the men who paint sylphs, to fall in love with some *bonne et brave femme*, heavy-heeled and freckled.

Bertha's behaviour towards me was such as to encourage all my illusions, to heighten my boyish passion, and make me more and more dependent on her smiles. Looking back with my present wretched knowledge, I conclude that her vanity and love of power were intensely gratified by the belief that I had fainted on first seeing her purely from the strong impression her person had produced on me. The most prosaic woman likes to believe herself the object of a violent, a poetic passion; and without a grain of romance in her, Bertha had that spirit of intrigue which gave piquancy to the idea that the brother of the man she meant to marry was dying with love and jealousy for her sake. That she meant to marry my brother, was what at that time I did not believe; for though he was assiduous in his attentions to her, and I knew well enough that both he and my father had made up their minds to this result, there was not yet an understood engagement—there had been no explicit declaration; and Bertha habitually, while she flirted with my brother, and accepted his homage in a way that implied to him a thorough recognition of its intention, made me believe, by the subtlest looks and phrases—feminine nothings which could never be quoted against her—that he was really the object of her secret ridicule; that she thought him, as I did, a coxcomb, whom she would have pleasure in disappointing. Me she openly petted in my brother's presence, as if I were too young and sickly ever to be thought of as a lover; and that was the view he took of me. But I believe she must inwardly have delighted in the tremors into which she threw me by the coaxing way in which she patted my curls, while she laughed at my quotations. Such caresses were always given in the presence of our friends; for when we were alone together, she affected a much greater distance towards me, and now and then took the opportunity, by words or slight actions, to stimulate my foolish timid hope that she really preferred me. And why should she not follow her inclination? I was not in so advantageous a position as my brother, but I had fortune, I was not a year younger than she was, and she was an heiress, who would soon be of age to decide for herself.

The fluctuations of hope and fear, confined to this one channel, made each day in her presence a delicious torment. There was one deliberate act of hers which especially helped to intoxicate me. When we were at Vienna her twentieth birthday occurred, and as she was very fond of ornaments, we all took the opportunity of the splendid jewellers' shops in that Teutonic Paris to purchase her a birthday present of jewellery. Mine, naturally, was the least expensive; it was an opal ring—the opal was my favourite stone, because it seems to blush and turn pale as if it had a soul. I told Bertha so when I gave it her, and said that it was an emblem of the poetic nature, changing with the changing light of heaven and of woman's eyes. In the evening she appeared elegantly dressed, and wearing conspicuously all the birthday presents except mine. I looked eagerly at her fingers, but saw no opal. I had no opportunity of noticing this to her during the evening; but the next day, when I found her seated near the window alone, after breakfast, I said, "You scorn to wear my poor opal. I should have remembered that you despised poetic natures, and should have given you coral, or turquoise, or some other opaque unresponsive stone." "Do I despise it?" she answered, taking hold of a delicate gold chain which she always wore round her neck and drawing out the end from her bosom with my ring hanging to it; "it hurts me a little, I can tell you," she said, with her usual dubious smile, "to wear it in that secret place; and since your poetical nature is so stupid as to prefer a more public position, I shall not endure the pain any longer."

She took off the ring from the chain and put it on her finger, smiling still, while the blood rushed to my cheeks, and I could not trust myself to say a word of entreaty that she would keep the ring where it was before.

I was completely fooled by this, and for two days shut myself up in my own room whenever Bertha was absent, that I might intoxicate myself afresh with the thought of this scene and all it implied.

I should mention that during these two months—which seemed a long life to me from the novelty and intensity of the pleasures and pains I underwent—my diseased participation in other people's consciousness continued to torment me; now it was my father, and now my brother, now Mrs. Filmore or her husband, and now our German courier, whose stream of thought rushed upon me like a ringing in the ears not to be got rid of, though it allowed my own impulses and ideas to continue their uninterrupted course. It was like a preternaturally heightened sense of hearing, making audible to one a roar of sound where others find perfect stillness. The weariness and disgust of this involuntary intrusion into other souls was counteracted only by my ignorance of Bertha, and my growing passion for her; a passion enormously stimulated, if not produced, by that ignorance. She was my oasis of mystery in the dreary desert of knowledge. I had never allowed my diseased condition to betray itself, or to drive me into any unusual speech or action, except once, when, in a moment of peculiar bitterness against my brother, I had forestalled some words which I knew he was going to utter—a clever observation, which he had prepared beforehand. He had occasionally a slightly affected hesitation in his speech, and when he paused an instant after the second word, my impatience and jealousy impelled me to continue the speech for him, as if it were something we had both learned by rote. He coloured and looked astonished, as well as annoyed; and the words had no sooner escaped my lips than I felt a shock of alarm lest such an anticipation of words—very far from being words of course, easy to divine—should have betrayed me as an exceptional being, a sort of quiet energumen, whom every one, Bertha above all, would shudder at and avoid. But I magnified, as usual, the impression any word or deed of mine could produce on others; for no one gave any sign of having noticed my interruption as more than a rudeness, to be forgiven me on the score of my feeble nervous condition.

While this superadded consciousness of the actual was almost constant with me, I had never had a recurrence of that distinct prevision which I have described in relation to my first interview with Bertha; and I was waiting with eager curiosity to know whether or not my vision of Prague would prove to have been an instance of the same kind. A few days after the incident of the opal ring, we were paying one of our frequent visits to the Lichtenberg Palace. I could never look at many pictures in succession; for pictures, when they are at all powerful, affect me so strongly that one or two exhaust all my capability of contemplation. This morning I had been looking at Giorgione's picture of

the cruel-eyed woman, said to be a likeness of Lucrezia Borgia.
I had stood long alone before it, fascinated by the terrible reality of that cunning, relentless face, till I felt a strange poisoned
sensation, as if I had long been inhaling a fatal odour, and was
just beginning to be conscious of its effects. Perhaps even then
I should not have moved away, if the rest of the party had not
returned to this room, and announced that they were going to
the Belvedere Gallery to settle a bet which had arisen between
my brother and Mr. Filmore about a portrait. I followed them
dreamily, and was hardly alive to what occurred till they had all
gone up to the gallery, leaving me below; for I refused to come
within sight of another picture that day. I made my way to the
Grand Terrace, since it was agreed that we should saunter in the
gardens when the dispute had been decided. I had been sitting
here a short space, vaguely conscious of trim gardens, with a city
and green hills in the distance, when, wishing to avoid the proximity of the sentinel, I rose and walked down the broad stone
steps, intending to seat myself farther on in the gardens. Just as
I reached the gravel-walk, I felt an arm slipped within mine, and
a light hand gently pressing my wrist. In the same instant a
strange intoxicating numbness passed over me, like the contin-
uance or climax of the sensation I was still feeling from the gaze
of Lucrezia Borgia. The gardens, the summer sky, the consciousness of Bertha's arm being within mine, all vanished, and
I seemed to be suddenly in darkness, out of which there gradually broke a dim firelight, and I felt myself sitting in my father's
leather chair in the library at home. I knew the fireplace—the
dogs for the wood-fire—the black marble chimneypiece with
the white marble medallion of the dying Cleopatra in the centre. Intense and hopeless misery was pressing on my soul; the
light became stronger, for Bertha was entering with a candle in
her hand—Bertha, my wife—with cruel eyes, with green jewels
and green leaves on her white ball-dress; every hateful thought
within her present to me. . . . "Madman, idiot! why don't you kill
yourself, then?" It was a moment of hell. I saw into her pitiless
soul—saw its barren worldliness, its scorching hate—and felt it
clothe me round like an air I was obliged to breathe. She came
with her candle and stood over me with a bitter smile of con-

tempt; I saw the great emerald brooch on her bosom, a studded serpent with diamond eyes. I shuddered—I despised this woman with the barren soul and mean thoughts; but I felt help-less before her, as if she clutched my bleeding heart, and would clutch it till the last drop of life-blood ebbed away. She was my wife, and we hated each other. Gradually the hearth, the dim library, the candle-light disappeared—seemed to melt away into a background of light, the green serpent with the diamond eyes remaining a dark image on the retina. Then I had a sense of my eyelids quivering, and the living daylight broke in upon me; I saw gardens, and heard voices; I was seated on the steps of the Belvedere Terrace, and my friends were round me.

The tumult of mind into which I was thrown by this hideous vision made me ill for several days, and prolonged our stay at Vienna. I shuddered with horror as the scene recurred to me; and it recurred constantly, with all its minutiæ, as if they had been burnt into my memory; and yet, such is the madness of the human heart under the influence of its immediate desires, I felt a wild hell-braving joy that Bertha was to be mine; for the ful-filment of my former prevision concerning her first appearance before me, left me little hope that this last hideous glimpse of the future was the mere diseased play of my own mind, and had no relation to external realities. One thing alone I looked towards as a possible means of casting doubt on my terrible con-viction—the discovery that my vision of Prague had been false—and Prague was the next city on our route.

Meanwhile, I was no sooner in Bertha's society again than I was as completely under her sway as before. What if I saw into the heart of Bertha, the matured woman—Bertha, my wife? Bertha, the *girl*, was a fascinating secret to me still: I trembled under her touch; I felt the witchery of her presence; I yearned to be assured of her love. The fear of poison is feeble against the sense of thirst. Nay, I was just as jealous of my brother as before—just as much irritated by his small patronizing ways; for my pride, my diseased sensibility, were there as they had always been, and winced as inevitably under every offence as my eye winced from an intruding mote. The future, even when brought within the compass of feeling by a vision that made me shudder, had still no more than the force of an idea, compared with the force of present emotion—of my love for Bertha, of my dislike and jealousy towards my brother.

It is an old story, that men sell themselves to the tempter, and sign a bond with their blood, because it is only to take effect at a distant day; then rush on to snatch the cup their souls thirst after with an impulse not the less savage because there is a dark shadow beside them for evermore. There is no short cut, no patent tram-road, to wisdom: after all the centuries of invention, the soul's path lies through the thorny wilderness which must be still trodden in solitude, with bleeding feet, with sobs for help, as it was trodden by them of old time.

My mind speculated eagerly on the means by which I should become my brother's successful rival, for I was still too timid, in my ignorance of Bertha's actual feeling, to venture on any step that would urge from her an avowal of it. I thought I should gain confidence even for this, if my vision of Prague proved to have been veracious; and yet, the horror of that certitude! Behind the slim girl Bertha, whose words and looks I watched for, whose touch was bliss, there stood continually that Bertha with the fuller form, the harder eyes, the more rigid mouth—with the barren, selfish soul laid bare; no longer a fascinating secret, but a measured fact, urging itself perpetually on my unwilling sight. Are you unable to give me your sympathy—you who read this? Are you unable to imagine this double consciousness at work within me, flowing on like two parallel streams which never mingle their waters and blend into a common hue? Yet you must have known something of the presentiments that spring from an insight at war with passion; and my visions were only like presentiments intensified to horror. You have known the powerlessness of ideas before the might of impulse; and my visions, when once they had passed into memory, were mere ideas—pale shadows that beckoned in vain, while my hand was grasped by the living and the loved.

In after-days I thought with bitter regret that if I had foreseen something more or something different—if instead of that hideous vision which poisoned the passion it could not destroy, or if even along with it I could have had a foreshadowing of that moment when I looked on my brother's face for the last time, some softening influence would have been shed over my feeling towards him: pride and hatred would surely have been subdued into pity, and the record of those hidden sins would have been shortened. But this is one of the vain thoughts with which we men flatter ourselves. We try to believe that the egoism within us would have easily been melted, and that it was only the narrowness of our knowledge which hemmed in our generosity, our awe, our human piety, and hindered them from submerging our hard indifference to the sensations and emotions of our fellows. Our tenderness and self-renunciation seem strong when our egoism has had its day—when, after our mean striving for a triumph that is to be another's loss, the triumph comes suddenly, and we shudder at it, because it is held out by the chill hand of death.

Our arrival in Prague happened at night, and I was glad of this, for it seemed like a deferring of a terribly decisive moment, to be in the city for hours without seeing it. As we were not to remain long in Prague, but to go on speedily to Dresden, it was proposed that we should drive out the next morning and take a general view of the place, as well as visit some of its specially interesting spots, before the heat became oppressive—for we were in August, and the season was hot and dry. But it happened that the ladies were rather late at their morning toilet, and to my father's politely-repressed but perceptible annoyance, we were not in the carriage till the morning was far advanced. I thought with a sense of relief, as we entered the Jews' quarter, where we were to visit the old synagogue, that we should be kept in this flat, shut-up part of the city, until we should all be too tired and too warm to go farther, and so we should return without seeing more than the streets through which we had already passed. That would give me another day's suspense—suspense, the only form in which a fearful spirit knows the solace of hope. But, as I stood under the blackened, groined arches of that old synagogue, made dimly visible by the seven thin candles in the sacred lamp, while our Jewish cicerone reached down the Book of the Law, and read to us in its ancient tongue—I felt a shuddering impression that this strange building, with its shrunken lights, this surviving withered remnant of medieval Judaism, was of a piece with my vision. Those darkened dusty Christian saints, with their loftier arches and their larger candles, needed the consolatory scorn with which they might point to a more shrivelled death-in-life than their own.

As I expected, when we left the Jews' quarter the elders of our party wished to return to the hotel. But now, instead of rejoicing in this, as I had done beforehand, I felt a sudden over-powering impulse to go on at once to the bridge, and put an end to the suspense I had been wishing to protract. I declared, with unusual decision, that I would get out of the carriage and walk on alone; they might return without me. My father, thinking this merely a sample of my usual "poetic nonsense," objected that I should only do myself harm by walking in the heat; but when I persisted, he said angrily that I might follow my own absurd devices, but that Schmidt (our courier) must go with me. I assented to this, and set off with Schmidt towards the bridge. I had no sooner passed from under the archway of the grand old gate leading an to the bridge, than a trembling seized me, and I turned cold under the mid-day sun; yet I went on; I was in search of something—a small detail which I remembered with special intensity as part of my vision. There it was—the patch of rainbow light on the pavement transmitted through a lamp in the shape of a star.

Chapter II

Before the autumn was at an end, and while the brown leaves still stood thick on the beeches in our park, my brother and Bertha were engaged to each other, and it was understood that their marriage was to take place early in the next spring. In spite of the certainty I had felt from that moment on the bridge at Prague, that Bertha would one day be my wife, my constitutional timidity and distrust had continued to benumb me, and the words in which I had sometimes premeditated a confession of my love, had died away unuttered. The same conflict had gone on within me as before—the longing for an assurance of love from Bertha's lips, the dread lest a word of contempt and denial should fall upon me like a corrosive acid. What was the conviction of a distant necessity to me? I trembled under a present glance, I hungered after a present joy, I was clogged and chilled by a present fear. And so the days passed on: I witnessed Bertha's engagement and heard her marriage discussed as if I were under a conscious nightmare—knowing it was a dream that would vanish, but feeling stifled under the grasp of hard-clutching fingers.

When I was not in Bertha's presence—and I was with her very often, for she continued to treat me with a playful patronage that wakened no jealousy in my brother—I spent my time chiefly in wandering, in strolling, or taking long rides while the daylight lasted, and then shutting myself up with my unread books; for books had lost the power of chaining my attention. My self-consciousness was heightened to that pitch of intensity in which our own emotions take the form of a drama which urges itself imperatively on our contemplation, and we begin to weep, less under the sense of our suffering than at the thought of it. I felt a sort of pitying anguish over the pathos of my own lot: the lot of a being finely organized for pain, but with hardly any fibres that responded to pleasure—to whom the idea of future evil robbed the present of its joy, and for whom the idea of future good did not still the uneasiness of a present yearning or a present dread. I went dumbly through that stage of the poet's suffering, in which he feels the delicious pang of utterance, and makes an image of his sorrows.

I was left entirely without remonstrance concerning this dreamy wayward life: I knew my father's thought about me: "That lad will never be good for anything in life: he may waste his years in an insignificant way on the income that falls to him: I shall not trouble myself about a career for him."

One mild morning in the beginning of November, it happened that I was standing outside the portico patting lazy old Cæsar, a Newfoundland almost blind with age, the only dog that ever took any notice of me—for the very dogs shunned me, and fawned on the happier people about me—when the groom brought up my brother's horse which was to carry him to the hunt, and my brother himself appeared at the door, florid, broad-chested, and self-complacent, feeling what a good-natured fellow he was not to behave insolently to us all on the strength of his great advantages.

"Latimer, old boy," he said to me in a tone of compassionate cordiality, "what a pity it is you don't have a run with the hounds now and then! The finest thing in the world for low spirits!"

"Low spirits!" I thought bitterly, as he rode away; "that is the sort of phrase with which coarse, narrow natures like yours think to describe experience of which you can know no more than your horse knows. It is to such as you that the good of this world falls: ready dulness, healthy selfishness, good-tempered conceit— these are the keys to happiness."

The quick thought came, that my selfishness was even stronger than his—it was only a suffering selfishness instead of an enjoying one. But then, again, my exasperating insight into Alfred's self-complacent soul, his freedom from all the doubts and fears, the unsatisfied yearnings, the exquisite tortures of sensitiveness, that had made the web of my life, seemed to absolve me from all bonds towards him. This man needed no pity, no love; those fine influences would have been as little felt by him as the delicate white mist is felt by the rock it caresses. There was no evil in store for *him:* if he was not to marry Bertha, it would be because he had found a lot pleasanter to himself.

Mr. Filmore's house lay not more than half a mile beyond our own gates, and whenever I knew my brother was gone in another direction, I went there for the chance of finding Bertha at home. Later on in the day I walked thither. By a rare accident she was alone, and we walked out in the grounds together, for she seldom went on foot beyond the trimly-swept gravel-walks. I remember what a beautiful sylph she looked to me as the low November sun shone on her blond hair, and she tripped along teasing me with her usual light banter, to which I listened half fondly, half moodily; it was all the sign Bertha's mysterious inner self ever made to me. To-day perhaps, the moodiness predomi-nated, for I had not yet shaken off the access of jealous hate which my brother had raised in me by his parting patronage. Suddenly I interrupted and startled her by saying, almost fiercely, "Bertha, how can you love Alfred?"

She looked at me with surprise for a moment, but soon her light smile came again, and she answered sarcastically, "Why do you suppose I love him?"

"How can you ask that, Bertha?"

"What! your wisdom thinks I must love the man I'm going to marry? The most unpleasant thing in the world. I should quarrel with him; I should be jealous of him; our *ménage* would be conducted in a very ill-bred manner. A little quiet contempt contributes greatly to the elegance of life."

"Bertha, that is not your real feeling. Why do you delight in trying to deceive me by inventing such cynical speeches?"

"I need never take the trouble of invention in order to deceive you, my small Tasso"—(that was the mocking name she usually gave me). "The easiest way to deceive a poet is to tell him the truth."

She was testing the validity of her epigram in a daring way, and for a moment the shadow of my vision—the Bertha whose soul was no secret to me—passed between me and the radiant girl, the playful sylph whose feelings were a fascinating mystery. I suppose I must have shuddered, or betrayed in some other way my momentary chill of horror.

"Tasso!" she said, seizing my wrist, and peeping round into my face, "are you really beginning to discern what a heartless girl I am? Why, you are not half the poet I thought you were; you are actually capable of believing the truth about me."

The shadow passed from between us, and was no longer the object nearest to me. The girl whose light fingers grasped me, whose elfish charming face looked into mine—who, I thought, was betraying an interest in my feelings that she would not have directly avowed—this warm breathing presence again possessed my senses and imagination like a returning siren melody which had been overpowered for an instant by the roar of threatening waves. It was a moment as delicious to me as the waking up to a consciousness of youth after a dream of middle age. I forgot everything but my passion, and said with swimming eyes—

"Bertha, shall you love me when we are first married? I wouldn't mind if you really loved me only for a little while."

Her look of astonishment, as she loosed my hand and started away from me, recalled me to a sense of my strange, my criminal indiscretion.

"Forgive me," I said, hurriedly, as soon as I could speak again; "I did not know what I was saying."

"Ah, Tasso's mad fit has come on, I see," she answered quietly, for she had recovered herself sooner than I had. "Let him go home and keep his head cool. I must go in, for the sun is setting."

I left her—full of indignation against myself. I had let slip words which, if she reflected on them, might rouse in her a suspicion of my abnormal mental condition—a suspicion which of all things I dreaded. And besides that, I was ashamed of the apparent baseness I had committed in uttering them to my brother's betrothed wife. I wandered home slowly, entering our park through a private gate instead of by the lodges. As I approached the house, I saw a man dashing off at full speed from the stable-yard across the park. Had any accident happened at home? No; perhaps it was only one of my father's peremptory business errands that required this headlong haste.

Nevertheless I quickened my pace without any distinct motive, and was soon at the house. I will not dwell on the scene I found there. My brother was dead—had been pitched from his horse, and killed on the spot by a concussion of the brain.

I went up to the room where he lay, and where my father was seated beside him with a look of rigid despair. I had shunned my father more than anyone since our return home, for the radical antipathy between our natures made my insight into his inner self a constant affliction to me. But now, as I went up to him, and stood beside him in sad silence, I felt the presence of a new element that blended us as we had never been blent before. My father had been one of the most successful men in the money-getting world: he had had no sentimental sufferings, no illness. The heaviest trouble that had befallen him was the death of his first wife. But he married my mother soon after; and I remember he seemed exactly the same, to my keen childish observation, the week after her death as before. But now, at last, a sorrow had come—the sorrow of old age, which suffers the more from the crushing of its pride and its hopes, in proportion as the pride and hope are narrow and prosaic. His son was to have been married soon—would probably have stood for the borough at the next election. That son's existence was the best motive that could be alleged for making new purchases of land every year to round off the estate. It is a dreary thing onto live on doing the same things year after year, without knowing why we do them. Perhaps the tragedy of disappointed youth and passion is less piteous than the tragedy of disappointed age and worldliness.

As I saw into the desolation of my father's heart, I felt a movement of deep pity towards him, which was the beginning of a new affection—an affection that grew and strengthened in spite of the strange bitterness with which he regarded me in the first month or two after my brother's death. If it had not been for the softening influence of my compassion for him—the first deep compassion I had ever felt—I should have been stung by the perception that my father transferred the inheritance of an eldest son to me with a mortified sense that fate had compelled him to the unwelcome course of caring for me as an important being. It was only in spite of himself that he began to think of me with anxious regard. There is hardly any neglected child for whom death has made vacant a more favoured place, who will not understand what I mean.

Gradually, however, my new deference to his wishes, the effect of that patience which was born of my pity for him, won upon his affection, and he began to please himself with the endeavour to make me fill any brother's place as fully as my feebler personality would admit. I saw that the prospect which by and by presented itself of my becoming Bertha's husband was welcome to him, and he even contemplated in my case what he had not intended in my brother's—that his son and daughter-in-law should make one household with him. My softened feelings towards my father made this the happiest time I had known since childhood—these last months in which I retained the delicious illusion of loving Bertha, of longing and doubting and hoping that she might love me. She behaved with a certain new consciousness and distance towards me after my brother's death; and I too was under a double constraint—that of delicacy towards my brother's memory, and of anxiety as to the impression my abrupt words had left on her mind. But the additional screen this mutual reserve erected between us only brought me more completely under her power: no matter how empty the adytum, so that the veil be thick enough. So absolute is our soul's need of something hidden and uncertain for the maintenance of that doubt and hope and effort which are the breath of its life, that if the whole future were laid bare to us beyond to-day, the interest of all mankind would be bent on the hours that lie between; we should pant after the uncertainties of our one morning and our one afternoon; we should rush fiercely to the Exchange for our last possibility of speculation, of success, of disappointment: we should have a glut of political prophets foretelling a crisis or a no-crisis within the only twenty-four hours left open to prophecy. Conceive the condition of the human mind if all propositions whatsoever were self-evident except one, which was to become self-evident at the close of a summer's day, but in the meantime might be the subject of question, of hypothesis, of debate. Art and philosophy, literature and science, would fasten like bees on that one proposition which had the honey of probability in it, and be the more eager because their enjoyment would end with sunset. Our impulses, our spiritual activities, no more adjust themselves to the idea of their future nullity, than the beating of our heart, or the irritability of our muscles.

Bertha, the slim, fair-haired girl, whose present thoughts and emotions were an enigma to me amidst the fatiguing obviousness of the other minds around me, was as absorbing to me as a single unknown to-day—as a single hypothetic proposition to remain problematic till sunset; and all the cramped, hemmed-in belief and disbelief, trust and distrust, of my nature, welled out in this one narrow channel.

And she made me believe that she loved me. Without ever quitting her tone of *badinage* and playful superiority, she intoxicated me with the sense that I was necessary to her, that she was never at ease unless I was near her, submitting to her playful tyranny. It costs a woman so little effort to beset us in this way! A half-repressed word, a moment's unexpected silence, even an easy fit of petulance on our account, will serve us as *hashish* for a long while. Out of the subtlest web of scarcely perceptible signs, she set me weaving the fancy that she had always unconsciously loved me better than Alfred, but that, with the ignorant fluttered sensibility of a young girl, she had been imposed on by the charm that lay for her in the distinction of being admired and chosen by a man who made so brilliant a figure in the world as my brother. She satirized herself in a very graceful way for her vanity and ambition. What was it to me that I had the light of my wretched provision on the fact that now it was I who possessed at least all but the personal part of my brother's advantages? Our sweet illusions are half of them conscious illusions, like effects of colour that we know to be made up of tinsel, broken glass, and rags.

We were married eighteen months after Alfred's death, one cold, clear morning in April, when there came hail and sunshine both together; and Bertha, in her white silk and pale-green leaves, and the pale hues of her hair and face, looked like the spirit of the morning. My father was happier than he had thought of being again: my marriage, he felt sure, would complete the desirable modification of my character, and make me practical and worldly enough to take my place in society among sane men. For he delighted in Bertha's tact and acuteness, and felt sure she would be mistress of me, and make me what she chose: I was only twenty-one, and madly in love with her. Poor father! He kept that hope a little while after our first year of marriage, and it was not quite extinct when paralysis came and saved him from utter disappointment.

I shall hurry through the rest of my story, not dwelling so much as I have hitherto done on my inward experience. When people are well known to each other, they talk rather of what befalls them externally, leaving their feelings and sentiments to be inferred.

We lived in a round of visits for some time after our return home, giving splendid dinner-parties, and making a sensation in our neighbourhood by the new lustre of our equipage, for my father had reserved this display of his increased wealth for the period of his son's marriage; and we gave our acquaintances liberal opportunity for remarking that it was a pity I made so poor a figure as an heir and a bridegroom. The nervous fatigue of this existence, the insincerities and platitudes which I had to live

through twice over—through my inner and outward sense—
would have been maddening to me, if I had not had that sort of
intoxicated callousness which came from the delights of a first
passion. A bride and bridegroom, surrounded by all the appliances of wealth, hurried through the day by the whirl of society,
filling their solitary moments with hastily-snatched caresses, are
prepared for their future life together as the novice is prepared
for the cloister—by experiencing its utmost contrast.

Through all these crowded excited months, Bertha's inward
self remained shrouded from me, and I still read her thoughts
only through the language of her lips and demeanour: I had still
the human interest of wondering whether what I did and said
pleased her, of longing to hear a word of affection, of giving a
delicious exaggeration of meaning to her smile. But I was conscious of a growing difference in her manner towards me; sometimes strong enough to be called haughty coldness, cutting and
chilling me as the hail had done that came across the sunshine
on our marriage morning; sometimes only perceptible in the
dexterous avoidance of a *tête-à-tête* walk or dinner to which I
had been looking forward. I had been deeply pained by this—
had even felt a sort of crushing of the heart, from the sense that
my brief day of happiness was near its setting; but still I
remained dependent on Bertha, eager for the last rays of a bliss
that would soon be gone for ever, hoping and watching for some
after-glow more beautiful from the impending night.

I remember—how should I not remember?—the time when
that dependence and hope utterly left me, when the sadness I
had felt in Bertha's growing estrangement became a joy that I
looked back upon with longing as a man might look back on the
last pains in a paralysed limb. It was just after the close of my
father's last illness, which had necessarily withdrawn us from
society and thrown us more on each other. It was the evening of
father's death. On that evening the veil which had shrouded
Bertha's soul from me—had made me find in her alone among
my fellow-beings the blessed possibility of mystery, and doubt,
and expectation—was first withdrawn. Perhaps it was the first
day since the beginning of my passion for her, in which that passion was completely neutralized by the presence of an absorb-

ing feeling of another kind. I had been watching by my father's deathbed: I had been witnessing the last fitful yearning glance his soul had cast back on the spent inheritance of life—the last faint consciousness of love he had gathered from the pressure of my hand. What are all our personal loves when we have been sharing in that supreme agony? In the first moments when we come away from the presence of death, every other relation to the living is merged, to our feeling, in the great relation of a common nature and a common destiny.

In that state of mind I joined Bertha in her private sitting-room. She was seated in a leaning posture on a settee, with her back towards the door; the great rich coils of her pale blond hair surmounting her small neck, visible above the back of the settee. I remember, as I closed the door behind me, a cold tremulousness seizing me, and a vague sense of being hated and lonely—vague and strong, like a presentiment. I know how I looked at that moment, for I saw myself in Bertha's thought as she lifted her cutting grey eyes, and looked at me: a miserable ghost-seer, surrounded by phantoms in the noonday, trembling under a breeze when the leaves were still, without appetite for the common objects of human desires, but pining after the moon-beams. We were front to front with each other, and judged each other. The terrible moment of complete illumination had come to me, and I saw that the darkness had hidden no landscape from me, but only a blank prosaic wall: from that evening forth, through the sickening years which followed, I saw all round the narrow room of this woman's soul—saw petty artifice and mere negation where I had delighted to believe in coy sensibilities and in wit at war with latent feeling—saw the light floating vanities of the girl defining themselves into the systematic coquetry, the scheming selfishness, of the woman—saw repulsion and antipathy harden into cruel hatred, giving pain only for the sake of wreaking itself.

For Bertha too, after her kind, felt the bitterness of disillusion. She had believed that my wild poet's passion for her would make me her slave; and that, being her slave, I should execute her will in all things. With the essential shallowness of a negative, unimaginative nature, she was unable to conceive the fact that sensibilities were anything else than weaknesses. She had thought my weaknesses would put me in her power, and she found them unmanageable forces. Our positions were reversed. Before marriage she had completely mastered my imagination, for she was a secret to me; and I created the unknown thought before which I trembled as if it were hers. But now that her soul was laid open to me, now that I was compelled to share the privacy of her motives, to follow all the petty devices that preceded her words and acts, she found herself powerless with me, except to produce in me the chill shudder of repulsion—powerless, because I could be acted on by no lever within her reach. I was dead to worldly ambitions, to social vanities, to all the incentives within the compass of her narrow imagination, and I lived under influences utterly invisible to her.

She was really pitiable to have such a husband, and so all the world thought. A graceful, brilliant woman, like Bertha, who smiled on morning callers, made a figure in ball-rooms, and was capable of that light repartee which, from such a woman, is accepted as wit, was secure of carrying off all sympathy from a husband who was sickly, abstracted, and, as some suspected, crack-brained. Even the servants in our house gave her the balance of their regard and pity. For there were no audible quarrels between us; our alienation, our repulsion from each other, lay within the silence of our own hearts; and if the mistress went out a great deal, and seemed to dislike the master's society, was it not natural, poor thing? The master was odd. I was kind and just to my dependants, but I excited in them a shrinking, half-contemptuous pity; for this class of men and women are but slightly determined in their estimate of others by general considerations, or even experience, of character. They judge of persons as they judge of coins, and value those who pass current at a high rate.

After a time I interfered so little with Bertha's habits that it might seem wonderful how her hatred towards me could grow so intense and active as it did. But she had begun to suspect, by some involuntary betrayal of mine, that there was an abnormal power of penetration in me—that fitfully, at least, I was strangely cognizant of her thoughts and intentions, and she began to be haunted by a terror of me, which alternated every now and then with defiance. She meditated continually how the incubus could be shaken off her life—how she could be freed from this hateful bond to a being whom she at once despised as an imbecile, and dreaded as an inquisitor. For a long while she lived in the hope that my evident wretchedness would drive me to the commission of suicide; but suicide was not in my nature. I was too completely swayed by the sense that I was in the grasp of unknown forces, to believe in my power of self-release. Towards my own destiny I had become entirely passive; for my one ardent desire had spent itself, and impulse no longer predominated over knowledge. For this reason I never thought of taking any steps towards a complete separation, which would have made our alienation evident to the world. Why should I rush for help to a new course, when I was only suffering from the consequences of a deed which had been the act of my intensest will? That would have been the logic of one who had desires to gratify, and I had no desires. But Bertha and I lived more and more aloof from each other. The rich find it easy to live married and apart.

That course of our life which I have indicated in a few sentences filled the space of years. So much misery—so slow and hideous a growth of hatred and sin, may be compressed into a sentence! And men judge of each other's lives through this summary medium. They epitomize the experience of their fellow-mortal, and pronounce judgment on him in neat syntax, and feel themselves wise and virtuous—conquerors over the temptations they define in well-selected predicates. Seven years of wretchedness glide glibly over the lips of the man who has never counted them out in moments of chill disappointment, of head and heart throbbings, of dread and vain wrestling, of remorse and despair. We learn *words* by rote, but not their meaning; *that* must be paid for with our life-blood, and printed in the subtle fibres of our nerves.

But I will hasten to finish my story. Brevity is justified at once to those who readily understand, and to those who will never understand.

Some years after my father's death, I was sitting by the dim firelight in my library one January evening—sitting in the leather chair that used to be my father's—when Bertha appeared at the door, with a candle in her hand, and advanced towards me. I knew the ball-dress she had on—the white ball-dress, with the green jewels, shone upon by the light of the wax candle which lit up the medallion of the dying Cleopatra on the mantelpiece. Why did she come to me before going out? I had not seen her in the library, which was my habitual place for months. Why did she stand before me with the candle in her hand, with her cruel contemptuous eyes fixed on me, and the glittering serpent, like a familiar demon, on her breast? For a moment I thought this fulfilment of my vision at Vienna marked some dreadful crisis in my fate, but I saw nothing in Bertha's mind, as she stood before me, except scorn for the look of overwhelming misery with which I sat before her. . . . "Fool, idiot, why don't you kill yourself, then?"—that was her thought. But at length her thoughts reverted to her errand, and she spoke aloud. The apparently indifferent nature of the errand seemed to make a ridiculous anti-climax to my prevision and my agitation.

"I have had to hire a new maid. Fletcher is going to be married, and she wants me to ask you to let her husband have the public-house and farm at Molton. I wish him to have it. You must give the promise now, because Fletcher is going to-morrow morning—and quickly, because I'm in a hurry."

"Very well; you may promise her," I said, indifferently, and Bertha swept out of the library again.

I always shrank from the sight of a new person, and all the more when it was a person whose mental life was likely to weary my reluctant insight with worldly ignorant trivialities. But I shrank especially from the sight of this new maid, because her advent had been announced to me at a moment to which I could not cease to attach some fatality: I had a vague dread that I should find her mixed up with the dreary drama of my life—that some new sickening vision would reveal her to me as an evil genius. When at last I did unavoidably meet her, the vague dread was changed into definite disgust. She was a tall, wiry, dark-eyed woman, this Mrs. Archer, with a face handsome enough to give her coarse hard nature the odious finish of bold, self-confident coquetry. That was enough to make me avoid her, quite apart from the contemptuous feeling with which she con-

templated me. I seldom saw her; but I perceived that she
rapidly became a favourite with her mistress, and, after the lapse
of eight or nine months, I began to be aware that there had
arisen in Bertha's mind towards this woman a mingled feeling of
fear and dependence, and that this feeling was associated with
ill-defined images of candle-light scenes in her dressing-room,
and the locking-up of something in Bertha's cabinet. My interviews with my wife had become so brief and so rarely solitary,
that I had no opportunity of perceiving these images in her
mind with more definiteness. The recollections of the past
become contracted in the rapidity of thought till they sometimes
bear hardly a more distinct resemblance to the external reality
than the forms of an oriental alphabet to the objects that suggested them.

Besides, for the last year or more a modification had been
going forward in my mental condition, and was growing more
and more marked. My insight into the minds of those around
me was becoming dimmer and more fitful, and the ideas that
crowded my double consciousness became less and less dependent on any personal contact. All that was personal in me
seemed to be suffering a gradual death, so that I was losing the
organ through which the personal agitations and projects of others
could affect me. But along with this relief from wearisome
insight, there was a new development of what I concluded—as
I have since found rightly—to be a prevision of external scenes.
It was as if the relation between me and my fellow-men was
more and more deadened, and my relation to what we call the
inanimate was quickened into new life. The more I lived apart
from society, and in proportion as my wretchedness subsided
from the violent throb of agonized passion into the dulness of
habitual pain, the more frequent and vivid became such visions
as that I had had of Prague—of strange cities, of sandy plains, of
gigantic ruins, of midnight skies with strange bright constella-
tions, of mountain-passes, of grassy nooks flecked with the afternoon sunshine through the boughs: I was in the midst of such
scenes, and in all of them one presence seemed to weigh on me
in all these mighty shapes—the presence of something
unknown and pitiless. For continual suffering had annihilated

religious faith within me: to the utterly miserable—the unloving and the unloved—there is no religion possible, no worship but a worship of devils. And beyond all these, and continually recurring, was the vision of my death—the pangs, the suffocation, the last struggle, when life would be grasped at in vain.

Things were in this state near the end of the seventh year. I had become entirely free from insight, from my abnormal cognizance of any other consciousness than my own, and instead of intruding involuntarily into the world of other minds, was living continually in my own solitary future. Bertha was aware that I was greatly changed. To my surprise she had of late seemed to seek opportunities of remaining in my society, and had cultivated that kind of distant yet familiar talk which is customary between a husband and wife who live in polite and irrevocable alienation. I bore this with languid submission, and without feeling enough interest in her motives to be roused into keen observation; yet I could not help perceiving something triumphant and excited in her carriage and the expression of her face—something too subtle to express itself in words or tones, but giving one the idea that she lived in a state of expectation or hopeful suspense. My chief feeling was satisfaction that her inner self was once more shut out from me; and I almost revelled for the moment in the absent melancholy that made me answer her at cross purposes, and betray utter ignorance of what she had been saying. I remember well the look and the smile with which she one day said, after a mistake of this kind on my part: "I used to think you were a clairvoyant, and that was the reason why you were so bitter against other clairvoyants, wanting to keep your monopoly; but I see now you have become rather duller than the rest of the world."

I said nothing in reply. It occurred to me that her recent obtrusion of herself upon me might have been prompted by the wish to test my power of detecting some of her secrets; but I let the thought drop again at once: her motives and her deeds had no interest for me, and whatever pleasures she might be seeking, I had no wish to baulk her. There was still pity in my soul for every living thing, and Bertha was living—was surrounded with possibilities of misery.

Just at this time there occurred an event which roused me somewhat from my inertia, and gave me an interest in the passing moment that I had thought impossible for me. It was a visit from Charles Meunier, who had written me word that he was coming to England for relaxation from too strenuous labour, and would like to see me. Meunier had now a European reputation; but his letter to me expressed that keen remembrance of an early regard, an early debt of sympathy, which is inseparable from nobility of character: and I too felt as if his presence would be to me like a transient resurrection into a happier pre-existence.

He came, and as far as possible, I renewed our old pleasure of making *tête-à-tête* excursions, though, instead of mountains and glacers and the wide blue lake, we had to content ourselves with mere slopes and ponds and artificial plantations. The years had changed us both, but with what different result! Meunier was now a brilliant figure in society, to whom elegant women pretended to listen, and whose acquaintance was boasted of by noblemen ambitious of brains. He repressed with the utmost delicacy all betrayal of the shock which I am sure he must have received from our meeting, or of a desire to penetrate into my condition and circumstances, and sought by the utmost exertion of his charming social powers to make our reunion agreeable. Bertha was much struck by the unexpected fascinations of a visitor whom she had expected to find presentable only on the score of his celebrity, and put forth all her coquetries and accomplishments. Apparently she succeeded in attracting his admiration, for his manner towards her was attentive and flattering. The effect of his presence on me was so benignant, especially in those renewals of our old *tête-à-tête* wanderings, when he poured forth to me wonderful narratives of his professional experience, that more than once, when his talk turned on the psychological relations of disease, the thought crossed my mind that, if his stay with me were long enough, I might possibly bring myself to tell this man the secrets of my lot. Might there not lie some remedy for *me*, too, in his science? Might there not at least lie some comprehension and sympathy ready for me in his large and susceptible mind? But the thought only flickered feebly now and then, and died out before it could become a wish. The horror I had of again breaking in on the privacy of another soul, made me, by an irrational instinct, draw the shroud of concealment more closely around my own, as we automatically perform the gesture we feel to be wanting in another.

When Meunier's visit was approaching its conclusion, there happened an event which caused some excitement in our household, owing to the surprisingly strong effect it appeared to produce on Bertha—on Bertha, the self-possessed, who usually seemed inaccessible to feminine agitations, and did even her hate in a self-restrained hygienic manner. This event was the sudden severe illness of her maid, Mrs. Archer. I have reserved to this moment the mention of a circumstance which had forced itself on my notice shortly before Meunier's arrival, namely, that there had been some quarrel between Bertha and this maid, apparently during a visit to a distant family, in which she had accompanied her mistress. I had overheard Archer speaking in a tone of bitter insolence, which I should have thought an adequate reason for immediate dismissal. No dismissal followed; on the contrary, Bertha seemed to be silently putting up with personal inconveniences from the exhibitions of this woman's temper. I was the more astonished to observe that her illness seemed a cause of strong solicitude to Bertha; that she was at the bedside night and day, and would allow no one else to officiate as head-nurse. It happened that our family doctor was out on a holiday, an accident which made Meunier's presence in the house doubly welcome, and he apparently entered into the case with an interest which seemed so much stronger than the ordinary professional feeling, that one day when he had fallen into a long fit of silence after visiting her, I said to him—

"Is this a very peculiar case of disease, Meunier?"

"No," he answered, "it is an attack of peritonitis, which will be fatal, but which does not differ physically from many other cases that have come under my observation. But I'll tell you what I have on my mind. I want to make an experiment on this woman, if you will give me permission. It can do her no harm—will give her no pain—for I shall not make it until life is extinct to all purposes of sensation. I want to try the effect of transfusing blood into her arteries after the heart has ceased to beat for some minutes. I have tried the experiment again and again with animals that have died of this disease, with astounding results, and I want to try it on a human subject. I have the small tubes necessary, in a case I have with me, and the rest of the apparatus could be prepared readily. I should use my own blood—take it from my own arm. This woman won't live through the night, I'm convinced, and I want you to promise me your assistance in making the experiment. I can't do without another hand, but it would perhaps not be well to call in a medical assistant from among your provincial doctors. A disagreeable foolish version of the thing might get abroad."

"Have you spoken to my wife on the subject?" I said, "because she appears to be peculiarly sensitive about this woman: she has been a favourite maid."

"To tell you the truth," said Meunier, "I don't want her to know about it. There are always insuperable difficulties with women in these matters, and the effect on the supposed dead body may be startling. You and I will sit up together, and be in readiness. When certain symptoms appear I shall take you in, and at the right moment we must manage to get everyone else out of the room."

I need not give our further conversation on the subject. He entered very fully into the details, and overcame my repulsion from them, by exciting in me a mingled awe and curiosity concerning the possible results of his experiment.

We prepared everything, and he instructed me in my part as assistant. He had not told Bertha of his absolute conviction that Archer would not survive through the night, and endeavoured to persuade her to leave the patient and take a night's rest. But she was obstinate, suspecting the fact that death was at hand, and supposing that he wished merely to save her nerves. She refused to leave the sick-room. Meunier and I sat up together in the library, he making frequent visits to the sick-room, and returning with the information that the case was taking precisely the course he expected. Once he said to me, "Can you imagine any cause of ill-feeling this woman has against her mistress, who is so devoted to her?"

"I think there was some misunderstanding between them before her illness. Why do you ask?"

"Because I have observed for the last five or six hours—since, I fancy, she has lost all hope of recovery—there seems a strange prompting in her to say something which pain and failing strength forbid her to utter; and there is a look of hideous meaning in her eyes, which she turns continually towards her mistress. In this disease the mind often remains singularly clear to the last."

"I am not surprised at an indication of malevolent feeling in her," I said. "She is a woman who has always inspired me with distrust and dislike, but she managed to insinuate herself into her mistress's favour." He was silent after this, looking at the fire with an air of absorption, till he went upstairs again. He stayed away longer than usual, and on returning, said to me quietly, "Come now."

I followed him to the chamber where death was hovering. The dark hangings of the large bed made a background that gave a strong relief to Bertha's pale face as I entered. She started forward as she saw me enter, and then looked at Meunier with an expression of angry inquiry; but he lifted up his hand as if to impose silence, while he fixed his glance on the dying woman and felt her pulse. The face was pinched and ghastly, a cold perspiration was on the forehead, and the eyelids were lowered so as to conceal the large dark eyes. After a minute or two, Meunier walked round to the other side of the bed where Bertha stood, and with his usual air of gentle politeness towards her begged her to leave the patient under our care—everything should be done for her—she was no longer in a state to be conscious of an affectionate presence. Bertha was hesitating, apparently almost willing to believe his assurance and to comply. She looked round at the ghastly dying face, as if to read the confirmation of that assurance, when for a moment the lowered eyelids were raised again, and it seemed as if the eyes were looking towards Bertha, but blankly. A shudder passed through Bertha's frame, and she returned to her station near the pillow, tacitly implying that she would not leave the room.

The eyelids were lifted no more. Once I looked at Bertha as she watched the face of the dying one. She wore a rich *peignoir,* and her blond hair was half covered by a lace cap: in her attire she was, as always, an elegant woman, fit to figure in a picture of modern aristocratic life: but I asked myself how that face of hers could ever have seemed to me the face of a woman born of woman, with memories of childhood, capable of pain, needing to be fondled? The features at that moment seemed so preternaturally sharp, the eyes were so hard and eager—she looked like a cruel immortal, finding her spiritual feast in the agonies of a dying race. For across those hard features there came something like a flash when the last hour had been breathed out, and we all felt that the dark veil had completely fallen. What secret was there between Bertha and this woman? I turned my eyes from her with a horrible dread lest my insight should return, and I should be obliged to see what had been breeding about two unloving women's hearts. I felt that Bertha had been watching for the moment of death as the sealing of her secret: I thanked Heaven it could remain sealed for me.

Meunier said quietly, "She is gone." He then gave his arm to Bertha, and she submitted to be led out of the room.

I suppose it was at her order that two female attendants came into the room, and dismissed the younger one who had been present before. When they entered, Meunier had already opened the artery in the long thin neck that lay rigid on the pillow, and I dismissed them, ordering them to remain at a distance till we rang: the doctor, I said, had an operation to perform—he was not sure about the death. For the next twenty minutes I forgot everything but Meunier and the experiment in which he was so absorbed, that I think his senses would have been closed against all sounds or sights which had no relation to it. It was my task at first to keep up the artificial respiration in the body after the transfusion had been effected, but presently Meunier relieved me, and I could see the wondrous slow return of life; the breast began to heave, the inspirations became stronger, the eyelids quivered, and the soul seemed to have returned beneath them. The artificial respiration was withdrawn: still the breathing continued, and there was a movement of the lips.

Just then I heard the handle of the door moving: I suppose Bertha had heard from the women that they had been dismissed: probably a vague fear had arisen in her mind, for she entered with a look of alarm. She came to the foot of the bed and gave a stifled cry.

The dead woman's eyes were wide open, and met hers in full recognition—the recognition of hate. With a sudden strong effort, the hand that Bertha had thought for ever still was pointed towards her, and the haggard face moved. The gasping eager voice said—

"You mean to poison your husband . . . the poison is in the black cabinet . . . I got it for you . . . you laughed at me, and told lies about me behind my back, to make me disgusting . . . because you were jealous . . . are you sorry . . . now?"

The lips continued to murmur, but the sounds were no longer distinct. Soon there was no sound—only a slight movement: the flame had leaped out, and was being extinguished the faster. The wretched woman's heart-strings had been set to hatred and vengeance; the spirit of life had swept the chords for an instant, and was gone again for ever. Great God! Is this what it is to live again . . . to wake up with our unstilled thirst upon us, with our unuttered curses rising to our lips, with our muscles ready to act out their half-committed sins?

Bertha stood pale at the foot of the bed, quivering and help-less, despairing of devices, like a cunning animal whose hiding-places are surrounded by swift-advancing flame. Even Meunier looked paralysed; life for that moment ceased to be a scientific problem to him. As for me, this scene seemed of one texture with the rest of my existence: horror was my familiar, and this new revelation was only like an old pain recurring with new circumstances.

º º º º º

Since then Bertha and I have lived apart—she in her own neighbourhood, the mistress of half our wealth, I as a wanderer in foreign countries, until I came to this Devonshire nest to die. Bertha lives pitied and admired; for what had I against that charming woman, whom everyone but myself could have been happy with? There had been no witness of the scene in the dying room except Meunier, and while Meunier lived his lips were sealed by a promise to me.

Once or twice, weary of wandering, I rested in a favourite spot, and my heart went out towards the men and women and children whose faces were becoming familiar to me; but I was driven away again in terror at the approach of my old insight—driven away to live continually with the one Unknown Presence revealed and yet hidden by the moving curtain of the earth and sky. Till at last disease took hold of me and forced me to rest here—forced me to live in dependence on my servants. And then the curse of insight—of my double consciousness, came again, and has never left me. I know all their narrow thoughts, their feeble regard, their half-wearied pity.

It is the 20th of September, 1850. I know these figures I have just written, as if they were a long familiar inscription. I have seen them on this page in my desk unnumbered times, when the scene of my dying struggle has opened upon me. . . .

THE COLD EMBRACE*

Mary E. Braddon
(1837–1915)

He was an artist—such things as happened to him happen sometimes to artists.

He was a German—such things as happened to him happen sometimes to Germans.

He was young, handsome, studious, enthusiastic, metaphysical, reckless, unbelieving, heartless.

And being young, handsome and eloquent, he was beloved.

He was an orphan, under the guardianship of his dead father's brother, his uncle Wilhelm, in whose house he had been brought up from a little child; and she who loved him was his cousin—his cousin Gertrude, whom he swore he loved in return.

Did he love her? Yes, when he first swore it. It soon wore out, this passionate love; how threadbare and wretched a sentiment it became at last in the selfish heart of the student! But in its first golden dawn, when he was only nineteen, and had just returned from his apprenticeship to a great painter at Antwerp, and they wandered together in the most romantic outskirts of the city at rosy sunset, by holy moonlight, or bright and joyous morning, how beautiful a dream!

They keep it a secret from Wilhelm, as he has the father's ambition of a wealthy suitor for his only child—a cold and dreary vision beside the lover's dream.

---

*From *Ralph the Bailiff, and Other Stories*, 1861.

So they are betrothed; and standing side by side when the dying sun and the pale rising moon divide the heavens, he puts the betrothal ring upon her finger, the white and taper finger whose slender shape he knows so well. This ring is a peculiar one, a massive golden serpent, its tail in its mouth, the symbol of eternity; it had been his mother's, and he would know it amongst a thousand. If he were to become blind tomorrow, he could select it from amongst a thousand by the touch alone.

He places it on her finger, and they swear to be true to each other for ever and ever—through trouble and danger—sorrow and change—in wealth or poverty. Her father must needs be won to consent to their union by-and-by, for they were now betrothed, and death alone could part them.

But the young student, the scoffer at revelation, yet the enthusiastic adorer of the mystical, asks:

"Can death part us? I would return to you from the grave, Gertrude. My soul would come back to be near my love. And you—you, if you died before me—the cold earth would not hold you from me; if you loved me, you would return, and again these fair arms would be clasped round my neck as they are now."

But she told him, with a holier light in her deep-blue eyes than had ever shone in his—she told him that the dead who die at peace with God are happy in heaven, and cannot return to the troubled earth; and that it is only the suicide—the lost wretch on whom sorrowful angels shut the door of Paradise—whose unholy spirit haunts the footsteps of the living.

The first year of their betrothal is passed, and she is alone, for he has gone to Italy, on a commission for some rich man, to copy Raphaels, Titians, Guidos, in a gallery at Florence. He has gone to win fame, perhaps; but it is not the less bitter—he is gone!

Of course her father misses his young nephew, who has been as a son to him; and he thinks his daughter's sadness no more than a cousin should feel for a cousin's absence.

In the meantime, the weeks and months pass. The lover writes—often at first, then seldom—at last, not at all.

How many excuses she invents for him! How many times she goes to the distant little post-office, to which he is to address his letters! How many times she hopes, only to be disappointed! How many times she despairs, only to hope again!

But real despair comes at last, and will not be put off any more. The rich suitor appears on the scene, and her father is determined. She is to marry at once. The wedding-day is fixed— the fifteenth of June.

The date seems to burn into her brain.

The date, written in fire, dances for ever before her eyes.

The date, shrieked by the Furies, sounds continually in her ears.

But there is time yet—it is the middle of May—there is time for a letter to reach him at Florence; there is time for him to come to Brunswick, to take her away and marry her, in spite of her father—in spite of the whole world.

But the days and the weeks fly by, and he does not write—he does not come. This is indeed despair which usurps her heart, and will not be put away.

It is the fourteenth of June. For the last time she goes to the little post-office; for the last time she asks the old question, and they give her for the last time the dreary answer, "No; no letter."

For the last time—for tomorrow is the day appointed for the bridal. Her father will hear no entreaties; her rich suitor will not listen to her prayers. They will not be put off a day—an hour; to-night alone is hers—this night, which she may employ as she will.

She takes another path than that which leads home; she hurries through some by-streets of the city, out on to a lonely bridge, where he and she had stood so often in the sunset, watching the rose-coloured light glow, fade, and die upon the river.

He returns from Florence. He had received her letter. That letter, blotted with tears, entreating, despairing—he had received it, but he loved her no longer. A young Florentine, who has sat to him for a model, had bewitched his fancy—that fancy which with him stood in place of a heart—and Gertrude had been half-forgotten. If she had a rich suitor, good; let her marry him; better for her, better far for himself. He had no wish to fet-

ter himself with a wife. Had he not his art always?—his eternal
bride, his unchanging mistress.

Thus he thought it wiser to delay his journey to Brunswick, so
that he should arrive when the wedding was over—arrive in
time to salute the bride.

And the vows—the mystical fancies—the belief in his return,
even after death, to the embrace of his beloved? O, gone out
of his life; melted away for ever, those foolish dreams of his
boyhood.

So on the fifteenth of June he enters Brunswick, by that very
bridge on which she stood, the stars looking down on her, the
night before. He strolls across the bridge and down by the
water's edge, a great rough dog at his heels, and the smoke from
his short meerschaum-pipe curling in blue wreaths fantastically
in the pure morning air. He has his sketch-book under his arm,
and attracted now and then by some object that catches his
artist's eye, stops to draw: a few weeds and pebbles on the river's
brink—a crag on the opposite shore—a group of pollard willows
in the distance. When he has done, he admires his drawing,
shuts his sketch-book, empties the ashes from his pipe, refills
from his tobacco-pouch, sings the refrain of a gay drinking-song,
calls to his dog, smokes again, and walks on. Suddenly he opens
his sketch-book again; this time that which attracts him is a
group of figures: but what is it?

It is not a funeral, for there are no mourners.

It is not a funeral, but a corpse lying on a rude bier, covered
with an old sail, carried between two bearers.

It is not a funeral, for the bearers are fishermen—fishermen
in their everyday garb.

About a hundred yards from him they rest their burden on a
bank—one stands at the head of the bier, the other throws himself down at the foot of it.

And thus they form the perfect group; he walks back two or
three paces, selects his point of sight, and begins to sketch a hurried outline. He has finished it before they move; he hears their
voices, though he cannot hear their words, and wonders what
they can be talking of. Presently he walks on and joins them.

"You have a corpse there, my friends?" he says.

"Yes; a corpse washed ashore an hour ago."

"Drowned?"

"Yes, drowned. A young girl, very handsome."

"Suicides are always handsome," says the painter; and then he stands for a little while idly smoking and meditating, looking at the sharp outline of the corpse and the stiff folds of the rough canvas covering.

Life is such a golden holiday for him—young, ambitious, clever—that it seems as though sorrow and death could have no part in his destiny.

At last he says that, as this poor suicide is so handsome, he should like to make a sketch of her.

He gives the fishermen some money, and they offer to remove the sailcloth that covers her features.

No; he will do it himself. He lifts the rough, coarse, wet canvas from her face. What face?

The face that shone on the dreams of his foolish boyhood; the face which once was the light of his uncle's home. His cousin Gertrude—his betrothed!

He sees, as in one glance, while he draws one breath, the rigid features—the marble arms—the hands crossed on the cold bosom; and, on the third finger of the left hand, the ring which had been his mother's—the golden serpent; the ring which, if he were to become blind, he could select from a thousand others by the touch alone.

But he is a genius and a metaphysician—grief, true grief, is not for such as he. His first thought is flight—flight anywhere out of that accursed city—anywhere far from the brink of that hideous river—anywhere away from remorse—anywhere to forget.

He is miles on the road that leads away from Brunswick before he knows that he has walked a step.

It is only when his dog lies down panting at his feet that he feels how exhausted he is himself, and sits down upon a bank to rest. How the landscape spins round and round before his dazzled eyes, while his morning's sketch of the two fishermen and the canvas-covered bier glares redly at him out of the twilight!

At last, after sitting a long time by the roadside, idly playing with his dog, idly smoking, idly lounging, looking as any idle, light-hearted travelling student might look, yet all the while acting over that morning's scene in his burning brain a hundred times a minute; at last he grows a little more composed, and tries presently to think of himself as he is, apart from his cousin's suicide. Apart from that, he was no worse off than he was yesterday. His genius was not gone; the money he had earned at Florence still lined his pocket-book; he was his own master, free to go whither he would.

And while he sits on the roadside, trying to separate himself from the scene of that morning—trying to put away the image of the corpse covered with the damp canvas sail—trying to think of what he should do next, where he should go, to be farthest away from Brunswick and remorse, the old diligence comes rumbling and jingling along. He remembers it; it goes from Brunswick to Aix-la-Chapelle.

He whistles to the dog, shouts to the postillion to stop, and springs into the *coupé*.

During the whole evening, through the long night, though he does not once close his eyes, he never speaks a word; but when morning dawns, and the other passengers awake and begin to talk to each other, he joins in the conversation. He tells them that he is an artist, that he is going to Cologne and to Antwerp to copy Rubenses, and the great picture by Quentin Matsys, in the museum. He remembered afterwards that he talked and laughed boisterously, and that when he was talking and laughing loudest, a passenger, older and graver than the rest, opened the window near him, and told him to put his head out. He remembered the fresh air blowing in his face, the singing of the birds in his ears, and the flat fields and roadside reeling before his eyes. He remembered this, and then falling in a lifeless heap on the floor of the diligence.

It is a fever that keeps him for six long weeks on a bed at a hotel in Aix-la-Chapelle.

He gets well, and, accompanied by his dog, starts on foot for Cologne. By this time he is his former self once more. Again the blue smoke from his short meerschaum curls upwards in the morning air—again he sings some old university drinking-song—again stops here and there, meditating and sketching.

He is happy, and has forgotten his cousin—and so on to Cologne.

It is by the great cathedral he is standing, with his dog at his side. It is night, the bells have just chimed the hour, and the clocks are striking eleven; the moonlight shines full upon the magnificent pile, over which the artist's eye wanders, absorbed in the beauty of form.

He is not thinking of his drowned cousin, for he has forgotten her and is happy.

Suddenly someone, something from behind him, puts two cold arms round his neck, and clasps its hands on his breast.

And yet there is no one behind him, for on the flags bathed in the broad moonlight there are only two shadows, his own and his dog's. He turns quickly round—there is no one—nothing to be seen in the broad square but himself and his dog; and though he feels, he cannot see the cold arms clasped round his neck.

It is not ghostly, this embrace, for it is palpable to the touch—it cannot be real, for it is invisible.

He tries to throw off the cold caress. He clasps the hands in his own to tear them asunder, and to cast them off his neck. He can feel the long delicate fingers cold and wet beneath his touch, and on the third finger of the left hand he can feel the ring which was his mother's—the golden serpent—the ring which he has always said he would know among a thousand by the touch alone. He knows it now!

His dead cousin's cold arms are round his neck—his dead cousin's wet hands are clasped upon his breast. He asks himself if he is mad. "Up, Leo!" he shouts. "Up, up, boy!" and the Newfoundland leaps to his shoulders—the dog's paws are on the dead hands, and the animal utters a terrific howl, and springs away from his master.

The student stands in the moonlight, the dead arms around his neck, and the dog at a little distance moaning piteously.

Presently a watchman, alarmed by the howling of the dog, comes into the square to see what is wrong.

In a breath the cold arms are gone.

He takes the watchman home to the hotel with him and gives him money; in his gratitude he could have given that man half his little fortune.

Will it ever come to him again, this embrace of the dead?

He tries never to be alone; he makes a hundred acquaintances, and shares the chamber of another student. He starts up if he is left by himself in the public room of the inn where he is staying, and runs into the street. People notice his strange actions, and begin to think that he is mad.

But, in spite of all, he is alone once more; for one night the public room being empty for a moment, when on some idle pretence he strolls into the street, the street is empty too, and for the second time he feels the cold arms round his neck, and for the second time, when he calls his dog, the animal shrinks away from him with a piteous howl.

After this he leaves Cologne, still travelling on foot—of necessity now, for his money is getting low. He joins travelling hawkers, he walks side by side with labourers, he talks to every foot-passenger he falls in with, and tries from morning till night to get company on the road.

At night he sleeps by the fire in the kitchen of the inn at which he stops; but do what he will, he is often alone, and it is now a common thing for him to feel the cold arms around his neck.

Many months have passed since his cousin's death—autumn, winter, early spring. His money is nearly gone, his health is utterly broken, he is the shadow of his former self, and he is getting near to Paris. He will reach that city at the time of the Carnival. To this he looks forward. In Paris, in Carnival time, he need never, surely, be alone, never feel that deadly caress; he may even recover his lost gaiety, his lost health, once more resume his profession, once more earn fame and money by his art.

How hard he tries to get over the distance that divides him from Paris, while day by day he grows weaker, and his step slower and more heavy!

But there is an end at last; the long dreary roads are passed. This is Paris, which he enters for the first time—Paris, of which he has dreamed so much—Paris, whose million voices are to exorcise his phantom.

To him to-night Paris seems one vast chaos of lights, music, and confusion—lights which dance before his eyes and will not be still—music that rings in his ears and deafens him—confusion which makes his head whirl round and round.

But, in spite of all, he finds the opera-house, where there is a masked ball. He has enough money left to buy a ticket of admission, and to hire a domino to throw over his shabby dress. It seems only a moment after his entering the gates of Paris that he is in the very midst of all the wild gaiety of the opera-house ball.

No more darkness, no more loneliness, but a mad crowd, shouting and dancing, and a lovely Débardeuse hanging on his arm.

The boisterous gaiety he feels surely is his old light-heartedness come back. He hears the people round him talking of the outrageous conduct of some drunken student, and it is to him they point when they say this—to him, who has not moistened his lips since yesterday at noon, for even now he will not drink; though his lips are parched, and his throat burning, he cannot drink. His voice is thick and hoarse, and his utterance indistinct; but still this must be his old light-heartedness come back that makes him so wildly gay.

The little Débardeuse is wearied out—her arm rests on his shoulder heavier than lead—the other dancers one by one drop off.

The lights in the chandeliers one by one die out.

The decorations look pale and shadowy in that dim light which is neither night nor day.

A faint glimmer from the dying lamps, a pale streak of cold grey light from the new-born day, creeping in through half-opened shutters.

And by this light the bright-eyed Débardeuse fades sadly. He looks her in the face. How the brightness of her eyes dies out! Again he looks her in the face. How white that face has grown! Again—and now it is the shadow of a face alone that looks in his.

Again—and they are gone—the bright eyes, the face, the shadow of the face. He is alone; alone in that vast saloon.

Alone, and, in the terrible silence, he hears the echoes of his own footsteps in that dismal dance which has no music.

No music but the beating of his breast. The the cold arms are round his neck—they whirl him round, they will not be flung off, or cast away; he can no more escape from their icy grasp than he can escape from death. He looks behind him—there is nothing but himself in the great empty *salle*; but he can feel— cold, deathlike, but O, how palpable!—the long slender fingers, and the ring which was his mother's.

He tries to shout, but he has no power in his burning throat. The silence of the place is only broken by the echoes of his own footsteps in the dance from which he cannot extricate himself. Who says he has no partner? The cold hands are clasped on his breast, and now he does not shun their caress. No! One more polka, if he drops down dead.

The lights are all out, and, half an hour after, the *gendarmes* come in with a lantern to see that the house is empty; they are followed by a great dog that they have found seated howling on the steps of the theatre. Near the principal entrance they stumble over—

The body of a student, who has died from want of food, exhaustion, and the breaking of a blood-vessel.

NOT TO BE TAKEN AT BED-TIME*
Rosa Mulholland
(1841–1921)

This is the legend of a house called the Devil's Inn, standing in the heather on the top of the Connemara mountains, in a shallow valley hollowed between five peaks. Tourists sometimes come in sight of it on September evenings; a crazy and weather-stained apparition, with the sun glaring at it angrily between the hills, and striking its shattered window-panes. Guides are known to shun it, however.

The house was built by a stranger, who came no one knew whence, and whom the people nicknamed Coll Dhu (Black-Coll), because of his sullen bearing and solitary habits. His dwelling they called the Devil's Inn, because no tired traveller had ever been asked to rest under its roof, nor friend known to cross its threshold. No one bore him company in his retreat but a wizen-faced old man, who shunned the good-morrow of the trudging peasant when he made occasional excursions to the nearest village for provisions for himself and master, and who was as secret as a stone concerning all the antecedents of both.

For the first year of their residence in the country, there had been much speculation as to who they were, and what they did with themselves up there among the clouds and eagles. Some said that Coll Dhu was a scion of the old family from whose hands the surrounding lands had passed; and that, embittered

---

*From *All the Year Round* (Dec. 1865)

by poverty and pride, he had come to bury himself in solitude, and brood over his misfortunes. Others hinted of crime, and flight from another country; others again whispered of those who were cursed from their birth, and could never smile, nor yet make friends with a fellow-creature till the day of their death. But when two years had passed, the wonder had somewhat died out, and Coll Dhu was little thought of, except when a herd looking for sheep crossed the track of a big dark man walking the mountains gun in hand, to whom he did not dare say "Lord save you!" or when a housewife rocking the cradle of a winter's night, crossed herself as a gust of storm thundered over her cabin-roof, with the exclamation, "Oh, then, its Coll Dhu that has enough o' the fresh air about his head up there this night, the crature!"

Coll Dhu had lived thus in his solitude for some years, when it became known that Colonel Blake, the new lord of the soil, was coming to visit the country. By climbing one of the peaks encircling his eyrie, Coll could look sheer down a mountain-side, and see in miniature beneath him, a grey old dwelling with ivied chimneys and weather-slated walls, standing amongst straggling trees and grim warlike rocks, that gave it the look of a fortress, gazing out to the Atlantic for ever with the eager eyes of all its windows, as if demanding perpetually, "What tidings from the New World?"

He could see now masons and carpenters crawling about below, like ants in the sun, over-running the old house from base to chimney, daubing here and knocking there, tumbling down walls that looked to Coll, up among the clouds, like a handful of jack-stones, and building up others that looked like the toy fences in a child's Farm. Throughout several months he must have watched the busy ants at their task of breaking and mending again, disfiguring and beautifying; but when all was done he had not the curiosity to stride down and admire the handsome penelling of the new billiard-room, nor yet the fine view which the enlarged bay-window in the drawing-room commanded of the watery highway to Newfoundland.

Deep summer was melting into autumn, and the amber streaks of decay were beginning to creep out and trail over the

ripe purple of moor and mountain, when Colonel Blake, his only
daughter, and a party of friends, arrived in the country. The grey
house below was alive with gaiety, but Coll Dhu no longer found
an interest in observing it from his eyrie. When he watched the
sun rise or set, he chose to ascend some crag that looked on no
human habitation. When he sailed forth on his excursions, gun
in hand, he set his face towards the most isolated wastes, dipping into the loneliest valleys, and scaling the nakedest ridges.
When he came by chance within call of other excursionists, gun
in hand he plunged into the shade of some hollow, and avoided
an encounter. Yet it was fated, for all that, that he and Colonel
Blake should meet.

Towards the evening of one bright September day, the wind
changed, and in half an hour the mountains were wrapped in a
thick blinding mist. Coll Dhu was far from his den, but so well
had he searched these mountains, and inured himself to their
climate, that neither storm, rain, nor fog, had power to disturb
him. But while he stalked on his way, a faint and agonised cry
from a human voice reached him through the smothering mist.
He quickly tracked the sound, and gained the side of a man who
was stumbling along in danger of death at every step.

"Follow me!" said Coll Dhu to this man, and, in an hour's
time, brought him safely to the lowlands, and up to the walls of
the eager-eyed mansion.

"I am Colonel Blake," said the frank soldier, when, having left
the fog behind them, they stood in the starlight under the
lighted windows. "Pray tell me quickly to whom I owe my life."

As he spoke, he glanced up at his benefactor, a large man with
a sombre sun-burned face.

"Colonel Blake," said Coll Dhu, after a strange pause, "your
father suggested to my father to stake his estates at the gaming-
table. They were staked, and the tempter won. Both are dead;
but you and I live, and I have sworn to injure you."

The colonel laughed good humouredly at the uneasy face
above him.

"And you began to keep your oath tonight by saving my life?"
said he. "Come! I am a soldier, and know how to meet an
enemy; but I had far rather meet a friend. I shall not be happy

till you have eaten my salt. We have merrymaking tonight in honour of my daughter's birthday. Come in and join us?"

Coll Dhu looked at the earth doggedly.

"I have told you," he said, "who and what I am, and I will not cross your threshold."

But at this moment (so runs the story) a French window opened among the flower-beds by which they were standing, and a vision appeared which stayed the words on Coll's tongue. A stately girl, clad in white satin, stood framed in the ivied window, with the warm light from within streaming around her richly-moulded figure into the night. Her face was as pale as her gown, her eyes were swimming in tears, but a firm smile sat on her lips as she held out both hands to her father. The light behind her touched the glistening folds of her dress—the lustrous pearls round her throat—the coronet of blood-red roses which encircled the knotted braids at the back of her head. Satin, pearls, and roses—had Coll Dhu, of the Devil's Inn, never set eyes upon such things before?

Evleen Blake was no nervous tearful miss. A few quick words—"Thank God! you're safe; the rest have been home an hour"—and a tight pressure of her father's fingers between her own jewelled hands, were all that betrayed the uneasiness she had suffered.

"Faith, my love, I owe my life to this brave gentleman!" said the blithe colonel. "Press him to come in and be our guest, Evleen. He wants to retreat to his mountains, and lose himself again in the fog where I found him; or, rather, where he found me! Come, sir," (to Coll), "you must surrender to this fair besieger."

An introduction followed. "Coll Dhu!" murmured Evleen Blake, for she had heard the common tales of him; but with a frank welcome she invited her father's preserver to taste the hospitality of that father's house.

"I beg you to come in, sir," she said; "but for you our gaiety must have been turned into mourning. A shadow will be upon our mirth if our benefactor disdains to join it."

With a sweet grace, mingled with a certain hauteur from which she was never free, she extended her white hand to the tall looming figure outside the window; to have it grasped and wrung in a way that made the proud girl's eyes flash their amazement, and the same little hand clench itself in displeasure, when it had hid itself like an outraged thing among the shining folds of her gown. Was this Coll Dhu mad, or rude?

The guest no longer refused to enter, but followed the white figure into a little study where a lamp burned; and the gloomy stranger, the bluff colonel, and the young mistress of the house, were fully discovered to each other's eyes. Evleen glanced at the newcomer's dark face, and shuddered with a feeling of indescribable dread and dislike; then, to her father, accounted for the shudder after a popular fashion, saying lightly: "There is someone walking over my grave."

So Coll Dhu was present at Evleen Blake's birthday ball. Here he was, under a roof which ought to have been his own, a stranger, known only by a nickname, shunned and solitary. Here he was, who had lived among the eagles and foxes, lying in wait with a fell purpose, to be revenged on the son of his father's foe for poverty and disgrace, for the broken heart of a dead mother, for the loss of a self-slaughtered father, for the dreary scattering of brothers and sisters. Here he stood, a Samson shorn of his strength; and all because a haughty girl had melting eyes, a winning mouth, and looked radiant in satin and roses.

Peerless where many were lovely, she moved among her friends, trying to be unconscious of the gloomy fire of those strange eyes which followed her unweariedly wherever she went. And when her father begged her to be gracious to the unsocial guest whom he would fain conciliate, she courteously conducted him to see the new picture-gallery adjoining the drawing-rooms; explained under what odd circumstances the colonel had picked up this little painting or that; using every delicate art her pride would allow to achieve her father's purpose, whilst maintaining at the same time her own personal reserve; trying to divert the guest's oppressive attention from herself to the objects for which she claimed his notice. Coll Dhu followed his conductress and listened to her voice, but what she said mattered nothing; nor did she wring many words of comment or reply from her lips, until they paused in a retired corner where the light was dim, before a window from which the curtain was withdrawn. The sashes were open, and nothing was visible but water; the night Atlantic, with the full moon riding high above a bank of clouds, making silvery tracks outward towards the distance of infinite mystery dividing two worlds. Here the following little scene is said to have been enacted.

"This window of my father's own planning, is it not creditable to his taste?" said the young hostess, as she stood, herself glittering like a dream of beauty, looking on the moonlight.

Coll Dhu made no answer; but suddenly, it is said, asked her for a rose from a cluster of flowers that nestled in the lace on her bosom.

For the second time that night Evleen Blake's eyes flashed with no gentle light. But this man was the saviour of her father. She broke off a blossom, and with such good grace, and also with such queen-like dignity as she might assume, presented it to him. Whereupon, not only was the rose seized, but also the hand that gave it, which was hastily covered with kisses.

Then her anger burst upon him.

"Sir," she cried, "if you are a gentleman you must be mad! If you are not mad, then you are not a gentleman!"

"Be merciful," said Coll Dhu; "I love you. My God, I never loved a woman before! Ah!" he cried, as a look of disgust crept over her face, "you hate me. You shuddered the first time your eyes met mine. I love you, and you hate me!"

"I do," cried Evleen, vehemently, forgetting everything but her indignation. "Your presence is like something evil to me. Love me?—your looks poison me. Pray, sir, talk no more to me in this strain."

"I will trouble you no longer," said Coll Dhu. And, stalking to the window, he placed one powerful hand upon the sash, and vaulted from it out of her sight.

Bare-headed as he was, Coll Dhu strode off to the mountains, but not towards his own home. All the remaining dark hours of that night he is believed to have walked the labyrinths of the hills, until dawn began to scatter the clouds with a high wind. Fasting, and on foot from sunrise the morning before, he was then glad enough to see a cabin right in his way. Walking in, he asked for water to drink, and a corner where he might throw himself to rest.

There was a wake in the house, and the kitchen was full of people, all wearied out with the night's watch; old men were dozing over their pipes in the chimney-corner, and here and there a woman was fast asleep with her head on a neighbour's knee. All who were awake crossed themselves when Coll Dhu's figure darkened the door, because of his evil name; but an old man of the house invited him in, and offering him milk, and promising him a roasted potato by-and-by, conducted him to a small room off the kitchen, one end of which was strewed with heather, and where there were only two women sitting gossiping over a fire.

"A traveller," said the old man, nodding his head at the women, who nodded back, as if to say, "he has the traveller's right." And Coll Dhu flung himself on the heather, in the furthest corner of the narrow room.

The women suspended their talk for a while; but presently, guessing the intruder to be asleep, resumed it in voices above a whisper. There was but a patch of window with the grey dawn behind it, but Coll could see the figures by the firelight over which they bent: an old woman sitting forward with her withered hands extended to the embers, and a girl reclining against the hearth wall, with her healthy face, bright eyes, and crimson draperies, glowing by turns in the flickering blaze.

"I do' know," said the girl, "but it's the quarest marriage iver I h'ard of. Sure, it's not three weeks since he tould right an' left that he hated her like poison!"

"Whilst, asthoreen!" said the colliagh, bending forward confidentially; "throth an' we all know that o' him. But what could he do, the crature! When she put the burragh-bos on him!"

"The *what?*" asked the girl.

"Then the burragh-bos machree-o? That's the spanchel o' death, avourneen; an' well she has him tethered to her now, bad luck to her!"

The old woman rocked herself and stifled the Irish cry breaking from her wrinkled lips by burying her face in her cloak.

"But what is it?" asked the girl, eagerly. "What's the burragh-bos, anyways, an' where did she get it?"

"Och, och! it's not fit for comin' over to young ears, but cuggir (whisper), acushla! It's a sthrip o' the skin o' a corpse, peeled from the crown o' the head to the heel, without crack or split, or the charm's broke; an' that, rowled up, and put on a sthring roun' the neck o' the wan that's cowld by the wan that wants to be loved. An' sure enough it puts the fire in their hearts, hot an' sthrong, afore twenty-four hours is gone."

The girl had started from her lazy attitude, and gazed at her companion with eyes dilated by horror.

"Marciful Saviour!" she cried. "Not a sowl on airth would bring the curse out o' heaven by sich a black doin'!"

"Aisy, Biddeen alanna! an' there's wan that does it, an' isn't the divil. Arrah, asthoreen, did ye niver hear tell o' Pexie na Pishrogie, that lives betune two hills o' Maam Turk?"

"I h'ard o' her," said the girl, breathlessly.

"Well, sorra bit lie, but it's hersel' that does it. She'll do it for money any day. Sure they hunted her from the graveyard o' Salruck, where she had the dead raised; an' glory be to God! they wold ha' murthered her, only they missed her thracks, an' couldn't bring it home to her afther."

"Whist, a-wauher" (my mother), said the girl; "here's the thraveller gettin' up to set off on his road again! Och, then, it's the short rest he tuk, the sowl!"

It was enough for Coll, however. He had got up, and now went back to the kitchen, where the old man had caused a dish of potatoes to be roasted, and earnestly pressed his visitor to sit down and eat of them. This Coll did readily; having recruited his strength by a meal, he betook himself to the mountains again, just as the rising sun was flashing among the waterfalls, and sending the night mists drifting down the glens. By sundown the same evening he was striding over the hills of Maam Turk, asking of herds his way to the cabin of one Pexie na Pishrogie.

In a hovel on a brown desolate heath, with scared-looking hills flying off into the distance on every side, he found Pexie: a yellow-faced hag, dressed in a dark-red blanket, with elf-locks of coarse black hair protruding from under an orange kerchief swathed round her wrinkled jaws. She was bending over a pot upon her fire, where herbs were simmering, and she looked up with an evil glance when Coll Dhu darkened her door.

"The burragh-bos is it her honour wants?" she asked, when he had made known his errand. "Ay, ay; but the arighad, the arighad (money) for Pexie. The burragh-bos is ill to get."

"I will pay," said Coll Dhu, laying a sovereign on the bench before her.

The witch sprang upon it, and chuckling, bestowed on her visitor a glance which made even Coll Dhu shudder.

"Her honour is a fine king," she said, "an' her is fit to get the burragh-bos. Ha! ha! her sall get the burragh-bos from Pexie. But the arighad is not enough. More, more!"

She stretched out her claw-like hand, and Coll dropped another sovereign into it. Whereupon she fell into more horrible convulsions of delight.

"Hark ye!" cried Coll. "I have paid you well, but if your infernal charm does not work, I will have you hunted for a witch!"

"Work!" cried Pexie, rolling up her eyes. "If Pexie's charrm not work, then her honour come back here an' carry these bits o' mountain away on her back. Ay, her will work. If the colleen hate her honour like the old diaoul hersel', still an' withal her love will love her honour like her own white sowl afore the sun sets or rises. That, (with a furtive leer,) or the colleen dhas go wild mad afore wan hour."

"Hag!" returned Coll Dhu; "the last part is a hellish invention of your own. I heard nothing of madness. If you want more money, speak out, but play none of your hideous tricks on me."

The witch fixed her cunning eyes on him, and took her cue at once from his passion.

"Her honour guess thrue," she simpered; "it is only the little bit more arighad poor Pexie want."

Again the skinny hand was extended. Coll Dhu shrank from touching it, and threw his gold coin upon the table.

"King, king!" chuckled Pexie. "Her honour is a grand king. Her honour is fit to get the burragh-bos. The colleen dhas sall love her like her own white sowl. Ha, ha!"

"When shall I get it?" asked Coll Dhu, impatiently.

"Her honour sall come back to Pexie in so many days, do-deag (twelve), so many days, fur that the burragh-bos is hard to get. The lonely graveyard is far away, an' the dead man is hard to raise—"

"Silence!" cried Coll Dhu; "not a word more. I will have your hideous charm, but what it is, or where you get it, I will not know."

Then, promising to come back in twelve days, he took his departure. Turning to look back when a little say across the heath, he saw Pexie gazing after him, standing on her black hill in relief against the lurid flames of the dawn, seeming to his dark imagination like a fury with all hell at her back.

At the appointed time Coll Dhu got the promised charm. He sewed it with perfumes into a cover of cloth of gold, and slung it to a fine-wrought chain. Lying in a casket which had once held the jewels of Coll's broken-hearted mother, it looked a glittering bauble enough. Meantime the people of the mountains were cursing over their cabin fires, because there had been another unholy raid upon their graveyard, and were banding themselves to hunt the criminal down.

A fortnight passed. How or where could Coll Dhu find an opportunity to put the charm round the neck of the colonel's proud daughter? More gold was dropped into Pexie's greedy claw, and then she promised to assist him in his dilemma.

Next morning the witch dressed herself in decent garb, smoothed her elf-locks under a snowy cap, smoothed the wrinkles out of her face, and with a basket on her arm locked the door of the hovel, and took her way to the lowlands. Pexie seemed to have given up her disreputable calling for that of a simple mushroom-gatherer. The housekeeper at the grey house bought poor Muireade's mushrooms of her every morning. Every morning she left unfailingly a nosegay of wild flowers for Miss Evleen Blake, "God bless her! She had never seen the darling young lady with her own two longing eyes, but sure hadn't she heard tell of her sweet purty face, miles away!" And at last, one morning, whom should she meet but Miss Evleen herself returning alone from a ramble. Whereupon poor Muireade "made bold" to present her flowers in person.

"Ah," said Evleen, "it is you who leave me the flowers every morning? They are very sweet."

Muireade had sought her only for a look at her beautiful face. And now that she had seen it, as bright as the sun, and as fair as the lily, she would take up her basket and go away contented. Yet she lingered a little longer.

"My lady never walk up big mountain?" said Pexie.

"No," said Evleen, laughing; she feared she could not walk up a mountain.

"Ah yes; my lady ought to go, with more gran' ladies an' gentlemen, ridin' on purty little donkeys, up the big mountains. Oh, gran' things up big mountains for my lady to see!"

Thus she set to work, and kept her listener enchained for an hour, while she related wonderful stories of those upper regions. And as Evleen looked up to the burly crowns of the hills, perhaps she thought there might be sense in this wild old woman's suggestion. It ought to be a grand world up yonder.

Be that as it may, it was not long after this when Coll Dhu got notice that a party from the grey house would explore the mountains next day; that Evleen Blake would be one of the number; and that he, Coll, must prepare to house and refresh a crowd of weary people, who in the evening should be brought, hungry and faint, to his door. The simple mushroom-gatherer should be discovered laying in her humble stock among the green places between the hills, should volunteer to act as guide to the party, should lead them far out of their way though the mountains and up and down the most toilsome ascents and across dangerous places; to escape safely from which, the servants should be told to throw away the baskets of provisions which they carried.

Coll Dhu was not idle. Such a feast was set forth, as had never been spread so near the clouds before. We are told of wonderful dishes furnished by unwholesome agency, and from a place believed much hotter than is necessary for purposes of cookery. We are told also how Coll Dhu's barren chambers were suddenly hung with curtains of velvet, and with fringes of gold; how the blank white walls glowed with delicate colours and gilding; how gems of pictures sprang into sight between the panels; how the tables blazed with plate and gold, and glittered with the rarest glass; how such wines flowed, as the guests had never tasted; how servants in the richest livery, amongst whom the wizen-faced old man was a mere nonentity, appeared, and stood ready to carry in the wonderful dishes, at whose extraordinary fragrance the eagles came pecking to the windows, and the foxes drew near the walls, snuffing. Sure enough, in all good time, the weary party came within sight of the Devil's Inn, and Coll Dhu sallied forth to invite them across his lonely threshold. Colonel Blake (to whom Evleen, in her delicacy, had said no word of the solitary's strange behaviour to herself) hailed his appearance with delight, and the whole party sat down to Coll's banquet in high good humour. Also, it is said, in much amazement at the magnificence of the mountain rescue.

All went in to Coll's feast, save Evleen Blake, who remained standing on the threshold of the outer door; weary, but unwilling to rest there; hungry, but unwilling to eat there. Her white cambric dress was gathered on her arms, crushed and sullied with the toils of the day; her bright cheek was a little sun-burned; her small dark head with its braids a little tossed, was bared to the mountain air and the glory of the sinking sun; her hands were loosely tangled in the strings of her hat; and her foot sometimes tapped the threshold-stone. So she was seen.

The peasants tell that Coll Dhu and her father came praying her to enter, and that the magnificent servants brought viands to the threshold; but no step would she move inward, no morsel would she taste.

"Poison, poison!" she murmured, and threw the food in handfuls to the foxes, who were snuffing on the heath.

But it was different when Muireade, the kindly old woman, the simple mushroom-gatherer, with all the wicked wrinkles smoothed out of her face, came to the side of the hungry girl, and coaxingly presented a savoury mess of her own sweet mushrooms, served on a common earthen platter.

"An' darlin', my lady, poor Muireade her cook them hersel',

an' no thing o' this house touch them or look at poor Muireade's mushrooms."

Then Evleen took the platter and ate a delicious meal. Scarcely was it finished when a heavy drowsiness fell upon her, and, unable to sustain herself on her feet, she presently sat down upon the door-stone. Leaning her head against the framework of the door, she was soon in a deep sleep, or trance. So she was found.

"Whimsical, obstinate little girl!" said the colonel, putting his hand on the beautiful slumbering head. And taking her in his arms he carried her into a chamber which had been (say the story-tellers) nothing but a bare and sorry closet in the morning but which was now fitted up with Oriental splendour. And here on a luxurious couch she was laid, with a crimson coverlet wrapping her feet. And here in the tempered light coming through jewelled glass, where yesterday had been a coarse rough-hung window, her father looked his last upon her lovely face.

The colonel returned to his host and friends, and by-and-by the whole party sallied forth to see the after-glare of a fierce sunset swathing the hills in flames. It was not until they had gone some distance that Coll Dhu remembered to go back and fetch his telescope. He was not long absent. But he was absent long enough to enter that glowing chamber with a stealthy step, to throw a light chain around the neck of the sleeping girl, and to slip among the folds of her dress the hideous glittering burragh-bos.

After he had gone away again, Pexie came stealing to the door, and, opening it a little, sat down on the mat outside, with her cloak wrapped round her. An hour passed, and Evleen Blake still slept, her breathing scarcely stirring the deadly bauble on her breast. After that, she began to murmur and moan, and Pexie pricked up her ears. Presently a sound in the room told her that the victim was awake and had risen. Then Pexie put her face to the aperture of the door and looked in, gave a howl of dismay, and fled from the house, to be seen in that country no more.

The light was fading among the hills, and the ramblers were

returning towards the Devil's Inn, when a group of ladies who were considerably in advance of the rest, met Evleen Blake advancing towards them on the heath, with her hair disordered as by sleep, and no covering on her head. They noticed something bright, like gold, shifting and glancing with the motion of her figure. There had been some jesting among them about Evleen's fancy for falling asleep on the door-step instead of coming in to dinner, and they advanced laughing, to rally her on the subject. But she stared at them in a strange way, as if she did not know them, and passed on. Her friends were rather offended, and commented on her fantastic humour; only one looked after her, and got laughed at by her companions for expressing uneasiness on the wilful young lady's account.

So they kept their way, and the solitary figure went fluttering on, the white robe blushing, and the fatal burragh-bos glittering in the reflection from the sky. A hare crossed her path, and she laughed out loudly, and clapping her hands, sprang after it. Then she stopped and asked questions of the stones, striking them with her open palm because they would not answer. (An amazed little herd sitting behind a rock, witnessed these strange proceedings.) By-and-by she began to call after the birds, in a wild shrill way startling the echoes of the hills as she went along. A party of gentlemen returning by a dangerous path, heard the unusual sound and stopped to listen.

"What is that?" asked one.

"A young eagle," said Coll Dhu, whose face had become livid; "they often give such cries."

"It was uncommonly like a woman's voice!" was the reply; and immediately another wild note rang towards them from the rocks above; a bare saw-like ridge, shelving away to some distance ahead, and projecting one hungry tooth over an abyss. A few more moments and they saw Evleen Blake's light figure fluttering out towards this dizzy point.

"My Evleen!" cried the colonel, recognising his daughter, "she is mad to venture on such a spot!"

"Mad!" repeated Coll Dhu. And then dashed off to the rescue with all the might and swiftness of his powerful limbs.

When he drew near her, Evleen had almost reached the verge

of the terrible rock. Very cautiously he approached her, his object being to seize her in his strong arms before she was aware of his presence, and carry her many yards away from the spot of danger. But in a fatal moment Evleen turned her head and saw him. One wild ringing cry of hate and horror, which startled the very eagles and scattered a flight of curlews above her head, broke from her lips. A step backward brought her within a foot of death.

One desperate though wary stride, and she was struggling in Coll's embrace. One glance in her eyes, and he saw that he was striving with a mad woman. Back, back, she dragged him, and he had nothing to grasp by. The rock was slippery and his shod feet would not cling to it. Back, back! A hoarse panting, a dire swinging to and fro; and then the rock was standing naked against the sky, no one was there, and Coll Dhu and Evleen Blake lay shattered far below.

IRREMEDIABLE*

Ella D'Arcy
(1856–1937)

A young man strolled along a country road one August evening
after a long delicious day—a day of that blessed idleness
the man of leisure never knows: one must be a bank clerk forty-
nine weeks out of the fifty-two before one can really appreciate
the exquisite enjoyment of doing nothing for twelve hours at a
stretch. Willoughby had spent the morning lounging about a
sunny rickyard; then, when the heat grew unbearable, he had
retreated to an orchard, where, lying on his back in the long cool
grass, he had traced the pattern of the apple-leaves diapered
above him upon the summer sky; now that the heat of the day was
over he had come to roam whither sweet fancy led him, to lean
over gates, view the prospect, and meditate upon the pleasures of
a well-spent day. Five such days had already passed over his head,
fifteen more remained to him. Then farewell to freedom and
clean country air! Back again to London and another year's toil.

He came to a gate on the right of the road. Behind it a footpath meandered up over a grassy slope. The sheep nibbling on
its summit cast long shadows down the hill almost to his feet.
Road and fieldpath were equally new to him, but the latter
offered greener attractions; he vaulted lightly over the gate and
had so little idea he was taking thus the first step towards ruin
that he began to whistle "White Wings" from pure joy of life.

*From *The Yellow Book: An Illustrated Quarterly* (1894).

185

The sheep stopped feeding and raised their heads to stare at him from pale-lashed eyes; first one and then another broke into a startled run, until there was a sudden woolly stampede of the entire flock. When Willoughby gained the ridge from which they had just scattered, he came in sight of a woman sitting on a stile at the further end of the field. As he advanced towards her he saw that she was young, and that she was not what is called "a lady"—of which he was glad: an earlier episode in his career having indissolubly associated in his mind ideas of feminine refinement with those of feminine treachery.

He thought it probable this girl would be willing to dispense with the formalities of an introduction, and that he might venture with her on some pleasant foolish chat.

As she made no movement to let him pass he stood still, and, looking at her, began to smile.

She returned his gaze from unabashed dark eyes, and then laughed, showing teeth white, sound, and smooth as split hazelnuts.

"Do you wanter get over?" she remarked familiarly.

"I'm afraid I can't without disturbing you."

"Dontcher think you're much better where you are?" said the girl, on which Willoughby hazarded:

"You mean to say looking at you? Well, perhaps I am!"

The girl at this laughed again, but nevertheless dropped herself down into the further field; then, leaning her arms upon the cross-bar, she informed the young man: "No, I don't wanter spoil your walk. You were goin' p'raps ter Beacon Point? It's very pretty that wye."

"I was going nowhere in particular," he replied; "just exploring, so to speak. I'm a stranger in these parts."

"How funny! Imer stranger here too. I only come down larse Friday to stye with a Naunter mine in Horton. Are you stying in Horton?"

Willoughby told her he was not in Orton, but at Povey Cross Farm out in the other direction.

"Oh, Mrs. Payne's, ain't it? I've heard aunt speak ovver. She takes summer boarders, don't chee? I egspeck you come from London, heh?"

"And I expect you come from London too?" said Willoughby, recognizing the familiar accent.

"You're as sharp as a needle," cried the girl with her unrestrained laugh; "so I do. I'm here for a hollerday 'cos I was so done up with the work and the hot weather. I don't look as though I'd bin ill, do I? But I was, though: for it was just stiflin' hot up in our workrooms all larse month, an' tailorin's awful hard work at the bester times."

Willoughby felt a sudden accession of interest in her. Like many intelligent young men, he had dabbled a little in Socialism, and at one time had wandered among the dispossessed; but since then, had caught up and held loosely the new doctrine—it is a good and fitting thing that woman also should earn her bread by the sweat of her brow. Always in reference to the woman who, fifteen months before, had treated him ill; he had said to himself that even the breaking of stones in the road should be considered a more feminine employment than the breaking of hearts.

He gave way therefore to a movement of friendliness for this working daughter of the people, and joined her on the other side of the stile in token of his approval. She, twisting round to face him, leaned now with her back against the bar, and the sunset fires lent a fleeting glory to her face. Perhaps she guessed how becoming the light was, for she took off her hat and let it touch to gold the ends and fringes of her rough abundant hair. Thus and at this moment she made an agreeable picture, to which stood as background all the beautiful, wooded Southshire view.

"You don't really mean to say you are a tailoress?" said Willoughby, with a sort of eager compassion.

"I do, though! An' I've bin one ever since I was fourteen. Look at my fingers if you don't b'lieve me."

She put out her right hand, and he took hold of it, as he was expected to do. The finger-ends were frayed and blackened by needle-pricks, but the hand itself was plump, moist, and not unshapely. She meanwhile examined Willoughby's fingers enclosing hers.

"It's easy ter see you've never done no work!" she said, half admiring, half envious. "I s'pose you're a tip-top swell, ain't you?"

"Oh, yes! I'm a tremendous swell indeed!" said Willoughby, ironically. He thought of his hundred and thirty pounds' salary; and he mentioned his position in the British and Colonial Banking house, without shedding much illumination on her mind, for she insisted:

"Well, anyhow, you're a gentleman. I've often wished I was a lady. It must be so nice ter wear fine clo'es an' never have ter do any work all day long."

Willoughby thought it innocent of the girl to say this; it reminded him of his own notion as a child—that kings and queens put on their crowns the first thing on rising in the morning. His cordiality rose another degree.

"If being a gentleman means having nothing to do," said he, smiling, "I can certainly lay no claim to the title. Life isn't all beer and skittles with me, any more than it is with you. Which is the better reason for enjoying the present moment, don't you think? Suppose, now, like a kind little girl, you were to show me the way to Beacon Point, which you say is so pretty?"

She required no further persuasion. As he walked beside her through the upland fields where the dusk was beginning to fall, and the white evening moths to emerge from their daytime hiding-places, she asked him many personal questions, most of which he thought fit to parry. Taking no offence thereat, she told him, instead, much concerning herself and her family. Thus he learned her name was Esther Stables, that she and her people lived Whitechapel way; that her father was seldom sober, and her mother always ill; and that the aunt with whom she was staying kept the post-office and general shop in Orton village. He learned, too, that Esther was discontented with life in general; that, though she hated being at home, she found the country dreadfully dull; and that, consequently, she was extremely glad to have made his acquaintance. But what he chiefly realized when they parted was that he had spent a couple of pleasant hours talking nonsense with a girl who was natural, simple-minded, and entirely free from that repellently protective atmosphere with which a woman of the 'classes' so carefully surrounds herself. He and Esther had 'made friends' with the ease and rapidity of children before they have learned the dread meaning of 'etiquette,' and they said good night, not without some talk of meeting each other again.

Obliged to breakfast at a quarter to eight in town, Willoughby was always luxuriously late when in the country, where he took his meals also in leisurely fashion, often reading from a book propped up on the table before him. But the morning after his meeting with Esther Stables found him less disposed to read than usual. Her image obtruded itself upon the printed page, and at length grew so importunate he came to the conclusion the only way to lay it was to confront it with the girl herself.

Wanting some tobacco, he saw a good reason for going into Orton. Esther had told him he could get tobacco and everything else at her aunt's. He found the post-office to be one of the first houses in the widely spaced village street. In front of the cottage was a small garden ablaze with old-fashioned flowers; and in a large garden at one side were apple-trees, raspberry and cur-rant bushes, and six thatched beehives on a bench. The bowed windows of the little shop were partly screened by sunblinds; nevertheless the lower panes still displayed a heterogeneous collection of goods—lemons, hanks of yarn, white linen buttons upon blue cards, sugar cones, churchwarden pipes, and tobacco jars. A letter-box opened its narrow mouth low down in one wall, and over the door swung the sign, "Stamps and money-order office," in black letters on white enamelled iron.

The interior of the shop was cool and dark. A second glass-door at the back permitted Willoughby to see into a small sitting-room, and out again through a low and square-paned window to the sunny landscape beyond. Silhouetted against the light were the heads of two women; the rough young head of yesterday's Esther, the lean outline and bugled cap of Esther's aunt.

It was the latter who at the jingling of the doorbell rose from her work and came forward to serve the customer; but the girl, with much mute meaning in her eyes, and a finger laid upon her smiling mouth, followed behind. Her aunt heard her footfall. "What do you want here, Esther?" she said with thin disap-proval; "get back to your sewing."

Esther gave the young man a signal seen only by him and slipped out into the side-garden, where he found her when his purchases were made. She leaned over the privet-hedge to intercept him as he passed.

"Aunt's an awful ole maid," she remarked apologetically; "I b'lieve she'd never let me say a word to enny one if she could help it."

"So you got home all right last night?" Willoughby inquired; "what did your aunt say to you?"

"Oh, she arst me where I'd been, and I tolder a lotter lies." Then, with a woman's intuition, perceiving that this speech jarred, Esther made haste to add, "She's so dreadful hard on me. I dursn't tell her I'd been with a gentleman or she'd never have let me out alone again."

"And at present I suppose you'll be found somewhere about that same stile every evening?" said Willoughby foolishly, for he really did not much care whether he met her again or not. Now he was actually in her company, he was surprised at himself for having given her a whole morning's thought; yet the eagerness of her answer flattered him, too.

"Tonight I can't come, worse luck! It's Thursday, and the shops here close of a Thursday at five. I'll havter keep aunt company. But tomorrer? I can be there tomorrer. You'll come, say?"

"Esther!" cried a vexed voice, and the precise, right-minded aunt emerged through a row of raspberry-bushes; "whatever are you thinking about, delayin' the gentleman in this fashion?" She was full of rustic and official civility for "the gentleman," but indignant with her niece. "I don't want none of your London manners down here," Willoughby heard her say as she marched the girl off.

He himself was not sorry to be released from Esther's too friendly eyes, and he spent an agreeable evening over a book, and this time managed to forget her completely.

Though he remembered her first thing next morning, it was to smile wisely and determine he would not meet her again. Yet by dinner-time the day seemed long; why, after all, should he not meet her? By tea-time prudence triumphed anew—no, he would not go. Then he drank his tea hastily and set off for the stile.

Esther was waiting for him. Expectation had given an additional colour to her cheeks, and her red-brown hair showed here
and there a beautiful glint of gold. He could not help admiring
the vigorous way in which it waved and twisted, or the little curls
which grew at the nape of her neck, tight and close as those of
a young lamb's fleece. Her neck here was admirable, too, in its
smooth creaminess; and when her eyes lighted up with such
evident pleasure at his coming, how avoid the conviction she
was a good and nice girl after all?

He proposed they should go down into the little copse on the
right, where they would be less disturbed by the occasional
passer-by. Here, seated on a felled tree-trunk, Willoughby
began that bantering, silly, meaningless form of conversation
known among the 'classes' as flirting. He had but the wish to
make himself agreeable, and to while away the time. Esther,
however, misunderstood him.

Willoughby's hand lay palm downwards on his knee, and she,
noticing a ring which he wore on his little finger, took hold of it.

"What a funny ring!" she said; "let's look?"

To disembarrass himself of her touch, he pulled the ring off
and gave it her to examine.

"What's that ugly dark green stone?" she asked.

"It's called a sardonyx."

"What's it for?" she said, turning it about.

"It's a signet ring, to seal letters with."

"An' there's a sorter king's head scratched on it, an' some
writin' too, only I carnt make it out?"

"It isn't the head of a king, although it wears a crown,"
Willoughby explained, "but the head and bust of a Saracen
against whom my ancestor of many hundred years ago went to
fight in the Holy Land. And the words cut round it are our
motto, 'Vertue vauncet,' which means virtue prevails."

Willoughby may have displayed some accession of dignity in
giving this bit of family history, for Esther fell into uncontrolled
laughter, at which he was much displeased. And when the girl
made as though she would put the ring on her own finger, asking, "Shall I keep it?" he coloured up with sudden annoyance.

"It was only my fun!" said Esther hastily, and gave him the

ring back, but his cordiality was gone. He felt no inclination to renew the idle-word pastime, said it was time to go, and, swinging his cane vexedly, struck off the heads of the flowers and the weeds as he went. Esther walked by his side in complete silence, a phenomenon of which he presently became conscious. He felt rather ashamed of having shown temper.

"Well, here's your way home," said he with an effort at friendliness. "Goodbye; we've had a nice evening anyhow. It was pleasant down there in the woods, eh?"

He was astonished to see her eyes soften with tears, and to hear the real emotion in her voice as she answered, "It was just heaven down there with you until you turned so funny-like. What had I done to make you cross? Say you forgive me, do!"

"Silly child!" said Willoughby, completely mollified, "I'm not the least angry. There, goodbye!" and like a fool he kissed her.

He anathematized his folly in the white light of next morning, and, remembering the kiss he had given her, repented it very sincerely. He had an uncomfortable suspicion she had not received it in the same spirit in which it had been bestowed, but, attaching more serious meaning to it, would build expectations thereon which must be left unfulfilled. It was best indeed not to meet her again; for he acknowledged to himself that, though he only half liked, and even slightly feared her, there was a certain attraction about her—was it in her dark unflinching eyes or in her very red lips?—which might lead him into greater follies still.

Thus it came about that for two successive evenings Esther waited for him in vain, and on the third evening he said to himself, with a grudging relief, that by this time she had probably transferred her affections to someone else.

It was Saturday, the second Saturday since he left town. He spent the day about the farm, contemplated the pigs, inspected the feeding of the stock, and assisted at the afternoon milking. Then at evening, with a refilled pipe, he went for a long lean over the west gate, while he traced fantastic pictures and wove romances in the glories of the sunset clouds.

He watched the colours glow from gold to scarlet, change to crimson, sink at last to sad purple reefs and isles, when the sudden consciousness of someone being near him made him turn round. There stood Esther, and her eyes were full of eagerness and anger.

"Why have you never been to the stile again?" she asked him. "You promised to come faithful, and you never came. Why have you not kep' your promise? Why? Why?" she persisted, stamping her foot because Willoughby remained silent.

What could he say? Tell her she had no business to follow him like this; or own, what was, unfortunately, the truth, he was just a little glad to see her?

"Praps you don't care for me any more?" she said. "Well, why did you kiss me, then?"

Why, indeed! thought Willoughby, marvelling at his own idiocy, and yet—such is the inconsistency of man—not wholly without the desire to kiss her again. And while he looked at her she suddenly flung herself down on the hedge-bank at his feet and burst into tears. She did not cover up her face, but simply pressed one cheek down upon the grass while the water poured from her eyes with astonishing abundance. Willoughby saw the dry earth turn dark and moist as it drank the tears in. This, his first experience of Esther's powers of weeping, distressed him horribly; never in his life before had he seen anyone weep like that, he should not have believed such a thing possible; he was alarmed, too, lest she should be noticed from the house. He opened the gate; "Esther!" he begged, "don't cry. Come out here, like a dear girl, and let us talk sensibly."

Because she stumbled, unable to see her way through wet eyes, he gave her his hand, and they found themselves in a field of corn, walking along the narrow grass-path that skirted it, in the shadow of the hedgerow.

"What is there to cry about because you have not seen me for two days?" he began; "why, Esther, we are only strangers, after all. When we have been at home a week or two we shall scarcely remember each other's names."

Esther sobbed at intervals, but her tears had ceased. "It's fine for you to talk of home," she said to this. "You've got something that is a home, I s'pose? But me! my home's like hell, with nothing but quarrellin' and cursin', and a father who beats us whether sober or drunk. Yes!" she repeated shrewdly, seeing the lively disgust on Willoughby's face, "he beat me, all ill as I was, jus' before I come away. I could show you the bruises on my arms still. And now to go back there after knowin' you! It'll be worse than ever. I can't endure it, and I won't! I'll put an end to it or myself somehow, I swear!"

"But my poor Esther, how can I help it? what can I do?" said Willoughby. He was greatly moved, full of wrath with her father, with all the world which makes women suffer. He had suffered himself at the hands of a woman and severely, but this, instead of hardening his heart, had only rendered it the more supple. And yet he had a vivid perception of the peril in which he stood. An interior voice urged him to break away, to seek safety in flight even at the cost of appearing cruel or ridiculous; so, coming to a point in the field where an elm-hole jutted out across the path, he saw with relief he could now withdraw his hand from the girl's, since they must walk singly to skirt round it.

Esther took a step in advance, stopped and suddenly turned to face him; she held out her two hands and her face was very near his own.

"Don't you care for me one little bit?" she said wistfully, and surely sudden madness fell upon him. For he kissed her again, he kissed her many times, he took her in his arms, and pushed all thoughts of the consequences far from him.

But when, an hour later, he and Esther stood by the last gate on the road to Orton, some of these consequences were already calling loudly to him.

"You know I have only £130 a year?" he told her; "it's no very brilliant prospect for you to marry me on that."

For he had actually offered her marriage, although to the mediocre man such a proceeding must appear incredible, uncalled for. But to Willoughby, overwhelmed with sadness and remorse, it seemed the only atonement possible.

Sudden exultation leaped at Esther's heart.

"Oh! I'm used to managing" she told him confidently, and mentally resolved to buy herself, so soon as she was married, a black feather boa, such as she had coveted last winter.

Willoughby spent the remaining days of his holiday in thinking out and planning with Esther the details of his return to

London and her own, the secrecy to be observed, the necessary legal steps to be taken, and the quiet suburb in which they would set up housekeeping. And, so successfully did he carry out his arrangements, that within five weeks from the day on which he had first met Esther Stables, he and she came out one morning from a church in Highbury, husband and wife. It was a mellow September day, the streets were filled with sunshine, and Willoughby, in reckless high spirits, imagined he saw a reflection of his own gaiety on the indifferent faces of the passersby. There being no one else to perform the office, he congratulated himself very warmly, and Esther's frequent laughter filled in the pauses of the day.

Three months later Willoughby was dining with a friend, and the hour-hand of the clock nearing ten, the host no longer resisted the guest's growing anxiety to be gone. He arose and exchanged with him good wishes and goodbyes.

"Marriage is evidently a most successful institution," said he, half-jesting, half-sincere; "you almost make me inclined to go and get married myself. Confess now your thoughts have been at home the whole evening."

Willoughby thus addressed turned red to the roots of his hair, but did not deny it.

The other laughed. "And very commendable they should be," he continued, "since you are scarcely, so to speak, out of your honeymoon."

With a social smile on his lips, Willoughby calculated a moment before replying, "I have been married exactly three months and three days." Then, after a few words respecting their next meeting, the two shook hands and parted—the young host to finish the evening with books and pipe, the young husband to set out on a twenty minutes' walk to his home.

It was a cold, clear December night following a day of rain. A touch of frost in the air had dried the pavements, and Willoughby's footfall ringing upon the stones re-echoed down the empty suburban street. Above his head was a dark, remote sky thickly powdered with stars, and as he turned westward Alpherat hung for a moment "comme le point sur un *i*," over the slender spire of St. John's. But he was insensible to the worlds about him; he was absorbed in his own thoughts, and these, as his friend had surmised, were entirely with his wife. For Esther's face was always before his eyes, her voice was always in his ears, she filled the universe for him; yet only four months ago he had never seen her, had never heard her name. This was the curious part of it—here in December he found himself the husband of a girl who was completely dependent upon him not only for food, clothes, and lodging, but for her present happiness, her whole future life; and last July he had been scarcely more than a boy himself, with no greater care on his mind than the pleasant difficulty of deciding where he should spend his annual three weeks' holiday.

But it is events, not months or years, which age. Willoughby, who was only twenty-six, remembered his youth as a sometime companion irrevocably lost to him; its vague, delightful hopes were now crystallized into definite ties, and its happy irresponsibilities displaced by a sense of care, inseparable perhaps from the most fortunate of marriages.

As he reached the street in which he lodged his pace involuntarily slackened. While still some distance off, his eye sought out and distinguished the windows of the room in which Esther awaited him. Through the broken slats of the Venetian blinds he could see the yellow gaslight within. The parlour beneath was in darkness; his landlady had evidently gone to bed, there being no light over the hall-door either. In some apprehension he consulted his watch under the last street-lamp he passed, to find comfort in assuring himself it was only ten minutes after ten. He let himself in with his latch-key, hung up his hat and overcoat by the sense of touch, and, groping his way upstairs, opened the door of the first floor sitting-room.

At the table in the centre of the room sat his wife, leaning upon her elbows, her two hands thrust up into her ruffled hair; spread out before her was a crumpled yesterday's newspaper, and so interested was she to all appearance in its contents that she neither spoke nor looked up as Willoughby entered. Around her were the still uncleared tokens of her last meal: tea-slops, bread-crumbs, and an egg-shell crushed to fragments upon a plate, which was one of those trifles that set Willoughby's teeth on edge—whenever his wife ate an egg she persisted in turning the egg-cup upside down upon the tablecloth, and pounding the shell to pieces in her plate with her spoon.

The room was repulsive in its disorder. The one lighted burner of the gaselier, turned too high, hissed up into a long tongue of flame. The fire smoked feebly under a newly administered shovelful of "slack," and a heap of ashes and cinders littered the grate. A pair of walking boots, caked in dry mud, lay on the hearth-rug just where they had been thrown off. On the mantelpiece, amidst a dozen other articles which had no business there, was a bedroom-candlestick; and every single article of furniture stood crookedly out of its place.

Willoughby took in the whole intolerable picture, and yet spoke with kindliness. "Well, Esther! I'm not so late, after all. I hope you did not find the time dull by yourself?" Then he explained the reason of his absence. He had met a friend he had not seen for a couple of years, who had insisted on taking him home to dine.

His wife gave no sign of having heard him; she kept her eyes riveted on the paper before her.

"You received my wire, of course," Willoughby went on, "and did not wait?"

Now she crushed the newspaper up with a passionate movement, and threw it from her. She raised her head, showing cheeks blazing with anger, and dark, sullen, unflinching eyes.

"I did wyte then!" she cried. "I wyted till near eight before I got your old telegraph! I s'pose that's what you call the manners of a 'gentleman,' to keep your wife mewed up here, while you go gallivantin' off with your fine friends?"

Whenever Esther was angry, which was often, she taunted Willoughby with being "a gentleman," although this was the precise point about him which at other times found most favour in her eyes. But tonight she was envenomed by the idea he had been enjoying himself without her, stung by fear lest he should have been in company with some other woman.

Willoughby, hearing the taunt, resigned himself to the inevitable. Nothing that he could do might now avert the breaking storm; all his words would only be twisted into fresh griefs.

But sad experience had taught him that to take refuge in silence was more fatal still. When Esther was in such a mood as this it was best to supply the fire with fuel, that, through the very violence of the conflagration, it might the sooner burn itself out.

So he said what soothing things he could, and Esther caught them up, disfigured them, and flung them back at him with scorn. She reproached him with no longer caring for her; she vituperated the conduct of his family in never taking the smallest notice of her marriage; and she detailed the insolence of the landlady who had told her that morning she pitied "poor Mr. Willoughby," and had refused to go out and buy herrings for Esther's early dinner.

Every affront or grievance, real or imaginary, since the day she and Willoughby had first met, she poured forth with a fluency due to frequent repetition, for, with the exception of today's added injuries, Willoughby had heard the whole litany many times before.

While she raged and he looked at her, he remembered he had once thought her pretty. He had seen beauty in her rough brown hair, her strong colouring, her full red mouth. He fell into musing . . . a woman may lack beauty, he told himself, and yet be loved. . . .

Meanwhile Esther reached white heats of passion, and the strain could no longer be sustained. She broke into sobs and began to shed tears with the facility peculiar to her. In a moment her face was all wet with the big drops which rolled down her cheeks faster and faster, and fell with audible splashes on to the table, on to her lap, on to the floor. To this tearful abundance, formerly a surprising spectacle, Willoughby was now acclimatized; but the remnant of chivalrous feeling not yet extinguished in his bosom forbade him to sit stolidly by while a woman wept, without seeking to console her. As on previous occasions, his peace-overtures were eventually accepted. Esther's tears gradually ceased to flow, she began to exhibit a sort of compunction, she wished to be forgiven, and, with the kiss of reconciliation, passed into a phase of demonstrative affection perhaps more trying to Willoughby's patience than all that had preceded it.

"You don't love me?" she questioned, "I'm sure you don't love me?" she reiterated; and he asseverated that he loved her until he despised himself. Then at last, only half satisfied, but wearied out with vexation—possibly, too, with a movement of pity at the sight of his haggard face—she consented to leave him. Only, what was he going to do? she asked suspiciously; write those rubbishing stories of his? Well, he must promise not to stay up more than half-an-hour at the latest—only until he had smoked one pipe.

Willoughby promised, as he would have promised anything on earth to secure to himself a half-hour's peace and solitude. Esther groped for her slippers, which were kicked off under the table; scratched four or five matches along the box and threw them away before she succeeded in lighting her candle; set it down again to contemplate her tear-swollen reflection in the chimney-glass, and burst out laughing.

"What a fright I do look, to be sure!" she remarked complacently, and again thrust her two hands up through her disordered curls. Then, holding the candle at such an angle that the grease ran over on to the carpet, she gave Willoughby another vehement kiss and trailed out of the room with an ineffectual attempt to close the door behind her. Willoughby got up to shut it himself, and wondered why it was that Esther never did anyone mortal thing efficiently or well. Good God! how irritable he felt. It was impossible to write. He must find an outlet for his impatience, rend or mend something. He began to straighten the room, but a wave of disgust came over him before the task was fairly commenced. What was the use? Tomorrow all would be bad as before. What was the use of doing anything? He sat down by the table and leaned his head upon his hands.

The past came back to him in pictures: his boyhood's past first of all. He saw again the old home, every inch of which was familiar to him as his own name; he reconstructed in his thought all the old well-known furniture, and replaced it precisely as it had stood long ago. He passed again a childish finger over the rough surface of the faded Utrecht velvet chairs, and smelled again the strong fragrance of the white lilac tree, blowing in through the open parlour-window. He savoured anew the pleasant mental atmosphere produced by the dainty neatness of cultured women, the companionship of a few good pictures, of a few good books. Yet this home had been broken up years ago, the dear familiar things had been scattered far and wide, never to find themselves under the same roof again; and from those near relatives who still remained to him he lived now hopelessly estranged.

Then came the past of his first love-dream, when he worshipped at the feet of Nora Beresford, and, with the whole-heartedness of the true fanatic, clothed his idol with every imaginable attribute of virtue and tenderness. To this day there remained a secret shrine in his heart wherein the Lady of his young ideal was still enthroned, although it was long since he had come to perceive she had nothing whatever in common with the Nora of reality. For the real Nora he had no longer any sentiment, she had passed altogether out of his life and thoughts; and yet, so permanent is all influence, whether good or evil, that the effect she wrought upon his character remained. He recognized tonight that her treatment of him in the past did not count for nothing among the various factors which had determined his fate.

Now, the past of only last year returned, and, strangely enough, this seemed farther removed from him than all the rest. He had been particularly strong, well, and happy this time last year. Nora was dismissed from his mind, and he had thrown all his energies into his work. His tastes were sane and simple, and his dingy, furnished rooms had become through habit very pleasant to him. In being his own, they were invested with a greater charm than another man's castle. Here he had smoked and studied, here he had made many a glorious voyage into the land of books. Many a homecoming, too, rose up before him out of the dark ungenial streets, to a clear blazing fire, a neatly laid cloth, an evening of ideal enjoyment; many a summer twilight when he mused at the open window, plunging his gaze deep into the recesses of his neighbour's lime-tree, where the unseen sparrows chattered with such unflagging gaiety.

He had always been given to much daydreaming, and it was in the silence of his rooms of an evening that he turned his phantasmal adventures into stories for the magazines; here had come to him many an editorial refusal, but here, too, he had received the news of his first unexpected success. All his happiest memories were embalmed in those shabby, badly-furnished rooms.

Now all was changed. Now might there be no longer any soft indulgence of the hour's mood. His rooms and everything he owned belonged now to Esther, too. She had objected to most of his photographs, and had removed them. She hated books, and were he ever so ill-advised as to open one in her presence, she immediately began to talk, no matter how silent or how sullen her previous mood had been. If he read aloud to her she either yawned despairingly, or was tickled into laughter where there was no reasonable cause. At first Willoughby had tried to educate her, and had gone hopefully to the task. It is so natural to think you may make what you will of the woman who loves you. But Esther had no wish to improve. She evinced all the self-satisfaction of an illiterate mind. To her husband's gentle admonitions she replied with brevity that she thought her way quite as good as his; or, if he didn't approve of her pronunciation, he might do the other thing, she was too old to go to school again. He gave up the attempt, and, with humiliation at his previous fatuity, perceived that it was folly to expect that a few weeks of his companionship could alter or pull up the impressions of years, or rather of generations.

Yet here he paused to admit a curious thing: it was not only Esther's bad habits which vexed him, but habits quite unblameworthy in themselves which he never would have noticed in another, irritated him in her. He disliked her manner of standing, of walking, of sitting in a chair, of folding her hands. Like a lover, he was conscious of her proximity without seeing her. Like a lover, too, his eyes followed her every movement, his ear noted every change in her voice. But then, instead of being charmed by everything as the lover is, everything jarred upon him.

What was the meaning of this? Tonight the anomaly pressed upon him: he reviewed his position. Here was he, quite a young man, just twenty-six years of age, married to Esther, and bound to live with her so long as life should last—twenty, forty, perhaps fifty years more. Every day of those years to be spent in her society; he and she face to face, soul to soul; they two alone amid all

the whirling, busy, indifferent world. So near together in sem-
blance; in truth, so far apart as regards all that makes life dear.

Willoughby groaned. From the woman he did not love, whom
he had never loved, he might not again go free; so much he recognized. The feeling he had once entertained for Esther,
strange compound of mistaken chivalry and flattered vanity, was
long since extinct; but what, then, was the sentiment with which
she inspired him? For he was not indifferent to her—no, never
for one instant could he persuade himself he was indifferent,
never for one instant could he banish her from his thoughts. His
mind's eye followed her during his hours of absence as pertina-
ciously as his bodily eye dwelt upon her actual presence. She
was the principal object of the universe to him, the centre
around which his wheel of life revolved with an appalling
fidelity.

What did it mean? What could it mean? he asked himself with
anguish.

And the sweat broke out upon his forehead and his hands
grew cold, for on a sudden the truth lay there like a written word
upon the tablecloth before him. This woman, whom he had
taken to himself for better, for worse, inspired him with a passion, intense indeed, all-masterful, soul-subduing as Love
itself. . . . But when he understood the terror of his Hatred, he
laid his head upon his arms and wept, not facile tears like
Esther's, but tears wrung out from his agonizing, unavailing
regret.

M'NEILLS' TIGER-SHEEP*
Jane Barlow
(1857–1917)

The feud between the Timothy O'Farrells and Neil M'Neills at Meenaclure was not of very long standing, for the dowager Mrs. O'Farrell and the elder Mrs. M'Neill, who had been by no means young when it began, were still to the fore, and not yet even considered to have attained "a great ould age intirely." This seems a mere mushroom-growth compared with some of our family quarrels, which have been handed down from father to son through so many generations that everybody regards them as a part of the established order of things in the world of their parish. Still, to the younger people, who had been but children at its birth, it seemed to have lasted a long while, and their juniors would have found a different state of affairs almost unthinkable. For them the origin of the enmity had already begun to loom dimly through a mist of tradition, which would tend as time went on to grow vaguer and falser, until at length nobody would be left who could give a clear account of what it was all about. So far, however, all the neighbours who were "any age to speak of" knew the rights of the case well enough. And this is what had happened.

It was a cloudless midsummer evening, perhaps twenty years back—nobody is overparticular about chronology at Meenaclure—and all the dogs and children were away out on the wild land

*From *A Creel of Irish Stories*, 1898.

towards the mountains, minding the sheep, to keep them from coming home and eating up the crops. From April to October that was every year their occupation, and a very engrossing one they found it. For the scraggy little sheep of the district are endowed with an appetite for green food worthy of any locust, added to a cleverness at taking fences that would discredit no hunter; and this makes them a constant peril to the painfully-tilled fields, whose produce they threaten like a sort of visibly-embodied blight. Luckily, it is one whose ravages can be averted by timely precautions; and therefore, as soon as potatoes are *kibbed,* and oats sown, the sheep are driven off to a discreet distance on the moors, whence they are prevented from returning by a strong cordon of wary mongrels and active spalpeens. The children of such places as Meenaclure find the sunnier half of the year a season of perpetual school-vacation, when the longest days are watched out to their last lingering glimmer among the tussocks and boulders, so that the morning seems to have begun ages and ages ago by the time one straggles home, three-parts asleep on one's feet, the flocks having already betaken them-selves to completer repose, or, recognising the unattainability of young green oats, having set their nibbling mouths safely up the swarded hill-slopes. For that night the fields may lie secure from marauding tresspassers.

On this particular day, however, owing to some remissness of the young M'Neills and their shrewd-visaged dog, who were all led away by the excitement of a rabbit-hunt, one of the sheep under their charge successfully eluded observation, and broke through the line, with two comrades presently pattering after her. With a wiliness well masked by her expression of meek fatu-ity, she slunk along unseen in furzy folds of the broken ground, and late in the afternoon had arrived near the forbidden pas-tures. There she lurked furtively for a while, fully determined to hop over the fence of Timothy O'Farrell's oatfield, the very first moment that nobody seemed to be about. This opportunity soon occurred, as the O'Farrells' holding lies somewhat apart in a slight hollow, which secludes it from the little cabin-cluster standing a bit higher round a curve in the long green glacis-like foot-slope of Slieve Gowran.

Thus it came to pass that when Timothy O'Farrell returned from turf-cutting on the bog with his sister Margaret and his brothers Hugh and Patrick, the first thing they noticed was an object like a movable grey boulder cropping up on the delicate sheeny surface of their oat-patch. Whereupon: "Be the powers of smoke," said Timothy, "if there isn't them bastes in it agin."

"Three of them, no less," said Margaret.

"M'Neills', you may bet your brogues," said Hugh.

"The divil doubt it," said Timothy. Patrick, who was a youth of action rather than speech, had already plunged head-foremost towards the scene of the trespass.

There were several reasons why doubts of the M'Neills' responsibility in the matter should be relegated to the divil. In the first place, the M'Neills owned more sheep than anybody else at Meenaclure, whereas the O'Farrells owned none; and secondly, the O'Farrells had sown an unusually extensive patch of oats, while the M'Neills had planted potatoes only. The tendencies of this situation are obvious. Again, the O'Farrells had more than once before undergone the like inroads, and on these occasions Neil M'Neill had not, Timothy considered, shown by any means an adequate amount of penitence. "Bedad, now," Timothy reported to his family, "he was cool enough over it. Maybe it's *his* notion of fine farmin' to graze his bastes on other people's growin' crops." A deep-rooted sentiment of respect, however, restrained him from uttering these sarcasms in public. For Timothy, though the head and father of a family, had seen not many more than a score of harvests; and Neil, a dozen years his senior, enjoyed a high reputation among the neighbours as a very knowledgeable man altogether. After the second incursion, it is true, Timothy's wrath had so far overcrowded his awe as to make him "up and tell" Neil M'Neill that "if he didn't mind his ould shows of sheep himself, he'd be apt to find somebody that'd do it in a way he mightn't like." Still, the affair went no further, and Timothy had soon reverted to his customary attitude of amicable veneration. But at this third repetition of the offence his anger could not be expected to subside so harmlessly.

Pat's shouts and flourishing gallop speedily routed the conscious-stricken sheep, and two of them whisked up the hill-side like thistledown on a brisk breeze; but the third, who was the ringleader, leaped the fence with so little judgment that she came floundering against Timothy, who grasped her dexterously by the hind-legs.

Now, to catch a Slieve Gowran sheep alive in the open is a rare and difficult feat—proverbially impossible, indeed, at Meenaclure; but Timothy and his brethren were at a loss how they should best turn this achievement of it to account. They felt that simply to let the creature go again would be a flat and unprofitable result, yet what else could they do with it? While they pondered, and their captive impotently wriggled, Hugh suddenly had an inspiration. It came to him at the sight of two large black pots, which stood beside a smouldering fire against the white end-wall of their little house. To an unenlightened observer, they might have suggested some gipsy encampment, but Hugh knew they betokened that his mother had been dyeing her yarn. The Widow O'Farrell was a great spinner, and a large part of the wool shorn in the parish travelled over her whirring wheel on its way to Fergus the weaver's loom. A few old sacks lying near the fire had contained the ingredients which she used according to an immemorial recipe. From the mottled grey lichen, *crottal*, which clothes our boulders with hues strangely like those of the fleeces browsing among them, she extracted a warm tawny brown; a flaky mass of the rusty black turf-soot supplied her with a strong yellow, and the dull-red bog-ore boiled paradoxically into black.

"Be aisy, will you, you little thief of the mischief," Hugh said to the sheep. "M'Neills' she is, sure enough; there's the mark. Musha, lads, let's give her a dab or so of what's left in the ould pots. 'Twould improve her apparance finely."

"Ay would it," said Timothy. "She's an unnathural ugly objic' of a crathur the way she is now. Bedad, they've a couple of barrels desthroyed on us."

"A few odd sthrakes of the black and yella'd make her look iligant," said Hugh. "Do you take a hould of her, Tim. Och, man, don't let her away, but lift her aisy. Maggie, did you see e'er a sign of the stick they had stirring the stuff wid? But it's apt to be cool enough agin now."

"Ah, boys dear, but it's ragin' mad M'Neills 'll be if you go for to do such a thing," Margaret said, half-scared, and blundering in her flurry on a wrong note, as she at once perceived. For her brothers promptly responded in a sort of fugal movement—

"And sure who's purvintin' of them? They're welcome, bedad, them, or the likes of them. Is it ragin'? Maybe it's raison they'll have before they're a great while oulder, musha Moyah." And they proceeded with all the greater enthusiasm to carry out their design, which became more ambitiously elaborate in the course of execution.

Early next morning, while the mountain-shadow still threw a purple cloak over the steep fields of Meenaclure, where all the dewdrops were ready to twinkle as soon as a ray reached them, and when Mrs. Neil M'Neill was preparing breakfast, which at this short-coming summer season consisted chiefly of Indian meal, her eldest daughter ran in to her with news. There was somethin', Molly said, leppin' about in the pigstye. Now, the M'Neills' stye just then stood empty, in the interval between the despatch of their last lean fat pig to Letterkenny fair and the hoped-for fall in the market-price of the wee springy which was to replace him. So Mrs. M'Neill said, "Och, blathers, child alive, what would there be in it at all?"

"But it's rustlin' in the straw—I heard it—and duntin' the door wid its head like," Molly persisted.

"Sure then, run and see what it is, honey," said her mother, who was pre-occupied with a critical stage of her porridge; and a piece of practical business on hand generally disposes us to adopt a sceptical attitude towards marvels. "Maybe one of the hins might have fluttered into it; but there's apter to not be anythin'."

Molly, whose mood was not enterprising, reinforced her courage with the company of Judy and Thady before she went to investigate; and a minute afterwards she came rushing back uttering terrified lamentations, whereof the burden seemed to be, "It's a tiger-sheep." Her report could no longer be disregarded, and the rest of the family were presently grouped round the low wall of the little lean-to shed, which did really contain an inmate of extraordinary aspect. Its form was that of a newly-shorn sheep, long-legged and lank-bodied like others of its race, but in colouring altogether exceptional. Boldly marked stripes of black and tawny yellow alternated all over it, with a brilliant symmetry not surpassed by the natural history chromograph which flamed on the wall of Rathflesk National School, and which now recurred to little Molly's mind in conjunction with the fact that the wearer of the striated skin "was a cruel, savage, wicked baste, that would be swallyin' all before it," whereupon she had shrieked "Tiger-sheep!" and fled from ravening jaws.

Her parents and grandparents, on the contrary, stood and surveyed the phenomenon with almost unutterable wrath. Traces of a human hand in its production were plain enough, for the beast had been fastened into the stye by a rope round her neck, which was further ornamented with long bracken-fronds and tufts of curiously-coloured wool, studiously grotesque. In fact, had she been mercilessly endowed with "the giftie," she would no doubt have suffered from a mortification as acute as was that of her owners, instead of trotting off quite satisfied, when once she was released and at liberty to resume her fastidious nibbling among the dewy tussocks.

"That's some divilment of the O'Farrells, and the back of me hand to the whole of them!" said Neil M'Neill, with clenched eyebrows. "Themselves and their blamed impidence, and their stinkin' brashes! The ould woman's niver done boilin' them up for her wool. It's slung about her head I wish they were, sooner than to be used for misthratin' other people's dacint bastes."

"'Deed now, thrue for you," said his mother. "Sure wasn't she tellin' me herself yesterday evenin' she'd been busy all day gettin' her yarn dyed, agin she would be knittin' the boys their socks? Gad'rin' the sut she said she was this good while. That's the way they done it—och, the vagabones!"

"It's a bad job," said old Joe M'Neill, shaking his despondent white head.

"I wouldn't ever ha' thought it of them," said Mrs. M'Neill. "On'y them boys is that terrible wild; goodness forgive them, there's no demented notion they mayn't take into their heads. But what at all could we do for the misfort'nit crather? Sure it's distressful to see her goin' about that scandalous figure. I can't abide the sight of her."

Our bogland dyes, however, are very fast, and for many a day that summer Mrs. Neil had to endure the apparition of the O'Farrells' victim, who of course became a painfully conspicuous object on the hillside, where she roamed blissfully unaware of how her owners' eyes followed her with with gloomy resentment, and of how their neighbours' children, catching up Molly's cry, shouted one to another derisively, "Och, look at M'Neills' tiger-sheep!" But long and long after the parti-coloured fleece had vanished for good and all, the effects of the outrage continued to make themselves felt in the social life of Meenaclure, where it must be owned that the inhabitants are rather prone to keep their grudges in the same time-proof wallet with their gratitudes. And the grudges, somehow, often seem to lie atop. In this case, moreover, the injury had an especial bitterness, because the M'Neills came of an old sheep-keeping class, whose little flock was an inheritance handed down, dwindling, through many generations, and whose main interests and activies had time out of mind turned upon wool, so that everything connected with it had acquired in their eyes the peculiar sanctity with which we often invest the materials and implements belonging to our own craft. A chimney-sweep has probably some feeling of disinterested regard for his bags and brushes. Accordingly, sheep were to them a serious, almost solemn subject, altogether unsuitable for a practical joke; and an insult offered to them was felt to strike at the honour of the family. Small blame to them, therefore, if, as the neighbours said, they were ragin' mad entirely, and turned a deaf ear to all pacific overtures.

The O'Farrells, to do them justice, admitted upon reflection that they had maybe gone a little beyond the beyonds, and were disposed to be apologetic and conciliatory. But when old Mrs. O'Farrell, one day meeting the two smallest M'Neills on the road, presented each of them with a pale brown egg, which she had just found in the nest of her speckled hen away down beside the river, the result merely was that her gifts were smashed into an impromptu omelet before the M'Neills' door, by the direction of the master of the house, who only wished the ould sinner had been there herself to see the way he'd serve that, or anythin' else she'd have the impidence to be sendin' into his place. And later on, when the feathery gold of the O'Farrells' oatfield had been bound in stooks, and the hobbledehoy Pat was despatched to inquire whether the M'Neills might be wantin' e'er a thrifle of straw after the thrashin' for darnin' their bit of thatch, the polite attention elicited nothing except a peremptory injunction to "quit out of that."

In taking up this attitude, the M'Neills had at first the support of their neighbours' sympathy, public opinion being that it was no thing for the O'Farrells to go do. But as time went on, people began to add occasionally that sure maybe they didn't mean any such great harm after all, and that they were only young boyoes, without as much sense among the whole of them as would keep a duck waddling straight. What was the use of being so stiff over a trifle? These magnanimous sentiments were, no doubt, strengthened by the fact that in so small a community as Meenaclure a permanent breach between any two families could not but entail some inconveniences upon all the rest. It was irksome, for instance, to bear in mind throughout a friendly chat that at the casual mention of a neighbour's name the person you were talking to would look "as bitter as sut" and freeze into grim dumbness; or to have to consider, should you wish for a loan of Widdy O'Farrell's market-basket, that you must by no means "let on" to her your intention of carrying home in it Mrs. M'Neill's grain of tea; or to be called upon to choose between the company of Neil M'Neill and Hugh O'Farrell on the way home from the fair, because neither of them, as the saying is, would look the same side of the road as the other. Such obligations lay stumbling-blocks in our daily path, and nip growths of good fellowship, and are generally embarrassing and vexatious. However, Meenaclure had to put up with this state of things for so many a long day that people learned to include it unprotestingly among their necessary evils.

Under these circumstances, it was of course only in the nature of things that the little M'Neills and O'Farrells, the smallest of whom had not been born at the time of the quarrel, should always put out their tongues at one another whenever they met. They regarded the salutation, indeed, as a sort of ceremonial observance, which could not be omitted without a sense of indecorum. Thus, one inclement autumn, when Patrick O'Farrell was no longer a hobbledehoy, but "as big a man as you'd meet goin' most roads," he went off to a *rabble,* that is, a hiring-fair, at Letterkenny, and took service for six months with a farmer away at Raphoe. On the day that he left Meenaclure, he happened, just as he was setting out, to meet Molly M'Neill, who had by this time grown into "a tall slip of a girl going on for sixteen," and they duly exchanged the customary greeting, Pat getting the better of her by at least half-an-inch of insult. But when he returned on a soft April evening, it chanced again that one of the first persons he fell in with was Molly. She was coming along between the newly-clad hedges of a narrow lane, and when he caught sight of her first he mistook her for his cousin, Norah O'Farrell, she looked so much taller than his recollections. But, on perceiving his error, he merely gave up his intention of saying, "Well, Norah, and how's yourself this great while?" and slunk past without making any demonstration whatever. Molly would hardly have noticed it, indeed, as when she saw him coming she began to minutely examine the buds on the thorn-bushes, and did not lift an eyelash while they were passing. Yet, as they went their several ways, Pat felt that he had somehow shirked a duty; and Molly, for her part, could not shake off a sense of having failed in loyalty to her family until she had relieved he conscience by announcing at home that she was "just after meetin' that great *ugly*-lookin' gomeral, Pat O'Farrell, slingein' down the road below Widdy Byrne's."

The year which followed this spring was one of bad seasons and hard fare at Meenaclure, and towards the end of it Pat O'Farrell came reluctantly to perceive that he could best mend his own and his family's tattered fortunes by emigrating to the States. His resolve, though regretted by all his neighbours, except of course the M'Neills, was considered sensible enough; and at the "convoy" which assembled according to custom to see him off on his long journey the general purport of conversation was to the effect that, bedad, everybody'd be missing poor Pat, but sure himself was the fine clever boy wouldn't be any time gettin' together the price of a little place back again in the ould

country. The M'Neills alone were of the opinion, expressed by
Neil's mother, that "the only pity was the rest of the pack weren't
goin' along wid Pat; unless, like enough, they'd be more than the
people out in those parts could put up wid all at onst, the way
they'd be landin' them back on us like a bundle of ould rubbish
washin' up agin wid the tide."

But surprise was the universal feeling when, about six months
later, it became known that Neil M'Neill's eldest child Molly had
also made up her mind to cross over the water. Her own family
were foremost among the wonderers; for Molly had always been
considered rather excessively timid and quiet—certainly the
very last girl in the parish whom one would have thought likely
to make such a venture. They half believed that when it came to
the point, "sorra a fut of her would go;" and they much more
than half hoped so, notwithstanding that their rent had fallen
into alarming arrears, and none of her brethren were old
enough to help. Molly, however, actually went, amid lamentations and forebodings, both of her own and other people's, all
alike unavailing to stop her. Mrs. Timothy O'Farrell said she'd
be long sorry to have a daughter of hers streeling off to the ends
of the earth. And I think that Molly's mother *was* long sorry,
poor soul, through many a lonesome day and anxious night.

After these two departures, things at Meenaclure took their
wonted course, a little more sadly and dully perhaps than
heretofore. Communications from abroad came rarely and
scantily, for neither of the absentees had much scholarship.
Their sheep-herding summers had greatly curtailed that, and it
would have been difficult to say whether Pat's or Molly's scrawls
were the briefer or obscurer. But not long after Molly M'Neill
had gone, one of Pat O'Farrell's letters contained an important
piece of news—nothing less than that he was "just about gettin'
married." He did not go into particulars about the match,
merely describing the future Mrs. Pat as the "'best little girl in
or out of Ireland," and opining that they mightn't do too badly.
His family were not overjoyed at the event, which might be considered to presage a falling off in remittances; and his mother
was much cast down thereby, her thoughts going to the tune of
"my son is my son till he gets him a wife." Still, she was not so

dispirited as to be past finding some solace in an innuendo; and she almost certainly certainly designed one when she took occasion to remark just outside the chapel door, where she had been telling the neighbours her news: "But ah, sure, I don't mind so long as he hasn't took up wid one of them black-headed girls I never can abide the looks of. And 'deed now there's no fear of that. Pat's just the same notion as myself, I know very well." For Mrs. Neil M'Neill was standing well within earshot, and, as everybody remembered, "there wasn't a fair hair on the head of e'er a one of her childer." However, Mrs. Neil proved equal to the emergency, and remarked, addressing Katty Byrne, that "It was rael queer the sort of omadhawns she'd heard tell of some girls, who, belike, knew no better, bein' content to take great lumberin' louts of fellers, wid the ugly-coloured hair on their heads like nothin' in the world except a bit of new thatch before it would be combed straight."

She spoke without any presentiment that she would soon have to go through much the same experience as old Mrs. O'Farrell; but so it was. For a week or two later came a letter from Molly stating that was "just after gettin' married." Her husband, who she said was earning grand wages, bore the obnoxious name of O'Farrell, but there was nothing strange in the coincidence, as the district about Meenaclure abounds in Farrells and Neills, and without prefixes of O and Mac; and it seemed only natural to suppose a similar state of things in New York. Nobody could deny that there were plenty of O'Farrells very dacint people. So Molly's mother mourned in private over an event which seemed to set a seal upon the separation between her daughter and herself; and in public was well pleased and very proud, laying great stress upon the fact that Molly had sent the money-order just as usual,—"Sorra a fear of little Molly forgettin' the ould people at all,"—and serenely scorning Mesdames O'Farrell's opinion that "when a girl had to thravel off that far after a husband, it was the quare crooked stick of a one she'd be apt to pick up."

After this Meenaclure received no very thrilling foreign news for about a twelve-month. Then one fine Sunday, the Widdy O'Farrell was to be seen sailing along Masswards, with her head held extremely high in its stiff-frilled cap and dark blue hood, and with a swinging sweep of her black homespun skirt, which betrayed an exultant stride. All her family, indeed, wore a somewhat elated and consequential air, which most of her neighbours allowed to be justifiable when she explained that she had become the happy grandmother of her Pat's fine young son: the letter with the announcement had come last night. This was indeed promotion, for her son Tim's children were all girls. With the congratulations upon so auspicious an event even old Mrs. M'Neill could mingle only subdued murmurs about brats taking after their fathers that weren't good for much, the dear knows. However, she had not long to wait for as good or better a right to strut chin in air, since it was with a great-grandmother's dignity that a few days later she could inform everybody of the arrival of Molly's boy. She would, I believe, have found it very hard to forgive Molly if the child had been merely a daughter.

This rivalry, as it were, between the estranged families in the matter of news from their non-resident members recurred with the same equipoised result on more than one similar occasion, and was extended even to less happy events. For instance, one time when Pat wrote in great distraction, and a wilder scrawl than usual, that the "three childer was dreadful bad wid the mumps, he doubted would they get over it," the next mail brought just such a report from Molly; which was rather awkward for her mother and grandmother, who had been going about passing the remark that "when childer got proper mindin' they never took anythin' of the sort."

At length, however, when perhaps half-a-dozen years had gone by, the balance of good fortune dipped decidedly towards the O'Farrells. One autumn morning a letter came from Pat to say that he and his family were coming home. He had saved up a tidy little bit of money, and meant to try could he settle himself on a dacint little bit of land; at any rate he would get a sight of the ould place and the ould people. Great was the rejoicing of the O'Farrrells. Whereas for the M'Neills at this time the meagre mail-bags contained no foreign letter, no letter at all, bad or good, let alone one fraught with such grand news. Molly's mother, it is true, dreamt two nights running that Molly had

come home; but dreams are a sorry substitute for a letter, especially when everybody knows, and some people remind you, that
they always go by contraries. So Mrs. Neil fretted and fore-
boded, and had not the heart to be sarcastic, no matter how
arrogantly the O’Farrells might comport themselves.

Then the autumn days shrivelled and shrank, and one morning in late November the word went round Meenaclure that the
Kaley that evening would be up at Fergus the weaver’s. This
meeting-place was always popular, Fergus being a well-liked
man, with a wide space round his hearth. And this night’s con-
versazione promised to be particularly enjoyable, as it had
leaked out that Dan Farrell and Mrs. Keogh and Dinny O’Neill
were concerned in what is at Meenaclure technically termed “a
join,” for the purpose of treating the kaleying company to cups
of tea. In fact, the materials for that refreshment, done up in
familiar purple paper parcels, lying on the window-seat, were
obvious to everybody who came into the room, though to have
seemed aware of them would have been a grave breach of manners. When all the company were mustered, and the fire was
burning its brightest, Fergus might well look round his house
with satisfaction, for so large an assembly seldom came together,
and universal harmony seemed to prevail. This was not disturbed by the fact that several both of the Timothy O’Farrells
and Neil M‘Neills were present, as by this time everybody thoroughly understood the situation, and the neighbours arranged
themselves as a matter of course in ways which precluded any
awkward juxtapositions of persons “who weren’t spakin’.”

It was a showery evening, with a wafting to and fro of wide
gusts, which made the Widdy O’Farrell wonder more than once
as she sat on the form by the hearth, with the Widdy Byrne
interposed buffer-wise between her and old Joe M‘Neill. What
she wondered was, whether her poor Pat might be apt to be
crossin’ over the say on such an ugly wild night. Just as Mrs.
Keogh, with an eye on the lid-bobbing kettle, was about to ask
Fergus if he might happen to have e’er a drop of hot water he
could spare her—that being the orthodox preface to tea-making
on the occasion of a join—the house-door rattled violently, and
opened with a fling. As nobody appeared at it, this was supposed

to be simply the wind's freak, and Fergus said to Mick M'Murdo, who sat next to it, "Musha, lad, be givin' it a clap to wid your fut." But at that instant a voice was heard close outside, calling as if to another person a little farther off, "Molly, Molly, come along wid you; they're all here right enough, and I wouldn't be keepin' the door open on them." Whereupon there was a quick patter of approaching feet, followed by the entrance of two bundle-bearing figures. As they advanced into the flickering light, it showed that the figures were a man and a woman, and the bundles children; and in another moment there rose up recognising shrieks and shouts of "Pat" and "Molly," and then everybody rushed together tumultuously across a chasm of half-a-dozen years.

"They tould us below at Widdy Byrne's that we'd find yous all up here," said Pat O'Farrell, "so we left the baby there, and stepped along. Och, mother, it's younger you're grown instead of oulder, and that's a fac'."

"And where's the wife, Paudyeen agra?" said Pat's mother; "or maybe she sted below wid the child?"

"And where's himself, Molly jewel?" said Molly's mother. "Sure you didn't come your lone?"

"Why, here he is," said Molly. "Pat, man, wasn't you spakin' to me mother?"

"Och, whethen now, and is it Pat O'Farrell?" his mother-in-law said with a half-strangled gasp.

"And who else would it be at all at all, only Pat?" said Molly, as if propounding an unanswerable argument.

"Mercy be among us all—and you niver let on—och, you rogue of the world—you niver let on, Patsy avic, it was little Molly M'Neill you'd took up wid all the while," said his mother.

"Sure I was writin' to you all about her times and agin," Pat averred stoutly.

Perhaps things might have turned out differently if people had not been delighted and taken by surprise. But as it was, how could a feud be conducted with any propriety when Mrs. Neil had unprotestingly been hugged by Pat O'Farrell, and when old Joe M'Neill and his wife and daughter were already worshipping a very fat small two-year-old girl, who unmistakably featured all the O'Farrells that ever walked? The thing was impossible.

For one moment, indeed, an unhappy resurrection seemed to be threatened. It was when everybody had got into a circle round the hearth, in expectation of the cups of tea, which were beginning to clatter in the background, and when Pat O'Farrell, who was talking over old times with Neil M'Neill, suddenly gave his father-in-law a great thump on the back, exclaiming with a chuckle, "Och, man, and do you remimber your ould sheep that we got in the oats, and gave a coloured wash to? Faix, but she was the comical objec'—'the tiger-sheep,' the childer used to call her." Whereupon all the rest looked at one another with dismayed countenances, as if they had caught sight of something uncanny. But their alarm was needless. For Neil returned Pat's thump promptly with interest, and replied, "Haw, haw, haw! Bedad, and I do remimber her right well. Och now, man alive, I'll bet you me best brogues that wid all you've been behouldin' out there in the States you niver set eyes on e'er a baste'd aquil her for quareness—haw, haw, haw!" And the whole company took up the chorus, as if minded to make up on the spot all arrears of laughter owing on that long unappreciated joke. Amid the sound of which I have reason to believe that there fled away from Meenaclure for ever the last haunting phantasm of the unchancy tiger-sheep.

OUT IN THE COLD°
Charlotte Riddell
(1832–1906)

Chapter I

Not many years ago there lived in an out-of-the-way Irish town a certain Miss Saridge. She had lived in the same town ever since her birth, therefore it might have been supposed no mystery unfathomable by her neighbours could attach itself with the blameless lady, at that period considerably more than middle-aged.

Such was not the case, however. The inhabitants of Crossdene frankly confessed they were unable to "make her out," and in the absence of knowledge concluded she must be a miser.

"Look how little she spends," they said, "and nobody but herself and a little maid to keep. No doubt she is putting by lots of money, saving and scraping, and for what?"

For what, indeed, should Miss Saridge scrape and save; deny herself new dresses, and wear old-fashioned bonnets; refuse to accept hospitality, and with equal pertinacity rarely ask anyone to have a cup of tea; buy no few furniture, and give but sparingly to any local charity? Crossdene might well ask this question, and lacking the ability to answer it, decide the spinster was a miser.

For some reason local report is very apt to say people who do

---

°From *Handsome Phil and Other Stories*, 1899.

not noise their affairs abroad are worth a lot of money which they hoard.

There is something captivating in the notion of hidden money, and many an otherwise kindly and well-disposed person took a morbid pleasure in imagining the bags of gold and piles of silver which would be found secreted in Miss Saridge's house when that lady joined the majority.

It never occurred to one single creature in the town as being within the bounds of possibility that Miss Saridge was conceal-ing, not her wealth but her poverty; that her frail body con-tained, not a sordid but a great spirit; that her life had been one long self-denial—a cheerful sacrifice of everything most women hold dear for the sake of those she loved; and that the meagre meals, the shabby dresses, the guarded charity, were but the outward and visible signs of a pride which could not have brooked help, and shrank from pity.

Annabel Saridge did not look in the least like a heroine. She was a woman of the Dresden Shepherdess pattern—with soft pink and white cheeks, blue eyes, pearly teeth, dainty figure, who had been pretty in her youth, and even in her age was gracious and sweet to look upon. There was a tradition in Crossdene that she had been engaged when in her teens to one of the Errins of Errin Court, but as she never referred to the matter, and the Errin family had long given place to the Ograms, who knew noth-ing of Miss Saridge, people at last came to regard the legend as a myth, "because, of course, she would have married one belonging to such great people, if there had been any truth in the story."

Like a tradition also it seemed to the new people who had come to the town long after Miss Saridge ceased to be young, when anyone learned in such matters spoke of Mr. Saridge as having been a celebrated man; but this was true beyond the pos-sibility of dispute, because Michael Saridge had won for himself a name and a position as the best Irish scholar of his time.

Further, his head was a complete encyclopaedia of useless knowledge—that is, of knowledge which can be of little use to the owner, and is, broadly speaking, of no use to anyone else.

Nevertheless, his books brought him in some money and much reputation—so much of the latter, indeed, that one morning there arrived a letter announcing he had been awarded a pension by the then Government of £200 a year, in recognition of his services to literature.

Those were the days when such pensions were bestowed as a reward for success, and not as a punishment for failure.

No author at that period was, together with the whole British public, informed that a pittance of fifty pounds annually would be doled out to him in consideration of "his insufficient means of support," and accordingly Mr. Saridge, though he was a proud man, did not feel humiliated by the grant, but received it thankfully, knowing it would enable him to pursue his researches with an easier mind. He did not insure his life, because he could not, having a disease which insurance companies—more particular then than now—considered perilous.

"Never mind, my dear," he said to his wife, cheerily; "I shall not die one day the sooner because 'The Sun' does not think fit to take me, and instead of paying that office a premium every year, we will put the money by, and then I shall know I can afford to have an amanuensis when I go blind."

"Let me be your amanuensis before you go blind!" exclaimed Annabel, who happened to be in the room.

"Pooh! child—you must keep your pretty eyes for something better than copying my crabbed writing," said the fond father, laying his hand lovingly on her "bonnie brown hair."

That was a very pleasant home where the Saridges dwelt, situated just outside Crossdene. Rent was cheap there, and they had a good roomy house, surrounded by a large garden, with a paddock beyond.

Mr. Saridge was not rich; all told he had, perhaps, with the Civil List pension, five hundred a year, which, however, seemed wealth to an Irishman at that time, when people lived comfortably but plainly; when the pleasures of existence had not become merely another name for its taxes; when a man without courting ruin might dare to visit and be visited; when, in a word, simplicity was the rule and grandeur the exception.

There was good society also then to be found in Crossdene. The Jardynes at the Rectory, the Muleons at the Hall, the Burlews at Mountain View, the Carrigans at Fir Hill, the Errins at Errin Court, all boasted plenty of young folks ready to join in any picnic, dance, or game. Mary Jardyne was Annabel Saridge's chosen friend. Many a happy day they spent together walking, talking, sketching, playing duets, wondering what the future might have in store for them.

In many respects Annabel's was an ideal girlhood, but it was soon over. First her lover—that legendary Errin in whose very existence modern Crossdene scarcely believed—died; then her father did actually go blind, and she had to spend hours each day in writing to his dictation; then her only brother went wrong, somehow, and many hoarded hundreds were needed to save him from disgrace. Her elder sister, the beauty upon whom her parents once built high hopes, had years previously run off with a subaltern who did not treat her well; so there was nothing but sorrow all around. But Annabel turned a brave face to their troubles.

"We have had our good time, mother, and shall we complain now?" she said; and then she would go to her own room and have a good cry, before coming down to transcribe her father's comments on "Leour-na-heery" or "The Book of Ballymote."*

Chapter II

There was one thing Annabel never told Mr. Saridge— namely, that she had a perfect passion for writing tales.

In the days of her youth, women who wrote were regarded with doubtful eyes by many admirable persons—as, indeed, they are regarded by several even to the present time; and at that precise period, for many reasons, it was scarcely to be expected that a man and a father, even though an excellent Irish scholar, should rise superior to his environment.

Annabel and her gentle mother, who, truth to tell, did not believe her daughter was possessed of any literary gift whatsoever, talked the matter over, and decided no mention of the unfortunate proclivity should be made to Mr. Saridge. If when

*Leour-na-heery (*Book of the Dun Cow*) is a medieval Irish work; *The Book of Ballymote* is an Irish manuscript produced circa 1391.

blessed with sight he objected to female authors—as "persons who had unsexed themselves"—to what portentous dimensions might not his aversion grow when unable to see at all?

He had become very irritable, moreover, since his blindness, and felt weary—weary of the monotonous life looming before him.

Where were the pleasant companions, the brilliant friends who had caused the wilderness of Crossdene to blossom like the rose? Gone never to return. Crossdene led to nowhere in those latter days, for another chief held sway at Errin Court—a chief who cared not for learned men, and for whom learned men cared not at all.

Therefore it came to pass that only about four times in the year, when compelled, by virtue of a post he held there, to visit Dublin, one great student heard the trumpet-call of his regiment, and slowly fell into place among his comrades as of old.

Under these circumstances it was most unlikely the afflicted gentleman should hear with equanimity that his daughter longed to enlist in the Amazon troop then slowly gaining recruits.

"If he thought you wanted to write books of your own, it would kill your poor father," said Mrs. Saridge with conviction.

"I am, indeed, afraid it might seem very hard to him," agreed Annabel, while a curious quiver passed over her pretty face. Perhaps she had hoped for a different answer from the parent she adored.

"If you *must* write," added Mrs. Saridge, "do not let anyone know."

It is thus loving wives and tender mothers "trim," my reader!

Annabel was obliged to "trim" also. She did not desire to kill her father, but it proved quite as impossible to combat her passion for scribbling. For hours each day she wrote at Mr. Saridge's dictation; then, while Mrs. Saridge read aloud, she sewed, and it was only when night came, and everyone else in the house had retired to rest, that the patient maiden reduced to words those fancies she had been silently evolving in her brain throughout the day.

It may have been the utter absorption and the perfect solitude which influenced her work. Who can tell? One thing only is certain, that afterwards competent critics said of one who never made her mark, who for some reason remained "out in the cold," that her style was so absolutely *sui generis* she might under different conditions have done just what she pleased.

Brimful of legend and fancy, with a heart which echoed to every tone of human feeling, with an eye which missed no beauty of nature, and an ear that caught every sound of joy and distress—what might she not have done for Ireland and herself had the fates been kinder? Hers was the daintiest and most sympathetic style. Anyone reading her stories now, can see the trembling hare-bell and inhale the primrose's faint scent; can wander in imagination over mountains clothed with the purple heather, and dip knee-deep in bracken down hillsides leading to valleys verdant as only those of the Emerald Isle can ever appear.

For not merely was the girl Irish, but she knew Ireland as few even born on the soil ever do.

The love of her native land permeated her whole soul. To her it seemed the fairest, finest isle created by God, and her pen, inspired by enthusiasm and knowledge, might indeed under favourable auspices have worked wonders for good.

Was it any marvel that, as the months went by, she felt she could refrain herself no longer, and must tell her stories to the world? that with her mother's consent she wrote a confidential letter to her girlhood's friend, Mary Jardyne?

Alas! how seldom do the friendships of youth outlive the years that witness their birth! The love and the liking may, and often do, survive, but it is only one time in ten thousand that the woman's faith mirrors the girl's fancy.

"A man is not without honour," etc.

Kindly, superficial, well-connected Mr. Jardyne, whose lines had fallen into pleasant places near London, must have known that statement by heart, and yet, when consulted by his daughter, who thought "dear Annabel was making a great mistake," could only suggest submitting manuscripts brimful of genius to the secretary of a straight-laced religious society. He did the best he knew and the result was *nil*.

"I am so sorry, darling," wrote Miss Jardyne, who enclosed the secretary's adverse note, "but you see."

"You see," echoed poor Mrs. Saridge.

"Yes, mother, but I shall not give up."

Then Mrs. Saridge sighed.

Persistent endeavour seemed dreadful to the mothers of that epoch.

Annabel did not give up. She tried the Dublin publishers without avail. But one sympathetic bookseller gave her good advice, and told her she had better send her work to London. Then came a time of weary waiting, of hope deferred, of rejection, of acceptance without any remuneration, of acceptance with the promise of payment, and at last—a guinea.

Mrs. Saridge was glad then the girl had not given up, but she was more glad when the sad day came that Mr. Saridge died, and the pension ceased, and his salary also, when they were left with scarcely any ready money, and had nothing to depend on but the very small private fortune that poor gentleman inherited from his father.

Misfortunes never come singly. Everything went wrong from the time mother and daughter entered the small house in a back street into which they moved when compelled to break up their old home. The postman never seemed to bring a letter that did not convey the intelligence of some fresh disaster.

Tom required help, and then Tom's widow and Tom's fatherless children; Adelaide also needed money. Finally, Mr. Saridge's small inheritance sank so much in value that when the necessity arose for realizing it only about one-third of its former worth could be obtained.

When the downhill descent is begun, the end becomes a mere matter of time. It was only because Annabel proved so brave and self-denying that Mrs. Saridge never really felt the pinch of absolute want. The wretched pittance left after helping Tom and Adelaide, and Tom's widow and Tom's children, sufficed to meet the expenses of Mrs. Saridge's long illness and pay for her funeral; then Annabel sat down in her lonely home to consider the future.

She was young no longer. Poverty had made her very proud, and solitude very shy. She could earn but little, and lack of success had taught her self-depreciation, but she was not unhappy or unthankful.

Literature has its compensations as well as its trials, and she had rarely time to brood over sorrows which might well have broken an idle woman's heart.

One morning in an early spring the fancy seized her to look at Errin Court once more. For years she had avoided the road which led past that place; but time is a great soother, and after years no sorrow holds a sting save some sorrow caused by sin.

This dear lady's gentle heart held no sin except that which every child of Eve brings into the world.

She stood and looked up the long avenue, where the elms were 'a mist of green'; she let her eyes wander across the noble park and rest on the sparkling river that gave life and variety to the landscape. How happy she had been there once upon a time! How long ago that fairy dream of love and truth ended! and yet how vividly it all came back to her as she turned aside and paced under the trees that skirted the demesne till she reached the top of the hill they—she and her young lover—had so often climbed together!

Then a great longing fell upon her to tell the story which hitherto had only been felt; from experience to repeat when old the solemn truth she had heard in her youth—

> "'Tis better to have loved and lost
> Than never to have loved at all."

She went home and began to write with more of the eager yearning felt in her teens than she had thought ever to experience again. As she wrote, the story—hers, and yet not hers—grew upon her, and for months she devoted every leisure moment to that which was a labour of delight.

When at last she laid down her pen she could not see the final words because of blinding tears.

It was the supreme effort of her life—the best thing she had ever written!

Next day she despatched her story, entitled "'Tis Better to have Loved and Lost,"* to the magazine which paid least badly of any she wrote for; then she began to wait.

---

*From *In Memoriam* (1850), by Alfred Lord Tennyson (1809–1892).

That was early in August, and it was not till the end of September she wrote again, and elicited an answer. The magazine had changed hands, and a new editor been appointed. He was out of town, and until his return nothing could be done with respect to Miss Saridge's manuscript, or the small cheque due for her last contribution. Though courteously worded, this was a blow, and one the author took greatly to heart—so greatly, indeed, that when week after week went by without bringing any further communication, she sank into such a state of despondency that she could scarcely do any work at all. Then there ensued a time when she and the little maid had to go on very short allowance indeed—Miss Saridge on the shortest, for she had ever thought first of others, last of herself. Much against her will, she was obliged to break into a sum of money she had painfully saved against that day which must arrive for all, when the windows would be darkened and she gone home! It was a dull, damp winter, and in the beginning of December the poor lady caught a chill, and had to take her to bed. It was weary work, lying there at first all alone, but after a while she grew indifferent. There were long hours, during the course of which she did not remember anything—even anxiety. She had not even energy enough to open her letters.

At last the rector's wife, missing her from church, called late one afternoon. She was new to Crossdene, and had not accepted the popular theory about Miss Saridge. Moreover, "whatever she may be," she said to her husband, "we ought to know her better than we do."

"My mistress is in bed, ma'am," the small maid informed her; "and asleep," she added.

"Is she ill, then?"

"She had had a cold."

"And who is seeing to her?"

"I am, ma'am; I took her up a cup of tea an hour ago, and she said it was beautiful."

"Tell her when she wakes that I shall come round again in about an hour," answered Mrs. Frenshaw, who went home along the unlighted street with a strange pain in her kindly heart. "The poor woman—the poor, poor soul!" she thought.

She had not reached the rectory gate ere a mighty knock woke all the echoes in Miss Saridge's humble home—a knock such as the little servant had never heard previously, and that caused her to run affrighted to the door.

"Does Miss Saridge live here?" asked a tall and portly lady, stepping into the tiny hall.

"Yes, ma'am, but—" began the child—for she was really nothing but a child—who saw by the light of a dip candle, which flickered in a direct draught, the grandest lady she had ever beheld—a lady dressed in a tailor-made cloth gown, a sealskin jacket, and a velvet bonnet, and who said, as the speaker paused and hesitated—

"But what?"

"Please, ma'am, she's in bed."

"That does not matter; she will see me. Give this card to her." And taking a gold pencil-case out of her bag, she added five words after the printed name.

"But she is asleep, ma'am."

"Then I will wait till she wakes."

Just at that moment there sounded the faint tinkle of a hand-bell, and the miniature maid, saying, "That is for me," ran up the staircase, closely followed by the stranger, who heard a weak voice ask—

"What was all that knocking about, Polly, and who is talking so loudly in the hall?"

"Forgive me, Annabel; I did not know you were ill," came in a low, hushed tone. "I am your old friend Mary Jardyne."

Conclusion

They had sat for a time hand locked in hand, speaking few words, but words that sufficed; then Mrs. Montrose, *née* Jardyne, went downstairs, and, opening the kitchen door, said to Polly—

"I am going to fetch a doctor, and shall take the key."

"Can't I run for him, ma'am?"

The small creature was always willing.

"No, I will go myself. I only came to tell you lest you might feel frightened."

She was back in five minutes, accompanied by the doctor, a young man, who looked very grave, when, after leaving his patient, he stood in the hall, lit only by that guttering dip, smoothing his hat with his hand thoughtfully.

"She is very low," he said, "and will require the greatest care."

"She shall have it."

There was no hesitation or shilly-shallying about Mrs. Montrose. Ere she had been in the shabby house an hour its whole aspect seemed different. A piled-up turf fire in the front parlour amazed passers-by, who saw the blaze through unshuttered windows. Polly had been sent for her mother, who in her turn had been sent to make purchases, and told to call at the hotel and order Mrs. Montrose's luggage to be brought up.

"For I am going to stay here till Miss Saridge is better," explained the lady, "and shall want a room prepared that I can sleep in, and you to remain here if possible."

"Save and keep us!" exclaimed the woman, as she hurried away; "was ever the like heard!"

Mrs. Frenshaw, when she returned, certainly thought the like never had been heard; it appeared to her a transformation scene to be sitting before a glorious fire in that mean room, listening while Mrs. Montrose, who looked twenty years younger than Miss Saridge, told how they had been friends when girls—"ages ago."

"We drifted apart, as people do somehow," said the lady, whose father once filled the position then occupied by Mr. Frenshaw. "I do not know why, for I never liked any friend so much as Annabel Saridge. Dear me," she went on dreamily, "what talks we used to have about our future! If I had only known what her future really was—if I *only* had known!"

"And why did you not?" asked Mrs. Frenshaw, with blunt directness.

"I have told you—we drifted apart. She took one side of the river and I the other."

"Yes, as in 'Divided,'" said Mrs. Frenshaw.

"Precisely."

"I do not think anything could divide me from an old friend."

"Ah! you have never lived in London; and besides, how could I know where she was—what she was doing?"

Mrs. Frenshaw remained silent.

"I should not have known now," went on Mrs. Montrose, "that the woman who wrote under the name of 'Anna Bell' was my old friend but for the accident that made my husband editor of *Trafalgar Square.* He wrote to Miss Saridge about a delightful novelette, a marvellous novelette, which was lying at the office, and when he received no reply, asked me if I had ever heard of anyone so called while my father was rector at Crossdene. Then everything came out, and he suggested that I should break my journey here on my way to Philipstown, where I was invited to spend Christmas."

"Is your husband, then, a relation of Sir Conlan Montrose?"

"Yes, he is a cadet of that family. As matters are, however, I shall not go to Philipstown, but stop here till Miss Saridge is well enough to return to London with me."

"I cannot understand why no one here ever imagined she wrote."

"Why should anyone imagine it? She kept everything so close. I asked the reason she published under a *nom de plume,* and she said she did not think her father would have liked her to do so under his—as if his stupid old books were for a moment to be compared with hers."

"He was a great scholar, Mr. Frenshaw says."

"No doubt, and lost his sight by poring over those awful Irish characters."

"He was a very learned man," persisted Mrs. Frenshaw.

Within a few days it was astonishing how green Mr. Saridge's memory became in Crossdene, how frequently his works were spoken of, how suddenly new-comers grew desirous of hearing everything about him and his daughter Mrs. Montrose could tell.

As for that lady, she won golden opinions by proving to herself the best nurse, Doctor Lanigan declared, he had ever seen.

"I would not have given that," he said, snapping his fingers, "for Miss Saridge's chance of recovery the first night I came here, and yet she has made wonderful progress, all owing to Mrs. Montrose's care. Such sense, such calmness, such devotion, I never met with."

Which statement seemed hard to many ladies in Crossdene who considered themselves good nurses, though not perhaps so expensively dressed as Mrs. Montrose!

Certainly Miss Saridge seemed going on excellently well. Mrs. Montrose had brought the best tonics possible with her. Instead of struggling poverty, chill neglect, utter loneliness, misery—recognition, companionship. It was a beautiful future Mrs. Montrose pictured. Not when Annabel, in the joy of her happy girlhood, dreamed dreams and saw visions, had she ever beheld anything more fair.

"It seems too good to be true," she would say sometimes, for years of disappointment had made her timid.

And then Mrs. Montrose's firm hand closed on the wasted fingers that had written so long for such wretched pay, and by a warm pressure silently declared the days of sorrow and shortness were ended.

"Only get well," said Mrs. Montrose.

"Am I not doing my best?" asked the invalid.

And she did do her best. If Mrs. Montrose were an ideal nurse, Miss Saridge was an ideal patient.

"I want to run up to Dublin to-morrow," said Mrs. Montrose one evening. "Will you do everything you are told while I am away?"

"Indeed I will."

"I shall be back by five o'clock."

"Do not hurry on my account."

The doctor called in the morning as usual, and found Miss Saridge's state extremely satisfactory. Later on she took her medicine, her beef-tea, her beaten-up eggs, without a murmur.

If Mrs. Montrose had been there herself nothing could have gone better till the afternoon; then—

"How is she?" was her friend's first inquiry when Polly opened the front door.

"She's sleeping beautifully, ma'am; she's ever so much better. She got up—she would, ma'am, though mother thought it risky—and she wrote, and wrote, till she was just tired out, when she said, 'I'll lie down now.'"

"She did what?" asked Mrs. Montrose, aghast.

"Wrote a lot, ma'am; said she must finish—"

Without answering by a word, Mrs. Montrose ran upstairs and entered the room; then Polly heard her calling shrilly—

"Fly for the doctor."

Polly never knew how she got out of the house and down the street and into the surgery, where Doctor Lanigan was just replacing a bottle on the shelf.

"Come," said the small maid, in her terror and excitement taking hold of his wrist, and almost dragging him onto the pavement.

"What is the matter, child?" he asked.

"I don't know—oh, I don't know! but she told me to fly for you, and I have!"

He did not wait even to get his hat, but rushed to the poor shabby house, where the door stood wide.

"I am afraid you are too late," said Mrs. Montrose from the landing.

He did not speak, but, passing her by, entered the familiar room. Miss Saridge was lying quite still, one arm—the right— thrown out a little. He took the tiny hand. What a morsel of a hand it was!

"She is dead!" he exclaimed. "How is this?"

Who could tell! From out the 'great for evermore' there came no voice or sound—only utter silence. For a minute Mrs. Montrose and the doctor stood looking at each other; then, scarcely knowing what he was doing, the latter placed his hand on the heart which could never beat again.

"Quite dead," he repeated, walking towards the hearth.

As he did so, he saw some sheets of paper lying on the floor, and mechanically stooped to lift them.

"The poor soul would get up to write," explained Mrs. Montrose in a whisper.

Then he held the sheets towards her, so that she could see there was no writing on them; nothing but a series of purpose-less scrawls such as a young child might have scribbled.

"I understand now," said Doctor Lanigan, after a pause. "Death was standing by her all the time."

And better so, perhaps; better that while her heart was warm with the glow of renewed friendship, while the fairy bells of hope and joy were making glad melody in her ears, while she was basking in the full sunshine of that unclouded happiness her life had for so long lacked, Death, "standing by," should lead her gently out of the cold forever.

GREAT-UNCLE McCARTHY[*]

E. Œ. Somerville (1858–1949)
and Martin Ross (1862–1915)

A resident Magistracy in Ireland is not an easy thing to come by nowadays; neither is it a very attractive job; yet on the evening when I first propounded the idea to the young lady who had recently consented to become Mrs. Sinclair Yeates, it seemed glittering with possibilities. There was, on that occasion, a sunset, and a string band playing "The Gondoliers," and there was also an ingenuous belief in the omnipotence of a godfather of Philippa's—(Philippa was the young lady)—who had once been a member of the Government.

I was then climbing the steep ascent of the Captains towards my Majority. I have no fault to find with Philippa's godfather; he did all and more than even Philippa had expected; nevertheless, I had attained to the dignity of mud major, and had spent a good deal on postage stamps, and on railway fares to interview people of influence, before I found myself in the hotel at Skebawn, opening long envelopes addressed to "Major Yeates, R.M."

My most immediate concern, as anyone who has spent nine weeks at Mrs. Raverty's hotel will readily believe, was to leave it at the earliest opportunity; but in those nine weeks I had learned, amongst other painful things, a little, a very little, of the methods of the artisan in the West of Ireland. Finding a house had been easy enough. I had had my choice of several, each with

[*]From *Some Experiences of an Irish R.M.*, 1899.

235

some hundreds of acres of shooting, thoroughly poached, and a considerable portion of the roof intact. I had selected one; the one that had the largest extent of roof in proportion to the shooting, and had been assured by my landlord that in a fortnight or so it would be fit for occupation.

"There's a few little odd things to be done," he said easily; "a lick of paint here and there, and a slap of plaster——"

I am short-sighted; I am also of Irish extraction; both facts that make for toleration—but even I thought he was understating the case. So did the contractor.

At the end of three weeks the latter reported progress, which mainly consisted of the facts that the plumber had accused the carpenter of stealing sixteen feet of his inch-pipe to run a bell wire through, and that the carpenter had replied that he wished the divil might run the plumber through a wran's quill. The plumber having reflected upon the carpenter's parentage, the work of renovation had merged in battle, and at the next Petty Sessions I was reluctantly compelled to allot to each combatant seven days, without the option of a fine.

These and kindred difficulties extended in an unbroken chain through the summer months, until a certain wet and windy day in October, when, with my baggage, I drove over to establish myself at Shreelane. It was a tall, ugly house of three storeys high, its walls faced with weather-beaten slates, its windows staring, narrow, and vacant. Round the house ran an area, in which grew some laurustinus and holly bushes among ash heaps, and nettles, and broken bottles. I stood on the steps, waiting for the door to be opened, while the rain sluiced upon me from a broken eaveshoot that had, amongst many other things, escaped the notice of my landlord. I thought of Philippa, and of her plan, broached in to-day's letter, of having the hall done up as a sitting-room.

The door opened, and revealed the hall. It struck me that I had perhaps overestimated its possibilities. Among them I had certainly not included a flagged floor, sweating with damp, and a reek of cabbage from the adjacent kitchen stairs. A large elderly woman, with a red face, and a cap worn helmet-wise on her forehead, swept me a magnificent curtsey as I crossed the threshold.

"Your honour's welcome——" she began, and then every door in the house slammed in obedience to the gust that drove through it. With something that sounded like "Mend ye for a back door!" Mrs. Cadogan abandoned her opening speech and made for the kitchen stairs. (Improbably as it may appear, my housekeeper was called Cadogan, a name made locally possible by being pronounced Caydogawn.)

Only those who have been through a similar experience can know what manner of afternoon I spent. I am a martyr to colds in the head, and I felt one coming on. I made a laager in front of the dining-room fire, with a tattered leather screen and the dinner table, and gradually, with cigarettes and strong tea, baffled the smell of must and cats, and fervently trusted that the rain might avert a threatened visit from my landlord. I was then but superficially acquainted with Mr. Florence McCarthy Knox and his habits.

At about 4.30, when the room had warmed up, and my cold was yielding to treatment, Mrs. Cadogan entered and informed me that "Mr. Flurry" was in the yard, and would be thankful if I'd go out to him, for he couldn't come in. Many are the privileges of the female sex; had I been a woman I should unhesitatingly have said that I had a cold in my head. Being a man, I huddled on a mackintosh, and went out into the yard.

My landlord was there on horseback, and with him there was a man standing at the head of a stout grey animal. I recognised with despair that I was about to be compelled to buy a horse.

"Good afternoon, Major," said Mr. Knox in his slow, sing-song brogue; "it's rather soon to be paying you a visit, but I thought you might be in a hurry to see the horse I was telling you of."

I could have laughed. As if I were ever in a hurry to see a horse! I thanked him, and suggested that it was rather wet for horse-dealing.

"Oh, it's nothing when you're used to it," replied Mr. Knox. His gloveless hands were red and wet, the rain ran down his nose, and his covert coat was soaked to a sodden brown. I thought that I did not want to become used to it. My relations with horses have been of a purely military character, I have endured the Sandhurst riding-school, I have galloped for an impetuous general, I have been steward at regimental races, but none of these feats have altered my opinion that the horse, as a means of locomotion, is obsolete. Nevertheless, the man who accepts a resident magistracy in the southwest of Ireland voluntarily retires into the prehistoric age; to institute a stable became inevitable.

"You ought to throw a leg over him," said Mr. Knox, "and you're welcome to take him over a fence or two if you like. He's a nice flippant jumper."

Even to my unexacting eye the grey horse did not seem to promise flippancy, nor did I at all desire to find that quality in him. I explained that I wanted something to drive, and not to ride.

"Well, that's a fine raking horse in harness," said Mr. Knox, looking at me with his serious grey eyes, "and you'd drive him with a sop of hay in his mouth. Bring him up here, Michael."

Michael abandoned his efforts to kick the grey horse's forelegs into a becoming position, and led him up to me.

I regarded him from under my umbrella with a quite unreasonable disfavour. He had the dreadful beauty of a horse in a toy-shop, as chubby, as wooden, and as conscientiously dappled, but it was unreasonable to urge this as an objection, and I was incapable of finding any more technical drawback. Yielding to circumstance, I "threw my leg" over the brute, and after pacing gravely round the quadrangle that formed the yard, and jolting to my entrance gate and back, I decided that as he had neither fallen down nor kicked me off, it was worth paying twenty-five pounds for him, if only to get in out of the rain.

Mr. Knox accompanied me into the house and had a drink. He was a fair, spare young man, who looked like a stable boy among gentlemen, and a gentleman among stable boys. He belonged to a clan that cropped up in every grade of society in the county, from Sir Valentine Knox of Castle Knox down to the auctioneer Knox, who bore the attractive title of Larry the Liar. So far as I could judge, Florence McCarthy of that ilk occupied a shifting position about midway in the tribe. I had met him at dinner at Sir Valentine's, I had heard of him at an illicit auction, held by Larry the Liar, of brandy stolen from a wreck. They

were "Black Protestants," all of them, in virtue of their descent
from a godly soldier of Cromwell, and all were prepared at any
moment of the day or night to sell a horse.

"You'll be apt to find this place a bit lonesome after the hotel,"
remarked Mr. Flurry, sympathetically, as he placed his foot in its
steaming boot on the hob, "but it's a fine sound house anyway,
and lots of rooms in it, though indeed, to tell you the truth, I
never was through the whole of them since the time my great-
uncle, Denis McCarthy, died here. The dear knows I had
enough of it that time." He paused, and lit a cigarette—one of
my best, and quite thrown away upon him. "Those top floors,
now," he resumed, "I wouldn't make too free with them. There's
some of them would jump under you like a spring bed. Many's
the night I was in and out of those attics, following my poor
uncle when he had a bad turn on him—the horrors, y' know—
there were nights he never stopped walking through the house.
Good Lord! will I ever forget the morning he said he saw the
devil coming up the avenue! 'Look at the two horns on him, says
he, and he out with his gun and shot him, and, begad, it was his
own donkey!"

Mr. Knox gave a couple of short laughs. He seldom laughed,
having in unusual perfection the gravity of manner that is bred
by horse-dealing, probably from the habitual repression of all
emotion save disparagement.

The autumn evening, grey with rain, was darkening in the tall
windows, and the wind was beginning to make bullying rushes
among the shrubs in the area; a shower of soot rattled down the
chimney and fell on the hearthrug.

"More rain coming," said Mr. Knox, rising composedly; "you'll
have to put a goose down these chimneys some day soon, it's the
only way in the world to clean them. Well, I'm for the road. You'll
come out on the grey next week, I hope; the hounds'll be meeting here. Give a roar at him coming in at his jumps." He threw
his cigarette into the fire and extended a hand to me. "Good-bye,
Major, you'll see plenty of me and my hounds before you're
done. There's a power of foxes in the plantations here."

This was scarcely reassuring for a man who hoped to shoot
woodcock, and I hinted as much.

"Oh, is it the cock?" said Mr. Flurry; "b'leeve me, there never was a woodcock yet that minded hounds, now, no more than they'd mind rabbits! The best shoots ever I had here, the hounds were in it the day before."

When Mr. Knox had gone, I began to picture myself going across country roaring, like a man on a fire-engine, while Philippa put the goose down the chimney; but when I sat down to write to her I did not feel equal to being humorous about it. I dilated ponderously on my cold, my hard work, and my loneliness, and eventually went to bed at ten o'clock full of cold shivers and hot whisky-and-water.

After a couple of hours of feverish dozing, I began to understand what had driven Great-Uncle McCarthy to perambulate the house by night. Mrs. Cadogan had assured me that the Pope of Rome hadn't a betther bed undher him than myself; wasn't I down on the new flog mattherass the old masther bought in Father Scanlan's auction? By the smell I recognised that "flog" meant flock, otherwise I should have said my couch was stuffed with old boots. I have seldom spent a more wretched night. The rain drummed with soft fingers on my window panes; the house was full of noises. I seemed to see Great-Uncle McCarthy ranging the passages with Flurry at his heels; several times I thought I heard him. Whisperings seemed borne on the wind through my keyhole, boards creaked in the room overhead, and once I could have sworn that a hand passed, groping, over the panels of my door. I am, I may admit, a believer in ghosts; I even take in a paper that deals with their culture, but I cannot pretend that on that night I looked forward to a manifestation of Great-Uncle McCarthy with any enthusiasm.

The morning broke stormily, and I woke to find Mrs. Cadogan's understudy, a grimy nephew of about eighteen, standing by my bedside, with a black bottle in his hand.

"There's no bath in the house, sir," was his reply to my command; "but me A'nt said, would ye like a taggeen?"

This alternative proved to be a glass of raw whisky. I declined it.

I look back to that first week of housekeeping at Shreelane as to a comedy excessively badly staged, and striped with lurid melodrama. Towards its close I was positively home-sick for

Mrs. Raverty's, and I had not a single clean pair of boots. I am not one of those who hold the convention that in Ireland the rain never ceases, day or night, but I must say that my first November at Shreelane was composed of weather of which my friend Flurry Knox remarked that you wouldn't meet a Christian out of doors, unless it was a snipe or a dispensary doctor. To this lamentable category might be added a resident magistrate. Daily, shrouded in mackintosh, I set forth for the Petty Sessions Courts of my wide district; daily, in the inevitable atmosphere of wet frieze and perjury, I listened to indictments of old women who plucked geese alive, of publicans whose hospitality to their friends broke forth uncontrollaby on Sunday afternoons, of "parties" who, in the language of the police sergeant, where subtly defined as "not to say dhrunk, but in good fighting thrim."

I got used to it all in time—I suppose one can get used to anything—I even became callous to the surprises of Mrs. Cadogan's cooking. As the weather hardened and the woodcock came in, and one by one I discovered and nailed up the rat holes, I began to find life endurable, and even to feel some remote sensation of home-coming when the grey horse turned in at the gate of Shreelane.

The one feature of my establishment to which I could not become inured was the pervading subpresence of some thing or things which, for my own convenience, I summarised as Great-Uncle McCarthy. There were nights on which I was certain that I heard the inebriate shuffle of his foot overhead, the touch of his fumbling hand against the walls. There were dark times before the dawn when sounds went to and fro, the moving of weights, the creaking of doors, a far-away rapping in which was a workmanlike suggestion of the undertaker, a rumble of wheels on the avenue. Once I was impelled to the perhaps imprudent measure of cross-examining Mrs. Cadogan. Mrs. Cadogan, taking the preliminary precaution of crossing herself, asked me fatefully what day of the week it was.

"Friday!" she repeated after me. "Friday! The Lord save us!" 'Twas a Friday the old masther was buried!"

At this point a saucepan opportunely boiled over, and Mrs. Cadogan fled with it to the scullery, and was seen no more.

In the process of time I brought Great-Uncle McCarthy down to a fine point. On Friday nights he made coffins and drove hearses; during the rest of the week he rarely did more than patter and shuffle in the attics over my head.

One night, about the middle of December, I awoke, suddenly aware that some noise had fallen like a heavy stone into my dreams. As I felt for the matches it came again, the long, grudging groan and the uncompromising bang of the cross door at the head of the kitchen stairs. I told myself that it was a draught that had done it, but it was a perfectly still night. Even as I listened, a sound of wheels on the avenue shook the stillness. The thing was getting past a joke. In a few minutes I was stealthily groping my way down my own staircase, with a box of matches in my hand, enforced by scientific curiosity, but none the less armed with a stick. I stood in the dark at the top of the back stairs and listened; the snores of Mrs. Cadogan and her nephew Peter rose tranquilly from their respective lairs. I descended to the kitchen and lit a candle; there was nothing unusual there, except a great portion of the Cadogan wearing apparel, which was arranged at the fire, and was being serenaded by two crickets. Whatever had opened the door, my household was blameless.

The kitchen was not attractive, yet I felt indisposed to leave it. None the less, it appeared to be my duty to inspect the yard. I put the candle on the table and went forth into the outer darkness. Not a sound was to be heard. The night was very cold, and so dark, that I could scarcely distinguish the roofs of the stables against the sky; the house loomed tall and oppressive above me; I was conscious of how lonely it stood in the dumb and barren country. Spirits were certainly futile creatures, childish in their manifestations, stupidly content with the old machinery of raps and rumbles. I thought how fine a scene might be played on a stage like this; if I were a ghost, how bluely I would glimmer at the windows, how whimperingly chatter in the wind. Something whirled out of the darkness above me, and fell with a flop on the ground, just at my feet. I jumped backwards, in point of fact I made for the kitchen door, and, with my hand on the latch, stood still and waited. Nothing further happened; the thing that lay there did not stir. I struck a match. The moment of tension turned to bathos as the light flickered on nothing more fateful than a dead crow.

Dead it certainly was. I could have told that without looking at it; but why should it, at some considerable period after its death, fall from the clouds at my feet? But did it fall from the clouds? I struck another match, and stared up at the impenetrable face of the house. There was no hint of solution in the dark windows, but I determined to go up and search the rooms that gave upon the yard.

How cold it was! I can feel now the frozen musty air of those attics, with their rat-eaten floors and wall-papers furred with damp. I went softly from one to another, feeling like a burglar in my own house, and found nothing in elucidation of the mystery. The windows were hermetically shut, and sealed with cobwebs. There was no furniture, except in the end room, where a wardrobe without doors stood in a corner, empty save for the solemn presence of a monstrous tall hat. I went back to bed, cursing those powers of darkness that had got me out of it, and heard no more.

My landlord had not failed of his promise to visit my coverts with his hounds; in fact, he fulfilled it rather more conscientiously than seemed to me quite wholesome for the cock-shooting. I maintained a silence which I felt to be magnanimous on the part of a man who cared nothing for hunting and a great deal for shooting, and wished the hounds more success in the slaughter of my foxes than seemed to be granted to them. I met them all, one red frosty evening, as I drove down the long hill to my demesne gates, Flurry at their head, in his shabby pink coat and dingy breeches, the hounds trailing dejectedly behind him and his half-dozen companions.

"What luck?" I called out, drawing rein as I met them.

"None," said Mr. Flurry briefly. He did not stop, neither did he remove his pipe from the down-twisted corner of his mouth; his eye at me was cold and sour. The other members of the hunt passed me with equal hauteur; I thought they took their ill luck very badly.

On foot, among the last of the straggling hounds, cracking a carman's whip, and swearing comprehensively at them all, slouched my friend Slipper. Our friendship had begun in Court, the relative positions of the dock and judgment-seat forming no obstacle to its progress, and had been cemented during several days' tramping after snipe. He was, as usual, a little drunk, and he hailed me as though I were a ship.

"Ahoy, Major Yeates!" he shouted, bringing himself up with a lurch against my cart; "it's hunting you should be, in place of sending poor divils to gaol!"

"But I hear you had no hunting," I said.

"Ye heard that, did ye?" Slipper rolled upon me an eye like that of a profligate pug. "Well, begor, ye heard no more than the thruth."

"But where are all the foxes?" said I.

"Begor, I don't know no more than your honour. And Shreelane—that there used to be as many foxes in it as there's crosses in a yard of check! Well, well, I'll say nothin' for it, only that it's quare! Here, Vaynus! Naygress!" Slipper uttered a yell, hoarse with whisky, in adjuration of two elderly ladies of the pack who had profited by our conversation to stray away into an adjacent cottage. "Well, good-night, Major. Mr. Flurry's as cross as briars, and he'll have me ate!"

He set off at a surprisingly steady run, cracking his whip, and whooping like a madman. I hope that when I also am fifty I shall be able to run like Slipper.

That frosty evening was followed by three others like unto it, and a flight of woodcock came in. I calculated that I could do with five guns, and I despatched invitations to shoot and dine on the following day to four of the local sportsmen, among whom was, of course, my landlord. I remember that in my letter to the latter I expressed a facetious hope that my bag of cock would be more successful than his of foxes had been.

The answers to my invitations were not what I expected. All, without so much as a conventional regret, declined my invitation; Mr. Knox added that he hoped the bag of cock would be to my liking, and that I need not be "affraid" that the hounds would trouble my converts anymore. Here was war! I gazed in stupefaction at the crooked scrawl in which my landlord had declared it. It was wholly and entirely inexplicable, and instead of going to sleep comfortably over the fire and my newspaper as a gentleman should, I spent the evening in irritated ponderings over this bewildering and exasperating change of front on the part of my friendly squireens.

My shoot the next day was scarcely a success. I shot the woods in company with my gamekeeper, Tim Connor, a gentleman whose duties mainly consisted in limiting the poaching privileges to his personal friends, and whatever my offence might have been, Mr. Knox could have wished me no bitterer punishment than hearing the unavailing shouts of "Mark cock!" and seeing my birds winging their way from the coverts, far out of shot. Tim Connor and I got ten couple between us; it might have been thirty if my neighbours had not boycotted me, for what I could only suppose was the slackness of their hounds.

I was dog-tired that night, having walked enough for three men, and I slept the deep, insatiable sleep that I had earned. It was somewhere about 3 A.M. that I was gradually awakened by a continuous knocking, interspersed with muffled calls. Great-Uncle McCarthy had never before given tongue, and I freed one ear from blankets to listen. Then I remembered that Peter had told me the sweep had promised to arrive that morning, and to arrive early. Blind with sleep and fury I went to the passage window, and thence desired the sweep to go to the devil. It availed me little. For the remainder of the night I could hear him pacing round the house, trying the windows, banging at the doors, and calling upon Peter Cadogan as the priests of Baal called upon their god. At six o'clock I had fallen into a troubled doze, when Mrs. Cadogan knocked at my door and imparted the information that the sweep had arrived. My answer need not be recorded, but in spite of it the door opened, and my house-keeper, in a weird *déshabille,* effectively lighted by the orange beams of her candle, entered my room.

"God forgive me, I never seen one I'd hate as much as that sweep!" she began; "he's these three hours—arrah, what, three hours!—no, but all night, raising tallywack and tandem round the house to get at the chimbleys."

"Well, for Heaven's sake let him get at the chimneys and let me go to sleep," I answered, goaded to desperation, "and you may tell him from that if I hear his voice again I'll shoot him!"

Mrs. Cadogan silently left my bedside, and as she closed the door she said to herself, "The Lord save us!"

Subsequent events may be briefly summarised. At 7.30 I was awakened anew by a thunderous sound in the chimney, and a brick crashed into the fireplace, followed at a short interval by two dead jackdaws and their nests. At eight, I was informed by Peter that there was no hot water, and that he wished the divil would roast the same sweep. At 9.30, when I came down to breakfast, there was no fire anywhere, and my coffee, made in the coach-house, tasted of soot. I put on an overcoat and opened my letters. About fourth or fifth in the uninteresing heap came one in an egregiously disguised hand.

"Sir," it began, "this is to inform you your unsportsmanlike conduct has been discovered. You have been suspected this good while of shooting the Shreelane foxes, it is known now you do worse. Parties have seen your gamekeeper going regular to meet the Saturday early train at Salters Hill Station, with your grey horse under a cart, and your labels on the boxes, and we know as well as *your agent in Cork* what it is you have in those boxes. Be warned in time.—Your Wellwisher."

I read this through twice before its drift became apparent, and I realised that I was accused of improving my shooting and my finances by the simple expedient of selling my foxes. That is to say, I was in a worse position than if I had stolen a horse, or murdered Mrs. Cadogan, or got drunk three times a week in Skebawn.

For a few moments I fell into wild laughter, and then, aware that it was rather a bad business to let a lie of this kind get a start, I sat down demolish the preposterous charge in a letter to Flurry Knox. Somehow, as I selected my sentences, it was borne in upon me that, if the letter spoke the truth, circumstantial evidence was rather against me. Mere lofty repudiation would be unavailing, and by my infernal facetiousness about the woodcock I had effectively filled in the case against myself. At all events, the first thing to do was to establish a basis, and have it out with Tim Connor. I rang the bell.

"Peter, is Tim Connor about the place?"

"He is not, sir. I heard him say he was going west the hill to mend the bounds fence." Peter's face was covered with soot, his eyes were red, and he coughed ostentatiously. "The sweep's after breaking one of his brushes within in yer bedroom chimney, sir," he went on, with all the satisfaction of his class in announcing domestic calamity; "he's above on the roof now, and he'd be thankful to you to go up to him."

I followed him upstairs in that state of simmering patience that any employer of Irish labour must know and sympathise with. I climbed the rickety ladder and squeezed through the dirty trapdoor involved in the ascent to the roof, and was confronted by the hideous face of the sweep, black against the frosty blue sky. He had encamped with all his paraphernalia on the flat top of the roof, and was good enough to rise and put his pipe in his pocket on my arrival.

"Good morning, Major. That's a grand view you have up here," said the sweep. He was evidently far too well bred to talk shop. "I thravelled every roof in this counthry, and there isn't one where you'd get as handsome a prospect!"

Theoretically he was right, but I had not come up to the roof to discuss scenery, and demanded brutally why he had sent for me. The explanation involved a recital of the special genius required to sweep the Shreelane chimneys; of the fact that the sweep had in infancy been sent up and down every one of them by Great-Uncle McCarthy; of the three ass-loads of soot that by his peculiar skill he had this morning taken from the kitchen chimney; of its present purity, the draught being such that it would "dhraw up a young cat with it." Finally—realising that I could endure no more—he explained that my bedroom chimney had got what he called "a wynd" in it, and he proposed to climb down a little way in the stack to try "would he get to come at the brush." The sweep was very small, the chimney very large. I stipulated that he should have a rope round his waist, and despite the illegality, I let him go. He went down like a monkey, digging his toes and fingers into the niches made for the purpose in the old chimney; Peter held the rope. I lit a cigarette and waited.

Certainly the view from the roof was worth coming up to look at. It was rough, heathery country on one side, with a string of little blue lakes running like a turquoise necklet round the base of a firry hill, and patches of pale green pasture were set amidst the rocks are heather. A silvery flash behind the undulations of the hills told where the Atlantic lay in immense plains of sunlight. I turned to survey with an owner's eyes my own grey woods and straggling plantations of larch, and espied a man coming out of the western wood. He had something on his back, and he was walking very fast; a rabbit poacher no doubt. As he passed out of sight into the back avenue he was beginning to run. At the same instant I saw on the hill beyond my western boundaries half-a-dozen horsemen scrambling my zigzag ways down towards the wood. There was one red coat among them; it came first at the gap in the fence that Tim Connor had gone out to mend, and with the others was lost to sight in the covert, from which, in another instant, came clearly through the frosty air a shout of "Gone to ground!" Tremendous horn blowings followed, then, all in the same moment, I saw the hounds break in full cry from the wood, and come stringing over the grass and up the back avenue towards the yard gate. Were they running a fresh fox into the stables?

I do not profess to be a hunting-man, but I am an Irishman, and so, it is perhaps superfluous to state, is Peter. We forgot the sweep as if he had never existed, and precipitated ourselves down the ladder, down the stairs, and out into the yard. One side of the yard is formed by the coach-house and a long stable, with a range of lofts above them, planned on the heroic scale in such matters that obtained in Ireland formerly. These join the house at the corner by the back door. A long flight of stone steps leads to the lofts, and up these, as Peter and I emerged from the back door, the hounds were struggling helter-skelter. Almost simultaneously there was a confused clatter of hoofs in the back avenue, and Flurry Knox came stooping at a gallop under the archway followed by three or four other riders. They flung themselves from their horses and made for the steps of the loft; more hounds pressed, yelling, on their heels, the din was indescribable, and justified Mrs. Cadogan's subsequent remark that "when she heard the noise she thought 'twas the end of the world and the divil collecting his own!"

I jostled in the wake of the party, and found myself in the loft, wading in hay, and nearly deafened by the clamour that was bandied about the high roof and walls. At the farther end of the loft the hounds were raging in the hay, encouraged thereto by the whoops and screeches of Flurry and his friends. High up in the gable of the loft, where it joined the main wall of the house, there was a small door, and I noted with a transient surprise that there was a long ladder leading up to it. Even as it caught my eye a hound fought his way out of a drift of hay and began to jump at the ladder, throwing his tongue vociferously, and even clambering up a few rungs in his excitement.

"There's the way he's gone!" roared Flurry, striving through hounds and hay towards the ladder, "Trumpeter has him! What's up there, back of the door, Major? I don't remember it at all."

My crimes had evidently been forgotten in the supremacy of the moment. While I was futilely asserting that had the fox gone up the ladder he could not possibly have opened the door and shut it after him, even if the door led anywhere, which, to the best of my belief, it did not, the door in question opened, and to my amazement the sweep appeared at it. He gesticulated violently, and over the tumult was heard to asseverate that there was nothing above there, only a way into the flue, and anyone would be destroyed with the soot——

"Ah, go to blazes with your soot!" interrupted Flurry, already half-way up the ladder.

I followed him, the other men pressing up behind me. That Trumpeter had made no mistake was instantly brought home to our noses by the reek of fox that met us at the door. Instead of a chimney, we found ourselves in a dilapidated bedroom, full of people. Tim Connor was there, the sweep was there, and a squalid elderly man and woman on whom I had never set eyes before. There was a large open fireplace, black with the soot the sweep had brought down with him, and on the table stood a bottle of my own special Scotch whisky. In one corner of the room was a pile of broken packing-cases, and beside these on the floor lay a bag in which something kicked.

Flurry, looking more uncomfortable and nonplussed than I could have believed possible, listened in silence to the ceaseless harangue of the elderly woman. The hounds were yelling like lost spirits in the loft below, but her voice pierced the uproar like a bagpipe. It was an unspeakably vulgar voice, yet it was not the voice of a countrywoman, and there were frowzy remnants of respectability about her general aspect.

"And is it you, Flurry Knox, that's calling me a disgrace! Disgrace, indeed, am I? Me that was your poor mother's own uncle's daughter, and as good a McCarthy as ever stood in Shreelane!"

What followed I could not comprehend, owing to the fact that the sweep kept up a perpetual undercurrent of explanation to me as to how he had got down the wrong chimney. I noticed that his breath stank of whisky—Scotch, not the native variety.

Never, as long as Flurry Knox lives to blow a horn, will he hear the last of the day that he ran his mother's first cousin to ground in the attic. Never, while Mrs. Cadogan can hold a basting spoon, will she cease to recount how, on the same occasion, she plucked and roasted ten couple of woodcock in one torrid hour to provide luncheon for the hunt. In the glory of this achievement her confederacy with the stowaways in the attic is wholly slurred over, in much the same manner as the startling outburst of summons for trespass, brought by Tim Connor during the remainder of the shooting season, obscured the unfortunate episode of the bagged fox. It was, of course, zeal for my shooting that induced him to assist Mr. Knox's disreputable relations in the deportation of my foxes; and I have allowed it to remain at that.

In fact, the only things not allowed to remain were Mr. and Mrs. McCarthy Gannon. They, as my landlord informed me, in the midst of vast apologies, had been permitted to squat at Shreelane until my tenancy began, and having then ostentatiously and abusively left the house, they had, with the connivance of the Cadogans, secretly returned to roost in the corner attic, to sell foxes under the ægis of my name, and to make inroads on my belongings. They retained connection with the outer world by means of the ladder and the loft, and with the house in general, and my whisky in particular, by a door into the other attics—a door concealed by the wardrobe in which reposed Great-Uncle McCarthy's tall hat.

It is with the greatest regret that I relinquish the prospect of writing a monograph on Great-Uncle McCarthy for a Spiritualistic Journal, but with the departure of his relations he ceased to manifest himself, and neither the nailing up packing-cases, nor the rumble of the cart that took them to the station, disturbed my sleep for the future.

I understand that the task of clearing out the McCarthy Gannon's effects was of a nature that necessitated two glasses of whisky per man; and if the remnants of rabbit and jackdaw disinterred in the process were anything like the crow that was thrown out of the window at my feet, I do not grudge the restorative.

As Mrs. Cadogan remarked to the sweep, "A Turk couldn't stand it."

LENA WRACE°
May Sinclair
(1863–1946)

She arranged herself there, on that divan, and I knew she'd
come to tell me all about it. It was wonderful, how, at forty-
seven, she could still give that effect of triumph and excess, of
something rich and ruinous and beautiful spread out on the bro-
cades. The attitude showed me that her affair with Norman
Hippisley was prospering; otherwise she couldn't have afforded
the extravagance of it.

"I know what you want," I said. "You want me to congratulate
you."

"Yes. I do."

"I congratulate you on your courage."

"Oh, you don't like him," she said placably.

"No, I don't like him at all."

"He likes you," she said. "He thinks no end of your painting."

"I'm not denying he's a judge of painting. I'm not even denying he can paint a little himself."

"Better than you, Roly."

"If you allow for the singular, obscene ugliness of his imagination, yes."

"It's beautiful enough when he gets it into paint," she said.
"He makes beauty. His own beauty."

"Oh, very much his own."

°From *The Dial* (July 1921).

"Well, *you* just go on imitating other people's—God's or somebody's."

She continued with her air of perfect reasonableness. "I know he isn't good-looking. Not half so good-looking as you are. But I like him. I like his slender little body and his clever, faded face. There's a quality about him, a distinction. And look at his eyes. *Your* mind doesn't come rushing and blazing out of your eyes, my dear."

"No. No. I'm afraid it doesn't rush. And for all the blaze—"

"Well, that's what I'm in love with, the rush, Roly, and the blaze. And I'm in love, *for the first time*" (she underlined it) "with a man."

"Come," I said, "come."

"Oh, *I* know. I know you're thinking of Lawson Young and Dickey Harper."

I was.

"Well, but they don't count. I wasn't in love with Lawson. It was his career. If he hadn't been a Cabinet Minister; if he hadn't been so desperately gone on me; if he hadn't said it all depended on me—"

"Yes," I said. "I can see how it would go to your head."

"It didn't. It went to my heart." She was quite serious and solemn. "I held him in my hands, Roly. And he held England. I couldn't let him drop, could I? I had to think of England."

It was wonderful—Lena Wrace thinking that she thought of England.

I said, "Of course. But for your political foresight and your virtuous action we should never have had Tariff Reform."

"We should never have had anything," she said. "And look at him now. Look how he's crumpled up since he left me. It's pitiful."

"It is. I'm afraid Mrs. Withers doesn't care about Tariff Reform."

"Poor thing. No. Don't imagine I'm jealous of her, Roly. She hasn't got him. I mean she hasn't got what I had."

"All the same he left you. And you weren't ecstatically happy with him the last year or two."

"I daresay I'd have done better to have married you, if that's what you mean."

It wasn't what I meant. But she'd always entertained the illusion that she could marry me any minute if she wanted to; and I hadn't the heart to take it from her since it seemed to console her for the way, the really very infamous way, he had left her.

So I said, "Much better."

"It would have been so nice, so safe," she said. "But I never played for safety." Then she made one of her quick turns.

"Frances Archdale ought to marry you. Why doesn't she?"

"How should I know? Frances's reasons would be exquisite. I suppose I didn't appeal to her sense of fitness."

"Sense of fiddlesticks. She just hasn't got any temperament, that girl."

"Any temperament for me, you mean."

"I mean pure cussedness," said Lena.

"Perhaps. But, you see, if I were unfortunate enough she probably *would* marry me. If I lost my eyesight or a leg or an arm, if I couldn't sell any more pictures—"

"If you can understand Frances, you can understand me. That's how I felt about Dickey. I wasn't in love with him. I was sorry for him. I knew he'd go to pieces if I wasn't there to keep him together. Perhaps it's the maternal instinct."

"Perhaps," I said. Lena's reasons for her behaviour amused me; they were never exquisite, like Frances's, but she was anxious that you should think they were.

"So you see," she said, "they don't count, and Norry really *is* the first."

I reflected that he would be also, probably, the last. She had, no doubt, to make the most of him. But it was preposterous that she should waste so much good passion; preposterous that she should imagine for one moment she could keep the fellow. I had to warn her.

"Of course, if you care to take the risk of him—" I said. "He won't stick to you, Lena."

"Why shouldn't he?"

I couldn't tell her. I couldn't say, "Because you're thirteen years older than he is." That would have been cruel. And it would have been absurd, too, when she could so easily look not a year older than his desiccated thirty-four.

It only took a little success like this, her actual triumph in securing him.

So I said, "Because it isn't in him. He's a bounder and a rotter." Which was true.

"Not a bounder, Roly dear. His father's Sir Gilbert Hippisley. Hippisleys of Leicestershire."

"A moral bounder, Lena. A slimy eel. Slips and wriggles out of things. You'll never hold him. You're not his first affair, you know."

"I don't care," she said, "as long as I'm his last."

I could only stand and stare at that; her monstrous assumption of his fidelity. Why, he couldn't even be faithful to one art. He wrote as well as he painted, and he acted as well as he wrote, and he was never really happy with a talent till he had debauched it.

"The others," she said, "don't bother me a bit. He's slipped and wriggled out of their clutches, if you like. . . . Yet there was something about all of them. Distinguished. That's it. He's so awfully fine and fastidious about the women he takes up with. It flatters you, makes you feel so sure of yourself. You know he wouldn't take up with *you* if you weren't fine and fastidious, too—one of his great ladies. . . . You think I'm a snob, Roly?"

"I think you don't mind coming *after* Lady Willersey."

"Well," she said, "if you *have* to come after somebody—"

"True." I asked her if she was giving me her reasons.

"Yes, if you want them. *I* don't. I'm content to love out of all reason."

And she did. She loved extravagantly, unintelligibly, out of all reason; yet irrefutably. To the end. There's a sort of reason in that, isn't there? She had the sad logic of her passions.

She got up and gathered herself together in her sombre, violent beauty and in its glittering sheath, her red fox skins, all her savage splendour, leaving a scent of crushed orris root in the warmth of her lair.

Well, she managed to hold him, tight, for a year, fairly intact. I can't for the life of me imagine how she could have cared for the fellow, with his face all dried and frayed with make-up. There was something lithe and sinuous about him that may, of course, have appealed to her. And I can understand his infatuation. He was decadent, exhausted; and there would be moments when he found her primitive violence stimulating, before it wore him out.

They kept up the *ménage* for two astounding years.

Well, not so very astounding, if you come to think of it. There was Lena's money, left her by old Weinberger, her maternal uncle. You've got to reckon with Lena's money. Not that she, poor soul, ever reckoned with it; she was absolutely free from that taint, and she couldn't conceive other people reckoning. Only, instinctively, she knew. She knew how to hold Hippisley. She knew there were things he couldn't resist, things like wines and motor cars he could be faithful to. From the very beginning she built for permanence, for eternity. She took a house in Avenue Road with a studio for Hippisley in the garden; she bought a motor car and engaged an inestimable cook. Lena's dinners, in those years, were exquisite affairs, and she took care to ask the right people, people who would be useful to Hippisley, dealers whom old Weinberger had known, and journalists and editors and publishers. And all his friends and her own; even friends' friends. Her hospitality was boundless and eccentric, and Hippisley liked that sort of thing. He thrived in a liberal air, an air of gorgeous spending, though he sported a supercilious smile at the *fioritura*, the luscious excess of it. He had never had too much, poor devil, of his own. I've seen the little fellow swaggering about at her parties, with his sharp, frayed face, looking fine and fastidious, safeguarding himself with twinklings and gestures that gave the dear woman away. I've seen him, in goggles and a magnificent fur-lined coat, shouting to her chauffeur, giving counter orders to her own, while she sat snuggling up in the corner of the car, smiling at his mastery.

It went on till poor Lena was forty-nine. Then, as she said, she began to "shake in her shoes." I told her it didn't matter so long as she didn't let him see her shaking. That depressed her, because she knew she couldn't hide it; there was nothing secret in her nature; she had always let "them" see. And they were bothering her—"the others"—more than "a bit." She was jealous of every one of them, of any woman he said more than five words to.

Jealous of the models, first of all, before she found out that they didn't matter; he was so used to them. She would stick there, in his studio, while they sat, until one day he got furious and turned her out of it. But she'd seen enough to set her mind at rest. He was fine and fastidious, and the models were all "common."

"And their figures, Roly, you should have seen them when they were undressed. Of course, you *have* seen them. Well, there isn't—is there?"

And there wasn't. Hippisley had grown out of models just as he had grown out of cheap Burgundy. And he'd left the stage, because he was tired of it, so there was, mercifully, no danger from that quarter. What she dreaded was the moment when he'd "take" to writing again, for then he'd have to have a secretary. Also she was jealous of his writing because it absorbed more of his attention than his painting, and exhausted him more, left her less of him.

And that year, their third year, he flung up his painting and was, as she expressed it, "at it" again. Worse than ever. And he wanted a secretary.

She took care to find him one. One who wouldn't be dangerous. "You should just see her, Roly." She brought her in to tea one day for me to look at and say whether she would "do."

I wasn't sure—what can you be sure of?—but I could see why Lena thought she would. She was a little unhealthy thing, dark and sallow and sulky, with thin lips that showed a lack of temperament, and she had a stiffness and preciseness, like a Board School teacher—just that touch of "commonness" which Lena relied on to put him off. She wore a shabby brown skirt and a yellowish blouse. Her name was Ethel Reeves.

Lena had secured safety, she said, in the house. But what was the good of that, when outside it he was going about everywhere with Sybil Fermor? She came and told me all about it, with a sort of hope that I'd say something either consoling or revealing, something that she could go on.

"*You* know him, Roly," she said.

I reminded her that she hadn't always given me that credit.

"*I* know how he spends his time," she said. "How do you know?"

"Well, for one thing, Ethel tells me."

"How does she know?"

"She—she posts the letters."

"Does she read them?"

"She needn't. He's too transparent."

"Lena, do you use her to spy on him?" I said.

"Well," she retorted, "if he uses her—"

I asked her if it hadn't struck her that Sybil Fermor might be using him?

"Do you mean—as a *paravent*? Or," she revised it, "a parachute?"

"For Bertie Granville," I elucidated. "A parachute, by all means."

She considered it. "It won't work," she said. "If it's her reputation she's thinking of, wouldn't Norry be worse?"

I said that was the beauty of him, if Letty Granville's attention was to be diverted.

"Oh, Roly," she said, "do you really think it's that?" I said I did, and she powdered her nose and said I was a dear and I'd bucked her up no end, and went away quite happy.

Letty Granville's divorce suit proved to her that I was right.

The next time I saw her she told me she'd been mistaken about Sybil Fermor. It was Lady Hermione Nevin. Norry had been using Sybil as a *"paravent"* for *her*. I said she was wrong again. Didn't she know that Hermione was engaged to Billy Craven? They were head over ears in love with each other. I asked her what on earth had made her think of her? And she said Lady Hermione had paid him thirty guineas for a picture. That looked, she said, as if she was pretty far gone on him. (She tended to disparage Hippisley's talents. Jealousy again.)

I said it looked as if he had the iciest reasons for cultivating Lady Hermione. And again she told me I was a dear. "You don't know, Roly, what a comfort you are to me."

Then Barbara Vining turned up out of nowhere, and from the first minute Lena gave herself up for lost.

"I'm done for," she said. "I'd fight her if it was any good fighting. But what chance have I? At forty-nine against nineteen, and that face?"

The face was adorable if you adore a child's face on a woman's body. Small and pink; a soft, innocent forehead; fawn skin hair, a fawn's nose, a fawn's mouth, a fawn's eyes. You saw her at Lena's garden parties, staring at Hippisley over the rim of her plate while she browsed on Lena's cakes and ices, or bounding about Lena's tennis court with the sash ribbons flying from her little butt end.

Oh, yes; she had her there. As much as he wanted. And there would be Ethel Reeves, in a new blouse, looking on from a back seat, subtle and sullen, or handing round cups and plates without speaking to anybody, like a servant. I used to think she spied on them for Lena. They were always mouthing about the garden together or sitting secretly in corners; Lena even had her to stay with them, let him take her for long drives in her car. She knew when she was beaten.

I said, "Why do you let him do it, Lena? Why don't you turn them both neck and crop out of the house?"

"Because I want him in it. I want him at any cost. And I want him to have what he wants, too, even if it's Barbara. I want him to be happy. . . . I'm making a virtue of necessity. It can be done, Roly, if you give up beautifully."

I put it to her it wasn't giving up beautifully to fret herself into an unbecoming illness, to carry her disaster on her face. She would come to me looking more ruined than ruinous, haggard and ashy, her eyes all shrunk and hot with crying, and stand before the glass, looking at herself and dabbing on powder in an utter abandonment to misery.

"I know," she moaned. "As if losing him wasn't enough I must go and lose my looks. I know crying's simply suicidal at my age, yet I keep on at it. I'm doing for myself. I'm digging my own grave, Roly. A little deeper every day."

Then she said suddenly, "Do you know, you're the only man in London I could come to looking like this."

I said, "Isn't that a bit unkind of you? It sounds as though you thought I didn't matter."

She broke down on that. "Can't you see it's because I know I don't any more? Nobody cares whether my nose is red or not. But you're not a brute. You don't let me feel I don't matter. I know I never did matter to you, Roly, but the effect's soothing, all the same. . . . Ethel says if she were me she wouldn't stand it. To have it going on under my nose. Ethel is so high-minded. I suppose it's easy to be high-minded if you've always looked like that. And if you've never *had* anybody. She doesn't know what it is. I tell you, I'd rather have Norry there with Barbara than not have him at all."

I thought and said that would just about suit Hippisley's book. He'd rather be there than anywhere else, since he had to be somewhere. To be sure she irritated him with her perpetual clinging, and wore him out. I've seen him wince at the sound of her voice in the room. He'd say things to her; not often, but just enough to see how far he could go. He was afraid of going too far. He wasn't prepared to give up the comfort of Lena's house, the opulence and peace. There wasn't one of Lena's wines he could have turned his back on. After all, when she worried him he could keep himself locked up in the studio away from her.

There was Ethel Reeves; but Lena didn't worry about his being locked up with *her.* She was very kind to Hippisley's secretary. Since she wasn't dangerous, she liked to see her there, well housed, eating rich food, and getting stronger and stronger every day.

I must say my heart bled for Lena when I thought of young Barbara. It was still bleeding when one afternoon she walked in with her old triumphant look; she wore her hat with an *air crâne,* and the powder on her face was even and intact, like the first pure fall of snow. She looked ten years younger and I judged that Hippisley's affair with Barbara was at an end.

Well—it had never had a beginning; nor the ghost of a beginning. It had never happened at all. She had come to tell me that: that there was nothing in it; nothing but her jealousy; the miserable, damnable jealousy that made her think things. She said it would be a lesson to her to trust him in the future not to go falling in love. For, she argued, if he hadn't done it this time with Barbara, he'd never do it.

I asked her how she knew he hadn't, this time, when appearances all pointed that way? And she said that Barbara had come and told her.

Somebody, it seemed, had been telling Barbara it was known that she'd taken Hippisley from Lena, and that Lena was crying herself into a nervous break-down. And the child had gone straight to Lena and told her it was a beastly lie. She hadn't taken Hippisley. She liked ragging with him and all that, and being seen about with him at parties, because he was a celebrity and it made the other women, the women he wouldn't talk to, furious. But as for taking him, why, she wouldn't take him from anybody as a gift. She didn't want him, a scrubby old thing like that. She didn't *like* that dragged look about his mouth and the way the skin wrinkled on his eyelids. There was a sincerity about Barbara that would have blasted Hippisley if he'd known.

Besides, she wouldn't have hurt Lena for the world. She wouldn't have spoken to Norry if she'd dreamed that Lena minded. But Lena had seemed so remarkably not to mind. When she came to that part of it she cried.

Lena said that was all very well, and it didn't matter whether Barbara was in love with Norry or not; but how did she know Norry wasn't in love with *her*? And Barbara replied amazingly that of course she knew. They'd been alone together.

When I remarked that it was precisely *that,* Lena said, No. That was nothing in itself; but it would prove one way or another; and it seemed that when Norry found himself alone with Barbara, he used to yawn.

After that Lena settled down to a period of felicity. She'd come to me, excited and exulting, bringing her poor little happiness with her like a new toy. She'd sit there looking at it, turning it over and over, and holding it up to me to show how beautiful it was.

She pointed out to me that I had been wrong and she right about him, from the beginning. She knew him. "And to think what a fool, what a damned silly fool I was, with my jealousy. When all those years there was never anybody but me. Do you remember Sybil Fermor, and Lady Hermione—and Barbara? To think I should have so clean forgotten what he was like. . . . Don't you think, Roly, there must be something in me, after all, to have kept him all those years?"

I said there must indeed have been, to have inspired so

remarkable a passion. For Hippisley was making love to her all over again. Their happy relations were proclaimed, not only by her own engaging frankness, but still more by the marvellous renaissance of her beauty. She had given up her habit of jealousy as she had given up eating sweets, because both were murderous to her complexion. Not that Hippisley gave her any cause. He had ceased to cultivate the society of young and pretty ladies, and devoted himself with almost ostentatious fidelity to Lena. Their affair had become irreproachable with time; it had the permanence of a successful marriage without the unflattering element of legal obligation. And he had kept his secretary. Lena had left off being afraid either that Ethel would leave or that Hippisley would put some dangerous woman in her place.

There was no change in Ethel, except that she looked rather more subtle and less sullen. Lena ignored her subtlety as she had ignored her sulks. She had no more use for her as a confidant and spy, and Ethel lived in a back den off Hippisley's study with her Remington, and displayed a convenient apathy in allowing herself to be ignored.

"Really," Lena would say in the unusual moments when she thought of her, "if it wasn't for the clicking, you wouldn't know she was there."

And as a secretary she maintained, up to the last, an admirable efficiency.

Up to the last.

It was Hippisley's death that ended it. You know how it happened—suddenly, of heart failure, in Paris. He'd gone there with Furnival to get material for that book they were doing together. Lena was literally "prostrated" with the shock; and Ethel Reeves had to go over to Paris to bring back his papers and his body.

It was the day after the funeral that it all came out. Lena and Ethel were sitting up together over the papers and the letters, turning out his bureau. I suppose that, in the grand immunity his death conferred on her, poor Lena had become provokingly possessive. I can hear her saying to Ethel that there had never been anybody but her, all those years. Praising his faithfulness; holding out her dead happiness, and apologizing to Ethel for talking about it when Ethel didn't understand, never having had any.

She must have said something like that, to bring it on herself, just then, of all moments.

And I can see Ethel Reeves, sitting at his table, stolidly sorting out his papers, wishing that Lena'd go away and leave her to her work. And her sullen eyes firing out questions, asking her what she wanted, what she had to do with Norman Hippisley's papers, what she was there for, fussing about, when it was all over?

What she wanted—what she had come for—was her letters. They were locked up in his bureau in the secret drawer.

She told me what had happened then. Ethel lifted her sullen, subtle eyes and said, "You think he kept them?"

She said she knew he'd kept them. They were in that drawer.

And Ethel said, "Well then, he didn't. They aren't. He burnt them. *We* burnt them. . . . We could, at least, get rid of *them!*"

Then she threw it at her. She had been Hippisley's mistress for three years.

When Lena asked for proofs of the incredible assertion she had *her* letters to show.

Oh, it was her moment. She must have been looking out for it, saving up for it, all those years; gloating over her exquisite secret, her return for all the slighting and ignoring. That was what had made her poisonous, the fact that Lena hadn't reckoned with her, hadn't thought her dangerous, hadn't been afraid to leave Hippisley with her, the rich, arrogant contempt in her assumption that Ethel would "do" and her comfortable confidences. It made her amorous and malignant. It stimulated her to the attempt.

I think she must have hated Lena more vehemently than she loved Hippisley. She couldn't, *then,* have had much reliance on her power to capture; but her hatred was a perpetual suggestion.

Supposing—supposing she were to try and take him?

Then she had tried.

I daresay she hadn't much difficulty. Hippisley wasn't quite so fine and fastidious as Lena thought him. I've no doubt he liked Ethel's unwholesomeness, just as he had liked the touch of morbidity in Lena.

And the spying? That had been all part of the game; his and Ethel's. *They* played for safety, if you like. They had *had* to throw Lena off the scent. They used Sybil Fermor and Lady Hermione and Barbara Vining, one after the other, as their *paravents*. Finally they had used Lena. That was their cleverest stroke. It brought them a permanent security. For, you see, Hippisley wasn't going to give up his free quarters, his studio, the dinners and the motor car, if he could help it. Not for Ethel. And Ethel knew it. They insured her, too.

Can't you see her, letting herself go in an ecstasy of revenge, winding up with a hysterical youp? "You? You thought it was you? It was me—*me*—ME. . . . You thought what we meant you to think."

Lena still comes and talks to me. To hear her you would suppose that Lawson Young and Dickey Harper never existed, that her passion for Norman Hippisley was the unique, solitary manifestation of her soul. It certainly burnt with the intensest flame. It certainly consumed her. What's left of her's all shrivelled, warped, as she writhed in her fire.

Yesterday she said to me, "Roly, I'm *glad* he's dead. Safe from her clutches."

She'll cling for a little while to this last illusion: that he had been reluctant; but I doubt if she really believes it now.

For you see, Ethel flourishes. In passion, you know, nothing succeeds like success; and her affair with Norman Hippisley advertised her, so that very soon it ranked as the first of a series of successes. She goes about dressed in stained-glass futurist muslins, and contrives provocative effects out of a tilted nose, and sulky eyes, and sallowness set off by a black velvet band on the forehead, and a black scarf of hair dragged tight from a raking backward peak.

I saw her the other night sketching a frivolous gesture—

THE DEMON LOVER°

Elizabeth Bowen
(1899–1973)

Towards the end of her day in London Mrs. Drover went round to her shut-up house to look for several things she wanted to take away. Some belonged to herself, some to her family, who were by now used to their country life. It was late August; it had been a steamy, showery day: at the moment the trees down the pavement glittered in an escape of humid yellow afternoon sun. Against the next batch of clouds, already piling up ink-dark, broken chimneys and parapets stood out. In her once familiar street, as in any unused channel, an unfamiliar queerness had silted up; a cat wove itself in and out of railings, but no human eye watched Mrs. Drover's return. Shifting some parcels under her arm, she slowly forced round her latchkey in an unwilling lock, then gave the door, which had warped, a push with her knee. Dead air came out to meet her as she went in.

The staircase window having been boarded up, no light came down into the hall. But one door, she could just see, stood ajar, so she went quickly through into the room and unshuttered the big window in there. Now the prosaic woman, looking about her, was more perplexed than she knew by everything that she saw, by traces of her long former habit of life—the yellow smoke-stain up the white marble mantelpiece, the ring left by a

---

°From *The Demon Lover and Other Stories*, 1945.

vase on the top of the escritoire; the bruise in the wallpaper where, on the door being thrown open widely, the china handle had always hit the wall. The piano, having gone away to be stored, had left what looked like claw-marks on its part of the parquet. Though not much dust had seeped in, each object wore a film of another kind; and, the only ventilation being the chimney, the whole drawing-room smelled of the cold hearth. Mrs. Drover put down her parcels on the escritoire and left the room to proceed upstairs; the things she wanted were in a bedroom chest.

She had been anxious to see how the house was—the part-time caretaker she shared with some neighbours was away this week on his holiday, known to be not yet back. At the best of times he did not look in often, and she was never sure that she trusted him. There were some cracks in the structure, left by the last bombing, on which she was anxious to keep an eye. Not that one could do anything—

A shaft of refracted daylight now lay across the hall. She stopped dead and stared at the hall table—on this lay a letter addressed to her.

She thought first—then the caretaker *must* be back. All the same, who, seeing the house shuttered, would have dropped a letter in at the box? It was not a circular, it was not a bill. And the post office redirected, to the address in the country, everything for her that came through the post. The caretaker (even if he *were* back) did not know she was due in London today— her call here had been planned to be a surprise—so his negligence in the manner of this letter, leaving it to wait in the dusk and the dust, annoyed her. Annoyed, she picked up the letter, which bore no stamp. But it cannot be important, or they would know . . . She took the letter rapidly upstairs with her, without a stop to look at the writing till she reached what had been her bedroom, where she let in light. The room looked over the garden and other gardens: the sun had gone in; as the clouds sharpened and lowered, the trees and rank lawns seemed already to smoke with dark. Her reluctance to look again at the letter came from the fact that she felt intruded upon—and by someone contemptuous of her ways. However, in the tenseness preceding the fall of rain she read it: it was a few lines.

Dear Kathleen: You will not have forgotten that today is our anniversary, and the day we said. The years have gone by at once slowly and fast. In view of the fact that nothing has changed, I shall rely upon you to keep your promise. I was sorry to see you leave London, but was satisfied that you would be back in time. You may expect me, therefore, at the hour arranged. Until then . . .   K.

Mrs. Drover looked for the date: it was today's. She dropped the letter on the bed-springs, then picked it up to see the writing again—her lips, beneath the remains of lipstick, beginning to go white. She felt so much the change in her own face that she went to the mirror, polished a clear patch in it and looked at once urgently and stealthily in. She was confronted by a woman of forty-four, with eyes starting out under a hat-brim that had been rather carelessly pulled down. She had not put on any more powder since she left the shop where she ate her solitary tea. The pearls her husband had given her on their marriage hung loose round her now rather thinner throat, slipping in the V of the pink wool jumper her sister knitted last autumn as they sat round the fire. Mrs. Drover's most normal expression was one of controlled worry, but of assent. Since the birth of the third of her little boys, attended by a quite serious illness, she had had an intermittent muscular flicker to the left of her mouth, but in spite of this she could always sustain a manner that was at once energetic and calm.

Turning from her own face as precipitately as she had gone to meet it, she went to the chest where the things were, unlocked it, threw up the lid and knelt to search. But as rain began to come crashing down she could not keep from looking over her shoulder at the stripped bed on which the letter lay. Behind the blanket of rain the clock of the church that still stood struck six—with rapidly heightening apprehension she counted each of the slow strokes. "The hour arranged . . . My God," she said, "*what* hour? How should I . . . ? After twenty-five years . . ."

* * *

The young girl talking to the soldier in the garden had not ever completely seen his face. It was dark; they were saying goodbye under a tree. Now and then—for it felt, from not seeing him at this intense moment, as though she had never seen him at all—she verified his presence for these few moments longer by putting out a hand, which he each time pressed, without very much kindness, and painfully, on to one of the breast buttons of his uniform. That cut of the button on the palm of her hand was, principally what she was to carry away. This was so near the end of a leave from France that she could only wish him already gone. It was August 1916. Being not kissed, being drawn away from and looked at intimidated Kathleen till she imagined spectral glitters in the place of his eyes. Turning away and looking back up the lawn she saw, through branches of trees, the drawing-room window alight: she caught a breath for the moment when she could go running back there into the safe arms of her mother and sister, and cry: "What shall I do, what shall I do? He has gone."

Hearing her catch her breath, her fiancé said, without feeling: "Cold?"

"You're going away such a long way."

"Not so far as you think."

"I don't understand?"

"You don't have to," he said. "You will. You know what we said."

"But that was—suppose you—I mean, suppose."

"I shall be with you," he said, "sooner or later. You won't forget that. You need to nothing but wait."

Only a little more than a minute later she was free to run up the silent lawn. Looking in through the window at her mother and sister, who did not for the moment perceive her, she already felt that unnatural promise drive down between her and the rest of all human kind. No other way of having given herself could have made her feel so apart, lost and foresworn. She could not have plighted a more sinister troth.

Kathleen behaved well when, some months later, her fiancé was reported missing, presumed killed. Her family not only supported her but were able to praise her courage without stint because they could not regret, as a husband for her, the man they knew almost nothing about. They hoped she would, in a year or two, console herself—and had it been only a question of consolation things might have gone much straighter ahead. But her trouble, behind just a little grief, was a complete dislocation from everything. She did not reject other lovers, for these failed to appear: for years she failed to attract men—and with the approach of her thirties she became natural enough to share her family's anxiousness on this score. She began to put herself out, to wonder; and at thirty-two she was very greatly relieved to find herself being courted by William Drover. She married him, and the two of them settled down in this quiet, arboreal part of Kensington: in this house the years piled up, her children were born and they all lived till they were driven out by the bombs of the next war. Her movements as Mrs. Drover were circumscribed, and she dismissed any idea that they were still watched.

As things were—dead or living the letter-writer sent her only a threat. Unable, for some minutes, to go on kneeling with her back exposed to the empty room, Mrs. Drover rose from the chest to sit on an upright chair whose back was firmly against the wall. The desuetude of her former bedroom, her married London home's whole air of being a cracked cup from which memory, with its reassuring power, had either evaporated or leaked away, made a crisis—and at just this crisis the letter-writer had, knowledgeably, struck. The hollowness of the house this evening cancelled years on years of voices, habits and steps. Through the shut windows she only heard rain fall on the roofs around. To rally herself, she said she was in a mood—and for two or three seconds shutting her eyes, told herself that she had imagined the letter. But she opened them—there it lay on the bed.

On the supernatural side of the letter's entrance she was not permitting her mind to dwell. Who, in London, knew she meant to call at the house today? Evidently, however, this had been known. The caretaker, *had* he come back, had had no cause to expect her: he would have taken the letter in his pocket, to forward it, at his own time, through the post. There was no other sign that the caretaker had been in—but, if not? Letters dropped in at doors of deserted houses do not fly or walk to tables in halls. They do not sit on the dust of empty tables with the air of certainty that they will be found. There is needed some human hand—but nobody but the caretaker had a key. Under circumstances she did not care to consider, a house can be entered without a key. It was possible that she was not alone now. She might be being waited for, downstairs. Waited for—until when? Until "the hour arranged." At least that was not six o'clock: six has struck.

She rose from the chair and went over and locked the door.

The thing was, to get out. To fly? No, not that: she had to catch her train. As a woman whose utter dependability was the keystone of her family life she was not willing to return to the country, to her husband, her little boys and her sister, without the objects she had come up to fetch. Resuming work at the chest she set about making up a number of parcels in a rapid, fumbling-decisive way. These, with her shopping parcels, would be too much to carry; these meant a taxi—at the thought of the taxi her heart went up and her normal breathing resumed. I will ring up the taxi now; the taxi cannot come too soon: I shall hear the taxi out there running its engine, till I walk calmly down to it through the hall. I'll ring up—But no: the telephone is cut off . . . She tugged at a knot she had tied wrong.

The idea of flight . . . He was never kind to me, not really. I don't remember him kind at all. Mother said he never considered me. He was set on me, that was what it was—not love. Not love, not meaning a person well. What did he do, to make me promise like that? I can't remember—But she found that she could.

She remembered with such dreadful acuteness that the twenty-five years since then dissolved like smoke and she instinctively looked for the weal left by the button on the palm of her hand. She remembered not only all that he said and did but the complete suspension of *her* existence during that August week. I was not myself—they all told me so at the time. She remembered—but with one white burning blank as where acid has dropped on a photograph: *under no conditions* could she remember his face.

So, whenever he may be waiting, I shall not know him. You have no time to run from a face you do not expect.

The thing was to get to the taxi before any clock struck what could be the hour. She would slip down the street and round the side of the square to where the square gave on the main road. She would return in the taxi, safe, to her own door, and bring the solid driver into the house with her to pick up the parcels from room to room. The idea of the taxi driver made her decisive, bold: she unlocked her door, went to the top of the staircase and listened down.

She heard nothing—but while she was hearing nothing the *passé* air of the staircase was disturbed by a draught that travelled up to her face. It emanated from the basement: down there a door or window was being opened by someone who chose this moment to leave the house.

The rain had stopped; the pavements steamily shone as Mrs. Drover let herself out by inches from her own front door into the empty street. The unoccupied houses opposite continued to meet her look with their damaged stare. Making towards the thoroughfare and the taxi, she tried not to keep looking behind. Indeed, the silence was so intense—one of those creeks of London silence exaggerated this summer by the damage of war—that no tread could have gained on hers unheard. Where her street debouched on the square where people went on living, she grew conscious of, and checked, her unnatural pace. Across the open end of the square two buses impassively passed each other: women, a perambulator, cyclists, a man wheeling a barrow signalized, once again, the ordinary flow of life. At the square's most populous corner should be—and was—the short taxi rank. This evening, only one taxi—but this, although it presented its blank rump, appeared already to be alertly waiting for her. Indeed, without looking round the driver started his engine as she panted up from behind and put her hand on the door. As she did so, the clock struck seven. The taxi faced the main road: to make the trip back to her house it would have to turn—she had settled back on the seat and the taxi *had* turned before she, surprised by its knowing movement, recollected that she had not "said where." She leaned forward to scratch at the glass panel that divided the driver's head from her own.

The driver braked to what was almost a stop, turned round and slid the glass panel back: the jolt of this flung Mrs. Drover forward till her face was almost into the glass. Through the aperture driver and passenger, not six inches between them, remained for an eternity eye to eye. Mrs. Drover's mouth hung open for some seconds before she could issue her first scream. After that she continued to scream freely and to beat with her gloved hands on the glass all round as the taxi, accelerating without mercy, made off with her into the hinterland of deserted streets.